HARD TARGET

The Works of Alan Jacobson

Novels

False Accusations

KAREN VAIL SERIES

The 7th Victim

Crush

Velocity

Inmate 1577

No Way Out

Spectrum

OPSIG TEAM BLACK SERIES

The Hunted

Hard Target

The Lost Codex

Short stories

"Fatal Twist"

(featuring Karen Vail)

"Double Take"

(featuring Carmine Russo & Ben Dyer)

For up-to-date information on Alan Jacobson's current and future novels, please visit his website, www.AlanJacobson.com.

HARD TARGET

AN OPSIG TEAM BLACK NOVEL

ALAN JACOBSON

Cover design by Alan Jacobson

Book cover text set in Caudex, copyright © 2011 by Hjort Nidudsson

Author photograph: Corey Jacobson

978-1-5040-1338-3

This edition published in 2015 by Open Road Integrated Media, Inc.
345 Hudson Street
New York, NY 10014
www.openroadmedia.com

For my uncle, Leonard Rudnick

At first I thought that the Leonard Rudnick of my childhood bore little resemblance to the Leonard Rudnick of *Hard Target*. But then I realized that both are doctors who care deeply about their patients, and both are good souls who would do anything for a person in need. Moreover, both overcame substantial adversities as youngsters to lead rewarding lives.

On a personal level, my uncle has had a profound effect on me, starting with my earliest childhood memories when we went fishing in Bay Shore, New York and caught a large . . . boot. That taught me that fishing was not the sport for me.

My uncle also introduced me to chiropractic. Chiropractic treatment not only cured my blinding migraine headaches, but it brought me across the country to California, where I started a rewarding career and met the most important person of my life. There have been other influences, too numerous to record here, but suffice it to say that my uncle's smile, humor, warmth, and wisdom have helped me become the person that I am today.

Unk, this one's for you.

HARD TARGET

". . . Whenever any Form of Government becomes destructive . . . it is the Right of the People to alter or to abolish it, and to institute new Government . . . it is their Right, it is their Duty, to throw off such Government, and to provide new Guards for their future Security."

—THOMAS JEFFERSON

The Declaration of Independence

"Our death is not an end if we can live on in our children and the younger generation. For they are us, our bodies are only wilted leaves on the tree of life."

—ALBERT EINSTEIN

Collected Papers of Albert Einstein © 1987

ELECTION NIGHT

November 7
10:57 PM EST

Everyone dies, it's just a matter of when. But Glendon Rusch, vice president of the United States, had always figured it would be a distant occurrence—three or four decades in the future. He had no way of knowing the events that would prove godlike in their finality were a mere three or four *minutes* away.

The Sikorsky VH-3 helicopter, one of only a dozen in the executive transport fleet out of Quantico, chopped its way through Virginia air space. Inside, in the relative quiet of the custom outfitted cabin, Rusch tapped his right foot, staring ahead at his wife, Macy, wanting the time to dissolve away like grains of sugar in hot coffee. Because the sooner the minutes passed, the sooner he'd know if his grueling two-year run for president would be the crown jewel in his career ring, or a nine hundred million dollar faux diamond.

"Too close to call," Rusch was told as they lifted off. But what the hell did that mean? He needed to talk with his campaign director. Just how close was "too close to call"? Was that statistical jargon for "It doesn't look good, but we're not mathematically eliminated"?

Rusch stole a glance at Macy's watch: could the last forty minutes have made a difference? He looked at the cabin phone ten feet away, willing it to ring. But would it bring good news or bad? He closed his eyes and let his head rest against the seatback. Stop obsessing.

Fatigue was dragging at every body part, trying to pull him into defeat. Like gravity, he fought it unconsciously, not permitting the lack of sleep and his weary mind to darken his thoughts. He needed to shift his attention elsewhere, if only for a moment or two.

Rusch looked at his daughter, Kelsey, who was strapped into seat number three to her mother's left along the cabin wall. She was staring with longing eyes at Sam Washburn, the Special Agent-in-Charge of the vice president's Secret Service detail. Washburn was a hunk, or so sixteen year-old Kelsey had said, and she had a crush on him. Rusch cleared his throat and caught his daughter's attention. He raised a disapproving eyebrow and tilted his head. She rolled her eyes in response, her face shading red as she turned away.

Rusch shared a smile with Macy. He remembered when Kelsey was only a newborn bundle wrapped in a drawstring nightgown, sleeping in his arms. Time passed much too quickly.

And yet, in times like these, it passed much too slowly.

The cabin phone rang. Rusch's heart rate surged.

Sam Washburn, a veteran of the executive detail and several election cycles, knew the importance of the call. He unbuckled and snatched up the handset, listened a moment, then handed the receiver to Rusch's senior campaign aide, Chris Sawyer.

Sawyer nodded and grunted, his eyes darting around as he digested the information being relayed to him over the phone. His gaze found Rusch, the aide's poker face giving away nothing—but his shoulders slumping slightly. Finally, he hung up the phone and said, "The polls are just about closed in Washington, Arizona, and California. And CNN's calling it." He waited a beat, then said, "We're in!"

Rusch closed his eyes and sighed relief. Macy took his hands in hers and squeezed. Rusch knew that of everyone on board, his wife was the most proud of him . . . with Kelsey a close second. He absorbed the moment, surrounded by those he loved dearly and who loved him, and he realized it didn't get any better than this. He blinked away the tears and found his voice.

"How long till touch down?" Rusch said, forcing the hoarse words from his throat.

"Five or six minutes," Sawyer said. "Big crowd waiting for us."

"Then where's that champagne? Pop the damn cork."

Sawyer snapped his heels together and sprung into a mock salute. "Yes sir, Mr. *President*."

Macy, seated across from her husband, leaned forward and wiped at his tears with a thumb. She spoke close to his ear: "I guess I'll find out tonight what it's like to sleep with the President of the United States. Not many women can make that claim."

"Probably more than you know," Rusch deadpanned, then planted a kiss on her hand. He leaned back, then blew a kiss to Kelsey as Sawyer ripped the foil from the Dom Perignon. With an audible pop, the cork exploded upward, frothy suds fizzling out of the bottle and crawling over Sawyer's hands like ocean foam. He stepped back to keep the champagne off his Allen Edmonds wingtips, then lifted the bubbly for everyone to see. "To Glendon Rusch, President of the United States!"

Sawyer reached forward to pour Rusch's glass, but the helicopter lurched hard to the right and the bottle flew from his hand. It shattered against a bulkhead, shards and spilled champagne showering the floor.

"What the hell was that?" Rusch shouted, his hands gripping the thick armrests.

But before anyone could venture a guess, a thunderous explosion blew the armored chopper aside like a plastic toy. Sawyer slammed into Washburn and the two men fell in tandem. The Secret Service agent tried to push Sawyer aside, but their tangled legs kept him buried beneath the man's weight.

A bright flash caught the edge of Rusch's peripheral vision. Through the window to his left, the blinding flare of the pulverized escort helicopter's flaming debris accelerated toward him.

"Sweet Jesus!" Rusch instinctively recoiled, bracing for impact.

The wreckage slammed against the VH-3, ripping a hole in the cabin's metal skin. The helicopter rotated out of control in a dizzying elliptical orbit, whipping its occupants about like an amusement park ride. The force dislodged the sprawled Sawyer and flung him into the wall like a rag doll—along with everything else that was not secured.

Glass from the demolished window littered Macy's bleeding face, her head flopping from side to side against the firm, upholstered seatback. "Macy . . . honey!" Rusch grabbed her wrist and gave a gentle tug. "Macy!"

She did not respond.

"Daddy—"

Kelsey. Her voice was barely audible over the wind and rotor noise, which was now deafeningly loud. Rusch turned toward his daughter, whose eyes were flushed with terror. Her thick auburn hair whipped fiercely in the violent wind. Straining against his seatbelt, Rusch reached forward and to his right, across the debris that littered the floor. "Sweetie—take my hand!"

Rusch knew the VH-3 was designed for maximum crash survivability, but logic told him that at five thousand feet, human flesh and bones in a free-falling metal coffin faced longer odds than he wanted to admit. What's more, there were only two crashworthy seats. And he and his wife occupied both of them.

Washburn's black suit jacket flapped furiously against his face as he wrapped a bloody arm around the adjacent bulkhead, desperately trying to right himself.

Despite numerous attempts, Rusch could not get hold of Kelsey's hand. He turned back to his wife, whose neck and shoulders were visibly soaked with blood.

"Macy, can you hear me? Answer me!"

Other than involuntary jostling, she did not move. He again twisted toward Kelsey and stretched as far as he could, but he still could not reach her. Waves of nausea began racking his intestines. He fought the urge to vomit as he reached down to his seatbelt and struggled with the buckle. But the stress of the moment—or the violent movement of the helicopter—made the simple task of releasing the clasp instantly complex.

Washburn was suddenly in front of him. "Do not remove your seatbelt, sir!"

"My daughter—"

"Her belt's secure," Washburn shouted over the din. "She's fine." Washburn grabbed hold of the two arms of Rusch's chair to keep himself from tumbling out the gaping hole in the side of the cabin. His face was inches from the president-elect's.

"Get me out of this damn seatbelt, Sam." Rusch continued to struggle with the latch. "Now!"

"My orders are to ensure your safety—"

The chopper lurched again, and a cold flash of air blasted against Rusch's face. The rotor blades roared louder, then the cabin went black. A red emergency light snapped on, but in the dizzying spin, Rusch could not steady his vision long enough to make out what was happening. One thing was clear, though: Washburn was no longer in front of him.

In the dim light, Rusch could barely see the outline of Macy's still body. Uncontrolled grief struck him in the chest like a powerful blow, evacuating his breath like a vacuum. As he turned toward Kelsey, fire exploded into the cabin. Intense heat seared his cheeks. He instinctively threw his hands up to shield his face, a pain unlike anything he'd ever experienced enveloping his fingers and arms.

Flames sprouted all around him, licking at the spilled champagne along the floor.

Rusch saw Washburn in the fire's flaring light, his feet suddenly ablaze. The Secret Service agent stumbled backwards as if practicing an awkward dance step, arms flailing the dead air. And before the scream could leave his throat, he was gone, sucked through the jagged opening that used to be the cabin wall.

The rumble of another blast rocked the helicopter. Angry flames devoured the interior. Like a runaway elevator, the craft was suddenly free-falling, and Rusch once again reached for his daughter's hand. But she wasn't there.

Her seat—along with that section of the bulkhead—was gone.

A man dressed in a black leather jacket sat on a motorcycle, its muffled engine purring quietly. Somewhere off in his thoughts, Alpha Zulu was aware that the surrounding brush and field straw could ignite against the searing heat of his bike's exhaust pipes. But none of that mattered. At this point, nothing would sully their plans. They were well past the point of turning back.

Zulu checked his chronograph, then strapped a panoramic night vision device over his eyes. Seconds later, he located his target. The chopper was rocking from side to side and flying erratically, spinning uncontrollably as it fell from the heavens. He yanked the light amplification unit away just as a white flash brightened the sky.

Zulu rooted a tracking device from his pocket and followed a blinking red light as it coursed the grid.

"Acquired the target," he said into his helmet-mounted encrypted two-way radio.

"Copy that," came the response.

The man seated behind him with his Timberlands curled over the rear footrests tapped him on his right shoulder. Time to go.

Zulu kicked the motorcycle into first gear as the VH-3 dropped from the lifeless night sky like a shot pheasant—a fiery, dying hulk heading for its final resting place.

Federal Bureau of Investigation
Washington Field Office - WFO
601 4th Street NW
Washington, D.C.

11:02 PM EST

FBI Supervisory Special Agent Aaron Uziel drummed his fingers on the armrest of his boss's guest chair. The office was finished with tan paisley wallpaper, walnut furniture, and a floor-to-ceiling, wall-to-wall entertainment cabinet. Playing across a forty-six-inch LCD television was ABC News Election Center, their pundits and anchors debating the latest presidential precinct tallies.

Uziel—"Uzi" to his colleagues and friends—stared vacantly at the images scrolling across the screen. A few moments earlier he had pulled his tired body out of the chair to lower the volume so he didn't have to listen to the repetitive drone of newscasters and so-called experts spinning their party's take on the evening's results.

He ran the back of his hand across the black stubble that had accumulated on his face since this morning. His wife had always said it gave him a rugged look, and with the sharp, pleasing angles of his face, he had to agree. He never had difficulty getting a date as a young teen, and the lingering stares he got as his face and lean body matured only numbed him to all the attention. But in the past several years, his face had lost its boyish good looks. Lines crisscrossed his forehead like roads on a street map. Stress lines were one thing: live long enough in today's type-A lifestyle and they accumulated like larvae on a corpse. But his were pain lines, formed from grief and deep-seated sadness . . . constant reminders of past tragedy. As if Uzi needed physical reminders. The emotional torment was enough, and it never gave him much of a reprieve.

The door swung open and Marshall Shepard lumbered in. Despite the relentless pressure that accompanied the assistant special agent-in-charge position, Shepard's ebony skin was the polar opposite of Uzi's: nearly wrinkle-free. His graying temples and creeping hairline were the sole overt signs of middle age. Shepard paused in front of his desk chair and removed his suit coat with a flourish, then draped it over the seatback.

"Well," Shepard said, "you pulled a real freakin' doozie this time, Uzi."

Uzi rubbed at his dark eyes with a finger. "Are you trying to be funny, or do you always rhyme this late at night?"

Shepard sat down heavily. The large chocolate brown leather chair groaned. "Serious heat's coming your way."

"I'm surprised it took this long."

Shepard massaged his temples. "My life just got a whole lot more complicated. Thanks a freakin' bunch."

"Look," Uzi said, shifting in his chair and pulling himself upright. "I did what I thought was right. Osborn— What he did was dangerous. It wasn't a little thing, Shep, it was big-time shit. And you know it. Could've gotten innocent people killed. It wasn't the first time."

Shepard waved a hand. "Yeah, I know the speech—"

"It's not a speech." Uzi was leaning forward now, his brow hard. "I did what was right, what I hope every agent would do if he or she was faced with the same situation." He paused, leaned back, then continued. "It was the right thing to do. I get paid to do a job and I did it."

"You don't get paid to rat out a colleague."

Uzi snorted. "You think I should've kept my mouth shut?"

Shepard looked away. "From my seat, you did the right thing. I just wish . . . I just wish it never happened. It's bad all around."

Uzi gave a conciliatory nod.

"I'm leaving him on the job. For now. You'll have to deal with that."

"Your decision. You're the boss."

Shepard shook his head. "You know I'd go to the end of the Earth for you, man. But some things I can't protect you from."

Uzi's eyes narrowed. "I don't need your protection. I can take care of myself."

Shepard rested two beefy elbows on his desk. "That's never been an issue. But this is different. It's not a criminal with a gun or a terrorist with a bomb . . . This is an enemy different from anything you've ever dealt with. The enemy's your own unit, and they're pissed as hell. They may never forgive you. You've gotta be prepared for that. That's a lot to deal with, on top of, well . . . you know."

"Not like I'll ever forget."

Shepard looked down. A moment of silence passed, then he asked, "And that brings me to why I wanted to meet with you. Whatever happened with that shrink?"

Uzi let his eyes wander to the television screen. "Stupid talking heads. None of 'em predicted such a close election. Not one of them."

"You never saw her, did you?"

Uzi tilted his head. "President Glendon Rusch. Has a ring to it, don't you think?"

"It'd be a good idea, especially because of what's happened. The shrink can help. Your plate's been full, and this Osborn thing's only going to make it . . . fuller."

Uzi tore his gaze from the television. "Thanks for the cliché. And for the advice."

"Here's the thing, Uzi. It's not advice. Not this time. It's mandatory. If you want to remain in Washington. If you don't, then it'll be up to your new ASAC to determine what should be done."

Uzi's eyes widened. "Shep, don't do this to me—"

"Your macho side doesn't want to spill your guts to a woman, fine. You want someone closer to home, fine. No excuses this time."

"Shep, please—"

"You should be thanking me for circumventing an EAP," Shepard said, referring to the FBI's in-house Employee Assistance Program that required a counselor to talk with an agent before sending him to a psychiatrist. "Besides, you did it to yourself. I'm just trying to keep my people happy. And right now they're not very happy. You need to get some help and I need to keep things under control. Control's important right now. For your sake."

Uzi bit his lower lip.

"I've got someone else for you to see."

"You'd really transfer me if I don't see a shrink?"

"And by see him, I mean actually *go*. Talk to him, work with him. For as long as *he* sees fit."

"What about what I think?"

"I've cut you a lot of slack the past few years, Uzi. I've given you a lot of leeway in how you run your unit. Time's come for you to do it my way."

Uzi looked away.

"Way I see it, you ratted out Osborn because what he did struck too close to home. He reminds you of yourself. That's it, isn't it?"

Uzi stood up and leaned his palms on Shepard's desk. "I don't need this bullshit. Especially now." His face had turned crimson and his eyes were wide. "I did what I did because it was right. DIOG says so," he said, referring to the Bureau's Domestic Investigations and Operations Guide. "So don't be giving me any psychological mumbo jumbo explanation about how my actions had some deeper meaning."

The two men stared at each other for a long moment.

"Sit. Down."

Uzi took his seat.

"You want to stay in Washington?"

"Yes."

"Thought so," Shepard said. "You'll be seeing Dr. Leonard Rudnick. You have an appointment with him tomorrow, eight o'clock." He reached into his drawer and tossed a business card in Uzi's direction.

Uzi scraped it off the desk. "Twenty-three eleven M Street. Two blocks from my house."

"Incentive to keep your appointments. Besides, he's a good man. You'll like him."

Uzi snorted. "Right."

The buzz on the phone made Uzi jump. Shepard lifted the handset and listened, his eyes narrowing, a noticeable layer of perspiration breaking out across his forehead. "Thank you," he whispered into the phone, then let the handset drop from his ear. His stunned gaze met Uzi's.

"What's wrong?" Uzi asked.

"Marine Two went down in a field forty miles from here." The two men were silent as they absorbed the impact of the statement. After a few seconds of silence, Shepard got to his feet. "Chopper's on its way to pick you up. Carolyn has the GPS coordinates. Get 'em and get out there. Now."

11:06 PM

Paramedic Dell Gibbons and his partner had just returned from a three-car pileup on the interstate when the call came over the radio: a helicopter had crashed in a field just inside their patrol sector. Gibbons had to pee and his stomach was grumbling. But he shoved the rig into gear and headed off toward the nighttime countryside.

The paramedics were followed by a fire truck, three "attack engines," and a couple of water tenders, sirens screaming as they rumbled down the roadway.

His partner leaned closer to the two-way radio that had spurted static a few seconds earlier. "Repeat?"

"That's Marine Two that went down," the dispatcher said. "The veep's chopper."

"The vice president?" Gibbons asked. "Holy shit." He had the feeling he was about to enter a scene on par with the medics who had responded to the shooting of President John F. Kennedy. Well, almost on par. He felt a part of history. All the offhand remarks his mother had made about him not pursuing her dream of him becoming a doctor would be silenced forever. He would be one of the few who had responded to the scene when Vice President Rusch's helicopter went down.

But as he tooled along the highway, he realized that his mother's silence would last but a moment. Then she would tell him he could have been the *doctor* called upon to treat the vice president instead of "just" the paramedic who had transported him to the hospital.

"I read an article about these helicopters in some military magazine," his partner said. "They got all kinds of special protection, lasers and shit like that. They can take enemy fire, even missiles, I think, and still keep flying."

"Yeah, well, this one ain't still flying."

Seven minutes after the call, Gibbons and his partner were first on the scene, arriving seconds ahead of the county sheriff and the fire trucks. The medics quickly surveyed the carnage, keeping a distance from the flames that stretched high into the sky, fed by an abundant supply of spilled Jet A fuel. Though less flammable than gasoline, the high performance kerosene burned very hot. Explosion wasn't merely possible, but likely.

The firefighters jumped from their rigs and deployed their heavy inch-and-a-half hoses across the vast area of burning debris. In less than a minute, water was pumping onto the wreckage, followed seconds later by aqueous film forming foam designed to cap the fire and flammable liquids by suffocating them.

In short order, they cleared a narrow path for Gibbons and his partner to begin their search for survivors. But before Gibbons could move ten feet, he saw something off to his right: a man on the ground, crawling, trying to get to his hands and knees, without much success . . . dangerously close to the tip of a swirl of violent flames.

"Over there," Gibbons yelled.

He and his partner were upon the man in seconds. They made a quick assessment, determined he was safe to move, then grasped him by both armpits and rolled him onto an adjacent spine board. After securing him with straps, they dragged the survivor away from the fire's blazing heat.

Gibbons grabbed a pair of shears from his belt and cut through what remained of the man's suit coat and dress shirt. "Sir, can you hear me?" he asked.

A groan in response, a half-hearted movement of his left arm.

"I'm a paramedic. We're gonna take good care of you."

The man's face was so badly burned Gibbons couldn't tell if he was thirty or fifty. "Starting a central line," Gibbons said.

"A central line? We never do that in the—"

"We've gotta infuse him now, no choice. We'll dress the burns and get him the hell out of here. Medevac?"

Seconds later, his partner lowered the two-way from his ear. "Three minutes."

Gibbons bit his lip as he worked, keeping his thoughts to himself. He was concerned about the extent of the burns covering the man's face, hands, and feet.

"Gib—I think I see someone else."

"Go," Gibbons said. He watched as his partner ran off in the direction of what appeared to be another prone body crawling slowly across the devastated landscape.

Gibbons finished establishing the IV, then noticed something shiny protruding from the partially burned suit coat he had cut away. He reached into the inside pocket and pulled out a blue and gold Waterman pen. It was thick and heavy, but well balanced. He rolled it between his fingers and saw something engraved on the barrel: "Vice President Glendon E. Rusch."

"Holy shit." He glanced over his shoulder, saw that no one was watching, and slipped the pen into his shirt pocket. Just in case his mother did not believe him.

11:39 PM

The wreckage was still partially ablaze, though the army of firefighters had the situation contained. Uzi stepped from the FBI's Black Hawk helicopter and ran toward the periphery of the crash site. He stopped at the outer border, taking in the carnage the way he'd been taught to view any crime scene: get the big picture first, then move inward for the details. He pulled a toothpick from his jacket pocket, stuck it in his mouth, and twirled it about with his lips and tongue.

Emergency personnel continued to wander the area, though at this point Uzi surmised the rescue aspect had concluded and they were now engaged in recovery efforts.

Uzi walked toward the concentration of investigators, which he estimated as numbering between fifty and sixty. The acrid stench of burning fuel mixed with smoldering electrical and mechanical parts flared his nostrils. He slid past a couple of workers who were placing klieg lights along the periphery, then knelt beside the first technician he came to, a woman in dark coveralls with "NTSB" written in white phosphorescent letters across her back.

He flashed his Bureau credentials and nodded at the ground she was examining. "Special Agent Aaron Uzi," he said, the toothpick bobbing on his lips. Years ago he got into the habit of truncating his last name during introductions, as most people botched it anyway. "I'm head of JTTF out of WFO," Uzi said, referring to the Joint Terrorism Task Force at the FBI's Washington Field Office.

"Angela Bonacelli, Aviation Go Team," she said. "Structures Specialist."

"What can you tell me?"

"I can tell you this A-triple-F makes it very hard to do my job."

"'A' what?"

"The foam. Good thing is it smothers everything in its path and puts out the fire. Bad thing is, well, it smothers everything in its path. And you're not supposed to disturb it or the fire'll start up again." She moved past a large piece of metal that was layered with foam and settled herself in a clearing beside loose dirt.

"Other than that," Uzi said, moving beside her.

Bonacelli spoke without looking up, suddenly fascinated by what lay in front of her, flicking at the soil with a small brush. "Both choppers crashed. Marine Two and its escort. Two survivors, from what I hear. A Secret Service agent and the vice president."

"You mean president-elect."

As she sifted through the dirt, she said, "Yeah."

"Anything else?"

"Wreckage is strewn over a very large area. Radar picked up pieces coming down ten miles from here."

"Ten miles? On a helicopter crash?"

"First of all, we've got two choppers. We don't know the sequence yet, but one could've gone down first, then the other. Leaves a much greater scatter pattern." Bonacelli shrugged. "It'll take a while before all the wreckage is sorted out."

"Still," Uzi mused. "Ten miles. Doesn't seem possible, unless . . ."

"Unless there was an explosion of some sort." Bonacelli nodded. "Disabling but not totally destructive. Debris falls, but the chopper stays aloft. Finally, she stalls or something else gives out, and she drops out of the sky."

"An explosion. Are you saying this was intentional?"

"Whoa," she said, holding her hands out in front of her. "I was just reporting the size of the debris field. My job is to gather evidence, Agent Uzi. In a case like this, someone else who gets paid a lot more than me determines what it all means."

"Theoretically. If there's an explosion that's not caused by a bomb, we're talking either mechanical or structural failure, right?"

"Right." She looked out at the smoldering wreckage. "What a mess." Almost to herself, she said, "How the hell could this have happened?"

Uzi turned away. It was exactly what he was wondering. From what he knew, the executive fleet of helicopters was meticulously maintained. Parts were replaced on a set schedule, whether or not they were worn. The human factor, however, was always something that needed to be ruled out: pilot error, improperly installed equipment, acts of terror. Until they had more information, it was ill advised to jump to conclusions.

But his mind was churning, nonetheless.

Uzi's tongue played with the toothpick as he glanced out over the field of burning embers and twisted metal. "Who's here? FAA, Hazmat, you guys, Secret Service, Marines . . ." He continued scanning the on-scene personnel, guessing affiliation by their dress and body language.

Bonacelli took a sample bag from her kit and scooped a trowel of dirt. "Defense Department, county sheriffs, and the executive branch medical team. I think that covers it."

"Shitload of people."

Uzi knew that in a crash scene such as this one, the National

Transportation Safety Board ran the show until they determined cause. If it was accidental, the FBI left NTSB to finish their analysis. If it was a criminal act, the Bureau took over. In a case involving the executive branch, parallel investigations ran in the background: DOD, Secret Service, the Marines— They all did their own thing. All agencies were supposed to run their findings through the NTSB, but turf wars often compromised the process.

Uzi's thighs were beginning to ache. He stood gingerly from his crouch, his old football knee clunking when he straightened it. Bonacelli rose as well.

"Who are your Powerplants and Systems Specialists?"

"John Maguire and Clarice Canfield," she said, twisting her torso to scan the milling bodies. "They're out there somewhere."

Uzi's glance followed hers and settled on a long-haired brunet in a business suit, walking slowly along the periphery. "Who's that?" He wasn't sure if he had said it aloud.

"Haven't the slightest. Not one of ours."

Uzi watched the woman take a few more steps, then turned back to Bonacelli. "Thanks. I'll catch you a little later, in case there's anything else you can tell me." Without waiting for a response, he made his way toward the brunet. Her skirt ended halfway down her thighs, curiously short for a November evening in Virginia. Then again, she might've been dressed for a night out, then ordered to report to the accident scene. Whatever the reason, Uzi wasn't complaining.

But as quickly as the hormones shot into his bloodstream, the guilt followed, like a radioactive tag searching out its target tissue. How could he lust after another woman?

He and Dena had been together since high school, from the moment he had first laid eyes on her cute ass. She always laughed when he told her that his first attraction to her involved her backside. In her mind, she had more intriguing features. But as Uzi had told her, you can never explain attraction. It's either there or it's not. And with Dena, it started with something physical—her behind—and quickly progressed to the most intangible of assets, her heart and soul.

As the brunet slinked toward him, the thought that he was no longer married flashed in his mind. He was widowed. It was an important distinction, he told himself, though it was one he had not been able to settle deep within his core. Rational thoughts and logic almost always got lost inside the emotional baggage of guilt.

As an internal war raged between his hormones and conscience, he found himself blocking the woman's path. Without meeting his eyes, she shifted her hips and deftly slithered around him.

"Have we met before?" He usually knew he was going to speak before words emerged from his mouth. In this case, something else had control over his body.

The woman turned slowly and looked at him, her lustrous hair falling across the left portion of her face. He could only make out the white of her right eye, as it reflected the burning embers along the ground.

"I'm sorry," he said, stepping toward her. "Aaron Uziel." He had used his full last name. Why? He couldn't remember the last time he'd done that. He suddenly felt hot, a layer of sweat blanketing his skin. He stood there facing her before awkwardly extending a hand.

She took it in a firm handshake, then released it. "FBI?"

His left hand found the FBI creds ID clipped to his coat. "Yeah, I'm here for the wreck. To investigate." *What the hell's wrong with me? Of course I'm here to investigate.*

"Well, good luck," she said.

Before he could object, or say something to prevent her from walking away, she turned and moved off in the opposite direction. Her hips seemed to gyrate rhythmically.

He shook his head, and an image of his beloved Dena popped into his mind.

"Hey, G-man."

Uzi turned and had to hold up a hand against the blisteringly bright klieg light illuminating the area. Standing there was Special Agent Karen Vail, a profiler with the Bureau's Behavioral Analysis Unit.

"Karen, what are you doing here?"

"My ASAC said to get my ass over here ASAP. So I got my ass over here. Luckily the rest of me decided to come along for the ride."

"I thought you're in the adult crimes unit."

"So you *were* paying attention." She play-punched his shoulder.

"I know some politicians behave like children, but last I checked, this *is* an adult crime."

Uzi grinned at her. "I've missed working with you, Karen."

"Actually, this should've been Art Rooney's case, but Rooney just went on medical leave. They assigned it to my partner, Frank Del Monaco. But he's caught up in traffic on the way back from New York. So you got me."

"Don't know Del Monaco."

"Let's just say you lucked out."

Uzi held up a hand. "Hey, any time I get a chance to work with you, I've got the four-leaf clover thing going."

"You're not Irish, Uzi."

Uzi jutted his chin back. "Are you holding that against me?"

"We all have our handicaps."

A man wearing an NTSB jacket brushed against Uzi's shoulder. "All right," Uzi said, "you know the drill. Put on those mind-reading sixth sense glasses, take a good look around, then tell me who did this."

"Mind if I click my heels three times first?"

Uzi puckered his lips and nodded. "So that's how you profilers do it."

"Hey, boychick!"

Uzi turned and saw a silhouetted figure moving toward him.

There was only one person who ever called him "boychick," a Yiddish term that meant "male buddy." A few more steps and his vision confirmed the approaching man to be Hector DeSantos, a Department of Defense covert operative. Tall and lean, with the coolest pair of tiny, rectangular-framed designer glasses Uzi had ever seen, DeSantos sauntered with the confidence of a battlefield soldier armed with an AK-47 and a belt full of ammo.

"Santa, my man. Long time." The two men bumped fists.

"I heard somewhere you were with the Bureau. How've you been?"

Uzi bobbed his head. "Been better. You?"

"Same here. It's been, what? Four, five years?"

"A little over six. Not that I'm counting."

DeSantos leaned around Uzi. "Is that—Karen?"

"I was wondering how long it was going to take you to notice me," Vail said.

"Hey," DeSantos said, holding up a hand. "I never have a problem noticing a beautiful woman. This oaf was blocking my view."

Uzi jutted his chin back. "Oaf?"

"Great to see you," DeSantos said as he gave Vail a hug.

Uzi dug both hands into his jeans pockets. "I'd never figure you two for friends. You're at, like, different ends of the personality spectrum. If there is such a thing."

"We worked a case together," Vail said.

"A pretty intense case," DeSantos said with a chuckle. "I gotta warn you, Uzi, she's a goddamn pistol."

Uzi tilted his head in appraisal. "I've always thought of her more as a shotgun."

DeSantos nodded. "Deadly at close range."

"Exactly."

Vail rolled her eyes. "Don't know about you two, but I've got work to do."

"Catch up with you later," Uzi said.

"Is that a promise?" She winked, then walked off.

"So." DeSantos waved a hand at the burning wreckage. "This your case?"

"Lucky me. What about you? You don't handle shit like this. Don't you still work in the basement, doing things nobody's supposed to know about?"

"I'm kind of on leave from the secret spy stuff. Better left for another time."

"Consider it left. So whaddya got on this crash? You always know where to bite to get through the gristle."

DeSantos chuckled. "Here's the scoop: Air Traffic Control received a communication from Marine Two at twenty-three hundred-oh-one. They thought something hit their tail rotor. About the same time Marine Three reported a bright flash from Two's aft, and then they thought something hit *them*. ATC had the two birds maintaining formation, so it's pretty clear they didn't hit each other. ATC was thinking maybe it was a piece of Two's tail rotor that hit Three. They instructed Two to head for Quantico. Few seconds later, Three lost contact with ATC. Last communication at twenty-three oh-two, Two reported a second jolt and a complete loss of control."

Uzi mulled this a moment. "Maybe we can get something more from Rusch and that Secret Service agent."

"The agent just bit the dust."

"Shit." He shifted the toothpick in his mouth. "Rusch?"

DeSantos shrugged. "Medevaced out. Burned pretty bad. How bad, I don't know yet."

"I assume they've activated COG," Uzi said, referring to the Continuity of Government plan that provided for a shadow government to run the country's infrastructure from a secure, hardened location in the event a terrorist attack wiped out Washington's buildings and leadership.

DeSantos consulted his watch. "They should be boarding the transport choppers right about now. Until we get a handle on what the hell's going on, Whitehall's not taking any chances."

Uzi glanced out at the wreckage. "Damn straight."

"This kind of hit has gotta be a well-planned, coordinated attack. What do you think—al-Qaeda? Can they still pull off something like this?"

Uzi grunted. "There are sixty-nine major terrorist organizations in the world. Al-Qaeda's a good place to start, but as to whether or not they could pull off something this complex, I don't know. Not only have we taken out bin Laden, we've eliminated some of their top planners. Latest thinking is that AQ's a loose collection of regional 'affiliate' groups that operate independently and use the AQ 'brand'—no relationship to one another except for name and ideology. The stuff we found in bin Laden's compound showed he was frustrated with those groups—they didn't always do what he told them to do. But how AQ operated before we killed bin Laden, and how they're operating now, could be different. Some think the leadership now sets the targets and their affiliates take care of business. Centralized decisions, decentralized execution."

DeSantos shoved both hands into his jacket pockets. "And to think, we're partially responsible for creating this beast."

"How do you figure?"

"We bankrolled bin Laden back in the eighties."

"Oh, that. Yeah, well, it's the Middle East. Your friend today is your enemy tomorrow. That I get . . . but what kills me is that while we're sending bin Laden two billion in taxpayer money to fight the Soviets, he was teaming up with a Palestinian Islamic member of the Muslim Brotherhood to build training camps in Pakistan. Al-Qaeda's birth."

"That shining moment in world history." DeSantos tilted his head. "Two billion? Was it that much?"

"Something like that. Soon as we realized what was going on, we cut them off and shut down the banks that handled their money, but—"

"That's when they started their own private banking system. The How— Howula?"

"*Hawala.* Yeah. Our sanctions worked, that was the good news. Bad news was it worked too well. It forced them to get their act together, form a more traditional centralized command and control structure. They used the illicit drug trade to develop affiliates and franchises in other countries. Bottom line—we had the right idea, but there was no way to know that freezing their money would force them to become a better organized, more professional organization."

"Kind of like no way we could know that funding bin Laden to fight off the Soviets in the eighties could lead to him blowing up the Twin Towers and killing almost three thousand Americans twenty years later. What's the saying? 'Seemed like a good idea at the time'? At least we finally got the fucker."

"Yeah, we got him. But I'm not sure how much good that really did. I mean, yeah, we avenged the thousands he'd killed. And taking him out may've disrupted the group and created a temporary leadership scramble. But in terms of impacting their effectiveness, not so much."

"Maybe," DeSantos said. "Maybe not. But if we go on the assumption that AQ is now more a network of franchised groups, what's your gut say about who we should be looking at?"

Uzi blew a mouthful of air through his lips. "Al-Qaeda in the Arabian Peninsula's generally considered the most dangerous, but close behind is Islamic Jihad of Yemen, Al-Qaeda in Iraq, Al-Qaeda

Organization in the Islamic Maghreb, al-Shabaab, al-Humat, Egyptian Islamic Jihad, Libyan Islamic Fighting Group, East Turkestan Islamic Movement. Maybe a handful of others."

"I asked about your gut, not our Ten Most Wanted."

As Uzi opened his mouth to reply, an electronic guitar sung from DeSantos's pocket.

DeSantos patted his jacket, found the BlackBerry, and brought it to his face. "Yeah." His eyes narrowed. "Okay." He listened a moment, then turned to Uzi. "So much for the obvious."

"We don't want it to be too easy. That'd be no fun." Uzi nodded at the phone.

"Not sure yet. Intel could be good, could be shit. I'll check it out, let you know." DeSantos's voice—and gaze—suddenly drifted beyond Uzi's shoulder. "Mm, mmm. Who's that?"

Uzi turned and immediately locked on the woman DeSantos was looking at. "Don't know. I ran into her a few minutes ago. My brain turned to mush."

"Yeah, well, my other brain ain't mush, I can tell you that." DeSantos tilted his head. "Fine looking thing."

"Aren't you married?"

"Last time I checked, a marriage license didn't come with blinders. Besides, Maggie and I have . . . an agreement."

"I don't think I want to hear it."

"You probably don't. Knowing you, it'd make your ears curl."

Uzi was staring at the woman, watching her lean frame as she moved amongst the wreckage. "Yeah," he said, not really hearing DeSantos's comment.

"You know, you gave me shit, but looks to me like your radar's locked in on the same target. You're married—and I know your wife ain't as understanding as Maggie."

"Yeah." Uzi tore his eyes from the woman. "I mean, no. It's— It's a long story."

DeSantos's gaze was again stuck to the woman's body like Crazy Glue. "Miniskirt and high heels. Strange shit to be wearing at a crash scene, don't you think?"

"Do me a favor, Santa. Get me her name and find out who she's with." Hoping his question wouldn't initiate a discussion, he quickly added, "It's for the investigation."

DeSantos dipped his chin and looked at Uzi over the tops of his glasses. "Right. 'The investigation.'"

Uzi saw three of his task force members approaching in the distance, led by Agent Hoshi Koh, his office confidante. He got their attention with the wave of a hand, then told DeSantos he would meet up with him later.

As DeSantos walked off to begin his own analysis, Uzi shoved his hands deep into the pockets of his long black leather coat and met his colleagues a few strides from the perimeter of the wreckage. He filled them in on what he knew—which wasn't much. As Uzi expected, with the exception of Hoshi, they gave him a cold reception. Word traveled fast in field offices, even one as large as WFO.

Uzi and his team split up to begin their respective tasks. While en route to the site, Shepard had called Uzi to inform him that two dozen additional agents had been dispatched off-site to work the crash's behind-the-scenes logistics: interviewing the executive transport division's mechanics, pulling maintenance records, amassing weather reports for the region, and visiting with Air Traffic Control in an effort to reconstruct the helicopter's flight path during its last fateful moments.

Uzi looked for investigators wearing NTSB coveralls and eventually located Clarice Canfield. She was a take-charge woman, five-foot-one in thick-soled boots and a short, military-style hairdo. They made introductions and canned the small talk.

"So what can you tell me about the aircraft?" Uzi asked.

"Which one, the VH-3 or the Super Stallion?"

"Let's start with the H-3."

"Walk with me," she said. "I've got to find what's left of the cockpit." She started moving, faster than Uzi had thought possible with such short legs. Uzi flicked on a small flashlight and followed close behind like a puppy.

"I can tell you anything you want to know about it," she said.

"I flew H-3s in the military, so I know about its older cousin. But I need to know everything you can tell me about this particular model, the executive fleet."

Canfield shrugged. "It's your basic Sikorsky masterpiece, souped up for VIPs. This model started transporting the executive staff with the Kennedy administration. Just about my favorite chopper. Thing's a bulldog. Energy-absorbing landing gear to increase crash survivability, self-sealing puncture-resistant fuel tanks. Even the seats are shielded. This thing can take twenty-three-millimeter shells and live to tell about it. But inside the cabin, it's luxury all the way. Even has a galley and restroom." She paused long enough to turn around to glance at Uzi. "I feel like a used car salesman."

Someone passing by caught Uzi's shoulder and spun him half around. He took a couple large steps to catch up to Canfield, who had continued walking. "Carries a dozen people?" he asked.

Canfield stopped abruptly, then knelt beside a pile of foam-covered twisted metal. "These have a crew of three, sixteen passengers. Top speed, a hundred-seventy knots. Range, four-hundred forty-five miles." She shined her flashlight on the wreckage, shook her head, then stood up.

"And the Super Stallion?"

"Also built by Sikorsky. CH-53. Three GE turbine engines, air-to-air refueling, max speed about the same as the H-3. It's the military's workhorse. Whatever you need it to do, it can do. Special ops, military transport, search and rescue, you name it. Coolest thing is it can carry sixteen tons of supplies, cargo, vehicles, artillery, and troops."

Uzi's eyebrows rose. "Sixteen tons?"

"Think of it as the most powerful helicopter we've got—on steroids."

"So the Stallion's a stud. How does something like that end up looking like . . . chopped meat?"

"Don't know enough yet to say."

"Come on, don't hold out on me. You must have some idea. You can't tell me you haven't already started formulating an opinion."

Canfield tilted her head, leaned closer to something on the ground, then straightened back up. "Can't draw any conclusions till we have all the evidence collected. You know the drill."

Uzi lifted his flashlight and lit his face from below. "Based on what you're telling me, both these choppers were designed to withstand attack. The Stallion's built like a fortress, the closest thing we've got to a flying tank. Seems to me nothing could take it down unless someone was aiming a Sammy at it. Am I right?"

She shrugged a shoulder, then looked away to avoid eye contact.

Uzi stepped to within a foot from her. "Could it have been a Sammy?" Not surprisingly, she did not answer. Uzi knew this was a sore subject. "Sammys," or SAMs, were shoulder-launched surface-to-air infrared heat-seeking missiles that traveled 1,500 miles per hour—but stood only five feet tall and weighed a stingy thirty-five pounds. Known terrorist groups had gotten hold of at least three hundred of them several years ago. Then there were the Chinese and Russian versions, which could've fallen into who-knew-whose hands, and the Iraqi SAMs unaccounted for after the US invasion.

"Clarice." Uzi waited until he had eye contact. "Could it have been a Sammy?"

"Not likely. You'd need several missiles striking the choppers at the same time. These birds are equipped with state-of-the-art anti-missile technology."

"Such as what?"

"Fast-blinking strobe lights, like the ones in nightclubs and discos. Infrared jamming. The strobes confuse the SAM's eye and throw the missile off course."

"We used to use a low-tech version: throw a hot flare out of the aircraft."

"Same principle. You mind?" She pushed away Uzi's flashlight, which had strayed toward her eyes. "They're also equipped with lasers so bright that they'd confuse the missile's guidance system. Kind of like blinding someone by pointing your flashlight in their eyes." She forced a smile, then crouched beside a small section of the chopper's metal skin. "Then there's IR-attenuating paint that dims the helicopter body's infrared signature."

She ran her own light over the fragment, which was nearly free of foam. "They also spread crucial helicopter components around the vehicle, and install backup copies. That way, the chopper's not as likely to be destroyed by a single missile."

Uzi nodded. He had forgotten about that. "What about the shell of the helicopter? What's it made of?"

"Aluminum alloy. But parts of it have been ballistically hardened. Tough, lightweight armor is placed around the body." Canfield shut off her light and replaced the fragment from where she had taken it.

Uzi stood there a moment, lost in thought. Finally, he said, "But bombs, strategically placed, could take these choppers down. Right?"

She forced her gaze back to his. Her eyes lingered there a long second, then she turned and walked away.

Uzi spent the next ninety minutes covering the crash site and talking with investigators. He kept asking questions designed to prod them into reaching preliminary conclusions as to causation. Though he would not hold any of them accountable for such early impressions, he wanted to get a jump on where to focus his investigation.

No matter who Uzi spoke to, no matter which agency they were with, he kept getting the same opinion: this did not look like mechanical or structural failure.

Either Clarice Canfield was wrong, and a shoulder-mounted missile had been successfully fired at the chopper, or a fuel tank exploded—or a bomb was detonated from inside the craft. Any of these possibilities, even a few years ago, would have raised eyebrows, even led some to chuckle. But after TWA-800's supposed gas tank catastrophe, and after discovering stolen SAMs and detailed al-Qaeda manuals in Afghanistan as well as bin Laden's own operational notes—not to mention security breaches at countless military bases—all three scenarios now made his list of possible explanations.

He approached DeSantos, who was crouching beside the NTSB Powerplants specialist, John Maguire. DeSantos had a bright white LED flashlight trained on a large piece of metal that Maguire was handling with rubber gloves.

"Boychick. Look what we've got here."

Uzi knelt beside DeSantos. "A hunk of aluminum. So what?"

"It's what this hunk of aluminum tells us that's got my interest." DeSantos elbowed Maguire. "Tell him."

"It's only preliminary, Hector. I don't know how accurate it is. I could be way off—"

"Tell him. Uzi's cool, you won't catch any heat if you're wrong."

Maguire hesitated, then sighed deeply. “First of all, best I can tell, there’s nothing here from the tail rotor. If this bird fell from the sky, as I would expect it to, all the pieces would be in a well-defined area. They’re not. That would lead me to believe that the tail rotor might be part of the debris that was picked up on radar a few miles back.” He looked at Uzi, as if willing him to draw a conclusion.

Before Uzi could speak, Maguire nodded at the piece of metal in his hands. “This is from the transmission housing.” He motioned to DeSantos to shine his flashlight on the fragment. “See this?” he asked, pointing with an index finger. “Right here.”

Uzi leaned closer, his warm breath fogging the chilled air. “What am I supposed to be seeing that I’m not?”

“The sharp, jagged edges.”

“Okay, yeah,” Uzi said. “And that means what?”

“When we look for mechanical fatigue, and therefore structural failure, we expect to see chafing of the metal. If we look closely, we can see cracks where the metal gave way. It breaks, and the bird falls from the sky. But there’s no chafing, no overt signs of cracking here. No signs of fatigue whatsoever. In fact, all these parts look damn well brand new.”

“So you’re saying it’s not structural failure.”

“That’s a conclusion I’m not willing to commit to just yet. What I’m saying is that I don’t see any signs of the parts being defective or worn. But there is evidence that something pushed against the transmission housing. Something very powerful and very sudden,” Maguire said.

“‘Something’ as in . . . what?” Uzi asked.

DeSantos said, “Man, you’re thick. A freaking bomb, that’s what.”

“But there’s something that disturbs me,” Maguire said.

Uzi frowned. “If it ‘disturbs’ you, I’m willing to bet it’s really going to upset me.”

Maguire placed the metal fragment where he’d found it. “Whoever did this used a sophisticated device to take down the vice president’s bird. As for the Stallion . . .” Maguire shrugged a shoulder. “Had to be something very powerful. And gaining access to these choppers is damn-near impossible.”

“The fact that they were able to do it is definitely alarming,” Uzi said. He studied Maguire's face a moment. "But . . . that's not what disturbs you."

"No," Maguire said. "If you've got a bomb, and you've gained access to the chopper, I could think of several more effective places to put it. Places that would've made it immediately drop out of the sky. Like the Stallion did. But if radar and the flight path check out, they flew Marine Two for almost five minutes after the first Mayday call."

"Let's go back to the Stallion for a minute. They took it down real fast. No fooling around there. What's its Achilles' heel?"

"Without a doubt, the Jesus Nut."

Uzi smiled out of the right portion of his face. "Excuse me? What the hell's a Jesus Nut?"

"I'm not being sacrilegious. It's the 'nut' that holds everything together at the top of the main rotor. Screw around with it, put a bomb on it, the bird's toast. Drops out of the sky."

"Which is what happened."

Maguire bobbed his head. "That's what we think happened, based on radar. We'll know more once I hear from the team assigned to that crash site. They're searching right now with infrared, but there's miles to cover. That said, if you want my opinion on the most effective way of bringing that chopper down in the middle of the Virginia countryside, that'd be it."

They were silent for a few seconds before Uzi spoke. "So whoever did this wanted the Stallion down quickly, but they wanted Marine Two to stay up awhile longer. Why?"

"There's no terror in a quick death," DeSantos offered. "Whoever did this not only wanted Rusch dead, he wanted him and his family to suffer the terror of his helicopter going down."

"So this might've been personal," Uzi said. His gaze met DeSantos's. "Looks like this is going to be my job for the next year or so."

"It would appear so."

A dust swirl rose from the ground a hundred yards to the north. Uzi, who had left DeSantos and Maguire moments ago, could tell a helicopter had landed, and seconds later the backlit silhouettes of a clot of men began moving toward the debris field. One of them had Marshall

Shepard's shifting gait. Another appeared to be FBI Director Douglas Knox—followed by an unusually large security detail—and another gentleman Uzi could not immediately identify in the murky darkness.

The men stepped into the bright klieg light aura that hovered above the crash site. Knox, wearing a dark suit and matching overcoat that contrasted with his thick head of gray hair, looked out at the firefighters hauling their equipment back to their rigs and the army of investigators combing the debris.

At this proximity, Uzi recognized the other official with Knox as Director of Central Intelligence Earl Tasset, which explained the large contingent of bodyguards: in addition to Knox's security detail, Tasset's Security Protection Officers were also along for the ride.

Tasset said a few words to Knox, shook his head in disapproval at the scene before them, then approached Uzi and Shepard. Tasset had pointed, petite features, John Lennon glasses, and above-the-collar wavy, salt-and-pepper hair with a tightly cropped goatee. Uzi always thought the guy looked more like a progressive college professor than a top spy master.

"Mr. Directors," Shepard said, "this is Special Agent Aaron Uziel, head of WFO's JTTF." Both men, each intimately aware of the Joint Terrorism Task Force, nodded.

Uzi shook Knox's gloved hand, then Tasset's. "An honor to meet both of you," Uzi said.

Knox's eyes roamed the area beyond Uzi's right shoulder. "Report."

"Everything's very preliminary at this point, sir, but my impression is that this was not an accidental downing. No overt signs of mechanical or structural failure. Not to mention they were both real tough birds."

"Anything point to a bomb?"

"There's some . . . suggestion that an explosive device was placed beside the transmission housing of the veep's chopper. But this is all very preliminary."

"Son of a bitch." Knox clenched his jaw. "Find these people, Shepard. Whatever resources you need, whatever it takes, I don't care." He turned to Uzi. "You've got nine days to get me an answer."

Uzi's eyebrows rose. "Nine days?"

"Yes sir," Shepard said quickly. "We'll have that information for you, not a problem."

"I want to be kept aware of everything you learn," Tasset said to Shepard. "The idea is to work together here, pool our intel."

Knox's scowl deepened. "I'm sure he's well aware of 'the idea,' Earl." Knox threw a cautious look at Uzi, then moved off to tour the wreckage. Tasset and his people followed.

As soon as they were out of earshot, Uzi spoke. "Shep, I can't guarantee we'll be any closer to solving this thing in nine weeks, let alone nine days."

"When the director tells you he wants something done, you do it, Uzi. No excuses, just answers. Answers."

Uzi frowned and turned away.

"You need something, let me know. More agents, just tell me how many. That's how this is going to work." When he didn't get a reply, Shepard put a reassuring arm around his friend's shoulders. "Hey, someone tried to kill the president-elect of the United States, Uzi. That's never happened before. This is major shit. And you get to be the guy in the middle of it all."

"Somehow that doesn't make me feel better, Shep." Uzi held up a hand before Shepard could respond. "I won't let you down."

"I know you won't." He tightened his large paw around Uzi's shoulder, then turned and headed off toward the director.

Uzi rolled his head back, ran his hands across his face . . . and wondered how he was going to deliver.

DAY ONE

3:06 AM

Uzi brought his fist up to his mouth as the yawn stretched his lips wide. Fatigue was not just announcing its arrival, it was propping up the pillows and begging him to find a bed. He needed a Turkish coffee—but at this time of night, in the middle of the countryside, that was not going to happen. He hugged his body tight as a shiver rippled through his shoulders.

He hadn't wanted to call his old contact. There were issues such a meeting would bring up, things he didn't want to discuss. But he needed information his former colleague might be able to provide; the man was dialed in, always was, and with a nine-day deadline, Uzi needed something to set him in the right direction, intel that could streamline his efforts and spark his investigation. If there was anyone who could do that, like jumper cables to a dead car battery, it was Nuri Peled.

Uzi sat beneath a grove of trees on a metal mesh bench in Pershing Park, an unexpected slice of suburbia two blocks from the White House. To his right and across the street stood the regal centenarian Willard InterContinental Hotel, the "crown jewel" of Pennsylvania Avenue. Uzi remembered reading that the term "lobbyist" had been coined in the Willard's grand lobby and that writers Mark Twain and Walt Whitman had once chosen it as a place to gather and socialize.

The dense tree canopy filtered what little moonlight trickled down amidst the weary glow of streetlamps dotting the park's multiple levels. Uzi checked his watch, then fought off another yawn. A welcome teeth-chattering breeze blew across his face and woke him a bit. He wished Peled would arrive soon.

Fifteen minutes past the hour, the stocky form of a man in a running suit sauntered up to the reflecting pond set into granite banks near the center of the park. Uzi nonchalantly gazed in the man's direction, positively identified his friend, and then pulled himself off the bench, headed toward the large bronze statue of General John Pershing, the park's namesake. Marbled charcoal granite walls surrounded the figure; historical World War I blurbs and battle tales etched the smooth rock face.

The patter from the pond's fountain masked surrounding noises—so well that Peled was able to make a silent approach. Uzi turned and took in the man's face. More lines creased the eyes and a few scraggly gray hairs sprouted beneath his knit cap, but otherwise Nuri Peled looked the same as the last time Uzi had seen him.

"I didn't think I'd hear from you again," Peled said, his voice as rough as a nail file.

Uzi looked away. "I'm with the Bureau now."

"We know." Peled rocked back and forth on his heels. "How have you been? Since, well . . . since you left."

"Fine. I've been fine."

To this Peled looked at Uzi for the first time, his clear, appraising eyes doing a quick calculation. "You're lying."

"I need some info," Uzi said. He glanced over his left shoulder and scanned the park's crevices. He faced the statue again, the high walls behind it effectively shielding their mouths from anyone attempting to lip-read from a distance. The fountain noise would foil parabolic microphones and other high-tech listening tactics. "Intel," Uzi said, "on hostiles back home."

A short chuckle blurted from Peled's throat. "That's a bit open-ended, my friend. Can you be more specific?"

"Relative to the US, anything major being planned the past few months?"

"There's always chatter."

"I'm not interested in chatter. Reliable intel, Nuri. You know what happened tonight. You know what I'm asking."

"I'm no longer with our former employer. A friendly ally, though. Not to worry." Now it was Peled's turn to check their surroundings. After a scouring look around, he turned back to Uzi and said, "Possibly some activity involving a radical Islamic group. A whisper on the wind that one of them has set up shop here. Haven't been able to verify any of that yet."

"This whisper. Related to the chopper bombing?"

"Can't say. But if they are here, they're quite good, very quiet. Unaffiliated with mosques or imams. Independent funding. At least, no known connections with traditional money sources."

"Best guess."

"Best guess is that I can't guess yet. If you don't mind some friendly advice, this one smells domestic. But that's just my gut. Other than the whisper—which may or may not be related—I'm not seeing anything that puts a foreign terrorist anywhere near your case. But I just started poking around. If they're here, I'll find them. I'll have to dig a little faster in light of tonight's . . . events."

"I appreciate that."

"You know me well enough to know I'm not doing it for you."

Uzi nodded contritely. "Of course."

"I miss working with you, Uzi."

"Yeah, well, things don't always turn out the way we expect them to, you know?"

Peled kicked at a pebble by his shoe, then said, "I'll contact you if I find anything."

Uzi stood there, considering the inadequacy of his own words, thinking how life can change from white to black in the tick of a second hand. He knew this meeting would refresh unpleasant memories, memories he could ill afford to sort through right now. He needed to focus on the task at hand. Directly in front of him stood General Pershing, hero of a war nearly a hundred years earlier. And now a different war in a different world, a war fought against an elusive enemy, without masses of troops or land, tanks or submarines. Brutal and deadly nonetheless.

Uzi turned to shake Peled's hand, but the man was gone. Only the empty cement plaza stared back at him, the white noise rush of the pond's fountain the lone sound of the sleeping city. A brisk breeze reminded him how tired he was. He turned and lifted heavy feet toward his car.

7:00 AM

Long murky shadows stretched across the sidewalk like tendrils from a hideous monster. The dark night stank of death, of destruction and terror. Uzi moved amidst the darkness, through Jerusalem's myriad alleys and hidden spots only he knew . . . scores of stray cats sensing his urgency and scurrying away as he approached.

His nerves were like rotten teeth, ready to crumble at the slightest hint of pressure.

The phone call from Nuri Peled had been short and laced with warning. "Go home, Uzi. Now." Peled then hung up and Uzi took off on foot. Driving a car this close to home was too risky. The chances of being followed were great, the ability to lose your pursuer difficult.

Uzi moved anonymously through the bustling Ben Yehuda with speed and efficiency, weaving among the raucous youth, musicians, and tourists. He cut across the dark Independence Park and emerged on Agron, the urgency in Peled's voice pushing him, driving him faster than was safe.

Go home, Uzi. Now.

What could possibly await him at home that would warrant Peled's attention? Had he discovered a bug buried in a wall of his apartment? Papers hidden away in his floorboards? He had no hidden papers.

Dena . . . Had Dena discovered something and called Gideon? Had something startled her? With Uzi having gone dark—officially an "important business trip" to his wife, while in reality a covert mission in Syria and then Gaza—Dena knew the protocol: call the private security line, and whoever answered would alert Gideon. Gideon would then dispatch someone to look in on his wife and daughter. Dena, of course, did not know who Gideon was, or who manned the private line . . . only that she was to call it at the slightest hint of trouble.

Trouble. Had something happened to Dena and Maya? It was a possibility too painful to even consider. Besides, it was highly unlikely. "They've got the best security anyone could have," Gideon Aksel had told Uzi when he signed on. "Your family will be safe. We live and die by procedure, my friend. Follow it to the letter and everything will be fine." Uzi had branded the rules into his brain like a technogeek embeds an encryption algorithm on a computer chip. And until yesterday's mission, he had always followed procedure. Always.

But now, as he turned the corner to his apartment building and took in the scene before him, his heart skipped and jumped and his stomach pumped his throat full of bile. Police cars—fire engine—ambulance. Living room window missing. No, not missing, blown out—

"Uzi!" Emerging from the front entrance of the building was Nuri Peled, his face as long and dark as the night's shadows.

Uzi moved toward his friend, though he didn't remember covering the distance. They stood toe to toe, Uzi searching his mentor's face for information. Peled only looked up toward the stairs. Uzi turned and flew up the steps, floating, an apparition navigating the air currents as he headed toward his apartment. Through the open front door—no, it was blown off its hinges—he saw a large figure, its back to him.

Gideon Aksel turned. His stout body was rigid, the lines in his leathered face deep. Thick arms wrapped across his chest. He took in Uzi's face, then turned back toward the kitchen.

Rubble lay scattered about the floor of Uzi's small apartment. His home.

Gideon's feet were firmly planted amongst the debris. But he was not looking into the kitchen. He was looking out the window at something below.

Intense fear exploded through Uzi's body like a jolt of electricity.

Dena. Uzi shouted it this time. "Dena!"

He started down the hallway to his right, his legs moving slowly, as though trudging through knee-deep mud.

"Maya?" His mind started to come around, adding things up, taking in the scene. Police. Fire. Bombed out window and door. Nuri Peled at the front, Gideon Aksel inside his apartment.

But his brain wouldn't put it together. Couldn't put it together. His vision mentally fogged like a roadblock to comprehension. And then, in front of him, tucked away in his bed—his own bed, goddamn it!—the bodies of his wife and three year old daughter, bound at the ankles and wrists, blood all over. Blood. Blood in the bed, their throats slashed, eyes still open, staring at—

Staring at him.

He turned away. Through the window, a young woman slithered off in the shadows. The scene was too emotionally painful to process. He wanted to touch his wife and daughter, to kiss them, to whisper "Open your eyes, you're dreaming—" But in that split second, the fog lifted. He knew. It struck him like a sharp blow to the throat. He needed another look, to be sure his optic nerves were telling the truth.

He forced himself to turn back toward their bodies. A glimpse and then his knees went weak and it all came flooding into him. Everything suddenly adding up, making frightening sense. A moan escaped his lips and he realized he was on the floor, knees drawn up to his chest, intense sorrow shuddering up his spine as if death itself had made the journey.

No tears flowed.

Emptiness. Pain . . . anger.

The pressure of a gentle hand against his shoulder. In the background, voices.

Nuri Peled: I'm sorry, Uzi, I'm so sorry.

Gideon Aksel: It's your own damn fault . . . Your own fault . . .

Air shot into his lungs, a sudden gasp of terror as he jolted awake in bed, perspiration oiling his skin slick and shiny. Uzi's alarm was normally tuned to a smooth jazz station, but he must have hit the wrong button when setting it, because this morning the blaring buzzer—which would've awoken an entire battalion—jarred him from sleep.

And just as well. He needed something to shake him awake. To purge the pain from his memory, if only for a little while.

Uzi got out of bed, showered, and dressed for work. As he knotted his tie, he fought off the familiar, gnawing sense of sadness. He moved slowly, feeling as if he'd hardly slept. He had gotten home from his meeting with Nuri Peled at 4 AM, but couldn't fall asleep till some time later. Then the nightmare. It wasn't the first—and after six years of recurring dreams, he was sure it wouldn't be the last.

He punched the Power button on the remote and saw the words "MSNBC News Special Report" fade from the TV, replaced by a full-screen view of President Jonathan Whitehall seated behind his Oval Office desk, hands folded, intense resolve hardening his brow.

"It's with a heavy heart that I come before you this morning," Whitehall began, "on the dawn of another chapter of terrorism that has struck our nation. In our war on terror, we've been relentless in our pursuit of those perpetrating these crimes against freedom and democracy. And we've seen a number of flawlessly executed successes. But as I've repeatedly stated, despite our best efforts to be vigilant, the likelihood existed that we'd not seen the last attack on American soil. That statement has unfortunately proven true.

"I must stress that we do not yet know the identities of those responsible for this latest assault. We must all show restraint while our various agencies conduct their investigations. But know one thing: as we've done in the past, we will find out who committed this horrific act of murder. And then we will bring them to justice—"

Uzi powered down the TV. He had heard the speech before—not word for word, but the sentiments, the tone, the rally-the-troops show of confidence that leaders worldwide had displayed so many times in the past. Bombs, death . . . terror. There never seemed to be a shortage of terror.

He shoved his Glock-22 .40 handgun into its holster in the small of his back, secured his knives, then grabbed his leather overcoat. As Marshall Shepard had not so gently ordered, he had an appointment with a psychologist. Though he would have loved to skip it—and use Douglas Knox's nine-day deadline as an excuse—it would merely be prolonging the inevitable. He would keep his appointment, but make it a brief meet-and-greet. If there was one thing Uzi didn't want to do, it was break a promise to Shepard.

The man had saved Uzi's skin a number of times, and had single-handedly vouched for him when the Bureau was considering his application to the Academy. Uzi's stint with Israel's Shin Bet General Security Services gave the Bureau pause—as did any applicant's prior work history with a foreign police force or intelligence group. But Shepard stressed the positives: Uzi's exceptional investigative prowess, his knowledge of, and firsthand experience with, terrorism—as well as his fluency in Arabic. In the end, Shepard's pitch made the difference. The Bureau desperately needed someone with Uzi's skill set. And Uzi needed the job, not just to support himself financially, but for the diversion it provided from his personal issues.

Still, as he walked down the street to the doctor's office, he could not get past the feeling that the therapy sessions were going to be a waste of time. Before leaving the house, Uzi called his office and asked Madeline, his secretary, to get him the lowdown on the shrink. His cell rang as he approached the front entrance of the building, an upscale ten-story office and residential mixed-use facility with a curved façade and open balconies to M Street below.

Madeline reported that Leonard Rudnick was short on stature but long on experience. He had worked as a consulting psychologist for the Bureau for seventeen years, and though in semi-retirement, his practice now consisted primarily of agents and support personnel.

"Oh, and one more thing," Madeline told him. "There's a special entrance for Bureau employees. A nondescript taupe door. You go in one door and leave a totally different way. For confidentiality."

"Taupe?"

"That's what I was told."

"You think I can still cancel?"

"Uzi . . ." she whined.

"Okay, okay, I'm going."

He hung up as he approached the elevator. Once again he had thoughts of ditching the appointment altogether. He did not like talking about himself or his feelings—two obstacles to successful therapy, based on what little he knew of the practice of psychology.

Uzi exited the elevator, then pushed through the door Madeline had mentioned. He took a seat in the small, cherry-paneled waiting area. His eyes wandered and his knee bounced. There weren't many things that made him nervous, but facing someone to whom he was supposed to bare his soul was clearly one of them. He reached into his pocket, pulled out a cellophane wrapped toothpick, and shoved the mint-flavored wood in his mouth.

A moment later, Leonard Rudnick emerged from his office, a smile broadening his thin face. As Madeline had said, Rudnick was short. By Uzi's estimate, five-foot-two. With shoes on.

Rudnick took Uzi's hand and shook it vigorously. "Pleased to meet you. I'm Leonard Rudnick. You're Mark Klecko—the plumber, right?"

Uzi eyed him suspiciously. "No, I'm— Wait, you're kidding, aren't you?"

Rudnick clapped him on the back and led him into the room. "Of course I'm kidding. An experienced psychologist never guesses at his patient's identity. I know you're Mark Klecko." Rudnick peered over his quarter reading glasses. "Sit, make yourself comfortable, Agent Uziel. I was just pulling your leg."

Uzi settled himself into a firm upholstered chair opposite the seat Rudnick claimed. "Please—call me Uzi."

"Do you happen to know my son Wayne, at the Behavioral Sciences Unit?" Rudnick asked as he crossed his legs.

"Haven't had the pleasure."

"Different world, I guess. Wayne's buried down in the bowels of the Academy, studying serial killers and other such upstanding citizens." He slapped his thigh. "So—Uzi—let's talk about why you're here."

"Because my boss said I had to come."

Rudnick smiled. "I see you can make jokes, too."

"I'm not joking."

The grin faded from Rudnick's face. "I see. Well, we've got some work to do, then."

"That's what my boss said."

The doctor's eyes brightened. "I like a patient with a sense of humor. Now, tell me, Uzi, how do you feel about your boss ordering you to come here?"

"Look, doc, I'm not into this touchy-feely, get-in-touch-with-your-emotions bullshit. I'm not that kind of guy, okay? I don't like to talk about how I feel. Sometimes I don't even like to think about how I feel."

Rudnick nodded, but did not say anything. When Uzi's gaze began to wander around the office, the doctor said, "Go on."

"Go on with what?"

"Why do you think you don't like to talk about yourself?"

Uzi shrugged. "I don't know. I just don't."

Rudnick nestled his chin in the palm of his left hand, his elbow resting on the arm of the chair. "Think about it a moment, okay? Think about why you don't like to talk about yourself."

Uzi began bouncing his knee. Rudnick's gaze dropped to Uzi's fidgeting leg, then came to rest on his patient's eyes. "Extra energy," Uzi said. "Used to drive my wife crazy."

"Oh, so you're married?"

Uzi looked away. "Yes."

"But the information I received said—"

"She's dead. I'm widowed."

"I see." Rudnick waited for elaboration. Uzi did not provide any. "So your wife, did she die of health-related causes, or was it an accident?"

Uzi stopped bouncing his knee. He did not want to get into this. "Neither. But if you don't mind, doc, I'd rather not talk about it."

"I see."

"That's annoying, you know that?"

"What is?"

"The way you kind of look at me and say 'I see.' You don't see anything. With all due respect, this is a complete waste of time. I don't know why I agreed to come." Uzi stood and turned toward the door.

"I believe your boss said you had to." Rudnick's voice was measured, matter-of-fact.

Uzi, facing the door with his back to Rudnick, sighed deeply. He put his hands on his hips. "I'm in the middle of an important investigation, so my time is a bit limited right now, Doctor." He hesitated, then said what was on his mind. "Besides, I disagree with my boss's assessment."

"Well, since you have your orders, and I have mine, and they both involve talking to each other, I suggest we do what we're supposed to do."

Uzi turned to face the doctor. "How often do we have to meet?"

"Four times this week, then three times a week."

"No offense, Doc, but I don't have time for that. I'm running the Marine Two investigation."

"Then you have a lot of people working for you. A little time here and there won't hurt. I'm sure Mr. Shepard wouldn't have . . . suggested you see me unless you really needed it. And I'm sure you could afford a little time out of your schedule. But how about this. Let's strike a balance—take it one session at a time and see how we progress. Fair enough?"

"How am I doing so far?"

A smile crept across Rudnick's lips. It seemed to round his entire face. "That depends. Do you like the truth, or do you want sugar-coated opinions?"

"I don't like bullshit, if that's what you mean."

"That's exactly what I mean," Rudnick said. "So here's the straight scoop, Uzi. You've got some serious issues and your boss sent you here to explore them. I don't have to tell you how you're doing because you already know. What would help is if you'd realize that I'm not here to hurt you, but rather to help you. You tell me something, it stays with me. No one will ever know what we've talked about.

"I think you'll find that once we pop the lid and start examining what's bothering you, you'll feel better—relieved, even. But you have to work with me, help me get to the roots buried beneath the surface. Can you help me do that?"

Uzi turned back to the door. "I'm not sure." He placed a hand on the knob. "When do I need to be back?"

"Tomorrow. Same time, before your workday starts. Again, balance is important. I don't want to take you away from your case."

As far as that goes, we're on the same page.

8:57 AM

The Walter Reed National Military Medical Center, known as the WRNMMC—because it wouldn't qualify as an official military institution without a government-mandated acronym—dated back to the War of 1812. At the time, the facility occupied a rented building adjacent to the Washington Navy Yard. During the next century, its name and location underwent numerous changes until it found a permanent home in 1938 on a 250-acre cabbage farm in Bethesda that would become, four decades later, one of the ten largest medical centers in the country.

The private ICU room was guarded round the clock by a bevy of Secret Service personnel. Doctors and nurses wore photo ID and had their thumbprints scanned each time they entered the room—or they weren't allowed in. Extraordinary measures, even for the military hospital, but after one nearly successful attempt on the president-elect's life, the Secret Service vowed it would also be the last.

Forty-nine-year-old Vance Nunn, slim without ever having seen the inside of a health club, sporting a thinning head of gray hair and facial jowls of a man ten years his senior, waited for the fingerprint identification system to, literally, give the green light. He pulled his surgical mask down, then tapped his foot impatiently, glancing to his left at the Secret Service agent assigned to him.

"Dick, this is ridiculous. Can't you just tell them who I am?"

"Sorry sir. Must be a glitch in the program. I'll make sure it's repaired so you don't have to go through this again next time."

Nunn took that as his answer. Of course Dick couldn't bypass procedures. After what had happened, everyone's actions were being examined with renewed scrutiny. It was post-9/11 hysteria all over again. Though Secret Service agents routinely followed procedure to the letter, the slightest transgression during a time of heightened domestic threat could result in reassignment to the contingent guarding foreign nationals. Nunn would not ask Dick to jeopardize his job.

Nunn and Glendon Rusch had come up through the ranks together, first as senators in neighboring Virginia and Maryland, then as governors of their respective states. As freshmen lawmakers, they had promised each other during a late-night drinking binge at Nunn's brownstone in Georgetown that if one of them ever ran for president, the other would be his running mate. Regardless of the political climate at the time, or who owed what favors to whom, they would somehow make their arrangement work. At least, that was the plan. But Nunn, of all people, knew that plans didn't always take root the way you thought or hoped they would.

Quentin Larchmont, another of their longtime political allies and Rusch's ever-present advisor, also figured into the equation—though in a subservient, or supportive, role, which played to his trusted friend's strengths. Larchmont, who long ago had ambitions of his own, seemed content to ride their coattails, though Nunn figured there had to be some resentment buried deep within. No matter. Both Nunn and Larchmont were good soldiers and, until recently, things had gone as they had always figured they would.

A noise down the hall caught Nunn's attention. A doctor wearing a large red ID tag entered the corridor. Nunn motioned for Dick to wait where he was, then moved to meet the doctor. He extended a hand and said, "Vance Nunn."

"Josh Farber. For what it's worth, congratulations on your victory, Mr. Nunn."

Nunn gave an obligatory nod. "Dr. Farber," he said, glancing around the corridor, "can I have a word with you?"

The doctor motioned to an empty room off the hall. As soon as they entered, Farber tilted his head in inquiry.

Nunn shifted the surgical gown he was instructed to wear and said, "I don't want you to take this the wrong way, Doctor, but I need to know how bad the vice president's condition is." He cleared his throat. "Specifically, whether or not he's going to survive."

Farber lifted an eyebrow. "Mr. Nunn, you have to understand that I can't discuss the vice president's medical status with you. Doctor-patient confidentiality—"

"I understand that under normal circumstances, your patient's condition is something you hold in the strictest confidence. But this situation is anything but normal. If he's not going to make it, I need to know as soon as possible. There isn't a lot of time before the new administration takes over, and a lot has to be done between now and then—not least of which is putting together a cabinet. If the president-elect is going to survive, there'll be one set of people chosen. If not, I'm going to bring in my own people. Glen is a dear friend. Believe me, I'm not trying to pry into his private life or do anything to harm him. But I've got the welfare of three hundred million Americans to worry about."

Farber sighed, then glanced around the darkened room. "Mr. Nunn, you've put me in a very difficult spot."

"Why don't you go ask him? He'll tell you it's okay to brief me on his condition."

Farber nodded slowly. "Please give me a moment."

The doctor disappeared into the hallway, and returned a few moments later. He set down his clipboard and leaned back against the wall, hands shoved into the deep pockets of his white coat. "Despite being in a crash-worthy seat, the vice president's got a fractured right hand and two fractured legs. Left tibia and the right tibia and fibula. But they're uncomplicated fractures and broken bones heal extremely well, so by comparison that's of little concern.

"He's got mostly first- and second-degree burns, which is the good news. The bad news is he's also got some nasty third-degree burns as well. Full thickness burns, open and weeping."

Nunn recoiled a bit at the image.

"The skin is the body's largest organ," Farber continued. "Normally, it sheds fluid all day to help maintain the body's temperature. When the skin is burned, it's even worse. The patient loses a great deal of fluid and sometimes we can't replace it fast enough. Other times finding the right fluid balance is tricky. We've infused the vice president with electrolytes and are watching him for infection."

Nunn rubbed at his chin. "Okay."

"I don't have to tell you his facial burns are going to be disfiguring. Fortunately, I think we'll be able to manage these fairly well with plastics. The idea is to make him look as normal as possible. We've already taken steps. The best surgeon in the country is en route from Los Angeles. Per his orders, we've excised small pieces of skin from other parts of the vice president's body and have them growing in tissue cultures. When they're ready, they'll be used for covering the wounds on his face. I won't lie to you, Mr. Nunn. This will be a long process. Rehab alone could last six months, if not more."

Nunn bowed his head. "Jesus."

"In the acute phase, we'll be debriding his wounds. Once the wounds are appropriately covered, we've got contractures to worry about, particularly where the injured skin crosses joints. Fortunately, there's very little joint involvement. If you're going to burn your hands, the best place to do it is on the palmar surface. If the backs of his hands had been burned, even gripping a pen would cause major pain—and take a year of therapy to accomplish."

Nunn lowered himself down into a hardwood chair at the small table. "How—" He stopped himself, thought a moment, then said, "How can he govern like this?"

"If he can endure a grueling presidential campaign, he's probably an extraordinary individual. In times like these extraordinary people do extraordinary things. But my concerns go beyond running the country. Between the psychological effects of the facial burns and the loss of his family, he's going to require substantial counseling and a good support network."

"Of course."

"Medically, he's fortunate, and I've tried to impart that fact to him."

Nunn's face crumpled into a one-sided squint. "You've got to be kidding."

"He's sustained minor burn damage to portions of his esophagus and larynx, but if it'd hit the lungs his prognosis would've been far worse—pulmonary edema can be quite serious because he'd have to be on a ventilator. No, given what happened—the explosions, a freefalling helicopter, the fire . . . He was very lucky. That's a tough concept when your family's dead, you're hooked up to tubes, we're peeling away layers of skin, and you're looking at permanent disfigurement. Fact is, this could've been much, much worse."

Nunn nodded solemnly, then rose tentatively from his chair. "Thank you, Doctor. I appreciate your candor."

Farber pushed away from the wall, grabbed his clipboard, and extended a hand. "The vice president has given me permission to keep you updated, so feel free to contact me if you have any questions on treatment requirements or timelines, things of that nature." Farber's phone vibrated, and he checked the display. "I've got to take this."

The doctor walked out, leaving Nunn alone. He stood there for a long moment, then headed toward Rusch's room. He nodded at Dick, who was still waiting beside the secured door.

"We should be okay now, sir."

"Then let's give it another shot." Nunn extended his finger, the device scanned his print and a few seconds later, the green light appeared.

"Door break, authorized entry," Dick said into his sleeve. He pushed it open and stepped aside.

Nunn pulled the blue paper mask into place, and then walked into the room. A Secret Service agent stood at attention along the far wall, a hand pressing against the earbud that coiled down along his neck and disappeared beneath the navy suit coat that was barely visible under his gown.

But Nunn's attention was drawn to the bed, where a heavily bandaged man lay. Only his eyes were visible—save for a nose hole and a slit where his swollen lips were coated with what appeared to be a thick layer of petroleum jelly.

"My god." The words rolled from Nunn's mouth without warning. He instantly wondered if the whirring machinery had drowned out his uncensored comment. Without lifting his gaze from Rusch, Nunn said, "Agent, can you give us a few moments?"

"Sorry, sir."

"Look," Nunn said, trying to keep his voice level, "I'm the vice president-elect, I'm not going to harm my friend and running mate."

"Yes, sir." The agent's demeanor remained impassive. "Sorry, sir."

Nunn sucked his bottom lip. Apparently, he was again asking the Secret Service to break with procedure, and that wasn't going to happen. He walked to Rusch's bedside and placed a light hand on his friend's shoulder. "Glen."

Rusch slowly turned his head to face Nunn. "They tell me I'm lucky," he said with great effort, his voice possessing all the smoothness of cracked cement.

Nunn leaned closer to hear. "Have you been briefed?"

Rusch's eyes glossed over, and he turned away. "They're dead."

"My deepest condolences, Glen. There's nothing I can possibly say other than I'm— I'm just so very sorry. I can't believe they're . . ." He choked back a sob. "That they're gone." He placed a hand atop his friend's shoulder.

"I want these fuckers caught. I want to do unspeakable things to them." Rusch turned to the Secret Service agent, who quickly averted his eyes. "But this can't be a personal vendetta, Vance. We have to show the world that no one can do this without suffering the consequences. We have to do it right. Bring them to justice."

Nunn glanced briefly at the hovering agent, then said, "I've spoken with Director Knox, and he assures me that everything that can be done will be done to find them."

Rusch closed his eyes. After a long moment, he said, "Whatever the Bureau does, it'll be so . . . insufficient. Nothing will bring back my family."

Nunn felt it was best to let that comment float on the air for a moment before continuing.

"Quentin's been fully briefed," he finally said. "I assume he's been by."

Rusch didn't reply.

"He and Jordan are researching our options. I'm sorry—I really don't mean to talk business, but I just wanted you to know we've got things covered. Take whatever time you need. Heck, we've got two months to get our house in order." He glanced again at the agent, then said, "Plenty of time."

Rusch remained silent. He was staring off at the ceiling, or the wall . . . Nunn wasn't sure which. But he knew what was on the president-elect's mind. And though they had plenty of time, the truth was that there was still a great deal that needed to be done.

Nunn gave Rusch's shoulder a gentle pat, then left the room.

9:39 AM

Following his brief visit with Dr. Rudnick, Uzi met with the task force members assigned to the chopper crash investigation. They occupied the command post on WFO's fourth floor, an expansive suite of six rooms constructed after 9/11 to bring all functions of a terror investigation into one centralized area. Its main room was equipped with five rows of ten state-of-the-art computer work stations and six forty-two-inch plasma screens, all overseen by the assistant director's command office through a floor-to-ceiling window that dominated the rear of the room.

Beyond the sliding glass doors along the left wall, an ever-expanding group of JTTF support personnel had set up shop. In the past few hours, dozens of agents from the Secret Service, ICE, US Marshals Service, Military Intelligence, National Security Agency, and CIA had reported to their new posts.

Uzi ran through introductions and assignments, then split them into groups that reconvened at the crash sites, with the lead agents remaining behind to monitor the computers.

At first light, the NTSB team working through the night completed an aerial survey that identified three distinct debris fields, the first and most distant one containing a majority of the Stallion's fuselage, the second containing portions of the Black Hawk's tail rotor, and the third consisting of what was left of the vice president's chopper.

The stench of burning brush, smoldering metal, and incinerated bodies hung on the thick, hovering mist.

DeSantos met Uzi as he climbed from his Chevy Tahoe, which Uzi parked at the perimeter of Crash Site C, the resting place of the VP's helicopter. "We've got three areas to cover," Uzi said.

"I'm dialed in. Been to the others already. And I've got some info for you."

Uzi walked with DeSantos toward a concentration of technicians, who were still scouring the wreckage. The flame retarding foam had dissipated, having done its job of suffocating the fire and superheated residue. Without the sudsy film blanketing the site, the debris scene was like an ancient city freshly unearthed by archeologists: what now lay bare before the investigators provided a more complete picture of what had happened. String grids divided the site into sections, enabling the technicians to document the exact location where each piece of evidence was found before being removed to the lab for analysis.

"That chick you wanted me to check out," DeSantos said. "Name's Leila Harel. CIA, Counterintelligence."

Uzi stopped walking. "The one with the body? CIA?"

"So I'm told. Her family's from Iraq but they moved to Israel to escape persecution. She speaks Farsi and Arabic fluently—"

"Probably how she got recruited in the first place."

"Exactly." DeSantos dodged a technician approaching on the run and shifted right, out of the path of other oncoming workers. "First posting was in Jordan. She did well, and now she's stateside."

"What do you know about Earl Tasset? What's he all about?"

"Real piece of work. Quiet, passive aggressive. People have a tendency to underestimate him, think he can be pushed around. But underneath it all, the guy's a pit bull. He and Knox have squared off more than Tyson and Holyfield. Results were usually the same. Both came out bloodied, but Knox won. Tasset's career CIA, worked his way up. Good strategist."

"So what's the friction with Knox about?"

"They're sharks feeding off the same food chain, boychick. When there's enough food—money for their budgets—neither cares how much each one eats. But when things tighten up, they start circling each other in the water, nibbling at each other's blubber. Sometimes it gets bloody."

Uzi snorted. "Nothing like uniting against a common enemy."

"They'll be okay. They know what they're doing. And I can tell you they're both committed to getting the job done."

They stepped around a roped-off grid and passed a couple of technicians collecting a soil sample. "Knox gave me nine days to find out who's responsible."

"Nine days?" DeSantos stopped along the edge of the crime scene. "Doesn't sound like Knox."

Uzi took up a position to DeSantos's right. "Meaning what?"

"Could've come from on high. Don't get me wrong, Knox wants answers as fast as the next bureaucrat. But he's been in the trenches with us. He knows you can't just pick a date and say, 'Time's up. Give me the answer.'"

"That is basically what he said."

"Gotta be a reason. Nine days . . . what's happening in nine days? Not eight, not ten. Nine."

Uzi thought a moment. "Beats me." He pulled out his smartphone and tapped the screen a few times. He threw his head back. "How did I not see this? International Conference on Global Terrorism."

"That changes things a bit. Does he think something's going to happen during the conference?"

"Or," Uzi said, "maybe he wants to use the big stage to make a high-profile announcement? Conference on terrorism, big terror attack on the US, bang—nine days later, the FBI catches the assholes."

"It would make you Fibbies look awfully good."

"And Knox," Uzi said. "Let's not forget politics. Frazier and Ali. Budgets and shark blubber."

"Tyson and Holyfield, not Frazier—" DeSantos eyed him over the tops of his glasses. "You making fun of me?"

"Whatever the reason," Uzi said, "it gives us less time. Conference starts at two." He swiped his finger across the screen, then slid the phone back into his pocket. He walked in a circle, pacing, lost in thought.

"What's with the pacing? What are you thinking?"

"I'm thinking we don't have a whole lot of time to solve this thing." He stopped and stroked the stubble on his cheek. "Okay. We attack it on a few fronts. First we pay a visit to Quantico and interview the flight crew and maintenance personnel who worked on the choppers, then get with CIA and NSA to see if they picked up any chatter they didn't process fast enough."

DeSantos was nodding at each of Uzi's suggestions, then added, "We also need to look into the backgrounds of the other people on the choppers. Just in case. It's easy to get myopic, too focused on Rusch as the target. That's the most obvious, but it could also be way off base."

"Already on it. Two members of my task force are meeting right now with the Special Agent in Charge of the Secret Service Presidential Protective Division. He's putting together a list of agents and staff who were aboard both choppers. There were also some journalists on the Stallion."

"Yeah, but journalists don't make enemies."

Uzi smirked.

"Okay, so they make enemies. But not the kind who'd go to the trouble of killing the VP just to knock off a White House press correspondent." DeSantos's gaze lingered somewhere behind Uzi. "Your curvaceous spook is approaching."

Uzi was tempted to look, but thought better of it. "Give me a few minutes, then we can head over to the base."

DeSantos grunted. "Go do your thing, boychick. I'll do mine. When you're ready, come get me." He winked, then walked off.

Uzi nonchalantly turned, caught sight of Leila Harel, and headed in her direction. She was wearing terrain-appropriate boots, with black form-fitting tights stretched from her narrow waist down her long legs to her ankles. Clutching a clipboard against her chest, she knelt to examine something on the ground.

"What do you see?" Uzi asked. He was standing behind her and just off to her left.

Without turning, she said, "Charred dirt." She lifted a handful and sifted it through her slender fingers.

He noted her manicured red nails, then said, "Charred dirt. Strange thing to find at a crash site, don't you think?"

Still facing the ground, she said, "No."

Uzi frowned. His attempt at humor passed right through her, like an apparition. "What agency are you with?"

She did not answer.

"If I had to guess, and that certainly seems to be the case, I'd say you look like CIA." He rubbed his chin in mock thought. "Yeah, I'd say CIA."

Leila tossed the rest of the dirt to the ground, then slowly uncoiled her legs and stood. "I thought you were here to investigate the wreck." She turned her body, shoulders first, followed by her hips and legs. The form-fitting tights were complemented by a red turtleneck that clung to her full breasts.

Uzi felt his eyes wander down to admire the sweater before he abruptly brought them up to her face. Her comment about him investigating the wreck was mocking him, taking his stammering remark from last night and throwing it back in his face. But after the split second of embarrassment, he realized that she had remembered exactly what he had said.

"There are a lot of things here to investigate, it would seem," he said with sudden confidence. As he held her gaze, he could see a slight wavering in her eyes. There was warmth buried inside, though she worked to keep it hidden. "So am I right, CIA?"

"You're very persistent, Agent Uziel."

And she remembered my name. "Call me Uzi."

"Calling you by a nickname would imply a certain casualness to our relationship that we don't have."

Uzi shrugged. "Not really. No one uses my last name, not even people who hate my guts."

Leila's phone began to ring. She reached into her shoulder-slung purse, answered the call, then turned her back on him. After waiting a few moments, Uzi walked off to find DeSantos.

"That thing I was working on." DeSantos held up his BlackBerry as Uzi approached. "Got something."

Uzi waited a beat, but DeSantos did not elaborate. "You gonna keep it a secret?"

DeSantos glanced around to make sure no one was nearby. His gaze still off somewhere, he said, "Word is that ARM had a hand in this."

Uzi chuckled. "ARM had a hand? Is that a joke?"

"No boychick, no joke. Reliable intel. American Revolution Militia."

"My focus since—well, since 9/11—has been foreign. Bureau's all about counterterrorism and counterintelligence. ARM's domestic. I'm a little thin here. Help me out."

DeSantos buttoned his wool overcoat while formulating his thoughts. "I pulled together some info this morning, so I've got the basics. They came together about thirty years ago. Dude named Jeremiah Flint started a chapter in West Virginia that grew slowly over time. Then Jeremiah was gunned down during a routine traffic stop in Arlington."

"That must've gone over real well."

"Better than you think. He became a martyr. The new guy who took over focused them, started running them as a business. We may have a copy of their charter on file. I'll pull it. Basically, they're like most militias: they don't like the government. They think everything should be handled at a local level. They dispute just about anything that restricts them or takes their money: the Constitution, the IRS, the Federal Reserve, our court system. You know the deal."

Indeed he did. Patriot groups like The Freemen, and disasters like Ruby Ridge and Waco were required reading at the Academy. "The JTTF keeps up on domestic threats, but we've had our eye on home-grown Islamic radicals. They travel in different universes than domestic militias."

What Uzi kept to himself was that the man in charge of his task force's domestic terrorism unit happened to be the agent he just put on report: Jake Osborn.

"So you said this is reliable intel. Where'd you get it?"

DeSantos twisted his neck in both directions, checking the area before answering. "OPSIG," he said, referring to the covert Operations Support Intelligence Group, the supersecret band of Special Forces players housed in the Pentagon's basement. It was a group that did not exist on paper, with members who often worked for a bogus corporation and carried false identification. Hector DeSantos's unofficial employer.

"And why would OPSIG be involved?"

"You should think about coming on board. With your background, you'd be in invaluable asset."

"Join OPSIG?" Uzi drew his chin back. "Are you recruiting me?"

DeSantos winked.

"I'm flattered. But not interested."

"Think about it, boychick. You're a natural. And you'd be doing a lot of good."

"I'm in charge of the JTTF. I do plenty of good. Besides, my head's not in the right place."

DeSantos looked him over, grabbed Uzi's chin and moved it left, then right. "Head's square over your shoulders. Looks good to me." He chuckled, then said, "Okay, fine. I get it."

"So the American Revolution Militia. What makes them different from all the other crazy groups out there?"

DeSantos smiled, then slipped both hands into his jacket pockets.

"Top of the list, my man, is that none of the others is suspected of trying to assassinate the vice president of the United States."

Leaving DeSantos's red Corvette at the crash site and taking Uzi's Tahoe, they drove to the ARM compound, a heavily wooded parcel set on gently undulating hills just east of Vienna, Virginia. While en route, DeSantos read Uzi a hastily prepared intelligence brief to give him a deeper sense of what—and who—they would be facing on their arrival. After finishing the three page summary, DeSantos suggested they arrive unannounced, even though he expected the guards to be on full alert because of the helicopters' downing—particularly if they'd had a hand in their demise.

Uzi stopped the car in front of the eight-foot-tall masonry wall topped with sharp razor wire. "They mean business," he said, eyeing the barricade.

DeSantos ripped open a Juicy Fruit pack and folded a stick into his mouth. "If they're anything like my source described, we ain't seen nothing yet."

Uzi continued on to the main entrance, a fortified wrought-iron, motor-driven gate on wheels. A guard shack stood on a concrete slab off to the side. As the Tahoe's tires crunched the gravel road near the gate, a man dressed in combat fatigues and thick Remington camo boots emerged from the shed with a submachine gun clutched between his hands. He took a position behind the gate, legs spread wide.

Uzi pulled his SUV up to the gate, then rolled down his window. He held open his credentials wallet, the ID and shield facing the paramilitary man. "We need to talk with Nelson Flint."

"Got yourself a warrant?" The man's voice was cigarette raspy, thick with a Southern accent.

Uzi frowned. "Do we need one?"

A click followed by a muted voice blurted from the man's radio transceiver. He pulled the device from a leather harness on his belt and brought it to his face. He listened a few seconds before lowering it and slipping it back onto his belt. "Someone'll be by to get you."

Uzi and DeSantos got out of the Tahoe and leaned against the fender, the guard fingering his weapon and staring at them with contempt. DeSantos nudged Uzi's forearm, then nodded at a small, round, black-and-gray device mounted above the guardhouse. "Surveillance camera," he said by Uzi's ear.

Uzi had already taken notice. "I count fourteen. And anticlimb sensors on the fencing, and ground-loop vehicle sensors in the pavement where we're parked." The chomp of rubber on gravel snared their attention. Along the curve just beyond a stand of mature pines, an olive green Humvee appeared amid a low-lying dust cloud.

DeSantos played with the Juicy Fruit between his front teeth. "Welcome wagon arrives."

The SUV pulled to a stop alongside the guard shack, and, on the parasoldier's signal, the pedestrian gate opened electronically. Uzi followed DeSantos through and they climbed into the Hummer's backseat beside a man with close-cropped black hair. DeSantos slammed the door, and the driver, also sporting a Marine-regulation hairstyle, accelerated. The escorts remained quiet during the brief drive to the compound's apparent headquarters, a rectangular two-story Civil War-era brick house with two large Ionic columns that swallowed the entrance.

The vehicle stopped beside the front porch. Uzi and DeSantos were ushered to the side of the structure, where two small wood steps rose to a separate entrance. They entered and moved through the kitchen into the dining room. Clearly used for meetings now, the worn oval table that dominated the space sat covered with neatly stacked file folders, five smartphones, and an equal number of laptops.

Each of the window panes on the far wall had the wavy and bubbled appearance of era-specific glass. Hanging on the eggshell walls were faux Wanted posters sporting the Federal Reserve Chairman's face, a Nazi flag, and a framed reproduction of the Declaration of Independence.

"The fuck you people want?"

The deep, southern drawl came from the hallway behind them. Uzi spun and saw two men clad in combat fatigues, one fireplug short and squat, the other tall and lanky. As they approached, Uzi extended a hand. "Special Agent Aaron Uziel." He indicated his partner. "Hector DeSantos."

The squat man looked Uzi in the eye but did not offer his hand.

Instead, he shook his head. "A kike and a spic. The fuck this country's coming to."

DeSantos tilted his head, appraising the two men. "You know, Uzi, they kind of remind me of Abbott and Costello."

The thin one crossed his arms. "Don't much care for your humor."

"Sorry if I offended you," DeSantos said. "We spics aren't very polite." He nudged Uzi with an elbow. "Stringbean here is Rodney McCourt. Half-pint's Nelson Flint, heir to the throne after his father passed on."

Flint's chest puffed. "You mean was murdered."

"Pull a gun on a law enforcement officer, bad shit happens," DeSantos said.

Flint rooted a cigarette from his pocket, then stuck it between his lips. "Guvament's been spying on us again, Rodney. Using their fancy satellites to intrude on the average citizen's right to privacy."

"That's right, Mr. Flint," Uzi said. "We know all about you. And you know a lot about us, too. Like why we're here."

"Haven't the slightest," Flint said with a straight face.

DeSantos smiled wryly. "I'm sure if you think about it, it'll come to you. You're a semi-intelligent person."

"Six months ago," Uzi said, "your man, Bryce Upshaw, told a reporter for the *Washington Times* that Vice President Glendon Rusch would be sorry if he didn't re-examine his views on the right to bear arms. *He'd be sorry*. Those were his words, Mr. Flint, not mine."

"And now the Veep's helicopter is blown out of the sky," DeSantos added. "We don't think it was a coincidence."

"Mr. Upshaw was not speaking for our organization."

"Of course not," DeSantos said. "That would cause some . . . trouble for you, wouldn't it?"

Flint's face shaded red. "Upshaw was a goddamn fool. He's no longer part of our organization."

Uzi and DeSantos shared a look. "Was he a fool because he said stupid things, or because he said things in public that were best left behind closed doors?" DeSantos glanced behind him at the entrance to the room. "These doors, in fact?"

Flint pulled the unlit cigarette from his lips, then pointed it at

DeSantos as he spoke. "You two fuckers are here because I allow you to be here. Don't push your luck. I give the word, my guards'll haul your asses off our property."

DeSantos took a step forward into Flint's space. He looked down on the diminutive man and said, "You're a coward, Flint. A small man with a small man's brain. The only way you or your father could ever amount to something was for you to start your own organization where you could be the boss. Anywhere else you'd be sweeping floors or sorting garbage."

Flint's face flushed. "You son of a bitch—"

"You have something to do with those choppers going down," DeSantos said. "And we're going to prove it."

Flint grabbed DeSantos by the collar and pushed him back against the wall. "Get the fuck off my land!"

Before Flint could react, DeSantos swiped the man's hands to the side and spun him around. Rodney moved toward them, but Uzi stepped to the right and blocked his path.

DeSantos pushed Flint's face against one of the windows as he snapped handcuffs on his wrists. "You've got a hard-on for the government? Fine. That's your right. But don't assault a federal officer. That's just stupid, even for you."

Flint struggled, his nose grotesquely deformed by the glass. Mucus sucked in and out of his right nostril as a tear ran down his cheek. "You're . . . on my property . . . asshole."

DeSantos pulled up on Flint's handcuffs and the man cried out in pain.

"Santa," Uzi whispered into his ear, "turn down the volume. Let him go."

DeSantos hesitated a second, then fished out a long black key from his pocket and unlocked the handcuffs. "If we find anything connecting you to that chopper blast, we'll be back with an arrest warrant. Then we'll be chatting on *my* property, asshole."

Uzi eyed the tall man behind him. "We'll be seeing you two again."

Telling the Humvee driver to go to hell, they hoofed it back to Uzi's SUV, taking the opportunity to survey the compound. A well-armed guard trailed at a distance, his purpose to offer assistance should his visitors encounter difficulty finding the way back to their car. Actually, he was almost assuredly tasked with ensuring they didn't take any unwelcome detours—or photos—while traversing the ARM property.

Uzi thought of the OPSIG intelligence DeSantos had shared with him: it suggested an as-yet undisclosed figure was involved with ARM, someone with the business sense and management skills that Nelson Flint didn't possess. After this brief meeting, Uzi agreed with the assessment: Flint was a figurehead. There had to be a string puller lurking behind the scenes.

Uzi flicked a glance over his right shoulder at their tail, and figured the man was out of earshot. "Our Nelson Flint wasn't very forthcoming."

"Didn't expect him to be. Idea was to piss on their land, stake out our territory for our next visit. Maybe we'll stop by again in a few days."

"Something tells me he won't let us in again."

A grin broadened DeSantos's face. "He won't have to."

"I don't wanna know what you have in mind." Uzi breathed in deeply. "Nice chunk of land they've got here. Smell the pine?"

DeSantos unwrapped another stick of gum and sniffed it. "I like this smell better."

"You gotta be kidding. Juicy Fruit?"

"Brian used to chew it all day. Every day. Can't get it out of my head. It's all I've got left."

"It's hard losing a partner. On the job?"

DeSantos nodded. "Took a bullet. A black op we were running for Knox." DeSantos shoved his hands deep into the pockets of his wool overcoat. His eyes roamed the trees and building façades. "CCTV cameras on the redwoods every thirty feet."

Uzi had been checking as well. "Standard resolution color, infrared motion sensors. Wired. Pretty basic stuff."

They walked a few more feet in silence before DeSantos continued. "Brian died the same day his wife gave birth to a baby girl. My goddaughter."

Uzi thought back to the gum and DeSantos's comment. "You took it hard."

It was a moment before DeSantos answered. "Still am."

12:03 PM
193 hours 57 minutes remaining

Uzi and DeSantos drove in silence to Quantico Marine Base, a trip Uzi was accustomed to making because the FBI Academy was located on the eastern portion of the same campus. The Marine Corps's history on this site was well rooted, dating back to its establishment in 1917 following America's entry into World War I. Quantico became one of the largest shipyards in the country.

Uzi pulled in line behind a dozen or so cars and waited to gain admittance to the base. A brick gateway stretched across both lanes of traffic, emblazoned with large block letters:

QUANTICO - CROSSROADS OF THE MARINE CORPS

"Never came through the main gate before," Uzi said. He eyed the stiff military formality of the checkpoint, then the granite-based commemorative statue of soldiers raising the American flag at Iwo Jima, just off to the right. "Definitely more . . . Marine-like than the FBI side of the base." He looked at DeSantos, whose gaze was off somewhere in the distance. "Ever been here?"

"A few years ago. Did some training with the top dog, Major Vasquez. The AMO, Aircraft Maintenance Officer. He's responsible for all the upkeep done on the executive helicopter fleet."

Uzi pulled up to the guard post, where they were greeted by a lance corporal dressed in a crisp, fresh uniform. They showed him their credentials, explained why they were there, and waited while the Marine made a call to obtain authorization.

A moment later, the man handed back their cred cases and admitted them onto the base.

The Marine Corps Air Facility, thirty miles and a stone's throw by helicopter from downtown DC, resided in a densely wooded Virginian paradise with its own marina off the Chesapeake, a private golf course, riding stable, recreation areas, sports leagues, youth centers, and school system.

As they drove along the main drag, Fuller Road, Uzi noticed what appeared to be residential apartments peeking through the trees about thirty yards to his left. "Base housing?"

"Nope. See that creek?" DeSantos asked, nodding at a shallow grass-covered bank with water tumbling through. "That's the boundary of the base. Twenty feet beyond that is Triangle, Virginia. Civilian neighborhood."

"No secured wall along the perimeter?"

"Hard to imagine, huh?"

"So," Uzi said, "anyone could walk right onto the base. Not even a chain-link fence to climb."

"The town of Quantico is civilian, too. Located a couple miles down the road. I guess you could just tell the guard at the main gate you were going into town and they'd have to let you in."

"Yeah, right."

DeSantos shrugged. "They probably figure you gotta be crazy to try something on a military base with a thousand armed Marines walking the grounds."

Uzi thought of the suicide bombers he'd encountered, the mass destruction of 9/11, the planned attack on Fort Dix. Problem was, these people *are* crazy. "How much further to HMX?"

"Couple minutes."

In addition to serving as the training facility for a plethora of Marine units, Quantico's least publicly known function was to house and operate Marine Helicopter Squadron One, the only operational fleet on the base. Officially coded HMX-1, the squadron's primary purpose was to provide helicopter transport for the president and vice president, as well as for cabinet members and foreign dignitaries as authorized by the Director of the White House Military Office. HMX-1 was where the ill-fated Marine Two and Marine Three flights had originated on election night, having pre-positioned earlier in the day closer to Washington.

As Uzi and DeSantos approached the air facility, encircled by nasty razor-wire-topped chain-link fencing, they came upon another security checkpoint. After again providing their credentials for verification, they waited while the sergeant-of-the-guard phoned Major Warren Vasquez to obtain permission for them to access the Cage Hangar.

Vasquez apparently gave the sergeant whatever authorization he required, because the gate opened and the guard returned their IDs. Uzi proceeded down a circular drive along the two-lane road, then parked his SUV across from the large brick barracks building, where both of them got out. "Even if someone got onto the base," DeSantos said, "getting into HMX is a different story."

They headed toward the Cage's entrance, where they were met by more guards. The corporal examined their credentials yet again, then informed them that Major Vasquez was en route.

As the guard pulled his two-way radio from a clip on his shoulder, a large, glistening bottle green and white helicopter approached in the distance. It hovered fifty yards away, the wind from the beating blades ruffling Uzi's hair and kicking up a windstorm of dust that cascaded outward from the ground beneath the chopper. Uzi held up a hand to shield his face and watched as the bird touched down on a red circular plank of wood set out on a grassy field that simulated the landing area on the White House lawn.

"That's a VH-3D," DeSantos said above the grind of the engines. "Presidential transport."

"I've seen photos." *And pieces.* "Beautiful bird."

DeSantos nodded. "They've got a dozen of them, all identical. Uh, they had a dozen."

Uzi covered his ears to lessen the whining thump of the rotors. "Damn noisy, though."

"Only on the outside. Sound dampers around the engines bring it down to less than seventy decibels inside. No louder than a car."

A man in dress blues with graying temples and a leathery, pocked face pulled in front of them. His formal demeanor evaporated when he caught sight of DeSantos. He climbed out of his SUV and grinned broadly.

"Santa. How've you been?" He threw his hand out and the two vigorously shook.

"I'm still breathing, so all's good. You?"

His grin sagged. "Doing well till yesterday."

"That's why we're here. Aaron Uzi, FBI." Uzi extended a hand and received a more subdued, official greeting. "We need to talk with you about the pilots who handled both birds that went down, the VH-3D and Super Stallion, as well as the maintenance personnel who've worked on them."

"I've got the information in my office." Vasquez turned to the Marine behind him. "Corporal of the Guard, provide these two gents with visitor badges."

After Uzi and DeSantos signed in, they were handed their red clip-on placards and escorted through the turnstile by Major Vasquez.

"HMX-1 is divided into two areas," Vasquez said as they walked. "A green side and a white side. Green is where new personnel are screened and observed when they're first assigned here. After they clear the background check, which can take a year, year and a half, they're transferred to The Cage—the white side—which operates and maintains the Executive Detachment. That's the fleet that transports the president and vice president, their wives, and high-ranking support staff."

"The Cage?" Uzi asked.

"It was once surrounded by a tall security fence," Vasquez said. "Looked like a cage. Now it's a modern looking metal hangar connecting those two red-brick buildings you saw outside that go back, I don't know, maybe fifty years. All together, the 150,000-square-foot building is where we store the dozen helicopters, support offices for Crew Chiefs, Flight Line Division Chiefs, and the AMO—Aircraft Maintenance Officer."

"Nice setup," Uzi said.

"Started out in '47 as an experimental Marine unit to test and evaluate military helicopters. Wasn't long before it became an important part of presidential transport after Eisenhower used a chopper for an emergency trip from Rhode Island to DC. He was hooked—very convenient and very fast. Bang, we started using helicopters to ferry around the executive staff."

"What's the 'X' stand for?" Uzi asked.

"Experimental. All new birds and their modified systems were tested and evaluated right here. Now we do it at Pax River, NavAir HQ over in Lexington Park."

As they entered the large hangar, Vasquez motioned with a sweeping wave of his hand. "Welcome to The Cage. Ever been inside here, Agent Uzi?"

"No, sir. Fascinating place, though." He craned his neck around the cavernous structure, which currently housed about ten aircraft.

"You got H-3's, like the one that went down," Vasquez said as he pointed to the far wall. "Some of the threes are still in service since the Kennedy administration. It's a tribute to our vigilant maintenance program that they've lasted so long."

Unless someone blows it up.

"Then you've got the newer members of the fleet, the VH-60s. We put them into commission around eighty-eight. These things are the real deal."

"Black Hawks," Uzi said. "I've flown them. Great bird."

"Yes they are," Vasquez said with a slight nod. "These may be a bit different than the breed you know. State of the art. Not as comfortable and roomy as the H-3, but we can fold these things up and pack 'em into the back of a C-5 and take them overseas. They're a crucial part of our emergency relocation service because of their versatility. We can mobilize them damn near immediately. Since you know the basic Black Hawk design, you know they're battle-hardened. Ours can take a hit from a twenty-millimeter shell and still keep flying."

Just then, the whine of a craft's rotors filled the hangar. Uzi and DeSantos glanced out the open doors and saw a VH-60 powering up. The noise began building as Vasquez placed his hands against their backs and ushered them to an office along the periphery of the Cage's interior.

Vasquez shut the door, muting the noise. Models of fighter jets and helicopters adorned his large desk, with framed commendations and photos of Vasquez mugging with three presidents, including a glossy 8-by-10 with Jonathan Whitehall, on the wall behind him.

"Gentlemen, please." He motioned to two chairs in front of his desk. "I've got some materials I can share with you. Documents prepared for our internal investigation."

DeSantos settled into his seat. "We'll need a list of all the mechanics and maintenance personnel who have clearance to be near those choppers."

"Got it right here. Just about to go out to the safety board. I can run a copy for you." He pressed a button on his desk phone and a lance corporal entered the room. "Two copies of each document," he said, holding the file out to the young man.

"What can you tell us about the pilots?" Uzi asked.

Vasquez's shoulders squared up. "The men assigned to HMX-1 are some of the best we have to offer, Agent Uzi. They go through rigid training in evasive maneuvers, zero-visibility and close-formation flying. We're like the post office. Neither rain nor snow nor sleet will keep us from our jobs. The president or veep need to go somewhere, we go. No questions asked." He looked down at his desk, hesitated, then continued. "As to the men who went down with their choppers, I can tell you each of them was an extremely competent, highly decorated pilot. No problems with any of them."

"Then let's talk about others who had access to the birds," Uzi said. "Crew chiefs and maintenance personnel. You looked over the list. Any cause for concern?"

"Same story goes. Best of the best. Crew chiefs and other maintenance personnel are selected for assignment to HMX-1 based on exceptional performance and integrity while assigned to squadrons of the Fleet Marine Force. Their competence is beyond reproach."

"I wasn't asking about their competence, sir. I was questioning their patriotism."

Vasquez and Uzi shared a long stare. Uzi knew that questioning a Marine's commitment to his country was tantamount to the worst insult one could muster.

DeSantos cleared his throat. "I don't think Uzi means any disrespect, Warren. We have reason to believe an explosive device was planted aboard the craft. Most likely here."

Vasquez's brow crumpled and his mouth slipped open. "What?"

"It's all preliminary, and of course confidential. But I think you realize there are tough questions that have to be asked. No one wants to be asking them, least of all us."

Vasquez's face softened. "I know that." His gaze drifted off to somewhere on his desk. He sighed deeply. "Damn." He reached for the phone, punched an extension, chewed his lip until someone answered. "Top, I need some info. Get your keester over here ASAP." He shook his head. "Then drop everything. Just get over here."

As he hung up the phone, Uzi said, "Let me ask the question I asked before. Given that new information, does anything about these men stand out? Anything at all?"

Vasquez thought for a moment. "Nothing. One thing I didn't mention earlier. These guys go through a Yankee White. Know what that is? Hector?"

"Very thorough background check for personnel who have regular contact with the president and veep. Includes an SSBI—Single Scope Background Investigation. Bottom line—they're looking for unquestioned loyalty to the United States."

"All well and good," Uzi said. "But we've got a set of facts that don't jibe."

Vazquez squinted. "Bombs. You sure?"

"It's preliminary," Uzi said. "Lab's working it up now. The debris was scattered over a large area, and the techs don't like to jump to conclusions. Especially in a case like this. Obvious question is, How could a bomb be planted on one of those choppers? It'd have to be done here, right?"

Vasquez shifted uneasily in his chair. "I don't see where else. But you need to understand something. These birds are treated like fine gems. They're polished inside and out. We have rigid procedures for anything and everything done to them."

"I didn't mean to imply you don't."

"We have built-in redundancies and checks and balances every step of the way. So after a mechanic completes his work, he signs a form indicating exactly what was done and how long it took. An inspector then checks his work to make sure it meets our highest standards. He signs a form stating he's checked it. Then a Collateral Duty Inspector gives it his once-over and a Quality of Work Inspector signs off on it."

Vasquez interlaced his fingers and rested them on the desk in front of him. "Then the crew chief acts like a mother hen, inspecting the aircraft and signing it off as fit for flight. The pilots then come out and take another look at it."

"You're assuming that the person who planted the bomb sabotaged the part he was assigned to repair or replace," Uzi said.

"He could've been assigned to replace a battery," DeSantos said, "then placed the explosive beneath the rotor assembly. No one would see it, and none of the follow-up inspections would catch it. The inspectors would merely see the new battery and sign off on it."

Vasquez was silent as he studied his desk.

"Is that possible, Major?" Uzi asked.

Vasquez looked up at Uzi. "Yes." Before he could elaborate, his phone buzzed. He listened, straightened, then said, "Send him in."

The door opened and revealed a man his late forties with a red grease rag in his left hand. "This is Master Sergeant Cole Conrad," Vasquez said. "We call him 'Top.' He's the Cage's Flight Line division chief. Participated in Desert Shield and Desert Storm with a Super Stallion squadron. Top here can tell you anything there is to know about these beasts." Vasquez indicated his guests with a nod of his head. "This is FBI Special Agent Uzi and Hector DeSantos, DOD."

"Master Sergeant," Uzi started, "I'm going to give you a hypothetical, and I want you to treat it with strict confidence. It's only a hypothetical, and if what I'm about to tell you is taken as the truth, a whole lot of shit'll be stirred up. We clear on that?"

"Very clear, sir."

"If I told you a bomb took down Marine Two and Three, what would you say about that?"

Conrad shifted his feet. "You asking me if it's possible?"

"Let's start with that," DeSantos said.

Conrad shrugged. "Yes, sir. Very possible."

Uzi glanced at DeSantos, then said to Conrad, "Possible because a bomb could take one of these things down?" Uzi asked. "Or possible because someone could gain access to the fleet?"

"The former, sir."

"Even the Super Stallion?"

"Even the 53s. Yes, sir."

"How would you do it?"

Conrad chafed his hands against the red grease rag. He looked over to Vasquez before answering. After getting a permissive nod, the master sergeant said, "A standard military M112 demolition block—that's only a pound and a quarter of C-4—placed on the rotor hub would cause her to drop like a rock, with no hope of recovery."

Recovery, Uzi knew, was another term for "autorotation," a way of regaining control of the craft with the tail rotor gone.

Conrad continued: "Assuming I had access to the explosive material, it'd be a relatively simple deal. In fact, I could take the Stallion down with only half a pound, really."

"Where would you put it?"

"Well, the pilot or crew chief always does a walk-around before the flight. So I'd want my explosive to be well concealed." He shoved his grease rag through a belt loop, then shrugged. "If the pilot's good, and we've got only the best here, he could set the bird down even without a tail rotor, so I'd probably put the explosive on the main rotor hub."

"Ever hear of the Jesus Nut?" Uzi asked.

Conrad smirked, then snorted. "'Course." His smile faded. "This bird isn't named the Super Stallion for nothing. It's the largest, most powerful and technologically advanced helicopter in the world. Its only weakness is the Jesus Nut. Every mechanic worth his salt knows that."

"So if a block of C-4 was placed near the Jesus Nut, no one would see it on their walk-around?"

Conrad nodded knowingly. "The thing about C-4 is that it can be molded into just about anything. If I was doing it, I'd shape and paint it to look like part of the rotor head assembly."

"How would you detonate it?" DeSantos asked.

After a moment's thought, Conrad said, "Radio detonator or timer. I'd choose a discrete radio channel and detonate it where and when I'd want to." He threw a nervous, sideways glance at Vasquez, then added, "Hypothetically, of course."

Uzi and DeSantos were quiet.

Conrad again looked to Vasquez, then back to Uzi. "Anything else I can help you with?"

"Anyone on your staff show any strange tendencies?" Uzi asked.

"Sir?"

"An affinity for molding C-4," DeSantos said. "Or sympathy for right-wing groups. Or anyone who's made derogatory comments about Glendon Rusch. That type of thing."

Conrad angled his eyes ceilingward for a moment, then said, "No one, sir."

DeSantos crossed his arms over his chest. "I know it's a tough question, Master Sergeant. I'd be asking you to rat on a colleague, which is something Marines just don't do. I understand that. But we need an honest answer."

The "rat on a colleague" remark made Uzi flash on his own situation with Osborn. Like a pinprick to a fingertip, the comment caused some pain.

"Yes, sir. If I think of anything, I'll let Major Vasquez know."

"Thanks, Top," Vasquez said. The Master Sergeant nodded, then left.

Uzi sat there in the silence thinking how it easy it would've been to blow up those choppers—something he wouldn't have thought possible fifteen minutes ago. But there were still too many unanswered questions that required leaps of logic to bridge all the gaps.

"How about work attendance?" DeSantos asked. "Drug problems, disciplinary actions?"

"Impeccable records. All of them. I wish I had a smoking gun, a problem Marine who'd been reprimanded, but you wouldn't find that here. There's really nothing I can think of. I assume you'll want to interview each of them?"

DeSantos nodded.

The major lifted the phone and selected the extension for the Maintenance Material Control Officer. "It's Vasquez. Assemble the maintenance personnel in The Cage in fifteen minutes." Vasquez listened for a second, then asked, "How late? . . . Yeah, I'll hold." He cupped the phone and took the copies from his assistant, who had just entered the major's office. He handed the papers to DeSantos and said, "All personnel on Alpha shift will be available for questioning. One of the men is reporting in late—" He turned back to the handset. "Are you sure?" Vasquez chewed his bottom lip. "Fine. Thank you, Gunner."

"Problem?" DeSantos asked.

"One of the men was due in late, but hasn't shown yet."

"Is that unusual?" Uzi asked.

"He's an hour and a half overdue. Yes, that's unusual, Agent Uzi. Very unusual."

Uzi and DeSantos shared an uneasy look. "Tell you what, Warren,"

DeSantos said. "Why don't we postpone our interviews with the flight crew. Uzi and I will check out your missing man."

"It's probably nothing." Vasquez stood, then shook his head. "Shit."

Uzi ended his call as they approached the Tahoe. "My people already did some legwork for us. They've assembled a spreadsheet with backgrounds on all the flight crew, including the crew chiefs and maintenance personnel. They're sending it through right now."

"Sending it through to where?"

Uzi held out his phone. "To this."

"Your phone?"

"This is no ordinary smartphone. I've rooted it—hacked it, modified it. Made it . . . smarter." Uzi winked. "Just a bit. I mean, just a byte."

DeSantos looked at him. "Is that some kind of computer joke?"

"It was supposed to be." They got into the SUV and Uzi fired up the engine. He navigated his phone's screens, then handed it to DeSantos. "Page down through the spreadsheet."

"Is this thing secure?" DeSantos asked, taking the device.

Uzi chuckled. "I'm using Serpent-Twofish-AES encryption, which is three ciphers in a cascade—"

"Uzi. Uzi—I don't know what that shit means." He quickly raised a hand. "And I don't wanna know. Brian was a technogeek. He thought a good time was finding a way to hack into government and corporate computer systems. I never had the head for any of that crap."

"I spent five years working on chip design for Intel. I led the team that designed and built the Pentium 4."

DeSantos winced. "Why do I attract people like you?"

"Other way around. People like us are attracted to know-nothings like you. Makes us feel superior. Besides, I'm not a total techie. My motorcycle's a thirty-year-old dinosaur. Suzuki 450. Air cooled engine. Sat in my parents' garage for a dozen years till I moved back to the States, dug it out, and gave it mouth to mouth." He flashed on the rides in the hot New York summers—frigid wind rippling his shirt, intense acceleration as he twisted the throttle, the engine roaring with power. When he had told Dena he missed his motorcycle, she forbid him from buying one in Israel because it was too dangerous. *If she only knew what I really did for a living.*

"Wife bought me a Harley last year for my fortieth."

Uzi eyed his partner. "Nice gift."

"That's what home equity lines are for. Guess I should be thankful we're not underwater," he said absentmindedly as he sifted through the names on Uzi's phone. "This shit's gonna take a while to go through."

"Start with our missing Marine."

"Corporal William Ellison." DeSantos continued scrolling through the document until he found the entry. "Got it. Lives on base, a lettered apartment on John Quick Road. Couple miles from here."

He gave Uzi directions, then started reading the backgrounder on Ellison.

Uzi departed the Air Facility, then turned onto Barnett Avenue. "Anything pop out?"

"Guy's a model soldier, like Warren said." His eyes flicked right and left through the summary. "Could be a dead end."

Uzi accelerated. "We'll find out real soon."

Uzi turned onto John Quick Road and drove up to the 2000 block, then pulled in front of Corporal Ellison's residence. The three-story, six-family base-issue apartment building, with its thirties-style architecture and red-brick masonry, reminded Uzi of the school he attended in New York.

Two anonymous-gray aluminum gang mailboxes rose from the sidewalk like sentries guarding the entrance. Concrete-and-wood park benches stood astride the front walkway.

A patrol car sat parked at the curb, its radio crackling with dispatch chatter. Uzi craned his neck to look at the cruiser through the passenger window. "Looks like we've got company."

"Marines wouldn't let the FBI get the jump on their investigation," DeSantos said. "Despite my relationship with Warren." He handed Uzi back his phone, then got out and followed his partner to the front door. "How much of a lead you figure they got on us?"

"If they were on patrol and passing by, five or ten minutes."

Uzi led the way across the threshold, holding out his credentials case as he encountered the first military police officer stationed in the entryway.

"FBI. Aaron—"

"I know who you are, sir." The MP was a couple of inches shorter than Uzi, but his crisp uniform and formal demeanor gave him an air of control. "They'll be done in a few minutes."

Uzi said, "We'll just head on in and look around. I'm sure Major Vasquez wouldn't mind."

"Ellison here?" DeSantos asked.

The MP, his jaw tight, answered with a terse, "No."

DeSantos shouldered past the officer, followed by Uzi. After passing through the hallway, Uzi and DeSantos split up, each taking opposite ends of the rectangular apartment. Five minutes later, Uzi entered the family room and caught DeSantos's eye. They walked out of the apartment building together and stopped behind the Tahoe. Uzi glanced over his shoulder to make sure the base police were not within earshot. "Anything?"

"Nothing," DeSantos said. "You?"

"There was a message. On his answering machine."

"I didn't hear anything."

"I lowered the volume. If this turns into something, I wanted to make sure this time we got the jump on our 'buddies.' With nine days to get to the bottom of this, we can't afford to waste time with turf battles."

Uzi glanced back at the apartment again before continuing. "It was a female voice." He pulled out his phone, tapped and swiped at the screen several times with a finger and said, "He's got a younger sister, lives off-base. Could've been her. She was reminding him of her doctor's appointment at eight. She also wanted him to pick up some groceries on the way to work."

DeSantos squinted. "Groceries? Strange favor to ask a brother, don't you think? Especially when he lives on base and she doesn't. Not exactly 'on the way.'"

"Maybe she's laid up and he's helping her out. Hence the doctor's appointment."

"Time stamp on the message?"

"Nope. Old microcassette deal. Rewind the tape to the beginning and record over the messages. It was right at the beginning, so it's recent. He's missing this morning, so maybe she left it last night."

DeSantos indicated the apartment with a nod of his head. "You got anything else you want to look at in there?"

"I'd rather go check in with the sister."

"Let's do it. Before our friends get the same idea."

"Don't worry about it." Uzi tapped his pocket, where the tape was safely buried. "For the moment, this is our lead."

Katherine Ellison lived in Dumfries, Virginia, a small, backward-leaning town fifteen miles from her brother's apartment. Her house was a dilapidated clapboard, with weeds and gravel in place of a lawn, and weathered siding that was once blue but had long lost most of its pigment. Still, the surrounding land was wooded and green, pleasant and quiet.

Uzi pulled against the curb, blocking the short driveway where a red Dodge Ram was parked. "Does the corporal own a pickup?"

"In fact, he does."

Uzi's eyebrows rose, an understated movement intended to punctuate the fact that Ellison was there and that something had to be amiss. "He hasn't called into work."

DeSantos thought for a second, then said, "Sister's ill and he took her to the hospital."

"His pickup is blocking the driveway."

DeSantos's eyes darted around as he sought another explanation. "They took her car, which was parked at the curb. Or an ambulance came and took both of them to the hospital. Or—"

"When you hear hoof beats," Uzi said, "think horses, not zebras." It was an old medical school saw his father had drummed into him: when presented with the unknown, first consider the most obvious explanation before turning to the obscure ones.

DeSantos reached beneath his jacket and pulled out his Desert Eagle. Uzi was doing the same with his Glock. "Ready?"

Uzi nodded, then quietly popped his car door. Crouching low, they hurried up the broken concrete walkway, hands on their weapons and eyes scanning the windows for movement. As they stepped onto the wood porch, a floorboard creaked loudly under their weight. Uzi winced.

They took positions on either side of the door. DeSantos pointed at the doorbell. Uzi shrugged. At this point, if a nefarious sort was inside, he'd probably know they were there. Uzi nodded for DeSantos to continue. He pushed the button and a tinny, high-pitched bell sounded.

A moment later, Uzi balled a fist and rapped on the flaking wood door. Nothing.

"Is that blood on the doorframe?" DeSantos asked.

"Where?"

"There." DeSantos indicated generally with a dip of his nose.

Uzi didn't see anything, then understood.

"Someone's life could be in danger," DeSantos said. "We'd better go in."

As Uzi opened his mouth to object, DeSantos kicked in the door.

Uzi swung into position, Glock held in front of him, knees bent, eyes darting around the interior. He slid in, followed by DeSantos. Pistols leading the way, they began clearing rooms.

It didn't take long for Uzi to find what they were looking for. "Santa! In here."

DeSantos appeared seconds later. His shoulders slumped in resignation as his eyes found the uniformed Marine lying faceup on the threadbare carpet. "Shit."

"Corporal Ellison, I presume."

DeSantos moved the man's arm with the tip of his Desert Eagle, and the nametag, now visible, confirmed Uzi's assumption. "Large caliber weapon." He got down on a knee to examine the gunshot wounds in the forehead and chest. "A forty-five with hollow point rounds, I'd guess."

"Shooter was standing about fifteen, twenty feet away. Over there," Uzi said, nodding toward the far end of the room. "Groceries are on the counter. Bag's from the base commissary."

"I love it when everything fits together."

"Sister?"

"Let's go see."

They walked together down the hallway, on alert with guns still drawn, though Uzi figured the killer was long gone. They entered the first room on the right.

"Oh, Jesus," DeSantos said.

In the bed sat a radiation-bald Katherine Ellison, a bullet hole in her forehead, the dark stare of death draped across her face.

While DeSantos briefed Vasquez by phone, Uzi called the field office and informed Marshall Shepard of what they had found at Katherine Ellison's house. The FBI forensics unit was dispatched immediately and arrived in twenty-five minutes. One of the task force members accompanied the lab techs, allowing Uzi and DeSantos to return to Corporal Ellison's apartment.

Upon their arrival, they began a methodical search of the Marine's residence. While DeSantos rifled through old papers and files, Uzi mentally walked through the facts of the case. Someone wanted Ellison and his sister dead. The questions were obvious: who and why? And more significantly, was there a connection to the downing of Marine Two?

Uzi sat down at a cabinet housing the corporal's computer and started poking at the keyboard.

A few minutes later, DeSantos gestured at the monitor. "Find anything with ARM letterhead?"

Uzi managed a laugh. "I have a feeling we're not gonna find any smoking guns in this case."

"No, guess not." DeSantos tossed the file onto the bed behind him. "Just smoking helicopter debris."

"We should bring his PC over to the lab, have CART go through it," Uzi said, referring to the Bureau's Computer Analysis Response Team. "There's all sorts of shit that gets buried on hard drives that people don't know about. They think because they delete something, it vanishes into thin air."

DeSantos nodded. "Brian once said the data's still there, but the computer can't find it."

"Your partner was right," Uzi said. "A computer's hard drive is like an index system. When you delete a file, it stays on the hard drive but its entry in the index is removed. The supersmart computer thinks it's gone, but good old low-brow human intelligence can find it."

DeSantos leaned back. "You admit that?"

"Hey, what's fair is fair." He nodded at the PC. "Can we take what we need, or do we have to clear it with Vasquez?"

"You have to clear it." The voice came from behind them, down the hall. Warren Vasquez appeared a second later. "Just submit an inventory of what you're taking," he said to Uzi. "And don't forget to copy me on every report you people generate."

"Of course," Uzi said. "We're all on the same side."

"Let's hope so," Vasquez said.

Uzi's head tilted. "What's that supposed to mean?"

Ignoring Uzi's comment, Vasquez tossed a glance at DeSantos. "I assume that answering machine tape will show up on the inventory, right?"

Uzi could feel a slight sweat break out across his back. "Of course."

Vasquez's eye twitched slightly. "Good," he said, then walked out.

Fifteen minutes later, Uzi ended a phone call, then found DeSantos in the garage. "Anything?"

"He was a gear-head, apparently." DeSantos swiveled his body, nodding at the mess of objects strewn before him. Car magazines, specialized tools, cases of synthetic oil."

"You're on your own for a while." He held up his phone. "Shepard just called. I was summoned to the White House—"

"Agent Uziel?" A suited man entered the garage and displayed his Secret Service credentials. "Please come with me."

"As I was saying," Uzi said to DeSantos as he backed away toward his escort. "The president wants a dialogue with me."

DeSantos cocked his head in bemusement. "A dialogue with the president? How quaint."

Uzi tossed DeSantos his keys. "Catch up with you later. Don't scratch the paint."

President Jonathan Whitehall stood on the sloping, manicured patch of grass behind the Oval Office, a puffy goose down vest snapped around his torso and a titanium putter clutched in his leather-wrapped hands. Several balls were arranged in a row in front of him. He was lining up a shot, seemingly oblivious to Uzi's presence.

Not wanting to disturb the president's concentration, Uzi stood off to the side, waiting for Whitehall to acknowledge him. He had been escorted to the Southwest Gate, then handed off to another set of agents who ushered him to the tip of the grass, turned, and left him there.

"How long are you just going to stand there, son?" Whitehall's voice had the southern drawl Uzi had become accustomed to hearing the past eight years.

Uzi felt like he should have been awed by the man's presence, or at least be a bit nervous because of the setting. He was on the president's turf—literally—and totally unprepared for this meeting. Had he known in advance, he would've worn a suit. Then again, maybe not.

Marshall Shepard's warning did not give him much to go on. All he was told was that the president wanted to see him. Innocuous enough. But Uzi had learned years ago that casual chats with powerful leaders could sometimes evolve into something much more significant . . . if not downright dangerous.

He stood with his hands shoved deep into his leather overcoat's pockets, legs spread wide, conveying relaxed confidence. "Didn't want to disrupt your shot, sir." Courtesy first and always.

"Nonsense," Whitehall said, his eyes still focused on the putter. "Is this the way you're running your investigation? Afraid to assert yourself?"

"There are very few things I'm afraid of, Mr. President."

Whitehall looked up and found Uzi's gaze. Uzi did not look away. Whitehall conceded the silent battle and straightened. Keeping the putter in his left hand, he walked the ten feet separating the two men. Though Whitehall had lost half an inch sometime between sixty and seventy, it did not make much difference: his physical stature was not where his strength lay.

Whitehall had the reputation of being a hard-hitting negotiator, a staunch conservative who held to strict Republican values, a politician who always played fairly—a rarity in Washington. Tough, but fair. A man many liked to hate, but admired. His brutally direct nature had gotten him into trouble, while earning trust and respect among foreign leaders. He once told the Chinese premier his tie was god-awful ugly, and smiled while doing it.

Uzi had never met Whitehall, but he had read enough of the man to know he was the sort of no-nonsense, straight-shooting leader for whom Uzi preferred to work.

He seemed to study Uzi's face with a thorough once-over glance, as if he were inspecting a soldier in boot camp. "This . . . incident with the vice president—my vice president—can't go unpunished. I want every fucking terrorist associated with this bombing strung up by his balls. If someone knew about it and didn't do anything to stop it, I want him held responsible, too. I want their wives hauled in. Their barbers, car mechanics. Nothing overlooked. Am I making myself clear?"

"I assure you, Mr. President, we're doing everything possible to get these cowards. We'll find them." Uzi's eyes darted around the periphery. "Sir, it's not my place to pass judgment, but are you sure it's a good idea to be out in the open like this? Since we don't know who's responsible—"

"You're right, son. It's not your place. I've been in meetings round the clock. I needed to clear my mind, get some fresh air. I've got a contingent of Secret Service agents who won't let me take a piss without following me into the goddamn bathroom. After Marine Two went down they shoved me into the PEOC and didn't let me out for five hours. I won't be held prisoner like that again. The president of the United States can't be hiding, cowering away in some protected safe room. It's degrading."

Although he had never been there, Uzi knew that the PEOC was the Presidential Emergency Operations Center, located below the East Wing. An elaborate bunker, it was designed to withstand all types of non-nuclear attacks while allowing the president to remain in communication with other government facilities.

Whitehall lifted his putter and pointed it at Uzi. "The leader of the greatest country in the world has to lead by example." The movement of the putter in front of Uzi's face provided the emphasis. "If 9/11 taught us anything, it was that we've got to get on with our lives, show the terrorists they haven't won. And this is how we go on living." He craned his head toward the clearing sky. "By taking a few minutes off to clear the mind and hit some balls on a damn fine afternoon." Whitehall seemed to be lost in thought for a moment as he stared at the moving clouds. "Damn fine afternoon, wouldn't you say, son?"

"Mr. President, you asked me here for a reason—"

"Focus on what you're paid to do. See the big picture. In case Mr. Shepard didn't make it abundantly clear, we're hosting the International Conference on Global Terrorism in eight days. I don't have to tell you the embarrassment this incident has caused us. We can't even deal with terrorism in our goddamn backyard, and we're supposed to be heading up the effort to contain it on a global basis." He shook his head. "Bastards."

Shepard had not, in fact, mentioned it. But as he and DeSantos had surmised, Knox's deadline was dictated by the conference. Uzi had been briefed three months ago on the security measures being implemented, but Homeland Security and the Secret Service were firmly in charge, and his unit was not involved in either the planning or execution, so it had slipped to the far reaches of his mind. Whitehall had a point . . . and perhaps the attempt on the vice president was not personal, as he had been thinking. Maybe it was meant to send a message.

Whitehall moved back to the line of balls. He spread his legs, swung the putter and popped the ball so hard it flew into the air and landed well beyond its intended target.

Uzi stood there, wondering if Whitehall was done talking to him. He wasn't going to wait much longer. Standing there was a sign of weakness. He counted to three, then said, "Thank you, Mr. President." As he started to walk off, Whitehall called after him.

"There's something else you should know."

Uzi turned and waited for the president to meet his gaze.

"The conference is a cover. It's a working meeting, don't get me wrong. But there are bigger issues at stake. Time-sensitive issues, political issues. Things that mean a great deal to me."

Uzi cocked his head and quickly moved closer to the president. The nearest Secret Service agent, blending innocuously into a row of bushes a few yards away, slowly inched forward, clearly taking notice of Uzi's movement.

When they reached whisper distance, Whitehall continued. "High-level peace talks between the Israelis and Palestinians. Unofficially sanctioned, totally clandestine. Special negotiators from each side are coming to town to nail down a blueprint for peace. 'Bout fucking time.

I don't intend to let this slip through my hands in the waning days of my presidency. No one, no one knows about this but me, the secretary of state, my Secret Service detail, and now you. And it has to stay that way, you understand me, son?"

Uzi suddenly found himself rigid, at attention, his head tilted slightly back, a posture assumed when being addressed by a drill sergeant. "Yes, sir."

"Both my national security advisor and Director Tasset tell me there're some Mideast extremist groups high up on our list of suspects."

Uzi fought to absorb this news without reaction. Tasset had said nothing to him at the crash site about foreign extremist involvement. And the CIA rep on his JTTF had not yet made that assertion. Perhaps it was merely a knee-jerk reaction to a bold terror event of such striking scale. With their focus now on ARM, he wondered if he should brief the president on the turn the investigation had taken. He decided to keep his mouth shut until he was more certain of his facts.

"Some of these groups have had ties to certain factions within the Palestinian leadership for years," Whitehall continued. "Hamas, for one. That's no surprise to you, I'm sure. But if they're responsible for the assassination attempt, I need to know that before I sit down at the table with these people. Because instead of brokering a landmark peace deal, I'll be telling them they have six hours to get their people to safety because we'll be bombing their fucking government buildings into a pile of rubble."

Whitehall let Uzi chew on that a bit while the crimson drained from his cheeks. He rolled his shoulders, then said, "So you know where I stand on this, son, I do not want this investigation to show Palestinian involvement. I want this peace deal. It's good for the Middle East and it's good for the long-term stability of world markets. It further isolates Iran, and it brings some calm to a region plagued by decades of violence. And it's good for America." He paused, looked out at the roses a dozen feet away. "And, it's good for me. If I can come away with a comprehensive peace deal, accomplish something no president's been able to accomplish, well, then, that would be a mighty pretty feather in my fishing cap."

Uzi squinted against the bright sky. Was Whitehall telling him not to do or say anything that might implicate the Palestinians, even if he later found that they were involved? Or was he conveying his hope that they were innocent—but that they'd suffer severe consequences if they had done the deed?

"Make no mistake," Whitehall said. "Whoever they are, the bastards who did this are going to pay, Agent Uziel. Whether it's in the courts, at the wrong end of a volley of Tomahawks, or in some back alley, they will pay for ruining my last days in office."

After nearly fifty years in politics, it appeared that Jonathan Whitehall's public and private personas had merged, shaped by political rhetoric and sound bites. Uzi felt like he needed a translator to cut through the chaff, to be clear what this man was truly asking him to do.

"My last two months will be a hallmark of my administration," Whitehall continued. "It's not always how you perform, it's how you leave the stage that people remember. I want to be remembered as a strong leader who led the people through a difficult time, who brought us out better than when we went in. Above all, it's imperative we show these terrorists that no one fucks with the United States of America and gets away with it. Getting bin Laden was a really good deal. But it's old news. This— This latest attack is now the story of the day, maybe of the decade. Each day these terrorists escape justice is an insult. Do you understand what I'm saying?"

Uzi definitely did not. At the same time, this was the president. He felt intense pressure to appear confident, competent, and up to the task. But he wasn't sure what that "task" actually was. He had to risk asking for clarification. "Sir, what exactly would you like me to do?"

Whitehall jammed his putter into the turf. "I want justice, goddamn it!" The president looked hard at Uzi. In a low voice, he said, "I don't care how you get it. Do things by the book, but if you have these fuckers by the balls, don't let 'em disappear into thin air while you jerk around with a judge trying to get a warrant, goddamnit. Just get the job done." His eyes coursed Uzi's face again, as if searching for something. "If you can't do that, tell me now and I'll find someone else who can."

Was the president directing him to shoot a suspect in cold blood if the "need" arose? Due process right there on the street? Uzi had taken orders like this in the past, but they were always backed by hard evidence and the corroborating proof of reliable intelligence.

He wondered why he was being asked to do this when Whitehall had a man, and a group, at his disposal who carried out such missions without concern for legal proceedings. DeSantos. OPSIG.

A stiff wind smacked Uzi in the face. He looked at the president a few feet away and realized the man was awaiting his response. It appeared Whitehall was ordering him to be judge and jury. Uzi wondered if he was, indeed, up to the task. His commanding officer was giving him his marching orders, and he was expected to comply. In the past, there was only one time when Uzi had questioned his superior, and it ended in disaster.

Still, Whitehall's demeanor gave him pause. Whatever Uzi did, he had to be damn sure he was right. There was a lot in play, a great deal at stake. Uzi nodded slowly. "You can count on me, sir." Then he turned and walked away, unsure of the methods by which he would act. But the president's admonition continued to bounce around his thoughts like a superball on speed.

Just get the job done.

5:01 PM
188 hours 59 minutes remaining

Alpha Zulu had the constitution of a retired Navy SEAL. Yet though he moved with the slyness of a wild cougar, he prided himself more on his chameleonic ability to reinvent his appearance and demeanor to suit his environment. But an innate sense of timing was his most valuable asset.

He was the ideal person for this job, even if his business partners had not known the depth of his talents when they first initiated contact.

Alpha Zulu had a real name, of course, but almost no one knew it. He had several aliases, including bogus credit cards he used once a month, checking accounts, and studio apartments in seedier parts of town with utility hookups set on automatic debit from the bank to give the appearance of regular activity. Whatever he couldn't do himself, he had a small group of confidants he could count on to legitimize his illusion. It was all about credibility and the ability to blend in—into society, into a crowd, into everyday life, without anyone noticing him.

And in spite of all the post-9/11 security hype, he still functioned with impunity. No one in law enforcement knew who he was or what he was up to. He literally operated off the radar.

Zulu parked his run-of-the-mill Ford Escort on Tracy Road in Kalorama Heights, three blocks from the home of Republican Congressman Gene Harmon. Harmon held a powerful position in the United States government: head of the House Select Committee on Intelligence. Harmon was privy to secrets a mere handful in the government knew, and when a covert mission was undertaken, he was one of only eight individuals who were informed of the action before it was launched.

Zulu moved in the shadow of early nightfall, timing it so that even the occasional streetlight did not awaken while he was in the middle of his maneuver. Carrying a small device that fit inside the housing of a standard cell phone, he stepped briskly past the columned entryway of the sprawling, four-story, five-thousand-square-foot brick-and-slate Victorian mansion.

He turned right into the sunken driveway, knelt to tie his shoe, and set down the rigged phone. He continued down Tracy Road another two blocks, then crossed the street and headed back toward the Harmon residence. His destination was a narrow easement between two well-maintained three-story homes, one of which had a realtor's sign sunk in the postage stamp lawn. While well-hidden, this location provided an unimpeded view of the congressman's garage.

Zulu removed two pointed snowshoes from his compact backpack and fastened them to his Timberlands. Walking with them provided a challenge, but it was a necessary precaution. He settled himself behind the black iron gate and blended into the fauna that filled the space: ivy and well-pruned privet hedges. He repositioned the ski mask, then pulled a pocket watch from his fanny pack.

This was no ordinary watch, however. It was custom-crafted in Switzerland, the mecca of time-constipated artisans whose creation of accurate timepieces approached sexual ecstasy. Commissioned by Zulu's group three years ago, the pocket watches were fashioned from Italian sterling silver, engraved with curls and whorls in a pattern that emphasized its classic—indeed timeless—style.

In the center of the lid was a gold-inlaid scorpion, its powerful oversize claws, jointed tail, and venomous stinger manifest evidence of its menacing lethality. Zulu related to the arachnid; he owned several species from around the world and bonded with them as some do dogs. His shared kinship and common modus operandi made the scorpion a logical choice for the group's unofficial crest.

Thirty-five minutes passed. Zulu, dressed in black neoprene pants and top, was doing his best to fend off the chilled temperature. Though it was no colder than forty degrees, remaining still and squatting in bushes stagnated the blood and numbed his extremities.

After Zulu rose to flex and extend his feet—contracting the calf muscles helped the circulation in his legs—Congressman Gene Harmon's garage door rolled up. The midnight blue BMW crawled forward, up the driveway's gentle incline. Zulu brought a pair of compact night-vision binoculars to his eyes, positively identified the congressman through the windshield, and prepared to trigger the device, waiting for the right moment. Timing, as always, was key.

He squeezed the button and a split second later, his task was complete.

4:52 PM
189 hours 8 minutes remaining

After retrieving his car, Uzi headed off to interview Glendon Rusch at the Walter Reed National Military Medical Center. After arriving, he was directed to Building 10, where he took the stairs to the ICU. After clearing the security protocols at the door to Glendon Rusch's room, he hesitated with his hand on the knob. He'd seen injured soldiers before, men whose faces were obliterated by mortar rounds, women and children whose flesh and body parts were strewn a block away by a suicide bomber's explosives. But no matter how many times he'd done it, facing a terror victim was never easy.

Uzi had been told the president-elect's ability to talk would be dictated by his level of sedation and pain tolerance. He didn't expect the interview to last long or provide a magic bullet lead, but he had to make the attempt.

After gowning, Uzi settled the mask over his face and pushed through the door. He took in the scene with one quick glance: blinking and quietly thumping machines monitored Rusch's vitals and infused his ravaged body with fluids. He let the door swing closed behind him, then nodded at the Secret Service agent and took a few steps to Glendon Rusch's bedside, a move that drew the patient's attention. He slowly turned his head and his gaze found Uzi's. Though Uzi could not see his face, he thought he read pain in his gray, medication-hazed eyes. Not physical pain, however. Emotional pain.

Uzi squared his shoulders and said, "Special Agent Aaron Uziel. FBI."

Rusch blinked, but said nothing.

"I'm sorry for your loss." The words tumbled from Uzi's lips, but hurt the instant they left his mouth. He hadn't considered what he would say to the man when he first saw him. Only the investigative questions he needed to ask had populated his thoughts. But he immediately felt the inadequacy of his impersonal condolence. Uzi had once been on the receiving end, and in his fragile state, it irritated him with each successive utterance, like a repeatedly chafed wound. He hoped his delivery was sincere, somehow stained with his own pain.

"What can I do for you, Agent?" Rusch's voice seemed labored, coarse, and fatigued.

"Mr. Vice President, as hard as this may be for you, I need to talk to you about what happened. In the helicopter." Uzi was unsure how he should refer to Rusch. Mr. Vice President? Mr. President-elect? He chose the safest one, figuring that at the moment Rusch had more problems to deal with than caring about what title an FBI agent used when addressing him.

Rusch nodded ever so slightly. Uzi took that as a signal to continue.

"Sir, we know that explosives took down both choppers—"

"Then you already know . . . as much as I do."

Uzi hesitated. "Is there anything you can add? Can you tell me what happened in the cabin?"

"I lost my wife and daughter." Each word was undercut by anguish. "Nothing else matters."

Uzi knew firsthand this man's pain. He searched for the right words. "There's nothing we can do to change that, sir, but we want to catch the people who did this. Bring them to justice."

After a moment's silence, Rusch said, "I don't remember much. I heard the explosion—or felt it, I guess. The escort was first. And then . . . us. Next thing I know, a medic's bent over me." His eyes shuttered closed. "I wish I could tell you more."

"Do you have any idea of who might've wanted you dead?"

Rusch focused his gaze again on Uzi. "You're assuming I was the target."

"At the moment, we're looking at everything, everyone. But you always start by giving the most obvious the most emphasis. Someone went through an awful lot of trouble and risk to pull this off. Given that, you're the obvious target."

Rusch looked away. "As a prosecutor, I went up against teamsters, mobsters . . . violent criminals. As governor I signed the death penalty into law." He took a drowsy breath, smacked his petroleum-glossed lips. "I was a bastard of a VP, fought people . . . on several volatile issues. Point is . . . the list of who'd want me dead is . . . is too long to even keep track of."

Uzi hoped Rusch would say more, but he merely shut his eyes. Uzi took the hint. He pulled a business card from his pocket and set it on the cabinet beside Rusch's bed. "Call me if you think of anything. Thank you for your time, sir." He turned and headed for the door.

"One thing," Rusch said, his pain-weary voice barely audible over the whirring medical equipment. "Catch the people responsible, Agent Uziel. Don't do it for me. Do it for my wife and daughter. For this great country of ours."

Uzi dipped his chin in acknowledgment, then left.

5:25 PM
188 hours 35 minutes remaining

Uzi stood a dozen feet from the charred and exploded remains of Congressman Gene Harmon's BMW. He leaned against the moss-covered distressed-brick wall, sucking on a toothpick as the crime scene techs combed the ruins.

He had barely made it out of Glendon Rusch's room when his cell phone rang.

"Better get your ass over to Kalorama Road," Shepard said.

"What's on Kalorama Road?"

"Not what, Uzi, who. Congressman Gene Harmon. Or what's left of him."

"Shit."

"Yes, shit. Big time shit. Director's out of his freakin' mind—"

"I'm on my way." After Shepard gave him the address, Uzi headed for the exclusive neighborhood where congressional representatives, ambassadors, and other foreign dignitaries resided. He made good time, but now that he was at the scene, he realized there was nothing for him to do but watch. And think.

He felt helpless. Though his better sense told him Gene Harmon was only the latest target of their anonymous assassin—or group of assassins—he needed to find the connection . . . that one strand of evidence that established a relationship between Rusch, Ellison, and Harmon. Then he could begin focusing on motive. And once he had motive, it would only be a matter of time before he fingered the Unknown Subject, or UNSUB.

At least in theory. In practice, nothing was easy. Nothing was merely "a matter of time." Often it was hard work, intuitive insight, and a lot of luck thrown into a pot and allowed to simmer. How long? Who the hell knew. Sometimes years.

He didn't have years. He had a little over a week.

Uzi pushed away from the brick wall. One of the technicians, a tall, thick woman with latex gloves stretched over pudgy fingers, held a piece of flat black plastic a few inches in length.

"What's that?" Uzi asked.

She held it higher, as if getting a better look at it would give him the answer. He shrugged.

"It's part of the injection mold of a cellular phone."

Uzi suddenly became aware of DeSantos beside him. He glanced at his partner, then turned back to the technician. "So it's an injection mold. The congressman had a cell phone. Who doesn't?"

She held a flashlight against the material and parallel powder burn striations became evident. "Most people don't have cell phones bearing evidence of an incendiary device. C-4 residue, I'd guess. But that's preliminary."

Uzi looked at DeSantos. "That might be our link."

"Remote device, detonated by a simple call," DeSantos said. "Leave the phone somewhere, in this case the driveway, and when your target drives over it, you make your call."

Uzi sucked some more on his toothpick, then said, "So that means our UNSUB was somewhere nearby, watching and waiting for the right time."

DeSantos nodded, then turned to assess the street. "There's a lot of tree cover. It's a short block. Even with NVGs, he'd need a clear view."

"Well, let's get started. Short block or not, this is gonna take a while."

It did not take as long as Uzi had thought. Within the hour, a Metro PD cop found prints in the moist dirt across the street from the congressman's house, in a narrow easement between two adjacent homes. The crime scene techs were on it immediately and made plaster castings.

If this was, in fact, where the killer knelt an hour or so prior, it was potentially the break for which Uzi had been hoping. At least they could estimate the suspect's height, weight, and gender, and possibly even determine where he bought his shoes. From such tiny bits of information, major leads were often born.

But for all he knew, the castings were merely an expensive reproduction of the gardener's work boots. His better sense told him otherwise. For now, he would have to wait—and hope.

6:30 PM
187 hours 30 minutes remaining

Quentin Larchmont stood just outside the impromptu press room at Glendon Rusch's transition headquarters—formerly the suite of offices used to direct his campaign—a short distance from the White House.

Larchmont, a low-level cabinet member in the Whitehall administration's first term, was poised to elevate his game—and political profile—under Rusch's presidency.

Starting now. The widely anticipated chief-of-staff title would distinguish him as a driving force in Rusch's administration, but there was no better way for him to shape his political personality than by appearing on national television, talking to the People when they were emotionally vulnerable. In the past, leaders were born by giving rousing speeches at critical moments, by rising above the fray and showing the stuff of which they were made. This was his chance to indelibly imprint his image in the photographic silver of public consciousness.

Normally the task would have fallen to Rusch's communications director or senior campaign advisor—but both perished in the crash. Someone on the president-elect's team had to go before the cameras to speak for Glendon Rusch, to reassure the public their newly elected leader was alive and well. Or, rather, that he was alive. The task fell to Larchmont.

He was not complaining.

Heart thumping, his breath a bit short, he closed his eyes, cleared his thoughts, and found his emotional balance. He entered the room and somewhere in the back of his mind became aware of the droning buzz of press-room chatter as he strode to the podium. The noise hushed as if a judge had rapped a gavel. This wasn't the Quentin Larchmont of his days as the translucent deputy commerce secretary. And it wasn't the campaign trail anymore. This was the Big Show.

He looked up and took in the three dozen reporters and foreign press correspondents in front of him and the campaign workers who had gathered behind them. Cameras clicked. He found the handful of television cameras in the back, then let his eyes wander the room.

"Good evening," he began. "It was my hope that President Rusch would be addressing all of you at a time of great joy and triumph, at the dawn of a new era, highlighting the strengths and beauty of the democratic institution: candidates campaign and debate, and then the American people cast their votes to choose who it is they want to lead them, who it is they want to set policy, who it is they trust with our well-being and the well-being of our families.

"But the underpinnings of this system of democracy, the bricks and mortar, if you will, is our right to vote. It is a right, a freedom that exists because hundreds of thousands of Americans spilled their blood defending the rights given us by visionaries, forefathers who walked this very land well over two hundred years ago. But as we've seen in the more immediate past, threats to our freedoms are all around us, poised to challenge our great democracy.

"Response to challenge is what separates greatness from irrelevance. We are a country of greatness made up of people who face adversity and meet those challenges head-on. Witness the events of the past two days. An attempt on our president-elect's life. The slaughter of more than a dozen innocent people. And now, the cold-blooded murder of Congressman Gene Harmon, a dedicated member of Congress. In our own way, we each grieve alongside their families, saddened by their loss." He paused, looked at his notes, then glanced up at the press corps.

"But in the wake of such challenges, we persevere and grow stronger. Because Marine Two and its escort went down on the eve of a great awakening. The American people are resilient, and they have spoken, loud and clear: Glendon Rusch was elected to lead the greatest country in the free world, and despite these unexpected obstacles, the United States remains a nation built on unshakable principles. No one—not terrorists nor ruthless dictators—can take that away. Nor can they weaken our resolve.

"I tell you now, as I told you several weeks ago: Glendon Rusch will be your next president. When I'd said it back in September it was a prediction, a display of our strength of conviction to win the White House. Today I say it as a declaration that despite the efforts of a criminal mind—or minds—President-elect Rusch lives.

He *will be* your next president." Cameras clicked again, in unison, as if on cue.

Larchmont shifted his weight slowly, carefully. "I want to reaffirm your belief in this extraordinary man. And to those people who did not vote for him, you are now witness to the stuff of which Glendon Rusch is made. What happened several thousand feet above the Virginia countryside is testament to his mettle. Two people survived the destruction of both helicopters, but only Glendon Rusch lived to talk about it. Some may say it's luck. But Glendon Rusch survived because that's just the sort of man Glendon Rusch is. He's a warrior, a survivor.

"He's a soldier fighting for what he believes is right. Whether that be in a free-falling helicopter or ordering our troops into battle against a terrorist regime, President Rusch will fight to uphold the principles I spoke of a moment ago, the ones that make our United States of America the greatest nation on Earth."

Larchmont bowed his head, counted to three for effect, then looked directly into the television cameras. "I promise you that we will persevere. We will catch those responsible.

"But this country is not just about retribution. We will continue to lead the world, to aid the sick, to help poor nations meet their food and healthcare needs, to assist those less fortunate.

"To do that we need a seasoned leader, one with vision, convictions, and perseverance. I assure you now our new president will be fit to govern. The transition will proceed. Not as smoothly as we'd anticipated, of course. Challenges stand in our way. But remember: our response to challenge defines us as a people. I assure you the United States of America will emerge stronger."

Larchmont looked out at the cameras. "Thank you all for your prayers. God bless."

Uzi made his way to the front of the large room, where Quentin Larchmont was shaking hands with a number of supporters who were clearly moved by his speech. Uzi flashed his credentials at the Secret Service agent, and the man permitted him into the hallway with Larchmont. "Sir, I'm Agent Uzi. FBI."

Larchmont gave Uzi a quick once-over, then turned away. "I've got a meeting in ten minutes, and we're several blocks away."

"As I told your assistant, I'm in charge of the task force responsible for finding the terrorists who did this, sir. She said you'd be able to talk with me for a few moments. If you've got more pressing matters, let me know when might be more convenient for your schedule." Uzi folded his arms. He was pissing on the ground in front of Larchmont, letting him know they were standing on his territory.

Larchmont's jaw muscles tightened. "I've got very little of value to offer you, Agent Uzi."

"With all due respect, Mr. Larchmont, it's best if I determine that."

Larchmont's face flushed, but he kept his cool and gestured to the corridor ahead of them. "Walk and talk?" He started down the hall, two Secret Service agents bringing up the rear.

"What did you think of my little speech?"

"Good show. Plenty of well-crafted sound bites."

Larchmont stopped walking and faced Uzi. His face was taut, his jaw jutting forward. "This incident could weaken the president-elect's image, damage his ability to lead. Others might see it as an opportunity to step on the United States when she's down. So I had to spin it. Right now I see myself as a kind of Secret Service agent: protecting the political life of the president at all costs. Need be, I'd gladly take a bullet and kill my career if it meant saving the president's. Now, what's on your mind?"

Uzi glanced at the Secret Service agents to gauge their response to Larchmont's comment. They remained stoic.

"As the president-elect's protector," Uzi said, "perhaps you can shed some light on who might want to kill him."

Larchmont chuckled. "A loaded question. No one specifically, if that's what you mean. Glendon Rusch is a very popular man. You saw what he did at the polls—"

"'No one specifically'?" Uzi asked. "Does that mean you know of someone in general?"

A smile broke Larchmont's leathery face. "That's very good. Sitting on my every word. Kind of like the press. Never thought of that before. The FBI and the press both scour your words for hidden meaning."

"There's always hidden meaning with politicians, since they generally say a lot about nothing. Safer that way."

Larchmont's smile faded. "There are all sorts of nuts out there, no shortage of religious fanatics or rogue leaders. Look at Iran—which tried to assassinate an ambassador here in DC—or North Korea, or—hell, even Russia's taken to killing officials and journalists they consider to be a threat. You want someone specific? No idea who'd want to kill Glendon Rusch. That better, Agent? Direct enough for you?" He shook his head, then resumed his stride toward the lobby.

Choosing not to follow Larchmont, Uzi stood at the edge of the hall with his hands shoved into his jacket pockets. "So you're at a loss to explain what happened," he called across the lobby. "No political motives, personal vendettas, nothing like that."

Larchmont's shoulders fell submissively. He turned slowly and said, "Explaining what happened is your job. Instead of bothering me, why don't you go do something useful?"

Larchmont, now a few feet from the office building's front door, motioned to one of the Secret Service agents. "Joseph, we'd better get going. My meeting." The agent spoke into a microphone embedded in his sleeve. "Pluto is ready to move."

Having walked to within a few yards of Larchmont, Uzi said, "We may need to talk again."

Larchmont gave Uzi a disgusted once-over. "On top of everything that's happened, we've got a cabinet to assemble. If anything *significant* comes up, you know where to find me."

7:27 PM
186 hours 33 minutes remaining

Uzi arrived at the Aquia Commerce Center with a mind full of questions. He parked and took the elevator up to the second floor and informed the receptionist seated behind the bulletproof glass he was there to see a profiler with the FBI's Behavioral Analysis Unit.

Moments later, the large wood door cracked open, Supervisory Special Agent Karen Vail's lightly freckled face bunching a bit with a broad grin. She stepped forward and greeted him with a warm hug. "Let's head back to my crypt, talk there."

Vail led the way down various hallways and stopped at her office, a ten-by-ten room filled with files and reports, topic-related textbooks packed onto bookshelves, and FBI binders containing research articles on serial killers and rapists, sexual sadism and psychopathy. Dominating the shelf was an oversize manual of Bureau operational guidelines.

In the far corner of the room, a human skeleton stood beside a framed photo of a teenager and a tall man standing in front of the Martin Luther King, Jr. memorial.

Uzi leaned back and appraised the office. "You really need an interior decorator. A bit morose in here, don't you think?"

"I tangle with serial killers and walk knee deep in their victims' blood and guts. Morose is my middle name." She settled into her desk chair. An LCD screen above her left shoulder displayed photos of a crime scene. "So how've you been?"

Uzi shrugged. "Been busy, which is good. Well, I guess in a sense having lots to do when you head up the terrorism task force is bad. But for my sanity, staying busy helps. You?"

"My life's been . . . very eventful the past several months. I complain, but no one seems to give a shit."

"I called, you know, after . . . the thing with Dead Eyes."

"I'm sorry I didn't call you back. I— There was a lot of healing, mentally and physically. I tried to take a vacation in Napa, and that, well, let's just say I'm still healing from that. Mentally and physically." She grinned. "And don't ask me about my time on Alcatraz."

"Alcatraz, huh? Sounds positively arresting."

"You have no idea. But the good news is that I met someone."

"An inmate?"

"No, dipshit. A LEO," she said, referring to a law enforcement officer. "Vienna dick who was on my Dead Eyes task force. He's now a DEA agent." She craned her neck back and indicated the framed wall photo.

Uzi sat down in the office chair in front of Vail's desk. "He looks very . . . hunky."

Vail smiled, a bit mischievously. "Something tells me you're not here about Robby."

"The chopper. I need some answers. And the identity of our UNSUB, too, if you can swing it."

Vail grabbed an envelope off her desk and held it up to her forehead. "He's forty-nine years old, works for the government, and his name is—"

"Okay, okay," Uzi said, holding out a hand. "I guess I deserved that."

"You know what I can and can't do."

"Karen, I thought you could do everything." He grinned broadly.

"Like I told you at the crash site, it's Frank Del Monaco's case. I was just covering. You want me to call him?" She reached for the phone.

"No," Uzi said. He leaned to his left and shut the door. "I'd rather work with you."

Vail watched the door click closed, then said, "Frank and I have had our differences, but I think he can do up a decent profile on this."

"I don't know Frank Del Monaco. I know Karen Vail. Check that. I trust Karen Vail."

"Frank and I are technically assigned to the West Coast. Normally, he and I wouldn't come within ten yards of this."

"Then I feel even more lucky to be sitting in your office discussing this case."

Vail shook her head. "You realize if I help you, it'll piss off Frank big time. Not that I mind doing that. That's not the problem. It's my unit chief and ASAC—"

"Off the record then. Between us, that's all."

Vail tossed the envelope back onto her desk and sighed. "This is going to come back to bite me in the ass, but what the hell. I've been bitten there before. What do you want to know?"

"Tell me about the bombers you profile."

"That's a pretty open-ended question, Uzi. You just want some generalities?"

"Let's start with that, then we'll see."

Vail pushed her chair back a bit and leaned her elbows on her desk. "Douglas used to say that to know the artist, you had to study his art. How a bomb is made tells us a lot about the maker, or the artist, if you will. Just like there are differences in serial killers and how they handle their victims, bomb makers treat their bombs differently—and it all has to do with their personality. Did they spend a lot of time constructing the bomb, or is it haphazard and thrown together?

"If we have multiple bombs to examine, we can derive a signature from them. That means we can tie the devices to the same person, because he would've put his own artistic touches into the bomb when making it. The more unusual the construction, the more we can narrow it down to a particular individual. On its most basic level, there's something we call ritual behavior, which refers to the things the UNSUB does that are unnecessary for the successful commission of his crime. So if the unknown subject's objective is to kill someone when the bomb explodes, then using an exotic type of welding style is totally unnecessary. That becomes part of his ritualized behavior across multiple crimes."

"Okay," Uzi said. "Let me stop you there. I doubt we'll get much from the bombs this guy used because we don't have an intact device to examine. Looks like they all used C-4, but in different ways. Let's assume for a second the same guy made them. How about the maker? Can you tell me anything about this guy?"

"My guess is that's what Frank is working on."

"No, you. Can you tell me anything about this guy?"

"Uzi, we're all trained to profile offender behavior. Frank's been on the case since he got back in town. I turned all my stuff over to him. He can answer your questions better than I could."

Uzi leaned forward. "Karen, not all profilers have the same skill sets and abilities. Some have book knowledge and training, and some are intuitive. It just comes to them. I've seen you work, I know that you're intuitive. Plus, I don't trust people easily. You, I trust."

Vail leaned back in her chair and rocked a bit. "If I help you, I'm going to get in trouble. How's that for an intuitive prediction?"

"Here's what we've got so far, which isn't much." He handed her a manila envelope. "Just give me what you can, okay? That's all I'm asking."

"I have a hard time saying no to you, Uzi. Why is that?"

Uzi stood, then grabbed the door knob. "Hey, you're the psych expert. But if I had to guess, I'd have to say it's my striking good looks."

8:34 PM
185 hours 26 minutes remaining

Uzi walked into Marshall Shepard's office ten minutes late. He pulled a fresh toothpick from Shepard's private stash in his top left desk drawer, and stuck the mint-spiced piece of wood between his lips.

"Do you always go rummaging around your ASAC's desk without his knowledge?"

The voice came out of nowhere. It was authoritarian and stern, but not excessively loud. Uzi nearly dropped the toothpick from his mouth. In that instant, he flashed on his childhood, when he was caught with a Playboy magazine he'd found in his father's drawer.

Standing in the doorway was FBI Director Douglas Knox.

Uzi cleared his throat, gained his wits, and tried to act as if the daylights had not just been plucked from his skin. "ASAC Shepard keeps toothpicks—"

"I'm not interested," Knox said, then entered the room and moved behind Shepard's desk. With a quick flick of his wrists, he fanned aside his suit coat and shoved his hands deep into his pants pockets. "Good that you're here. I need to bring you up to speed on what I've set in motion the past couple of hours. I've assigned a total of three hundred agents to this case. Four squads—"

"And I've also tasked each member of the JTTF with naming additional agents from their own agencies," Uzi said.

"Very good." Knox began pacing behind Shepard's desk. "I've asked Assistant Director Yates to put together an interagency unit—the Marine Two Task Force—or M2TF, to support the efforts of JTTF. Hector's a logical choice to sit on it, and he'll report directly to me and the secretary of defense. Within the hour, the Rapid Deployment Logistics Unit will have found a place to hunker down. It'll be staffed with another two hundred agents from NSA, CIA, DOD, Secret Service, and Homeland Security. It'll run concurrent with your investigation and report directly to ADIC Yates."

Knox stopped talking, but continued pacing behind the desk. "Homeland Security is monitoring everything. I have a standing phone appointment with Secretary Braun twice daily to keep us both up to speed. Until we know more, we're treating this as an act of terrorism. It could also turn out to be personal revenge, or even a politically motivated assassination. The term 'terrorist' has become a colloquialism for anyone with radical ideas and I don't want it thrown around unnecessarily. Not until we have some proof."

"Our operating definition of a terrorist has been someone who kills or intimidates innocent people," Uzi said. "And if the target was in fact Glendon Rusch, they took a whole bunch of other people with him in their attempt. That fits the definition close enough for me."

Knox stopped and turned on his heel, facing Uzi. "Was the target president-elect Rusch?"

"I don't know yet, sir. It's a starting point. When you hear hoof beats—"

"Think horses. I'm familiar with the saying. You keep chasing the horses, Agent Uziel, but I don't want the zebras or bulls getting out of the pen either till we're sure they're not involved."

"Yes, sir."

"How does all this tie in with Congressman Harmon's murder?"

Uzi shrugged. The congressman's body was barely cold. Did Knox really expect him to have answers? "No compelling, direct evidence the two are related. Yet."

Knox resumed his pacing. "Then indirect."

Uzi thought of mentioning the possible C-4 connection, but until he got more info from the lab, he decided to keep it to himself. Instead, he said, "We've got some things in motion. But my gut tells me they're related."

"Your gut? That's all we've got?"

"At the moment." Uzi shifted his weight. "I can't manufacture evidence—"

Knox's head snapped up. He stopped moving, his cold eyes penetrating Uzi's, as if he were trying to bore right through his skull and peer into his brain. "I'm not suggesting you do, Agent. Just get me answers. The right answers."

Get me the right answers? What the hell does that mean? Was it a plea for Uzi to bring him the correct suspect, or the correct suspect for Knox's needs? He flashed back on his conversation with the president, the ambiguous innuendoes leaving him at a loss to fully understand what he was saying. *Or am I reading too much into it?* Heeding his boss's prior advice, Uzi merely nodded at Knox, then added, "Of course, sir."

"Director Knox," Shepard said, lumbering into the room. "Started without me. Good. I was talking with the lab—"

"Yes. Fine. I was just informing Agent Uziel here about the expansion of his task force."

Shepard gave Uzi a serious look, as he would any other field agent who was not his personal friend. Turning back to Knox, he said, "Just so you know, Mr. Director, Command Post is now staffed and operational. Revised plan calls for JTTF to hit three-hundred—"

"ADIC Yates has kept me fully briefed," Knox said with a wave of his hand. "But let me make something perfectly clear, Mr. Shepard: the number of bodies we've got assigned to this case doesn't matter if we don't break it. And soon. I don't want a failed investigation on my watch."

Shepard answered without hesitation. "Yes, sir."

Uzi shuffled the toothpick in his mouth but did not say anything. He was busy observing the interplay between Knox and Shepard.

"You have a problem with this?" Knox was focused on Uzi, his gaze deep and stern.

"Not at all. It all makes perfect sense."

Knox squinted a bit, no doubt trying to read the body language and attitude that underscored Uzi's comment. He turned back to Shepard. "I'd like an update by oh-nine hundred."

Shepard sat down heavily into his seat. "I hope to have something substantive to report by then."

"Make sure you do." Knox turned and left the room, failing to make eye contact with Uzi on the way out.

"He doesn't like me," Uzi said after the door had clicked shut.

"Douglas Knox doesn't like most people in the Bureau. I should say, he doesn't trust most people in the Bureau. I think it's been the same wherever he's been. It's his way of keeping his distance. Part of the power trip."

"How come you're not into that scene?"

Shepard reached into his drawer to pull out a toothpick. "You been in my desk again?"

"You didn't answer my question."

"I am into the power trip scene. That's why I'm an Assistant Special Agent in Charge. *In Charge*, get it? That's all about power, my friend. And within a couple years I plan to drop the 'assistant' from my title. Difference between me and the director is that I don't believe in stabbing people in the back to get where you want to go."

"You believe in a frontal assault."

"Exactly, exactly right." Shepard shoved the toothpick into his mouth. "So you think you can handle this, three hundred guys under your watch, some of 'em who hate your guts?"

"First of all, they're not all male, and second of all, yeah. I can handle it. The task force is designed to compartmentalize everything."

"It's also designed to have everything and everyone funneled to you. You will be interfacing with a lot of these people. You will."

"Not a problem," Uzi said.

"Don't let me down," Shepard said. "Just don't let me down." He leaned back in his chair. "Tell me where we stand."

"Working on a number of things. A buddy of mine from the Pentagon is poking around with me. Hector DeSantos."

"I know."

Uzi hesitated—Shepard clearly had his sources—then said, "Hector's sharp. We make a good team."

"Don't forget you've got two hundred ninety-nine other team members."

Uzi reached into his pocket and pulled out a stack of message slips. "They won't let me forget. Can I go now? I've got some calls to return." He stood up and started for the door.

"I heard you kept your appointment with the shrink."

Uzi turned, his hand on the knob. "I made you a promise. I keep my word."

Shepard let a smile creep across his lips. The toothpick poked through. "I know you do."

DAY TWO

8:01 AM
173 hours 59 minutes remaining

When Uzi walked into his office, he found that a new stack of message slips had accumulated on his desk. He spent nearly three hours returning calls when Madeline, his assistant, handed him another note.

"I thought you might want to see this one right away," she said. "The results are back on some of the evidence from Congressman Harmon's home."

Uzi arrived at the lab twenty minutes later.

He sat on a stool beside the FBI lab technician, Keisha Beekert. Clad in a white lab coat, the prematurely gray Beekert nudged a pair of reading glasses higher onto the bridge of her nose, then indicated the counter in front of her where several castings of the assailant's footprints rested.

"Do you see the problem?" she asked.

Not being an expert at reading plaster, he hesitated. As his eyes started their second pass over the castings, Beekert lifted one and cradled it in her hands.

"Here. What kind of shoe does this look like to you?"

Uzi tilted his head, appraising the large plaster chunk. "One belonging to Bigfoot?"

"I might accept that answer, because it would appear that your suspect is over eight feet tall judging by the size of his shoe."

Uzi thought of a joke dealing with men and their shoe size, but didn't want to get nailed with a sexual harassment suit. "What kind of shoe does it look like to you?" he asked instead.

"A Redfeather Women's Performance 21 snowshoe."

"A snowshoe," Uzi said. "But there's no snow on the ground."

Beekert looked at him over the tops of her glasses, probably wondering if he was dense or stupid.

Uzi decided to put her concerns to rest. "So you're saying the UNSUB used snowshoes to mask his shoe make and size. So we can't track him that way."

"Sharp guy you're dealing with here."

"Wait a minute. You said it was a women's snowshoe."

"So you're pretty sharp yourself. Yes," Beekert said, "that is what I said. According to the manufacturer, it's got 'an innovative V-tail tapered design with an Aircraft 6-series aluminum frame.' Rated for up to 175 pounds. But judging by the depth of most of the imprints, I'd estimate this person to be north of 200 pounds. A rather hefty woman, I'd say."

"A fact the manufacturer might be pleased to learn. They can expand their market." He shrugged. "To heftier women."

Beekert twisted her mouth in disappointment.

"Okay," Uzi said, "I get your point. You're saying that either this was a very large female assassin, or a slightly-larger-than-average male hit-man. The latter is more likely."

"I wouldn't want to draw conclusions for you. My job is merely to point out the facts."

"And the fact is, this guy is good. Very good."

"Wish I could've helped you more."

Uzi pushed off the stool. "Me, too."

2:05 PM
167 hours 55 minutes remaining

Following a classified briefing at the Strategic Information and Operations Center, Uzi was leaving the Hoover Building's garage when he saw Karen Vail's red hair inside a Bureau-issue Dodge Stratus. She rolled down her window and pulled up alongside him.

"I've been doing some more thinking on the Marine Two downing."

"Oh, yeah? I thought this was Frank Del Monaco's case."

"You want my help or not?"

Uzi smiled. "Go on."

"Can't talk right now. Gotta drop off some papers. Meet me at the coffee house across the road from my office. Gargoyles. Give me about an hour."

"I'll be there."

Karen Vail walked into Gargoyles ninety minutes later. Uzi was seated at a table watching the door and waiting for her, an empty cup of espresso in front of him. He had been returning calls, mowing through his message slips and emails when he saw Vail by the door. He set his phone on the table and leaned back in his seat.

"You didn't tell me there were a couple of gun-related homicides connected to this case," she said before her buttocks had hit the chair.

Uzi squirmed a bit. "Until we get some more evidence, I can't say they're—"

"My gut says they're related. You seem to trust my gut, so what that's worth, I'm not exactly sure. Any case, to your bomber. I think I can give you some general parameters. But we're clear this is unofficial. I don't even want you giving me shit if it turns out I'm wrong."

"No shit." He wiggled his fingers. "Spill."

"Okay, here's what I think." She looked at his empty cup, then stood up. "I need some coffee first."

She led the way to the counter, Uzi following, feeling like a kid who couldn't wait to open his birthday present. "Come on now, don't keep me in suspense—"

"Can I get you anything, Agent Vail?" the man behind the counter asked.

Uzi raised his right brow. "Guess you come here a lot."

"Shut up," Vail said to Uzi. She looked at the counterman. "The usual. And my friend will have some coffee grinds."

"Black," Uzi said. "Lots of sugar." He looked at Vail. "'Cause I'm so sweet."

Vail rolled her eyes.

"Another espresso, please," he said. The man moved off to prepare their drinks.

Vail leaned her buttocks against the counter and faced Uzi. "So here's what I think. That big chopper, the Super Stallion? What a name, typical macho male thing."

"Karen—"

"Okay. First thing you have to understand about bombings is that victimology is critical: who is the victim—or more specifically, who's the target? Remember the Centennial Park bombing? The big problem was trying to figure out who the guy was trying to kill. It was a directional bomb, we could tell that much, but there were a lot of potential targets in the vicinity: several different corporate tents, families, a security guard— We didn't know what his intent was, so we couldn't accurately assess what this offender was all about.

"In your case, is it the US government this guy is pissed at? Or the Marines? Or was it meant to embarrass the manufacturer of the helicopters? Once we know who the target was, we can begin the process of trying to answer why. Why this target, why now, why here? Why did he place the bomb on the helicopter? There was a specific reason for that. Why not just put a bomb under the target's car—he'd probably have easier access and less risk. All depends on who the target was.

"You also have to ask why he hit these helicopters and not others. Was he trying to draw attention by using a high-profile event?" She stopped and waited for him to respond. He said nothing. "You hear what I'm saying? Go down the wrong road, you'll be way off base."

The counterman placed the two drinks on a tray and slid it over to the register. Uzi handed the man a ten. While waiting for his change, he said, "Okay, disclaimers are out of the way. I know you're sticking your ass out here. Just tell me what you can."

Vail sighed. "They're more than disclaimers. There are some critical pieces of information we don't have."

"Understood." He took the change from the man and led the way to their table. He sat and sipped his coffee, waiting for her to continue.

Vail tipped her mug back and took a sip. "The Stallion was blown out of the sky. A cleverly disguised device, placed strategically at the only weak point this machine has, takes the thing right down. That can mean the UNSUB was really pissed at one or more of the inhabitants and wanted to pulverize them. But since there was another chopper involved that didn't need to be taken down, I don't think the Stallion was the target. The type of strike on the Stallion leads me to believe they wanted it out of the way, that it wasn't important. It's there for protection, right? Wipe out the guard and you can have your way with your weaker target. Serial killers work the same way.

"Which brings me to the Black Hawk. According to the file, the tail rotor was taken out first. I asked around, and I was told that a really good pilot can fly a chopper with just the main rotor. And the people who fly the Executive Fleet are really good. So assuming the bomber knew that—and I think he must have, otherwise why bother with the tail rotor, he could've taken the thing down like he did the Stallion—there was something at play here."

"Whoever did this," Uzi said, "wanted his target to experience fear before he died."

Vail raised the cup toward her lips. "Very good. Did your analytical logic skills come from your engineering background or the Bureau's renowned training?"

"Neither. I'm just naturally brilliant."

Vail choked on her sip of coffee. "Sorry, I didn't mean to laugh." She dabbed her mouth with a tissue. "Seriously, though. I think you should focus on the inhabitants of the Black Hawk. Find out who Glendon Rusch is, what he stands for. Not just what the media reports, but behind the scenes. Talk to congressmen, find out who hated whom."

"You feel this could've been an inside job?"

"It *was* an inside job, Uzi. First of all, that was a pretty sophisticated bomb, molded to fit the exterior surface. The labs on the explosive will be super important. We don't have an intact device, so the next best thing is reconstructing the bomb by the stuff blown off in the periphery. They do a photospectral analysis of the pieces and chemical residues to determine the type of material it was made from. If the preliminary theory is right, and it's C-4 or Semtex, you're dealing with limited availability. They could've stolen it from the Army or imported it from overseas. Either route involves extensive preparation and resources, indicating a more sophisticated offender."

"Everything points to C-4."

"Good. What you've given me so far indicates substantial planning and forethought. Whoever did this didn't download a recipe off the Internet and cook up a fertilizer bomb in his kitchen, then leave it in a backpack by a park bench. C-4 planted on helicopters that transport the president and vice president of the United States means a sophisticated operator.

"But more important than that," Vail continued, "the main question has to be, How could someone plant bombs on US Marine helicopters used for transporting the executive staff? It's a question of access. The logical conclusion is that one of the mechanics had to have been involved."

Uzi sipped his espresso. "We reached the same conclusion."

"Which provides a link, circumstantial of course, but a link nonetheless, to your murdered Quantico mechanic."

"See, I knew you were smarter than everyone else said you were."

Vail grinned. "I won't let you bait me. Charm works better, anyway."

"I didn't think someone who stares at dead bodies all the time could be so beautiful."

Vail nodded slowly. "That's a good start. I'll take more."

"Later. Let's go on. What else can you tell me?"

Vail drank from her cup, and then set it down. "Bombers like this are often loners. Maybe this mechanic hated the government." She held up a hand. "I know what you're thinking, he worked for the government, and he was considered the best of the best, or else he wouldn't have gotten this assignment. I agree, but I can't tell you how many times we've discovered that members of our Armed forces harbored deep-seated anger toward the country and everything it stands for. Think Timothy McVeigh. And he's not the only one—not by a long shot. Nidal Hasan's a slightly different example, but an example nonetheless."

"So this guy was a closet anarchist."

"Something like that."

"We're looking at ARM. You know anything about them?"

"Just that Nelson Flint is a bloodsucking good-for-nothing parasite who should be behind bars."

"I hate it when you hold back," Uzi said. "Someone on my task force thinks they're involved."

Vail cocked her head. "Here's the thing with that. Typically bombers don't work in groups. When hate-mongers get together, it's usually to talk about their complaints, kind of like group therapy, a misery-loves-company type thing. Makes them feel powerful. But they don't usually gather to act on their gripes. That said, there are notable exceptions, especially in recent history. Militia groups, for one. A recent example is that Hutaree 'Christian warrior' militia, which planned to use homemade bombs against federal agents."

Uzi sipped some more espresso. "I don't want to miss something important. Before I sell myself on the militia angle, tell me about bombers in general."

"Some guidelines?"

"Yeah. Like the loner thing. What else—Do they fit into some kind of generalized behavioral mindset?"

"To know the artist, study his art, remember? Bombing is passive-aggressive; the scum suckers who engage in this type of behavior are nonconfrontational. They set the bomb and go away. Poisoners and snipers are the same way. No direct contact with their victims. So when you generalize about who would do something like this, you think of someone who feels they were slighted by their company. So they go into a store and poison the food: others get sick. It's all done to embarrass the manufacturer."

"Can you be a little more specific? About our bomber."

Vail lifted the coffee to her lips. "So you want me fully out on the limb, huh? If the branch breaks—"

"I'll take full responsibility."

Vail put her mug down and thought a moment. "White male, forty-five to fifty, probably living on his own, but he has some support system, a person or persons he can confide in. Contrary to what I said a moment ago about loners, I think your guy's part of a group, an organized militia. He's neat, clean, very disciplined. Good attention to detail.

"Like I said, bombers tend to shy away from face-to-face confrontation, which is why they use a bomb instead of a knife or gun. But I don't think that's the case here. Just the opposite. I don't think it's about avoiding a confrontation; he thought—right or wrong—that this was simply the best way for him to accomplish his goal. He's above-average intelligence. Drives an older SUV or a pickup. Dark or muted color so he doesn't attract attention." She took another sip. "I feel like I'm so far out on the limb that the tree is about to tip over. Satisfied?"

Uzi took a swig from his cup, lost in thought. Finally, he looked up. "Yeah, yeah. Great. I appreciate it." His smartphone vibrated. He rummaged through his jacket pocket, pulled out the Nokia, and answered it. He listened a second, then said, "I'm on it. Text me the address. Be there ASAP." He stood up and planted a kiss on Vail's forehead. "Gotta run. I may call you again on this."

"Frank Del Monaco. Call him. It's his case, remember?"

"Yeah, whatever. I'll be in touch." He turned and ran out of the café.

4:29 PM
165 hours 31 minutes remaining

Uzi arrived at the Capitol Athletic Club twenty-five minutes later. Five of his task force members were there, along with DeSantos, who Uzi had called from his car while en route.

"Santa," Uzi said, bumping his colleague's fist with his own. "What's the deal?"

"Dead lobbyist. Russell Fargo. Midlevel partner with McKutcheon Winchester. That's all I know."

Uzi turned and caught the attention of Agent Hoshi Koh, who was leaning over the dead man's body in the ten-by-ten steam room. In a brief email he had dashed off to her earlier in the day, Uzi put Hoshi in charge of the group investigating the Ellison murder.

He squeezed his way into the room. A scent he had never before experienced—the coppery bitterness of blood mixed with eucalyptus oil—made his nostrils flare.

"You want to know what I think?" Hoshi asked.

"First I want to know why we were called. How is this guy related to our investigation?'

"He may not be. But Metro PD's reporting all murders to Shepard. JTTF is now the big deal. Suspicious stuff comes to us, just in case. Didn't he tell you?"

"Guess he left that part out. I'm only in charge. No reason for me to know the details." Uzi glanced around the room, noticed the blood-smeared tile. "So this guy was seated over there," he said, nodding at the far wall. "Gets clipped in the chest, then in the head, or vice versa, falls face first and lands here."

"Seems reasonable to me," Hoshi said.

DeSantos walked into the room and glanced around. Uzi introduced him to Hoshi and played out the murder in his mind while DeSantos and Hoshi exchanged pleasantries.

"Okay," Uzi said. "Now I'd like to know what you think."

Hoshi turned toward the reclining corpse, then tilted her head to the side as if she were appraising a sculpture. "I think this guy pissed somebody off."

Uzi stood there, waiting for more. He looked at DeSantos, who shrugged. "That's all you think?" Uzi asked.

"I think about my ex-husband when I'm horny, but I don't think you need that detail."

"You're right."

A thirty-something man in a grey Sears suit walked into the locker room, scribbling a note on his pad.

DeSantos indicated the guy with a slight nod. "Metro dick who caught the case. Name's Zambrano."

Uzi followed his partner out of the steam room and extended a hand. "Aaron Uzi." Uzi's credentials case, folded outward and protruding from his pocket, screamed FBI in bold letters.

Zambrano looked up and shook his hand. "Yeah. Good to meet you."

"We'll make sure you get copied on all our reports," Uzi said. "You'll do the same?"

"Hey, turf wars have their place. This isn't one of 'em."

Uzi squinted, sizing this guy up. *Turf wars have their place?* He handed the detective a blue, gold-embossed FBI business card. "We'll touch base with you before we take off."

"Yeah. Good," Zambrano said, then buried his face in his notepad as he moved off toward the steam room.

Uzi shared a look of bewilderment with DeSantos, then took his partner aside. "You get the lowdown on this Fargo dude?"

"As soon as I get back to my office, I'll know what flavor ice cream he liked."

"I'd be more interested in whether he's got any links to ARM, Ellison, Harmon, Rusch, or anyone else on that copter. And Rusch's wife. We need to look into Macy Rusch. Maybe she was getting some action on the side."

"Jilted lover blows up the VP and a bunch of Marines? Not even the *Enquirer* would run something like that."

Uzi shrugged. "It's another 'i' to dot." Then the sight of Leila Harel entering the locker room snagged his attention.

Uzi slapped DeSantos on the chest, then headed toward Leila. He covered the distance between them in three long strides.

"Hello again."

"Agent Uzi," she said offhandedly, glancing around his body at the grouping of Metro PD cops, FBI agents and crime-scene techs. "What a surprise."

"Just what I was thinking," he said, leaning slightly to his left to block her gaze.

Her lips twisted. "Excuse me," she said, then grabbed his arm and attempted to move him aside.

Whoa. Her touch shuddered through him. Just like the first time he'd met Dena—she brushed against his shoulder as she squeezed by him. And it changed his life forever.

"I can tell you everything you want to know," Uzi said. "How about a late dinner?" He glanced at the wall clock. "Eight-thirty, Founding Farmers. I've got a couple people working the case you should coordinate with."

Leila's gaze shifted to Uzi's face.

Is that the first time she actually looked into my eyes?

"What?" she asked.

"Dinner. Eight-thirty. Founding Farmers."

She stared at his face for a long moment, then nodded and pushed past him.

Uzi stood there and watched Leila walk away. He wished they'd be meeting alone, but perhaps it was better this way: less guilt.

1924 PENNSYLVANIA AVE NW
8:26 PM
161 hours 34 minutes remaining

Located a few blocks from the White House and adjacent to the International Monetary Fund in the heart of DC, Founding Farmers sat at the heart of the nation's circulatory system.

But the restaurant didn't merely specialize in power lunches and dinners; it featured fresh foods from the country's family farms, ranches, and fisheries.

Uzi passed through the polished stainless steel storefront and into the wood-inspired environs: raw butcher-block style tables and paneled walls and floors, with billowy, cloud-shaped light fixtures hanging from the second-story ceiling.

He sat at the bar, leather overcoat neatly folded and draped over his left forearm, watching Paul, the maître d, handle the guests as they entered. It was clear who'd been there before and who hadn't by their facial expressions upon glimpsing the interior's striking décor.

Leila entered and her head swiveled in all directions, taking in the colorful surroundings. Uzi slid off the barstool and greeted her.

"Our table's upstairs. Follow me." He led her by the elbow up the staircase, where small ceramic birds hung from the high ceiling.

He thought of telling Leila that she looked lovely—hot is the word he would've used, because it was true—but he knew that would be the wrong way to frame the evening. Correct or not, he believed it. Wearing a form-fitting red dress and a simple yet elegant pearl necklace topped off by a black cashmere cape loosely draped about her bare shoulders, she looked as good as that first time he had seen her at the crash site. Two-inch heels and long, slender thighs made it appear as if her legs went on forever, and brought her closer to Uzi's six-foot-two.

Uzi led her to their table in front of a large window that overlooked 20th Avenue NW. Karen Vail was seated with her back to them. When she felt Uzi's tap on her back, she rose and gave Leila a quick once-over. She squinted confusion, glanced at Uzi, and asked Leila, "You always wear your finest dress to a business meeting? Or did I miss the memo?"

Leila unfurled her cape and said, "This isn't my finest dress. But thank you for the compliment."

Vail crumpled her brow again. "Right."

Uzi cleared his throat, unsure what to make of their verbal sparring. *Where the hell's Santa?* "Leila Harel, meet Karen Vail. Karen's with the BAU."

Leila nodded acknowledgment. "Are you on the task force?"

"Hell yeah," Uzi said. "Karen's the best profiler we've got."

Vail stifled a laugh. "I *am* very good—but not the best. And I'm not on the task force. I'm just filling in for a colleague. As a favor."

"And what can you offer us as a profiler? This seems a bit out of your league."

Before Vail could fire off a barb in reply, a waiter greeted them.

"Clarence," Uzi said. "Good to see you." *And just in the nick of time.*

"Been a while," the middle-aged man said. They made small talk for a moment, then Clarence conveyed their specials, which featured roasted chicken salad with Trixie's mayonnaise, dried blueberries, Bibb lettuce, and golden beets. "I'll be back to take your order in a bit. No rush."

"We're waiting for one more, actually," Uzi said.

By the time Clarence walked off, Vail had clearly decided to let Leila's comment pass, and instead provided her with a professional, though concise, overview of the information she had discussed with Uzi.

"You people are known for serial killers," Leila said. "Just how is this going to help us find the bomber?"

"We people," Vail said between clenched teeth, "handle a variety of cases, from threat assessment to serial killers, rapists, arsonists, child abductors, and, yes, even those pillars of society, bombers."

Uzi inched forward uncomfortably in his chair. "Having an accurate profile will help us narrow down our suspect pool and tell us where to focus our investigation."

Leila hiked her brow. "No offense, but I don't see it. We don't even have the devices. They're in a million pieces scattered across how may square miles?"

"That definitely makes it more difficult," Vail said, "but not impossible. It just means we need to be more creative."

"Creative?" Leila turned to Uzi. "We need facts, not guesswork. Because if our guesses are wrong—"

"That's not what Karen meant."

"Uzi," Vail said, "I'm capable of speaking for myself. And yes, I meant creative. We don't always have the necessary forensics to identify our offender. So we have to use our heads to find the information other ways." Vail's BlackBerry buzzed. She pulled it from her belt, glanced at the screen, and then rose from her chair. "Gotta run. But thanks—it's been lovely. I'm sure dinner would've been better than the company." She forced a smile and gathered up her black sweater.

Uzi rose awkwardly from his chair. "Wait— You really have to go?"

"A case I was tricked into taking, for lack of a better term. Some football player. He was bludgeoned and his dick was cut off. We've got another vic."

Uzi winced. "Couldn't you have left out the part about the severed penis?"

"I can brief Hector on my own," Vail said, then turned to Leila. "Nice meeting you. Let's not do it again real soon."

Vail walked off toward the staircase.

Uzi sat down hard in his seat. "She's working this case as a favor to me, Leila. You didn't have to antagonize her."

Leila pursed her moist, glossed lips. "Sorry if I wasn't more accepting of her . . . theories. I just think it's going to be of limited value. I hope she didn't take it personally."

Uzi snorted. "Don't worry about it. Karen doesn't get mad. She gets *even*."

Clarence returned with a wine list in hand. "May I suggest something, or would you like to take a look for yourself?"

"Just a glass for me," Uzi said. "I've got a lot of work to do after dinner."

Clarence raised a brow and glanced at Leila. "Indeed."

"No," Uzi said with a grin. "Real work, Clarence."

"I'm sure it will be, Mr. Uzi. But we have your favorite Cabernet—Galil Mountain, from the Golan."

Uzi twisted his mouth into a mock frown. "You're like the serpent, Clarence. Tempting me." He gestured toward Leila. "Okay by you?"

"I'll give it a shot."

As Clarence headed off, Uzi's Nokia buzzed. He checked the screen and groaned. "Gotta be kidding."

"Problem?" Leila asked.

"Hector cancelled. Has to put out a fire."

"Hector?"

Uzi placed his phone on the table. "The other task force member who was joining us."

"So, Agent Uzi," she said, leaning forward on her elbows and tilting her head. "It's down to you and me."

"Please, just call me 'Uzi.'"

"Do you always pick up women at crash sites . . . Uzi?"

Uzi glanced from side to side. "Did I miss something?"

"I'm with the CIA. I'm trained to smell a setup better than most dogs sniff bombs."

"No setup, Leila. This was supposed to be a working dinner. I'd no idea Karen would catch a case and that Hector would cancel. But to answer your question about picking up women at crash sites, it's been at least a couple of years since I've done that." He smiled, then moved back to allow the busboy to place a plate of bread on the table. "Homemade cornbread with honey butter. Try some. It's to die for."

"Look at the facts," Leila said, ignoring Uzi's comment. "Here we are, just you and me, having dinner at a trendy restaurant. A romantic atmosphere. With wine on the way."

"Actually, the wine is served," Clarence said, turning the bottle to display the label for Uzi's inspection. Uzi indicated that Clarence should show it instead to Leila, and the server complied.

Leila, whose gaze was still locked on Uzi, diverted her eyes to the wine and nodded.

Clarence produced a polished chrome corkscrew, and with three twists and a pull, the Cabernet was breathing. He poured a small amount into Leila's glass and waited while she swirled it, then watched as she took a satisfying sniff before swishing a mouthful across her palate.

She glanced up at Clarence and said, "Very earthy. And a hint of dark chocolate. Excellent."

Uzi raised an eyebrow.

"I have an affinity for Cabs."

Clarence poured the two glasses, set the bottle down, and melted into the background.

Uzi reached for his glass and took a sip. He knew the vintage well and Leila was right about the flavors. Like Leila, Dena's palate could differentiate between coveted and lesser desirable vintages. The parallels between the women hijacked his thoughts for a brief moment and he saw Dena sitting across from him, the neckline of her red dress plunging a bit lower than Leila's, displaying a tantalizing hint of cleavage.

Uzi set down his glass. "Where did you acquire your taste for wine?" he asked.

Leila took another sip and let her eyes roam the room.

After a prolonged silence, Uzi said, "You don't like personal questions."

"Not really, no."

"Then we'll keep it to business for now. CIA. Counterintelligence?"

She dabbed at her lips with the napkin. "I'm looking into the crash. Like you."

"But you can't discuss it."

"I'm limited in what I can say. I'm sure you understand."

"The idea's to pool information, Leila. If there was a takeaway lesson from 9/11, that's it right there." She had no response, so he continued. "Guess that means we're back to personal stuff. Are you married?"

"Not anymore."

Uzi grabbed a piece of cornbread and placed it on his plate. He pulled off a corner and asked, "But you were. Divorced or widowed?"

"Divorced."

"Children?"

"No."

Uzi nodded, wishing the one-word responses would morph into more thoughtful answers. It was beginning to feel like an interrogation. "Siblings?"

"One brother." She pointed to the small plate by Uzi's elbow. "How's the bread?"

"Good," he said. "It's always good."

They spent the next hour sparring and discussing elements of the crash, Uzi supplying some of the facts they had amassed and hoping for an in-kind exchange from Leila. But she did not offer up the detailed intel he felt the CIA should have developed by now. To be fair, however, neither had those members of his task force who were with the Agency.

They eventually settled onto the more neutral ground of complaining about bureaucracy and sharing stories of the battle scars each had endured during the rise to their current positions. Underlying the evening, however, was the sense that the attraction Uzi felt was mutual—at one point he caught her reflection in a mirror watching his butt when he got up to use the restroom.

After arguing over who should pay the bill—they ended up splitting it—Uzi rose from his chair. "Can we do this again?" he asked as he helped place the cape onto her shapely shoulders.

"The work part or the part where your friends cancel and it's just you and me?"

"The part where my friends cancel."

She pursed her lips, a slight smile tickling the corners of her mouth. Looking out at the lights on 20th Avenue beyond the window, she said, "I think so."

Less than an enthusiastic response, but for now he would accept it. "Great. I'll call you."

He pulled out his Nokia and entered her number into his contacts list. Then he watched her walk out into the chilled DC night.

"She's quite beautiful," Clarence said behind Uzi's shoulder.

Uzi did not bother to turn around. "Yeah," he said. "I noticed."

DAY THREE

6:58 AM
151 hours 2 minutes remaining

Uzi pushed through the maple-framed glass doors to Leonard Rudnick's building, ascended the paneled lobby's steps, and then ran up the five flights to the doctor's special entrance. He preferred taking the stairs whenever possible—not because he didn't like elevators, but because his grandmother had ingrained in him the value of exercise. She religiously walked several flights daily to and from her fifth-story Brooklyn apartment, well into her nineties.

He took a few deep breaths to calm his lungs, then walked into the small waiting room, where he found Rudnick standing with the door open.

"Right on time," the doctor said.

Uzi followed Rudnick into his office and sat down heavily in his chair. "Look, Doc, I don't know if this is going to work. This case is taking all my time. Even meeting at seven AM . . . I need to keep my mind focused on the investigation—"

"Are you the only agent working this case?"

Uzi snorted. "We're up to about five hundred. But I'm in charge of more than half of them, and there're leads I'm following up myself."

"I understand. That's a tremendous amount of responsibility. Some thrive on it. But I want to know about you. Tell me what brought you to the FBI," Rudnick said with a casual wave of a hand.

Uzi blinked, realizing the doctor had just gently, yet abruptly, changed the subject.

"Was it the prestige?" Rudnick asked.

Uzi sighed in concession. He pulled a protein bar from his leather jacket and tore it open. "Breakfast. Hope you don't mind."

Rudnick gestured for him to continue. "I understand your time is short. Eating and talking is fine. So, to my question."

Uzi swallowed, then said, "I needed a job, and I wanted something that would fit with my professional background." He took another bite from the bar.

"I see. But that could describe a lot of jobs."

"The Bureau has a great retirement plan," he said as he chewed.

Rudnick grinned, as did Uzi. But then the doctor's face hardened as he leaned elbows onto knees and said, "I think it's time we talked about what happened to your family."

It was the most direct Rudnick had been, and in the instant the doctor finished his sentence, Uzi felt a surge of fear rattle his body. Had Rudnick been a boxer, he would've been dinged for hitting below the belt.

Uzi knew his body language had betrayed him. His eyes had widened, if only for a second, and then he had looked away. He swallowed hard. "If you know to ask," Uzi said, "then you already know what happened."

Rudnick remained stone-faced. "That's not how this works, Uzi. What I know or don't know is ultimately unimportant. But let me put you at ease. I was only told that you suffered a terrible family tragedy, and that as a result you moved back to the United States."

Uzi nodded but did not speak. The two of them sat there in silence, Uzi's gaze directed at the carpet, his mind sifting through tortured memories.

"It will help to talk about it."

Uzi looked down at the protein bar, no longer felt like eating, and shoved it back in his pocket. "I don't think I can."

"I see," Rudnick said. "How about I ask you a question I usually ask my patients who've gone through a 'terrible family tragedy.' He interlocked his fingers and leaned back. "Why haven't you committed suicide?"

"What?"

"Your answer could prove valuable in shaping our treatment."

Uzi's eyes found the ceiling. He didn't even know how to approach such a question.

"Have you ever considered it? Suicide?"

"The answer to your question, Doctor, is that I don't know. I don't know why I didn't commit suicide."

"Okay. Some people have an answer for me, and others, well, others discover the answer in the weeks that follow. So let's start with something a bit easier. Were you born in Israel?"

Uzi began bouncing his right knee. "My father was. He met my mother on a visit to New York and ended up staying there. I was born in Queens but he moved us back to Israel after I turned three. When I was about ten, we started living in both places. My aunt, who lived in Brooklyn, had Cerebral Palsy, and my mom didn't wanna be so far away from her.

"So we lived in New York during the school year and Israel during the summers. After doing my three years in the IDF, I ended up staying there. I got my degree from Braude College of Engineering." He laughed. "Because of my performance with the defense forces, my first job offer actually came from the Shin Bet security service. It's like our FBI. I was with them for three years before Intel offered me a full-time position working on the first NetBurst microarchitecture CPUs. They'd just opened Fab18, a new manufacturing facility in Israel and I had an 'in' through a friend, so it was perfect." He stopped, reflected for a moment. "Around that time, my father had also gotten sick, so my mother had all she could handle."

"And then what?"

"Spent almost five years with Intel as a design engineer. Five really good years. And then one day, things changed."

Rudnick sat patiently. But Uzi did not elaborate. "What changed?" he finally asked.

Uzi pulled a cellophane wrapped toothpick from his pocket and tore it open. He stuck it in his mouth and played with it between his tongue and teeth. "I ran into someone from my childhood. This man was very special to me, kind of like a hero. Other kids had Batman, or

Superman, but this guy was real." Uzi rolled the toothpick around a bit, then said, "Ever hear of Rafi Eitan?"

"The man who ran the operation that captured Adolf Eichmann."

Uzi's eyebrows rose. "Yes. I didn't think an American would know his name."

Rudnick's expression did not change. "The Nazis held special meaning for me. Why do you bring him up?"

"Rafi was a neighbor of mine. On summer afternoons he used to sit in front of his house and tell me and my friends about the time they kidnapped Eichmann and brought him back to Israel to stand trial. It was an incredibly daring operation, filled with intrigue and the sexiness of a good spy novel. Only this mission was real, and the peace it brought to the survivors ran deep. And it proved to the world that Israel's intelligence agency was a player, capable of anything." Uzi stared off for a moment. "I remember sitting there as a kid the first time he told the story. I was mesmerized. I knew then I wanted to be a Mossad agent."

"But instead you went into technology."

"My first year with the Shin Bet, I put in an application to the Mossad, figuring it was a sure thing. But I was rejected."

"Do you know why?"

"They don't tell you. You just never hear from them."

Rudnick rose from his chair and took a water pitcher from his desk. He poured Uzi a glass. "How did that make you feel?"

"I thought I was good at what I did, and I had this burning desire to serve. I felt it was something I was born to do." He took the drink from Rudnick.

"But how did it make you feel?" Rudnick locked eyes with Uzi.

Uzi shrugged. "Angry, I guess. Left out. Like someone was preventing me from doing something I really wanted to do. And that just made me more determined." He gulped some water. "One day when I was with Intel, I went home to visit my mom and I found Rafi in his backyard welding scrap metal into these really cool sculptures. We talked for several hours, late into the night. He told me about missions he'd been on, what he'd been doing after he'd retired. But then he asked me why I never went to work for Mossad. I told him I'd been rejected." Uzi paused for a moment. "What I tell you stays here, right?"

"Doctor-patient confidentiality is the cornerstone of trust in a relationship like ours."

Uzi nodded slowly. He didn't know if he should continue, but his instincts told him he could trust Rudnick. Besides, the doctor would have no reason to betray him. "A few days later," Uzi said, "I got a call from Gideon Aksel, the director general himself, asking me to come to his office for a meeting." He took another drink. "Rafi had vouched for me. And when Rafi Eitan vouches for you, they listen. I resigned from Intel the next day." Uzi set the glass down, then stole a glance at the wall clock. "Look, Doc—I really don't have time for this. Fifteen minutes is all I can give you today."

Rudnick's shoulders slumped. "I feel like we're making some good progress here. How 'bout you give me another fifteen, hmm?"

Uzi rose from the chair, unwilling to verbally concede that talking about the past had felt good. "Too much going on." He gave Rudnick a pat on the shoulder, then turned and walked out.

8:19 AM
149 hours 41 minutes remaining

The encrypted cell phone had already rung five times. Echo Charlie knew he wouldn't be dumped into voicemail, so there was no disadvantage in letting it ring.

Charlie leaned his car seat back and waited. He rolled down his window, took a deep breath, and closed his eyes. The sweet scent of cherry blossoms was absent from the winter air, replaced by barren branches and musty bay odors blowing off the Chesapeake. No matter. He did not need flowers and breathtaking landscapes. Power and influence were more intoxicating than Mother Nature—and vastly more significant than sensory input, which only diverted his focus.

"It's me," Charlie said when the phone was finally answered. He rolled up his window and dropped his head down, in case someone was trying to read his lips.

Alpha Zulu said, "Go ahead."

"We need our G-man monitored more closely. Controlled. Need be, he might have to be dealt with quickly."

"We can handle your G-man. We know things."

Charlie checked his scorpion-engraved pocket watch, always aware of the length of the call. Though it theoretically could not be traced, he was not taking any chances that the CIA or NSA had developed new ways of unscrambling the transmission and eavesdropping on his conversation. Technology changed so fast it was best not to take the risk.

"Our package is ready to be dropped off," Alpha Zulu said. "It's packed neatly and waiting to be delivered."

"Deliver and install. And make sure it works before you leave the job site."

"Our associate will see to it. I'll contact you after the job's complete."

Charlie ended the call, then stared out at the choppy Chesapeake water. There was no substitute for power.

None at all.

9:45 AM
148 hours 15 minutes remaining

Alpha Zulu sat beside Oscar Delta in the doctor's parking lot of the Walter Reed National Military Medical Center, eyes slowly moving in a grid pattern, left to right, from the farthest areas to the closest. Observing, watching.

Finally, keeping his gaze on the landscape before him, he said, "We're good. Go."

Oscar Delta shifted his weight in the bucket seat and pulled out his cell phone, then tapped out a message:

table set. invite the guests.

Delta pulled on his baseball cap, and then slipped on a pair of sunglasses. Ten minutes later, he popped open his door and walked to the visitor's parking lot, where a black Hyundai Dynasty was waiting. After a final glance around the vicinity, he slid behind the steering wheel and moved the car onto the hospital complex. His orders were to park the vehicle in a specific location and then move to an area where he would be capable of observing the aftereffects.

He locked the doors and peeled off his thin leather gloves while hiking the planned two hundred steps toward his perch. Once in position, he sent a text to Zulu:

great seats. cant wait for the show to start

9:32 AM
148 hours 28 minutes remaining

Uzi pulled out of the FBI Washington Field Office parking garage, having just completed a briefing with most of the task force agents. Despite the pressure he was under, he felt refreshed and energized. Moreover, he had a sharper awareness of the things around him, as if he'd just gotten over a cold and could smell the pot of fresh-brewed coffee.

He hadn't felt that way in years—six years, in fact. As he turned onto Pennsylvania Avenue, he realized that it had to do with his session with Rudnick. He now understood, intellectually at least, that the more he tried to contain his feelings, the more elusive their underlying meaning became.

Could talking about your problems be so liberating that it permeates your attitude toward everything? He was instantly grateful for Shepard's insistence that he start treatment, though he was still cautiously optimistic the effect would last. And he had no idea if he would even be able to keep his next appointment. Or the one after that.

Uzi parked his car near the National Mall and walked along Madison Drive, eyes roaming the area for DeSantos. He located him a moment later, sitting on a park bench thumbing through an edition of the *Post* and chewing a piece of gum.

"Got any more?" Uzi asked, settling down next to him.

DeSantos folded the paper in quarters, pulled out a pack of Juicy Fruit, and offered it to his partner. "I haven't been able to find anything linking Harmon, Fargo, and Ellison, or any of them to Rusch. About the only thing they had in common was their NFA membership." DeSantos looked off at the Washington Monument in the near distance.

"National Firearms Alliance?" Uzi asked. "That's interesting."

"No, it's not. I was just throwing that out because I didn't have anything else to say."

"Serious? They were all NFA members?"

"Them and seven million others." DeSantos blew on his hands. "It's not a crime. They do some good."

"They do more harm."

"Not worth the debate, my friend." DeSantos tucked the folded *Post* beneath his arm, then stood. "Point is, it's not a big deal that they're all members."

Uzi rose and followed in step as they crunched down the fine gravel path, heading west toward the monument.

"I'll bet my salary that every single person associated with ARM is an NFA member."

"So what? I bet they belong to the NRA, too." DeSantos shook his head. "You're trying to create a link where there isn't any."

"Far-right militias and NFA are in bed with each other. That fact can't be ignored."

"First," DeSantos said, "I'd verify that little assumption before calling it a fact. But fine, don't ignore it. Look into it. I just don't think there's anything there."

"Rusch is pro-gun control because of what happened to his sister. Killed by an illegal thirty-eight special. Robbery attempt—"

DeSantos held up a hand, then stopped walking. "She wasn't killed by a gun, Uzi. She was killed by the asshole who pulled the trigger."

"That's a classic NFA argument."

"Look, boychick. All I'm saying is that if a guy takes a hammer to his best friend, we don't talk about banning hammers. We prosecute the guy who swung it."

"And all I'm saying is that Rusch is not NFA's best friend." He waited to read DeSantos's blank face. When DeSantos didn't react, Uzi continued. "Motive. They had a reason to eliminate him."

"Now you're way out in left field."

"No, go with me on this." Uzi thought for a second, allowing the theory to form. "Let's say the NFA was concerned about Rusch's gun-control agenda. The only way to prevent a disaster—from their point of view—is to get rid of him. They find an ally in ARM and launch their plan."

"Too much of a leap for me. This isn't a goddamn spy movie, Uzi. And this isn't the Middle East. Don't forget we work for the US government. Like it or not—and I usually don't—there are legal and political checks and balances. There needs to be proof of a connection, a solid case. Not some hare-brained theory about the NFA and right-wing militias plotting to kill the next president of the United States."

"This from the guy who's been on more black ops than the government will admit to? You know what's out there, what's possible. Even with 9/11, America's only gotten a taste of the twisted minds these terrorists have. You and I . . . We've seen it up close." Uzi paused, looked away. "And personal."

DeSantos's moment of pause told Uzi that his partner agreed with him.

"Still," DeSantos finally said, "we don't have enough to go on."

Uzi chomped on the gum, his thoughts churning in unison. "So we need to dig some more. Find those connections."

"No," DeSantos said, poking at Uzi's leather jacket with an index finger. "You need to find those connections. I've got some other things I'm looking into."

Uzi started to object when his smartphone began ringing. He listened for a second, then caught DeSantos's eyes with his own. "Let's go," he said, jogging toward his Tahoe.

"What's going on?"

Uzi chirped his remote and the doors unlocked. "Tell you on the way."

Uzi put his magnetic light on the roof and drove like an Israeli, zipping through traffic and arriving at the National Military Medical Center in under fifteen minutes. He had been told that Glendon Rusch remembered something about the explosion and thought it might help their investigation.

As they approached, the fifteen-story tower of Building One rose like the guardian of the hospital complex, appearing like it did on any other dreary Maryland day.

Uzi turned his credentials wallet inside out and slipped the end into his coat's breast pocket so his Bureau ID was visible. Because of his olive complexion, slight accent and casual dress, he did not want to be profiled incorrectly by the military police. On high alert with heightened tensions, the scene could get ugly very fast.

They cleared security and hurried through the lobby—but before they could make it to the elevators, the ground shook. In the next split second, Uzi wasn't sure what he felt first—the concussive force against his chest, the rumble of the floor, or the sensation of being weightless and flying backward through the air.

The ear-shattering burst thumped his tympanic membrane like a punch to the nose: numbness at first, followed by the sequelae of pain and muffled hearing.

He gathered himself up from the floor, fine soot and shit coating his tongue and face—and looked around for his partner. "Santa," he shouted. He thought he shouted it—the strain on his throat felt like it—though he was not sure. "Santa!"

He got to his feet and saw DeSantos a few yards to his left, slowly getting up.

"You okay?"

DeSantos staggered, then caught himself. "I've just been knocked into a wall by a fucking bomb. No, I'm not okay. You?"

"I'm in one piece and I can kinda sort hear. All things considered, I feel great."

The wall behind them was partially missing, smoky daylight filtering through. Off in the distance, multiple car alarms wailed, followed seconds later by sirens. They stumbled through the rubble and emerged in the parking lot, where chunks of displaced asphalt littered the road. Piles of pulverized tempered glass covered the ground as if a dump truck had spilled a load of sparkling diamonds.

"Jesus," DeSantos said as they walked, leaning against one another for support.

"What do you want to bet the target was Rusch?"

"Better he's the target than the victim."

A physician in a white lab coat came rushing toward them. "You two okay?"

Uzi waved him off. "Fine. Shaken, not stirred."

DeSantos play-slapped his shoulder. "Shaken, not stirred? If I didn't know you better, I'd think the explosion caused some brain damage."

Uzi smirked. "Let's go check on Rusch."

Slowly, as their balance was still lacking, they took the stairs—which were littered with concrete fragments and glass shards. The fire door was twisted, but they were able to pry it open enough to squeeze through.

As they headed down the hall, Uzi's phone rang. "Phone works."

"That's a good sign," DeSantos said.

"Except that it's my boss. That's *not* a good sign." He brought the handset to his ear.

"Uzi," Shepard said, "get over to the military hospital, get over there right now."

Uzi thumbed the volume switch and maxed it out. "Let me guess. There's been another explosion."

"You already know?" Shepard asked. "Who called you?"

"DeSantos and I were onsite. Pretty fucking intense. Almost took us out— Too close for my taste. We're on our way to Rusch's room."

"A team will be there in five minutes. Keep me posted."

"DeSantos and I are fine, by the way. Thanks for asking." Uzi disconnected the call and shoved the Nokia into his pocket.

The two Secret Service agents guarding the door pulled their handguns as Uzi and DeSantos approached. "Get down. Get down now!"

Uzi glanced at his credentials case—but it was no longer attached to his jacket. "We're on the job," Uzi said, raising his hands above his head. "FBI. JTTF. SSA Uziel and DeSantos, DOD." *I hope these guys know their government acronyms.*

"Creds?" the agent said, voice strong and urgent. Still amped up.

"Musta been knocked off during the explosion."

"Got mine," DeSantos said. He held up his right hand and said, "Gonna reach into my jacket pocket. Slowly, okay?" He pulled it out and tossed it to the man's feet.

The agent examined it a moment, then pressed an index finger to his ear and read the information to the guy on the radio. A long moment later, he waved them through.

They took folded paper gowns and masks from an adjacent stainless steel cart, put them on, and pushed through the door.

Glendon Rusch was lying in bed, a phone pressed against his ear. "Yes, Mr. President. Thank you for the call. I appreciate that. I will."

The agent by his side took the handset and hung it up.

Rusch turned his head toward Uzi and DeSantos.

"Hector DeSantos. DOD." He started to extend a hand, then withdrew it, no doubt realizing that Rusch's upper limbs were completely bandaged.

"Are you okay?" Uzi asked.

"I'm not sure how to answer that."

Uzi had forgotten how raspy Rusch's voice was. Between that and his muffled hearing, he had to concentrate to make out what the man was saying.

"If you mean the explosion, I'm fine. My window's bulletproof glass. Woke me from a nightmare is all. Any casualties?"

"Don't know yet, sir. We came to check on you first."

"I've got several agents who are glued to my side. I don't need another two on my case."

Actually, you've got about five hundred on your case. "You asked to see me. Something you remembered about the helicopter."

"Remembered?" Rusch asked. "What on earth are you talking about? I already told you everything I know."

Uzi pulled his phone and checked the call history. It appeared to be a Bureau number, from the Washington Field Office.

"I'm sorry we bothered you," Uzi said. He gave DeSantos a jerk of his head and they left Rusch's room.

"What the hell was that about?" DeSantos asked.

"First thoughts . . . We were lured here."

"Yeah, no shit. You think this—this attack was about us?"

After dumping their gowns and masks, Uzi led the way back down the littered staircase to the ground floor, all the while working it through his head. "I still think Rusch was the target—but whoever's behind this wanted us to either witness it firsthand, or—"

"They figured they could take out three for the price of one."

Uzi found his creds amongst the dusty rubble in the lobby, then force-yawned a couple of times. "I think my hearing's coming back."

"We were lucky. Close enough to have a blast but not too close to have gotten blasted into a million pieces."

"If it was about us," Uzi said, "who'd have motive? Only one I can think of."

"ARM," DeSantos said. "They either followed us here, or—"

"Made the phone call that brought us here."

DeSantos shook his head. "I don't know. What's the number in your call history?"

"Someone from inside WFO. But caller IDs can be cloned if you know what you're doing," Uzi said as they stepped out into the parking lot.

The swirling red lights of emergency and law enforcement vehicles whipped across the remaining first-floor windows of Building 10. Uniformed workers rushed about, some gathering toolkits to begin documenting the scene, others already on hands and knees collecting evidence.

It was a sight Uzi was all too familiar with, having lived through the bloody, suicide-bomb-laden Palestinian uprisings in Israel. The scene brought back memories.

"You okay?" DeSantos asked. "You don't look too good."

"I'm fine."

"You look all pale and clammy—"

"Really—I'm fine."

They moved further into the carnage, taking care not to disturb the scene. Uzi knelt beside the first forensic technician they passed. "Any thoughts?"

The man glanced down at Uzi's creds. "My experience with scenes like this, given the blast pattern, says a car bomb."

A loud whistle came from an area closest to the building. "Over here."

Uzi and DeSantos followed a contingent of agents to the area of interest. A twisted and hollowed-out black Hyundai sedan rested against the hospital's façade.

Uzi contorted his torso to peer into the warped metal hulk. "This the source?"

"Looks like it," the technician said. "But for the moment, that's only a working theory. We're just getting started here."

"Anyone bite it?" DeSantos asked.

"Two on the first floor, I think. And someone in the lobby."

Uzi gestured at the car. "Car bomb means you put the explosive where, trunk?"

The technician shrugged. "Could be multiple places, depending on what you want to accomplish. For this, trunk would be a good place to start." They moved toward the back of the vehicle. He peered in and examined the damage to the surrounding metal, which sported sharp and angry flanges that curled outward. "If I had to guess, C-4. Packed right here, supplemented with some other type of explosive." He swiveled, took in the immediate area. "Took out part of the street, some windows and part of the building, but . . ."

"But what?" Uzi asked.

"If their target was the vice president, either they didn't know where he was, or they just plain used the wrong explosive."

"Good point," DeSantos said. "If they used AMFO—ammonium nitrate-fuel oil mixture—the ingredients are easy to get and it'd give them a large explosion capable of causing vertical damage to a building."

"That's what McVeigh used," Uzi said.

"More importantly, C-4 is high order and does a good job of blowing things around. AMFO's low order and brings things *down*."

Uzi took another look at the extent of the damage. "So if Rusch was the target, they used the wrong tool for the job. Unless *we* were the job."

"Could also be that this *was* related to Rusch and they used the C-4 because that's what they had available and it's what they're familiar with. They may not be sophisticated bomb makers."

"Or the people responsible are in big trouble because they didn't get the job done the first time when they took down Marine Two." The voice came from behind them.

Uzi turned. It was Leila.

"Leila. This is Hector DeSantos. Hector, Leila Harel."

"Hector." Leila tilted her head back. "You're the wingman."

"The— What?"

"Nothing," Uzi said, shaking his head at Leila, fighting back a smile.

"I've gotta go check on . . . something," DeSantos said, jerking a thumb over his shoulder. "Meet up with me at the car."

Uzi settled his gaze on the bombed-out vehicle twenty feet away. "I had a good time last night."

"Glad to hear it."

Uzi faced her. "Did you?"

She let a thin smile spread her lips. "Yes."

"Good." Uzi squared his shoulders. "What are you doing for lunch?"

"Today?"

Uzi consulted his watch. "As in right now."

Leila looked around, as if thinking of a reason to decline. "I just got here. I haven't had time to evaluate the crime scene."

"I can brief you over lunch."

"How about we do dinner tomorrow night, and then I can stay here and look around, and I won't feel like I've shirked my responsibilities."

"I admire your work ethic. Dinner it is. Any place in particular?"

"There's a Mediterranean place I know off Constitution in Fairfax. Amir's. Not as fancy as that farmer's place, but it's my type of food."

Uzi was so focused on the beauty of her face that he was hardly listening to what she was saying. "Okay. When and where?"

Leila's eyes narrowed. "That place I was just talking about. Amir's. In Fairfax."

"Right."

She smiled knowingly. "Say tomorrow, seven PM."

"Okay. 'Tomorrow, seven PM.'" He grinned. They both laughed.

"See you then."

As he watched her stride away, DeSantos's approaching voice grabbed his attention. "Are we all squared away? Did you exchange any information with her, or just lots of hormones?"

"Hormones," Uzi said. "No info." They turned and headed for his car. "We're having dinner tomorrow. Some Mediterranean place in Fairfax."

"Amir's," DeSantos said. "Great food. You'll like it."

Uzi pulled out his keys and winked at his partner. "I'm not going there for the food."

6:16 PM
139 hours 44 minutes remaining

The chilled evening descended quickly. While Uzi spent the afternoon hours going through emailed reports his task force agents had submitted, the hours melted into a clearing sunset. He was making steady progress when his phone line began blinking. He'd turned off the ringer hours earlier and his secretary had already gone home. He picked up the receiver, but no one was there.

Uzi set it down and turned his attention to another intra-office email. Ten minutes later, a message from Agent Hoshi Koh caught his eye: "I might have something. Call me ASAP."

Uzi lifted the handset, but before he could dial, Hoshi was standing in his doorway, her hand poised to knock.

"I was just about to call you," he said as he set the phone back in its cradle.

"I tried your line twice, and then your cell. But you didn't answer."

"I turned off the ringers. What's up?"

Hoshi took a seat on his guest chair and reclined. "You really wanna know?"

Uzi tilted his head. "Hoshi, it's late, I'm tired, and my brain is about to close up shop for the night. So if you've got something, speak up or hold it till tomorrow."

"I thought you saved the grouch for everyone else and your charming side for me."

"Sorry. I really am exhausted." Uzi leaned back in his large leather office chair and rubbed his right eye with the knuckle of his fist. "So . . . you found something?"

"Yeah, a guy who used to work with Ellison until a month ago, when he was transferred to Pax River, a different branch of HMX. Lieutenant Brad Wheeler. From what I've been able to gather, Wheeler hated Ellison's guts. They had more than one knock-down drag-out off base. Had something to do with Wheeler's transfer."

"Wonder why Vasquez didn't tell us about that." He noted Hoshi's crumpled brow. "The Aircraft Maintenance Officer at HMX. He had every chance to tell us about Wheeler's beef— Shit, he probably had a hand in the transfer."

"You want me to follow up?"

"I'll have Hector do it. He and Vasquez go back aways." Uzi thought a moment. "His sheet?"

"Clean."

"Figured. Wouldn't be at HMX if he had any marks. But you like this guy for Ellison."

"He's got to be looked at."

"I agree. So where's the problem?"

Hoshi shifted in her seat. "A buddy of Ellison's at Quantico told us Wheeler recently purchased a forty-five."

"Same caliber used on Ellison and his sister."

"Could be coincidence and mean nothing, but—"

"Anyone talk to this guy?"

"I did. Alibi is weak. Says he was in bed, sick. I checked with Pax River, and he did call in sick. But no doctor's visit before or after. No script, but a bunch of over-the-counter meds. Showed me a credit card receipt from CVS the day before the murder. I spoke with the store, and the receipt was for meds. But buying cold medicine and calling in sick doesn't mean jack." She received a nod from Uzi. "Other than that, I didn't get much from him. Too damn disciplined."

"Yeah, well, he's a Marine." Uzi rocked a bit in his chair, thinking. Then: "Gun records?"

Hoshi folded her arms across her chest and smiled wanly. "I knew you'd get to that sooner or later. In this case, later."

"Thanks for the vote of confidence."

"The director won't allow us to access the NICS," she said, referring to the National Instant Criminal Background Check System, the federal audit log utilized by gun dealers to conduct background checks on gun purchasers. "So the gun records might tell us a nice story, except that I can't get at them."

Uzi squinted. "That makes no sense. We need those records. What's his problem?"

"You really want to know?"

Uzi rose from his chair and stretched. "Hoshi, do you realize that every time I ask for your opinion, you answer me with a question?"

"Do I?" She caught herself and laughed. "Sorry." She glanced over her right shoulder, then lowered her voice. "I've had my eye on Knox for a long time. I just don't trust the guy. I've always felt he's had his hands in the NFA's coffers."

At the mention of the National Firearms Alliance, Uzi's ears perked up. "Like how?"

"To the tune of four-hundred thousand for his last senatorial reelection bid before he became director."

Uzi whistled. "That's a lot of money."

"That's a lot of influence," Hoshi said.

Uzi's eyes were roaming the room, but he was seeing nothing. He was thinking, putting this latest puzzle piece together with the others he'd inherited in the Rusch investigation. "Okay," he finally said. "So I need to get with Shepard on this, see if he can chat up the attorney general, get him to talk some sense into our esteemed director. I mean, we're all on the same side, right?" He shook his head. "Kind of strange for the head of the top law enforcement agency in the world to prevent his own agents from doing their jobs."

"I just came from Shepard's. He's still here, if you want to talk to him."

"Let's do that." He moved out from behind his desk and strolled through the doorway. "Anything come up on Gene Harmon?"

"How so?"

"Being chair of the House Select Committee on Intelligence, I figure the guy could've rattled a cage or two. See if he was involved in any unusually sensitive or controversial decisions the past couple of years."

"May be tough to get that kind of info. Closed-door congressional stuff."

"I'm sure you'll find a way." He received a reluctant nod from Hoshi, then continued: "Put some people on his life. Known acquaintances, relatives, friends—especially ambassadors, foreign heads of state, that sort of thing."

"Already being done."

"And follow up on this Wheeler dude. Talk to his buddies, see what else we can dig up on the guy."

"Speaking of digging up . . ." She handed him a message slip with a name and phone number scrawled across it. "A source of mine, works for a group that keeps tabs on gun-control issues. Gun Violence Center. He's got some info for you."

"You already spoke to him?"

"Let's just say I've got an open line to him. He usually knows what's going to happen before it does. Must have good intuition."

"Or good sources. Is he legit?"

"Thoroughly vetted. Totally clean. Graduated from UC Berkeley with a law degree, went to work for a huge firm in San Francisco but hated it. Became a PI specializing in cases that had a legal slant. Did that for eleven years, then moved east a decade ago."

"Moved east? Why?"

"Found his calling in certain political issues. Figured best place to be is here."

"You're comfortable with him?"

"Don't take my word for it. Talk to him, decide for yourself."

Uzi shoved the message slip into his pocket as he entered Marshall Shepard's office.

Shepard was on the phone, his elbows resting on the desk and his face buried in his large hands. Uzi and Hoshi took seats in front of him and waited.

"Yeah, do that," Shepard said. "Keep me informed." He pulled off the headset, then slammed it down on his desk. "Christ. That guy drives me up a wall. Up a freakin' wall." His face seemed to take in the presence of Hoshi—and the significance of her visit. "She told you," Shepard said to Uzi.

"What do you make of it?"

"Just got back from a briefing with the director. I was going to fill you in."

"Now's a good time."

Shepard looked at Hoshi. "What did you tell him?"

Hoshi's cheeks flushed, and Uzi realized he should have come alone.

"Just what we discussed, sir."

"If Koh here told you what she knows," Shepard said, "you probably know most of it. Director is placing some restrictions on our investigation."

Uzi found a toothpick on Shepard's desk. He pulled it from the wrapper and stuck it in his mouth. "You talk as if it's not a big deal."

"It's not, Uzi, it's not. There are bigger issues for us to deal with."

"He's our chief, but he's handcuffing us. We need those gun records."

"We've had roadblocks in investigations before. We'll find other ways of getting the info."

Uzi shared a look with Hoshi, whose face remained neutral. She was clearly uncomfortable with Uzi's challenging Shepard.

"Hoshi," Uzi said, "why don't you go finish that background sheet on Wheeler?"

Hoshi checked her watch, then glanced up at Shepard for his approval.

"Go," he said with the flick of a large hand.

She gathered herself and left the room.

As the door clicked shut, Uzi turned back to Shepard. "She's afraid of you, you know."

Shepard twisted his lips. "Most of my agents are. Except you. Why is that?"

"Because I know your secret. You've got a heart as big as your head." Shepard growled. Uzi got the impression that if his boss had been a Rottweiler, he'd have bared his teeth. "Back to Knox. Who else was in on this meeting?"

Shepard looked away. "The attorney general."

"That must've been fun. Cats and dogs." Uzi chuckled. "Did Coulter lay into him?"

"The Attorney General didn't have much of anything to say. He asked a few questions for clarification, but that was it." Shepard lifted a shoulder. "Maybe this whole NICS thing is Coulter's idea to begin with."

"You think?"

"Who the hell knows. They're both very conservative, Uzi. Strict interpretation of the Second Amendment."

Uzi held the tip of his nose and leaned forward.

"What's wrong?"

"Second Amendment or not, something stinks, Shep. And it's bad, whatever it is."

Shepard held up a big paw. "Let it stink. You just stay away from it. It's the fucking director, for Christ's sake. You've got enough problems—and enough on your plate."

Uzi could feel Shepard's eyes glaring at him. But he was lost in thought.

"Uzi, did you hear me? Did you hear what I said? Leave it alone."

Uzi rose from his chair and headed out.

"Where are you going?" Shepard barked.

Uzi stepped through the door, not bothering to stop as he called out over his shoulder, "To clear some room on my plate."

6:58 PM
139 hours 2 minutes remaining

After finishing with Shepard, Uzi grabbed his jacket and walked two blocks from the office toward that once ubiquitous, yet now rare, convenience: a pay phone. He pulled out the message slip Hoshi had given him and stood there, deciding if he wanted to call—and if he did, what he would say.

Figuring he had little to lose, he punched in the cell number for Hoshi's contact, Tad Bishop. The phone rang three times, but as Uzi entertained thoughts of hanging up—

"Bishop."

Uzi dipped his chin. Good tradecraft. Always. "Mr. Bishop, I was given your name by a friend. She told me you've got a good handle on the gun lobby."

"A bit of an understatement, but I won't hold that against you."

"Good, because I've got some questions for you."

"Not over the phone."

"Fine," Uzi said. "Meet me in the park behind Bureau of Printing and Engraving, off Wallenberg Drive. Go to the fireplug along Wallenberg and wait there."

"It'll take me about twenty minutes," Bishop said.

"I'll be the tall, dark, handsome guy in the leather overcoat."

"And I'll be the bald guy who's been thinking of dieting but can't seem to find the time."

Uzi stood in the plaza of the United States Holocaust Museum, down the block from the Bureau of Printing and Engraving. Finally, forty minutes after they had first spoken, a rotund man ambled up to the traffic light stanchion.

"You're late," Uzi said.

"I had to check you out. It took longer than I thought."

Uzi looked at him with raised eyebrows.

"You didn't think I'd just show up to meet someone who calls me and says, 'Meet me in a park to discuss the gun lobby' without doing a little due diligence."

Uzi pursed his lips. "Fair enough."

He lowered his voice. "I'll cut right to the chase. You want to know about the director, right? We're coming out with a report on Douglas Knox tomorrow. I'll make sure you get a copy, or if you want, you can download it from our website."

"But that doesn't tell the whole story," Uzi said.

Bishop turned and crossed Raoul Wallenberg Place, Uzi at his side. "I don't know if we'll ever know the whole story. But no, some things were left out of the report. I believe in what we do, but I know there are limits to the buttons we push. We want to stay alive, so there are certain lines we don't cross. If there's something that falls outside those lines, I tell Agent Koh and let her deal with it."

Uzi felt the moist dirt of the park grass giving a bit beneath his loafers. He stepped back onto the sidewalk and continued a few more paces in silence. "Consider me an extension of Agent Koh. I'll make sure any information you give me can't be traced back to you." When he got no objection, Uzi continued. "Let's start with some easy questions. Is Knox a member of the NFA?"

"Yes."

Uzi nodded. He figured as much. "How do you feel about that?"

"Over the years, congressmen have served on the NFA's board of directors. That's bad enough. But the director of the FBI? He should be squeaky clean. No ties to any group, organization, or corporation that could color his judgment on the issues he has to face while doing his job."

"How's NFA different from the NRA? I'm sure plenty of conservative politicians are NRA members."

"Different animal," Bishop said. He stopped walking and faced Uzi. "They've also got lines that shouldn't be crossed, and the NRA respects that line. But the NFA's a different story. Twenty years ago, when they were more concerned with the rights of hunters, it wasn't a big deal. But since then, the NFA's morphed into a political animal, a huge lobby group with substantial resources and a slab of new turf. They became the foot soldiers of the far right. The sales force, so to speak."

"I'm going to remain neutral on the merits of the NFA's beliefs and intentions," Uzi said. "I don't want my personal views to affect our discussion one way or the other. But tell me more about the NFA's leadership base. What motivates these people?"

Though Bishop was a good six inches shorter than Uzi, when the man looked up at him and their eyes met, even in the darkness Uzi could sense the fire that brewed there.

"What I hear you asking is how aggressive they'd get, right?" Uzi gave a slight nod, and Bishop continued. "These people want to win. They're respected members of the community, every one of them. Their backgrounds are clean, at least as far as law enforcement is concerned. Some have ties to fringe groups but their association is unofficial, carefully protected."

"But you know about them, these connections."

"I know about them, but I don't know the specifics. And don't ask me how I know."

Uzi glanced around the park, always on guard, always exercising caution. He lowered his voice. "I assume you had a defection from within their ranks."

"You understand the situation well," Bishop said.

"So you don't know who these 'fringe groups' are."

"No." Bishop's eyes narrowed. "And I'm better off not knowing."

"I hear you," Uzi said. "How about some perspective, then. How does all this tie in to President-elect Rusch?"

"It's a miracle Rusch made it this far."

"What do you mean by 'made it'?"

"That he won the election. Rusch is a problem. When his sister was killed three years ago, he went through an epiphany. He suddenly realized what we'd been preaching for the past fifteen years. That guns kill." Bishop wiped at his nose with a gloved hand. The temperature had dipped to the high thirties, and standing around was making it feel several degrees colder.

Bishop turned and started walking again, headed toward Independence Avenue. Uzi followed. "Rusch was a major challenge to the party. He was VP in a conservative administration that successfully defended against another 9/11. The economy was humming along and there was a steady growth in employment. They'd held the White House for eight years, but Whitehall was a goner on term limits. With his approval rating still in the seventies, they knew they had a strong shot at another four years—and Rusch was their ticket. But he had to be corralled. The main power brokers in the party sat him down and explained it all to him. They told him they needed him to be a team player or his career in politics would be over."

"But Rusch came out against the gun lobby."

"Big time. He played ball, rallied the party behind him. But the peace didn't last long. He didn't intend to make it a campaign issue, but a reporter with the *New York Times* asked the question during one of Rusch's rallies in October. Remember?"

"Typical campaign chatter, that's all that stuff ever is. I usually ignore it. Anyone can spin or promise anything to get elected—and the media plays right into it. Character is what counts."

"The reporter asked Rusch where he stood on gun control. He couldn't lie, because he knew the issue would come back to bite him in the ass later. So he danced around it. But during the last debate Gibson pressed him on it and Rusch officially came out against the gun lobby. At that point, a week before the election, there was nothing the party could do. He was their candidate." Bishop sniffled, rubbed his hands together. "The media made a big thing of it, of course, but it was nothing compared to what went on behind the scenes."

"And you know this, how?"

"Don't ask me that. But if it makes you feel any better, my sources are solid. And I always verify what they tell me. The last thing I want is to start rumors or say anything I'd have to go back on later. It would destroy my credibility. And in this business, credibility is everything."

"Go on," Uzi said. They had crossed Independence and were headed toward the brilliantly lit Washington Monument.

"What no one knew is that the National Firearms Alliance got involved. They'd given three million dollars to the Republicans over the past several years, and that bought them a lot of influence. Like I said before, the NFA became a clandestine leader of the conservative right wing. They pushed Rusch to the edge but couldn't get him to budge.

"Problem was, the NFA needed the right-wing as much as the right wing needed them. And in the end, both were powerless to stop Rusch. If he lost, the conservatives were out of power. If he won, they were scared shitless that he'd team with congressional Democrats to pass strict new gun laws. And with three Supreme Court judges about to retire or kick the bucket, you can bet Rusch's appointees will see things the way he does. The long debate over interpretation of the Second Amendment would be settled. Rusch would see to that."

Bishop let his theory hang in the thick air as his shoes crunched against the walkway.

Uzi felt his heartbeat kick up a notch, his body suffusing with euphoric anticipation. It was an emotion he hadn't felt in several years—and even then, he'd only experienced it a handful of times—the sudden realization that he had stumbled onto something far larger than the original mission he'd been assigned. He tried to keep his voice even and restrained. "So you're saying it'd be in their best interest if Glendon Rusch wasn't in the picture." He had chosen his words carefully, making it seem like a casual remark rather than a suggestion of motive for assassinating the man who had been elected the next president of the United States.

Bishop glanced sideways at Uzi. "They don't pay me enough to draw such conclusions."

They pay me enough. Uzi shook Bishop's hand, and then headed off into the darkness.

8:05 PM
137 hours 55 minutes remaining

Uzi went back to his office, too wired to go home. Forget about eating or sleeping. If there was validity to what Bishop had said, he knew the best place to be was at his desk, tapping away on his keyboard.

He exited the elevator, held his ID card in front of the sensor, and the electronic lock clunked loudly. After pushing through the thick glass doors, he made his way down the hall. A hint of movement by Hoshi's cubicle brought him to her desk.

"I didn't mean you should finish that report tonight," Uzi said.

She looked up, her eyes glazed from concentration. "I had nothing better to do. Might as well work."

"A beautiful woman like you has nothing to do? Impossible."

The skin flushed beneath her high cheekbones. "Yeah, yeah, yeah. You need something, don't you."

Though the sentiment behind his comment was genuine, he did, in fact, need her assistance. "You feel like going on a mission with me?"

She leaned back in her chair. "What kind of mission?"

He raised his eyebrows, then indicated that she should follow him. They walked over to his office and sat down beside his computer. "I met with your pal Bishop. He made some rather interesting assertions. I figured I'd dig a little, see what I could uncover. Other than the guys in cybercrime, you're the only other person here who knows her way around a computer network."

"What do you want me to do?"

Uzi pulled a laptop from behind his desk, taking care not to mess the papers that were arranged in their bins according to due date and level of complexity. He plugged it into an outlet and booted up. "You take the laptop and I'll be on my terminal. Let's see what we can find out."

Hoshi's eyes narrowed. "Find out about what?"

Uzi summarized Bishop's information, then pointed to his laptop. "You take the executive leadership of the NFA and I'll take our esteemed director. Let's start there. See where it leads us."

Hoshi swiveled her chair to face the screen and went to work.

Two hours later, Uzi rose from his seat and stretched toward the ceiling. "I'm hungry. You?"

Hoshi fought off a yawn. "I could use some coffee." She looked at Uzi's LCD monitor and inched closer. "What's that?"

Uzi turned to find a blinking red cursor beside a short paragraph of text. "Hmm. Interesting." He re-read the few sentences, then leaned back to consider what he'd seen. "I ran a little program I wrote last year. It takes a set of facts, like people's names and other identifying info—SSNs, drivers license numbers, whatever you've got—and compares it to other people in a given database, using the parameters you set for the search."

Hoshi squinted at him. "You wrote a program that could do all that?"

Uzi shrugged. "In my spare time." He realized what that might say about his lack of a social life, but he was more interested in the information he had just discovered. "So I gave it certain names to compare. I wanted it to tell me if it found any crossover relationships. And here we go," he said, pointing to the screen. "It found one between Douglas Knox and Skiles Rathbone, president of the NFA. They grew up in the same neighborhood, went to the same high school and college, and graduated the same year."

"Yeah, and that means what? Guilty by association? Guilty of what?"

Another blinking light grabbed Uzi's attention before he could answer. He looked at the screen, read the information, and grabbed for his cell phone.

"Who are you calling?" Hoshi asked.

"A partner in crime." He moved the handset to his mouth as the line connected. "Hey. We need to talk."

Hector DeSantos hesitated. "Like some time tomorrow, or first thing in the morning—"

"Like now. It's important. But not over the phone."

DeSantos groaned. "Fine. Come by my place. But I've got company." He gave Uzi directions and hung up.

"Get yourself a coffee, then keep on that," he said, waving a finger at his laptop. "Play with my program some more, see what you find."

"Looking for anything in particular?"

"Find me connections. Anything linking our two dead bodies, Rusch and Marine Two, the NFA, Knox, Coulter . . . and throw ARM into the mix for good measure."

Hoshi bit her lip.

"Think of this as just any old investigation. Forget the names for a minute, who these people are. We have a responsibility to look into anyone and everyone. If you thought I was involved, I'd expect you to be pulling my sheets. Understand?"

"Whether or not I understand isn't the issue. The director and attorney general—you think they'd understand if they found out what we were doing?"

Uzi looked away. "Call my cell if you find anything. Save everything into an encrypted file and email it to me. I'll look at it later."

Hoshi's pleading eyes made Uzi feel guilty for a moment. But he knew he was doing the right thing—an investigation was an investigation, regardless of the players involved. When a trail was laid down, it was his responsibility to follow that trail, no matter where it might lead.

He kept telling himself that as he made his way to the parking garage.

10:33 PM
135 hours 27 minutes remaining

Uzi nosed his Tahoe up to the brick security booth at Hector DeSantos's Beekman Place condominium in Adams Morgan. The immaculately groomed, trendy townhouse complex looked like an architect's attempt to bring small-town neighborhood sensibilities to the nation's capital. But its rural community flavor was primarily a function of aesthetics; Uzi surmised these units figured prominently on each homeowner's statement of net worth.

Uzi gained access to the development from a pudgy guard wearing a faux tin badge pinned to a polyester white shirt frayed around the collar. After the black iron gate pivoted open, Uzi drove into the private street and parked in a guest slot beside a row of young oaks.

As he got out of the car, the tone of his Nokia bleated from his pocket. He answered it as he made his way down the brick sidewalk that ran the length of the attached townhouses.

"Hey, it's your buddy—Danny Carlson."

Uzi instantly dug the name from his memory. Danny Carlson was Nuri Peled's cover. "Danny, my man, what's the word?"

"I'm not finding anything. I've been digging—under beds and rocks, in drawers and closets, you know the deal. Turning up all sorts of stuff, but nothing that'd help you."

Uzi stopped at the base of a small staircase and leaned against the wrought-iron railing. "I'm not surprised. It's looking domestic."

"What did I tell you?" Peled said.

"Yeah, well, at least we got a chance to see each other again. I'm sorry I lost touch. I kind of shut down. Just so I could go on. You know?"

"I do, my friend. And I'm sorry I let you lose touch. That was my mistake. Let's not let that happen again. Agreed?"

A smile spread Uzi's lips. "Yeah. Agreed."

"It was good seeing you again, Uzi. Anything comes up, I'll let you know."

Uzi ended the call, then continued up the steps to DeSantos's townhouse. Before he could knock, the front door opened and his partner invited him into the tiled entryway. A burst of laughter escaped from the adjacent kitchen area.

"Sorry to bust in on you so late. This could be important."

DeSantos waved a hand and did his best to deflect Uzi's concern. "What's up?"

"Oh, you're right!" A woman in tight jeans emerged from the kitchen with a glass of wine in her hand. "He *is* a stud."

She moved into the entryway and eyed Uzi from a few feet away, her body angled perpendicular to his, her head following the path of her eyes: from his feet up to his face.

"This is Maggie," DeSantos said. Uzi expected him to show a hint of embarrassment, but then remembered who he was dealing with, and the DeSantos's "open" relationship.

Uzi extended a hand. "Glad to meet you, Maggie."

She took his hand, squeezed it, and giggled. Her eyes widened slightly.

"And this is Trish and her daughter, Presley. My goddaughter," DeSantos said, squaring his shoulders with pride. The toddler was draped atop her mother's chest, arms dangling loosely over Trish's shoulders.

Uzi nodded to them; the sight of the two-year-old girl, lying sleepily against her parent, triggered thoughts of Maya. He shuddered inside. "I'm . . . I'm really sorry to barge in like this."

"Nonsense," Trish said. "We were just getting ready to go. Pres was asleep on the couch, and I've gotta get her into bed before she wakes up for good."

As Trish kissed Maggie good-bye, DeSantos gently stroked the girl's hair. The munchkin hunched her shoulders as if being tickled, then turned slowly and saw DeSantos. Her eyes squinted as a smile broadened her face. She reached out and gave her godfather a big hug and kiss.

Uzi grinned at the sight of his tough partner melting under the little girl's touch. He knew the feeling, but the memories were too painful, and he forced them aside.

"I'm going to walk them out," Maggie said.

The door closed and DeSantos motioned Uzi down the hall. "So you found something."

They entered the kitchen, a large square with stainless steel appliances, a temperature-controlled wine cabinet, and honey-stained wood floor. Maggie obviously liked peppers, as the red chilies adorned the frilly curtains, wallpaper, placemats—even the magnets on the refrigerator.

Uzi pulled out his smartphone. "Is your place clean?"

"Don't bother. I check it every day. We're fine."

Uzi hesitated, but acquiesced and put the handset away. "Yes, I found something. Maybe." He took a seat at the butcher block table and reclined in the chair, his hands shoved into the deep pockets of his overcoat. "I met with a guy tonight who thinks that Knox is in bed with the NFA."

DeSantos rolled his eyes. "Not this again."

"Hear me out. This guy says the NFA has become the strong-arm of the far right. They've given huge bucks to cover their interests in the White House. Everything was cool till Rusch's sister was murdered. Then he went on this crusade, switched policy, and came out against the gun lobby." He shrugged. "Maybe the NFA was furious and came up with a solution to their problem."

"And killing the vice president was their solution?"

"I'm thinking that if he lost the election, they wouldn't have set off the device. But as soon as they called the race, Rusch was a liability that had to be eliminated. Vance Nunn is a staunch conservative and he's never spoken out against the gun lobby. Easy choice. They decided to take their chances with Nunn."

DeSantos was quiet as he processed what Uzi had told him, no doubt running it through his bullshit filter. Finally, he asked, "And what do you think this has to do with Knox?"

"Knox is a member of the NFA. He went to school with Skiles Rathbone, NFA's top dog. Best I can tell, they grew up together."

"Well, that does it for me. Let's get an arrest warrant for the fucking FBI director because he went to the wrong school and grew up in the wrong town." DeSantos stood up. "Christ, Uzi, you sound like some whacked-out conspiracy nut. This guy you talked with. I bet he's one, too."

"Bishop's a straight shooter. I felt him out. He was careful of what he said and refused to jump to conclusions without proof. He seemed responsible, not some nut bent on making a point at all costs." He paused a second, as if suddenly convincing himself of his feelings about the man.

"Uzi. You've been in law enforcement a long time. You know the unwritten rule. Never trust an informant."

"Because they're usually criminals who'd lie or cheat to save their own asses. But this guy isn't a criminal. His sheet's clean. Well educated, upstanding citizen—"

"Who might have a hidden agenda of his own."

Uzi shook his head. "I believe him."

"What, that these guys were from the same neighborhood?"

"No, that info I got on my own."

The front door opened and Maggie walked in. "Brrr. It's cold out there." Arms banded across her chest, she shivered her way into the kitchen, looked at Uzi and DeSantos and seemed to sense the tension in the air. She backed out slowly. "Cold in here, too. I'm going to bed."

DeSantos did not look at her. He was still staring at Uzi. "I'll be up in a minute."

Uzi knew the comment was directed more at him than at Maggie.

She disappeared. DeSantos slid the kitchen door closed.

"Uzi, I've known Douglas Knox for fifteen years. I've worked under him both officially and unofficially. I gotta tell you, if you're suggesting a link between Knox and the attempted assassination of Glendon Rusch . . ." His voice tailed off. "You're wasting your time. Knox doesn't always play by the rules. No doubt about that. He's signed off on black ops that no one else knows about, or wants to know about, or will ever find out about. You know the score."

Uzi nodded.

"But everything Knox has done has been for the benefit of his country. Never for personal interests. Assassinating the veep is . . . That's sacred, know what I mean? You don't cross that line."

"I can't just ignore what I've found." Uzi rubbed at his temples. "There's not much to go on, I know. Just some sketchy stuff. But it set off my radar. I need to dig a little more, just to be sure. If he's clean, no harm. If not . . ." Uzi shrugged. "Let's see where it leads us."

"There's no 'us' in this. You go down this path, you do it alone. I can't— I won't investigate Douglas Knox."

Uzi stood. "I hear you. I'd probably do the same if the situation were reversed." He held out his fist and DeSantos reluctantly tipped it with his own. Uzi turned toward the door.

"Just be careful. Knox's guys, they look out for him."

Uzi stopped and turned back to DeSantos. “OPSIG.”

DeSantos looked away. “Close the door on the way out,” he said.

Uzi hesitated, then turned and left.

DAY FOUR

7:00 AM
127 hours remaining

Uzi walked into Leonard Rudnick's office and sat down, his gelled hair still slick from a shower. Though talking about his feelings was outside Uzi's comfort zone, doing it so early, when his defenses were still weak from cobwebs on the brain, bothered him even more. If his previous visit hadn't gone so well, he might have thought twice about showing up.

Too much to do, too much to think ab—

"So," Rudnick said. He reclined slightly, facing Uzi. "Any answers yet on the question I posed to you last time? About suicide—or, perhaps better phrased, your reason for living?"

Uzi sighed. "I haven't had a whole lot of time for introspection. This case—"

"Then tell me," Rudnick said. "How do you feel about loyalty?"

"Loyalty?" Uzi jutted his chin back. "In what context? I had a dog once, he was pretty loyal. We loved him. He protected us."

"What does loyalty mean to you? At work."

"You can't have an organization like the Bureau without loyalty. Fidelity, Bravery, Integrity. That's our motto."

"Yes," Rudnick said. "Rings a bell." He smiled. Uzi did not.

"Look, doc, if you've got a point to this, I'd really appreciate if you could get to it. This talking in circles isn't my way. I told you that when we first met."

"So you did. Very well. You had an incident recently with Agent Osborn."

Uzi's eyes rolled ceilingward. "He blatantly violated procedure, and it could've had catastrophic consequences. And it wasn't the first time. But instead of referring him for an OPR," he said, referring to the Office of Professional Responsibility, "I brought it to the attention of my ASAC."

"His actions endangered others?"

"They had a suspect holed up. Osborn was told to stand down, but when the guy bolted Osborn engaged him in a gunfight. Innocents were in the vicinity. Women and children."

"Women and children." Rudnick absorbed this, nodding slowly. "And how did reporting Agent Osborn sit with your colleagues?"

"I didn't have his back. They made it real clear they weren't too happy with me."

Rudnick tilted his head, apparently waiting for Uzi to elaborate. He did not. So they both sat there, Rudnick looking at Uzi and Uzi doing his best to go along with Rudnick's game plan without calling it a session and walking out.

Finally, Uzi spoke. "Look, doc. I really don't have time for this—"

"How did their reaction make you feel?"

Uzi lifted a shoulder. "It is what it is. They don't need to be my best buds, just my colleagues."

"And if you were on a case where they had to watch your back . . ."

"I'd expect them to do their jobs best they can. Regardless of who's in danger."

"No emotion in the equation," Rudnick said.

Uzi considered this a moment. Of course, Rudnick was right. "What's your point?"

"You are very direct, Uzi." Rudnick leaned forward onto the armrests of his chair, ran his tongue across his lips, and said, "My point is that we all have to coexist with people in life. It doesn't matter if they're coworkers, or friends, relatives, spouses . . . even the checker in the grocery store. We're a race that thrives on human interactions. We have to make an effort to communicate with the people in our life, and to realize they have feelings just like you and me."

"Doc, this guy didn't follow orders. Do you understand what that means, what the significance of that is?" Uzi realized he was out of his seat and shouting. He sat back down and cleared his throat.

Rudnick stared at his patient. "Tell me."

Uzi looked away. "When people don't follow protocol, you can't rely on them, you can't predict outcomes. Things spiral out of control. People get killed. Innocent women and children get killed." Uzi swiped at a tear that was losing its grip on his eyelid.

Rudnick sat there, locked on Uzi's face, no doubt analyzing his little tirade. After a few moments of silence, he said, "Uzi, I think there's more here to examine than just Agent Osborn's actions on a maneuver in the field last week. What do you think, hmm?"

Uzi sniffled, took an uneven breath, his gaze buried in the carpet at his feet. "There's nothing to examine. This case is taking all my energy, that's all. I'm tapped out."

"Tell me about the innocent women and children that get killed when procedures aren't followed." Rudnick's voice was calm and melodic as usual, but there was an underlying force beneath its surface.

"Nothing. It was nothing. I didn't mean anything by it."

Rudnick sat there, said nothing.

The time ticked by, a million images and thoughts blurring through Uzi's mind. *How could he understand? How could I begin to explain?* "Rules are made to be followed," Uzi finally said. "There's a reason for them. They're tested in the field, modified when they don't work."

"Is that the official Bureau position, or your own personal feelings?"

"The Bureau likes order, protocol. They have a four-thousand-page procedural manual."

"I get the impression that you take these . . . rules very seriously, perhaps more seriously than most. Was it always that way? With the Mossad?"

Uzi's head snapped up. Instinctively, he glanced around the room to see if anyone was listening. Of course, they were alone. "The Mossad has nothing to do with this. Even if it did, I couldn't discuss it with you."

Rudnick's brow crinkled. "Remember, Uzi, that whatever we discuss here is confidential. I couldn't tell anyone even if I wanted to."

Uzi's mouth curled into a frown. "I respect your ethics. I just— I just can't trust them with certain things."

Rudnick's face flushed. "I make that statement with a depth that goes beyond usual doctor-patient confidentiality—which should be enough by itself to allay your fears."

"Tell you what, doc. You tell me a secret. Something about yourself that means a great deal. Something you wouldn't want anyone else to know."

"I don't see—"

"If I know something about you, and you know something about me, we each have motivation to keep the secret. Standard fare in intelligence. Kind of like having someone by the balls." Uzi forced a smile.

For the first time, Rudnick looked uncomfortable. He seemed to shrink into himself. His shoulders slumped, his head shifted forward, and his eyes appeared to lose their brilliance. He sat like that for a long moment, then started speaking without looking at Uzi. "Very well. But I cannot explain why this is something that carries great meaning to me. I must show you. May I?"

Uzi shrugged.

Rudnick slid back his sport coat sleeve, unbuttoned his shirt button, and extended his forearm in Uzi's direction.

Uzi remained back in his chair, glancing at the doctor's thin, age-spotted skin and scraggly gray arm hairs with modest interest. But when he saw what was there, he immediately leaned forward. "Is that—"

"A tattoo? Yes. A concentration camp number? Yes again. Buchenwald."

Their gazes met. Uzi suddenly saw his doctor in a different light. "You're a survivor?"

Rudnick grunted. "I guess that describes my entire life, not just my time as a Nazi prisoner."

Uzi leaned back. "And this is a secret?"

"It's deeply personal, Uzi. Something I can't explain and wouldn't want to, if given the opportunity. I lost my mother and father, my two sisters, and my aunt and uncle. Everyone dear to me was taken, right before my eyes. Every possession lost, every value destroyed." He stared off at the wall behind his patient before continuing. "If I were as good a patient as I am a psychologist, I'd have gone for counseling decades ago. Let's just say no one knows what you now know. Aside from my son and late wife, no one has seen this tattoo." Rudnick pulled his sleeve down and fumbled with the button. "I showed you this as proof that I also would not do anything to jeopardize the security of the State of Israel." Having refastened the button, he shrugged his sport coat back into position. "Though I have to tell you," he said with a hint of amusement, "most people accept doctor-patient confidentiality as proof of my silence."

"I'm not most people."

"There's another reason why I showed that to you, Uzi." Rudnick leaned forward, resting his elbows on the chair arms. "Following orders blindly is not always desirable. If there's one thing of value we learned from the Nazis, it's that. I doubt Mr. Shepard would argue. I also happen to know for a fact that every FBI agent I've ever known or treated has bent the rules at one time or other. It's the intent that matters."

Uzi looked away. He did not like being cornered. "The situations are totally unrelated."

"Unrelated, yes," Rudnick said. "But the underlying concepts are the same."

"You don't understand, you can't understand. You can't possibly understand."

"Try me."

"No."

"Try me, Uzi."

"No, I . . . I can't."

"How long can you go on with this bottled up inside you? How long until your body, your mind can't take it anymore?"

Uzi looked away; his face felt flushed. "You've held it in for decades. Why can't I?"

"No," Rudnick said. "I treated it. I knew how to deal with it and I did so. Even though seeking outside counsel would've been better, what I did worked for me. But we're not here to talk about my treatment. We're here for yours." The doctor paused, then said, "Perhaps now is the time to return to that question I asked you, the one about your reason for living."

Uzi shook his head slowly. "I'm going to leave if you don't change the subject."

"Just talk to me, Uzi. I promise you it'll help—"

"It won't help anything!" Uzi was on his feet again, hands grasping clumps of hair. He turned and began to pace. "Why are you doing this to me?"

Rudnick stood and blocked his patient's path. He grabbed Uzi's wrists and said, "*I'm* not doing anything. You're doing it to yourself." His volume had risen to match Uzi's.

Uzi stood there, burnt-red emotion coloring his face, his knees shaking. "Don't you see? If I'd followed orders, if I'd done as instructed and followed protocol, my wife and daughter would still be alive today!" He was a volcano erupting. He had reached critical mass and there was nothing he could do to stop it. The emotions flowed out of him, hot and painful lava overriding everything in its path.

Chest heaving, on his knees, weeping. At his side was Rudnick, the doctor's hands wrapped around his patient's head, steadying it against his small chest. "That's it," he said calmly as Uzi's body shuddered. "Just let it out."

Uzi blubbered like a child, the tears cascading down his cheeks.

"We can now begin our work," Rudnick said. "And you can now begin to live the rest of your life."

8:21 AM
125 hours 39 minutes remaining

Uzi walked into his office, sunglasses blocking his bloodshot eyes. Hoshi was still bent over the laptop. Without saying a word, he moved behind his maple desk and sat down. Hoshi tapped away, apparently engrossed in her work.

"Tell me you went home last night," Uzi said.

"I crashed on the couch. Woke up around five, went downstairs and did a half hour on the treadmill, then showered and went back to work." She hit a few keys, then sat back and appeared to notice Uzi for the first time.

"You're wearing sunglasses."

"You're so damned perceptive, Hoshi. That's why I keep you around."

"You look really cool, you know? But—"

"Don't ask why I'm wearing them."

Hoshi turned back to her screen. "You probably got into a brawl last night. Don't want to admit you got clocked."

Uzi did not answer. He turned to his screen and checked his email. "Did you find anything?"

Hoshi reached for her tea cup and took a sip.

Uzi looked over the sundry items Hoshi had laid out across his desk's return—lipstick, lotion, hairbrush, cell phone, a pill case, an iPod—and that was just the top layer. "Just . . . make yourself at home."

"Thanks. But the offer's a little late. I already have."

Uzi smirked. "No shit."

Hoshi swiveled her foot out from beneath her buttocks and sat up straight. "I put together a document with everything we know about William Ellison."

"Anything significant?"

"The doc is cleverly named 'Ellison Profile.' Take a look. Pretty boring, if you asked me. But," she said, "you can get a lot of work done when no one's around. It's so quiet. No interruptions." She took another sip of tea. "I've got people on my team doing some more digging, but I stepped back and looked at this Ellison murder. Sister's ill, he's obviously the caregiver, or at least the responsible party, and the pressure starts to build along with her medical costs. But she doesn't have any health insurance. So what does he do?"

"Takes some money on the side."

"Right. So I figure, follow the money." She took another drink from her mug. "I sifted through the paperwork we got from his apartment, but there's nothing there. I'm now at the point where I have to get out the shovels."

"You need some warrants."

"Yup."

"I'll get you what you need."

She logged off the laptop, then swiped her forearm across the desk to corral all her items into a pile that she then dumped into her purse. Starting for the door, she said, "This teamwork shoulder-to-shoulder thing works pretty well. We should do it more often." She stopped in the doorway and drew his attention. "And I meant what I said. Those glasses are way cool." She winked at him, then left.

8:45 AM
125 hours 15 minutes remaining

Uzi emailed the information Hoshi had assembled on William Ellison to Karen Vail at the BAU. He didn't know if it would help them refine their bomber profile, but he had nothing to lose.

As he picked up the phone to return the list of calls that had accumulated, Madeline informed him that Hector DeSantos was on the line.

"I need your help," DeSantos said.

"I'm there," Uzi said, relieved that their disagreement over Knox did not damage their friendship. "What do you need?"

"Pick me up in twenty," DeSantos said. "We're going fishing."

As Uzi pulled out of the Pentagon parking lot, DeSantos told him they were returning to the ARM compound. Over the next ten minutes, the bare bones of an action plan began taking shape.

Uzi popped a toothpick into his mouth, tossing the wrapper into the small garbage pail he kept beside his seat. The mint flavor was strangely calming. "So you want to draw this guy out."

"I've got this feeling he's dirty. But they're good, very careful. They bury things pretty deep. I figure if we take them off their game, show up unexpected, rattle them a bit, we might come away with something."

Uzi winced. "Three words: Waco. Ruby Ridge. I'm not sure this is such a good idea. How aggressive are you planning to get?"

"I'm not going to incite a riot. I just want to turn up the heat on Flint, make him sweat. People who are under the gun tend to take action—and make mistakes. We plant the seed, then watch which way it grows."

"See who they contact."

"Exactly. Let them lay down breadcrumbs for us."

Uzi glanced sideways at his partner. "What if this leads to Knox?"

"It won't. That's the reason I want to do this. To prove you wrong."

"Except that there's no way we'll get in to bug the place."

DeSantos waved a hand. "Who needs bugs? I've got buddies at Crypto City."

"NSA?"

"They've got all sorts of cool eavesdropping satellites, shit like that."

"And of course you have a court order."

DeSantos winked at Uzi, then turned away and looked out his window.

They arrived at the American Revolution Militia compound expecting a confrontation. Uzi pulled his SUV up to their iron gate and honked with a heavy hand. The guard moved out from inside his booth, then grabbed the submachine gun slung around his right shoulder. With both hands grasping the weapon's handles, he took a position in front of them, feet spread and eyes narrow.

DeSantos got out of the truck and slammed the door. "Tell Flint his Fed buddies, Agents Spic and Kike, are back."

"I don't take orders from you, asshole."

DeSantos kept his voice restrained, yet firm. "Get Flint out here. Now. Or we'll park our truck, pitch a tent, and set up camp."

A filtered voice crackled over the man's two-way radio. With his eyes locked on DeSantos, the guard shifted the gun to his right hand and keyed the mike with his left.

DeSantos looked over at Uzi, who was focused on the other men standing about thirty yards back, at the edge of a stand of redwoods, Kalashnikov rifles of their own at the ready.

Uzi got out of his car and stood with the door open. His discomfort with this fishing expedition had spiked into the red zone. It had been years since he had been in enemy territory, behind the lines, outside the confines of law and order. Yet at the moment, he stood on the very brink of anarchy. He thought of his discussion with Rudnick over following rules and obeying orders, and wondered how far DeSantos could bend those rules before they started breaking.

He wiped his brow with a sleeve, the movement being watched with scrutiny by the unfriendlies across the way.

"Santa—"

"We're fine, Uzi. Just be cool."

A moment later, a Hummer pulled into view and stopped in a cloud of loose dirt. Nelson Flint emerged, in dress uniform, followed by an underling who brought up the rear. Flint stepped up to the gate opposite DeSantos. He lit a cigarette nonchalantly, a man whose confidence was boosted by the firepower behind him.

Flint sucked hard on his Marlboro, then blew the smoke out the left side of his mouth. "Maybe you didn't understand me last time. You boys ain't welcome here. Unless you got yourselves a warrant. Got one of them bogus documents?"

DeSantos shrugged. "Well, we kind of made a wrong turn, and . . . here we are."

"The fuck you want?" Flint asked.

DeSantos pulled a stick of Juicy Fruit from his pocket and folded it into his mouth. "I detect a little attitude there, Nellie." He tossed the spent wrapper through the gate at Flint's feet.

"That Juicy Fruit makes you look real tough, G-man."

DeSantos took a step forward.

Uzi knew that taking issue with DeSantos's deceased partner's gum was the wrong tack, even though Flint could not possibly know the significance behind it. He cleared his throat. "Santa, tell the man what we came here to tell him." The comment seemed to refocus DeSantos, but he still stood there, squinting at Flint, hatred floating on the air like teargas.

After a long moment, Uzi pressed ahead: "We know about your connections to the NFA." He watched for Flint's reaction. The man's eyes quickly locked on Uzi. Direct hit.

"You don't know shit, 'cause if you did, you wouldn't be standing on the other side of the fence like fags. You'd be on my property, crawlin' all over this place."

"That's where you're wrong, Mr. Flint. We're not storm troopers.

We don't just bust in. There are rules we have to follow. But we do have some good stuff brewing. The background files we're amassing on William Ellison and Russell Fargo are leading us right here. See, what you don't comprehend is that we've got an army of agents trolling the supersecret databases the government keeps on everyone. They're going through everything with a fine filter, and they've been sifting out little pieces to the puzzle. Pretty soon, before you know it, we'll have enough to see the whole picture. That's when we come busting in."

"All talk, is all." Flint turned and took a step toward his Hummer.

"We're connecting the dots. We know about Skiles Rathbone and his connection to—"

"Uzi," DeSantos shouted, "that's enough. He'll find out when the time is right."

Uzi looked at DeSantos, then hesitated for a moment before acquiescing. Uzi stepped closer to the gate, only a few feet away and outside the earshot of the other armed men. "We're after the bigger fish, Mr. Flint," he said in a low voice. "Help us out now and you'll get the deal. They'll get fried. If you send us away and we find out the info ourselves, or if one of the others sings first, the deal's off the table."

Flint took a couple of steps toward the gate, then sucked a long drag on his Marlboro, appearing to consider the offer. But then he pulled the cigarette from his mouth and flicked it through the bars at Uzi, who swatted it away. "Fuck you, Fibber. Get away from my land." He turned and got into his Hummer, the truck leaving a cloud of dust in its wake.

10:59 AM
123 hours 1 minute remaining

Uzi dropped DeSantos at the gate of the Pentagon, preferring to keep off its visitor logs until he could be sure how deep the potential Douglas Knox/National Firearms Alliance bond extended. With Knox's roots well entrenched in super-secret black ops groups, Uzi figured the director had to be aligned to some extent with NSA-types—officially or unofficially.

Leaving DeSantos to work that end of the investigation—it was, after all, DeSantos's area of expertise—he broke away to meet with Karen Vail, who had left a voicemail five minutes earlier.

The profiling unit's receptionist buzzed the security doors and Uzi proceeded down the maze of hallways to Vail's office. He stepped in and saw Vail sitting at her desk, her elbow on the armrest and her chin nestled in her hand.

Uzi took a seat in the chair beside her wall of bookshelves and crossed a leg over his knee. "What's wrong?"

"I think the branch is about to break."

Before Uzi could ask for clarification, a man walked in with a scowl on his face. His attention was focused on Uzi.

"Agent Uziel. I'm Thomas Gifford. ASAC of the behavioral analysis units."

Uzi sensed this visit was not going to be cordial, so he did not offer his hand to shake. "We've met," Uzi said, leaving the comment ambiguous to retain an advantage. If he knew or remembered something Gifford didn't, it would bother the man and give Uzi a sense of control.

"Agent Vail has been doing some work for you," Gifford said.

"We've talked about a case, yeah. She was helping me understand a few things from a behavioral perspective. But I wouldn't say it was for me. It's for the Bureau. For the investigation into the veep's assassination attempt."

"There's a protocol around here, Agent Uziel. The unit chief and I assign the cases. Agents don't get to call their friends and have them do work for them. Understand?"

The word "protocol" sent a dart into Uzi's heart. He of all people understood the importance of following procedures. He did not know how to respond.

"Frank," Gifford called down the hall, into the adjacent office. "A minute." He turned back to Uzi. "Frank Del Monaco is the agent assigned to this case."

"With all due respect, sir, I did not mean to cause problems. Agent Vail was at the crash site. I have a relationship with her. I trust her abilities, and trust is an important issue with me."

A heavyset man appeared in the doorway behind Gifford. Gifford nodded at Uzi's comment but was clearly not swayed by his explanation. "It's not her job to get touchy-feely with the law enforcement officers she serves. Our entire unit is trustworthy, with all the abilities Agent Vail has." Gifford took a step into the cramped office and indicated Frank Del Monaco with a dip of his chin. "This is Frank Del Monaco. Frank, this is Agent Uziel. He's from WFO, head of JTTF, running the task force investigating the chopper incident."

Del Monaco nodded at Uzi, whose arms were folded across his chest.

Gifford continued, "Because of all the work Agent Vail's done behind my back, and because of the amount of time invested in this case, I'm going to allow her to remain on. She'll work with Agent Del Monaco."

"Aren't they partners anyway?" Uzi asked.

"That didn't sound like an apology," Gifford said sternly.

Uzi held up a hand. "I won't muddy the protocol again, sir. I apologize and accept full responsibility for dragging her into this. In all fairness, she told me right up front I should be speaking with Agent Del Monaco."

"Did that make you feel better, getting it off your chest?" Gifford glanced at Vail, who still had her chin buried in her hand, eyes examining the carpet. "I've dealt with Agent Vail how I've seen fit—in essence, you've boiled some water and stuck her hand in it. Maybe next time you'll consider the consequences."

Gifford was now twisting the dagger he'd thrown earlier. Uzi struggled to shrug off what Gifford was saying.

"It won't happen again."

"No, Agent Uziel, it won't. I've spoken with ASAC Shepard and made sure of it. You guys come to us for help, we'll give you everything we've got. Just don't run over my toes again or this'll be the last time you see the inside of my unit." He pushed past Del Monaco and left the room.

Del Monaco frowned at Uzi, then followed Gifford's exit.

Uzi exhaled, then rubbed his forehead. "Sorry."

"My fault. When I told you 'no,' I should've meant it."

"How bad?"

Vail shrugged. “Nothing I won’t get over. Gifford needs me. We’ve had our rows in the past, much worse than this one, and we’ve gotten past it. I’m dealing with it. Besides, I’m dating his son. That kind of limits the blows.” Vail cringed. “So to speak.”

“I think I’ll leave that one alone.” Uzi sat forward in the chair. “Anything you can tell me on the stuff I sent over?”

Vail rested her elbows on her desk. “Lots. I pulled in a guy from ATF. Turk Roland. He’s with ABIS, their Arson and Bombing Investigative Services subunit.”

“He as good as you?”

“If we’re talking bombs, he and Art Rooney are the best. Rooney’s out on medical. We call Roland the Turkmeister.”

“The Turkmeister?”

“He just co-authored a new study for the NCAVC,” she said, referring to the National Center for the Analysis of Violent Crime. “I read through it, learned a lot.”

“So maybe getting you into trouble was a good thing.”

“Let’s not go there.” She pulled a file from a stack beside her computer and splayed it open. “Here’s the deal. As much research as there is on serial killers, there’s very little on bombers. That’s why this new study was so important. Basically, bombers are classified by motive. There’re several categories, from experimentation to vandalism, excitement, revenge, diversion, political-ideological, and criminal enterprise. Let’s focus on the last two, since my impression is that whoever’s done this is operating in a group and has gone through significant effort to blow up the veep’s choppers. The planning alone rules out a lot of our potential suspect pool.”

“Cool. Then what does that leave us with?”

“Assuming we’re not dealing with some Middle Eastern terrorist sect, bombers in general tend to be white males, averaging five-ten, a hundred eighty-five pounds. Your UNSUB will likely have one or more body tattoos. He might have some form of disfigurement because of accidents while building or testing his bombs. So look for facial scarring or missing fingers.”

“So we’re looking for an average white guy with tattoos and missing fingers. Shouldn’t be too hard to find. Reminds me of this play I once saw about a one-eyed woman from Guadalajara with a wooden leg."

Vail tilted her head. "Are you mocking me?"

Uzi leaned forward in his seat and rested his forearms on his knees. "Yes. I'm making fun of you, but this is good stuff. Go on."

"I take my work very seriously."

"Me too. Go on."

Vail eyed him for a moment, then continued. "He'll live in a middle-class neighborhood. He'll be heterosexual. You've got about a fifty-fifty chance that he's married. If he is, he'll have one to three kids."

Uzi's eyebrows rose. "You're shitting me."

"Here's the kicker. Unlike serial killers, these guys tend to come from fairly stable home environments. Your UNSUB's parents earned a decent living, and both parents were probably present through his childhood. In fact, he likely had a warm relationship with both of them, though it was a bit better with the mother—"

Uzi began lifting papers and file folders, as if searching for something.

Vail stopped talking and watched Uzi rifle through her desk. "Uh, what the hell do you think you're doing?"

"I'm looking for your crystal ball."

She turned away. "Look, Uzi, you've been through this process before. You know what a profile consists of."

"He'll have one to three kids? He had a warm relationship with his mother, but less so than his father? Come on. I mean, how accurate do you think this is?"

"I can only tell you what the research shows. Like I said, we know much more about serial killers. And this isn't my area of expertise. But after talking with Turk, I have confidence that this info is in the ballpark. Besides, this is only meant as a way to narrow the field a bit, not hand you the name and address of your offender."

Uzi sighed. "Okay. What else?"

"Your UNSUB will have a good relationship with his kids, and probably with his wife, too, but that's not as certain. He'll be bright, and educated through high school—maybe even some college. But socially he'll be an underachieving loner."

"What about religion?"

"Most likely Protestant. Possibly Baptist. Not fervent, but it does matter to him."

"I was just kidding."

"Actually, I thought it was an excellent question."

"Oh yeah? Then I was serious." He winked, then asked, "What about military service?"

"Are you joking now or serious?"

He dipped his chin and eyed her from an angle. Squinting, he said, "Serious."

"Then it's another good question. There doesn't seem to be a hugely significant association with military service, though a fair percentage, maybe thirty percent of known bombers, did serve. Army and Marines. But I think a better way of looking at it is that these people do tend toward a fascination with explosive devices, ordnance, ammunition, and so on. Whether your UNSUB officially recognized these interests in an organized military fashion might not be the case. But I would look first at the military and use it as a comparative database."

"Organized military fashion. So he might've gotten his kicks elsewhere, like with a militia?"

"Yes."

"And the 'underachieving loner'—socially—that would also fit with a militia."

"Could," she corrected. "Could fit. Remember, these are guidelines, not absolutes." She paused, glanced at her notes, then rocked her head back. "All that said, here's something that'll sound the radar. Bombing is the assassination method of choice for militia groups."

Uzi's eyebrows rose. "Is that right?"

"If you look back thirty years," she said, consulting her notes, "they've typically used bombs to get even with their enemies. Pipe bombs, fertilizer bombs, even artillery. But C-4 would be relatively new for them. At this point, I should tell you that profiling them might be a tad bit harder because you're dealing with group behaviors."

"Does this throw your profile out the window?"

"Not necessarily. And we could still be talking about an individual here."

"Then let's go on. Will he be employed?"

"Yes. Chances are good he's in a decent financial position. First of all, he used C-4. He had to have gotten it from somewhere. Unless he stole it—which ATF would know about—it'd require money and contacts—which again could suggest an organized group. Groups provide the ability to pool resources and influence. And the comfort to draw up and execute such an aggressive plan."

While Uzi considered what she had said, Vail glanced again at her notes.

"Here's something that may be of immediate help. It's likely your guy did time as a juvenile. Probably even multiple felonies, which might help narrow things. As an adult, he's probably had three felony arrests."

"So he's a guy who'd been in our system."

"Yeah, but there's a caveat here. If he is with a group, the bomb maker is the one who's been in the system. The top dogs might not show up in our database. But—"

"We'll get the guy with the dirty fingernails to roll on his bosses."

"Look for bombing/explosive and burglary/robbery offenses. If he did do time, that'll likely be the deal."

"Are these guys like serial killers— Will any power rape type of thing show on their sheets?"

She shook her head. "Even though there's often a sexual component to some bombers' motives, rape or sexual assault isn't their vice."

"Okay," Uzi said. "Let's step back a second. I think we can assume this bomber is part of a group, and this group has political/ideological motives, or is interested in revenge. Agreed?"

Vail shifted in her seat. "The branch is creaking."

"William Ellison was a bright guy. Could he have been our bomber?"

"He certainly had access, and he had intimate knowledge of the mechanical aspects of the helicopter, more than enough to take the thing down. But is he the guy who built the bomb? Maybe. Not necessarily. From the info you faxed me, Ellison fits certain aspects of the profile. But he also falls outside it in a lot of ways. Big thing is that he didn't have a criminal history. He was single, didn't appear to be in a significant relationship, and his childhood was not exactly what you'd call stable or warm and fuzzy. There was a note in there about his father, who skipped when little William was two."

"I saw it."

"And given his high-end job at the Marine base, I assume he wasn't missing any fingers."

"No disfiguring marks, either," Uzi said. "And he didn't have any overt government inclinations or he would've failed the Yankee White background check. It's pretty intense." He thought a moment, then said, "Can we assume that Ellison was the one who placed it?"

"Best not to deal in assumptions. Logic is better. So let's look at it logically based on your scenario. Bottom line, the day after the chopper is taken down, Ellison's erased. Professional job from what I saw in the file. Nothing personal in the crime scene. Just a surgical hit. Very clean."

"Which suggests and supports the group theory."

"Forgetting their reliance on bombs to eliminate their enemies, I'd agree. Go with what you've got and deal with the facts: Ellison worked on the choppers, the choppers exploded, then Ellison is eliminated. Logic suggests it was done to cover their tracks. Who's pulling the strings?"

"ARM?"

Vail sighed, leaned back in her chair. "Prime suspect. But you need proof. A smoking gun."

"More like discarded C-4."

Vail closed her file. "I think you've got enough to run with."

"Maybe." Uzi reached over and closed the door and lowered his voice. He was about to take a risk, but he trusted Vail and believed that whatever he told her would remain between them. "I've got another theory. Douglas Knox, the NFA and ARM."

Vail's eyebrows rose. Her eyes darted from side to side as she processed what Uzi was suggesting. "Conspiracy?"

Uzi shrugged.

"For what reason? I mean, that's big stuff, Uzi."

"Glendon Rusch's pro-gun-control policy." He briefly recapped his meeting with Bishop, then sat back and waited for her response.

She twisted her lips in thought. "Well, as conspiracy theories go, it's intriguing. Up there with Oliver Stone's JFK theory. But we're not talking Hollywood here. You have to actually prove it."

"I'm not stupid. I know it'll be next to impossible. These people know how to cover their asses. And Knox has deep contacts just about everywhere you look."

"Have you floated something by the AG?"

Uzi had not thought of going straight to Winston Coulter. He was, after all, head of the Department of Justice, and the DOJ was the FBI's parent, so to speak. If Coulter authorized an investigation, Knox's displeasure—and resulting heat—would fall on Coulter, not on Uzi. And with Uzi's new reputation for blowing the whistle, hiding behind the AG's shield was fine with him.

"Think I should?"

"I don't know. Probably best to wait till you've got something more . . . explosive." She squinted. "Sorry—couldn't resist."

"What do you think of my theory?"

"Honestly?"

Uzi made a face. "No, lie to me."

"Fine," Vail said. "It scores pretty high on my bullshit radar." She leaned forward. "I'm not saying it's not what's going on here, but a few accusations and numbers thrown around by a guy who may be a paranoid conspiracy nut himself . . . I'd need more than that to even consider it. I dealt with Knox once, and he was firm but fair, and at the end of the day, supportive. I don't know him near well enough to draw up anything even resembling a behavioral profile, but going just on gut instinct, I can't see him being part of a conspiracy to assassinate the president-elect."

Uzi twisted his lips in disappointment, but knew she was right. His proof was as thin as his theory was compelling. But that was just it: it was a theory. He needed evidence—and until he got some, he was nowhere.

2:32 PM
119 hours 28 minutes remaining

Uzi's cell was ringing. He set his iPad onto the dashboard, having finished dictating his thoughts on the salient parts of Vail's profile. While trying to keep his left hand on the wheel and one eye on the interstate, he fished through his overcoat, which was folded beside him. By the time he rooted out the phone, the caller had left a voicemail: it was Madeline telling him to report immediately to the attorney general's office.

He returned Madeline's call, hoping she could provide some background on the meeting. She could not. Uzi left a message for Shepard, then exited the interstate and arrived at the Department of Justice several minutes later. He checked in with Winston Coulter's personal assistant, then turned to take a seat. But before he was able to sit, the woman told him the attorney general was ready to see him.

Uzi hesitated a moment, trying to figure out the reason for the meeting. Not only was it called at the last minute, but Winston Coulter was notorious for making people wait, a trait Uzi figured was part of the power game a lot of Washington bureaucrats played. Yet Uzi had been ushered in the moment he arrived.

Given the peculiarity of the situation, Uzi's interest was piqued, to say the least. But maybe this visit, whatever its purpose and no matter how unprecedented, would give him the opportunity to discuss the restrictive order Knox had placed on them in accessing the NICS database.

Uzi walked into the spacious office, where a portly Winston Coulter sat behind his desk chattering on the phone. He did not acknowledge Uzi's presence, keeping his gaze fixed on the ceiling. Uzi immediately realized that standing in someone's office while he ignored you was infinitely more intimidating than waiting by yourself in a comfortable anteroom.

Uzi stood there a moment, then began to peruse the wall hangings. Certificates, law degrees and decrees, the usual photo ops with politicians. The office, though personalized, contained all the trappings and decorations Uzi had seen a hundred times.

"No, he's here now," Coulter said. "I'll take care of it. Thanks for the heads up, Victor." Coulter slammed down the phone and met Uzi's gaze. "Agent, seems we've got a bit of a problem."

Uzi stepped closer to the large maple desk, but did not sit. "With what, sir?"

"I just got off the phone with Victor Ripclaw. You know who Victor Ripclaw is, Agent?"

"Name rings a bell, but I can't—"

"Victor Ripclaw is the managing partner with Hayes Patino Sinclair Ripclaw. You've heard of that law firm, haven't you?"

"One of the largest on the east coast." *And one with enough clout to be able to pick up the phone and get through to the attorney general of the United States.*

"Exactly right, Agent. You know why Mr. Ripclaw called me?"

"Sir, with all due respect, if we could get to the point—"

"His client is Nelson Flint. Is that blunt enough for you?"

Uzi closed his mouth. That was a revelation of significance. "Nelson Flint's with Hayes Patino Sinclair Ripclaw? Doesn't that strike you as odd, sir?"

"Whether it strikes me as odd or not, Agent Uziel, is irrelevant. Mr. Ripclaw is quite upset over your two visits to Mr. Flint's place of business."

"It's a right-wing militia compound, sir. I wouldn't exactly call it 'a place of business.'"

"You didn't call it a place of business. I did. And the point, Agent Uziel, is that you should not have been there unless you had a warrant."

"With all due respect, sir, the first time we were there they gave us access voluntarily. The second time we never set foot on their property. Regardless of what their Madison Avenue lawyer claimed, we didn't need a warrant. We just went there to ask questions during the normal course of our investigation."

"With your guns drawn?"

"We did not draw our weapons, sir."

"That's not what I was told."

"I don't know who—"

"Listen here, Agent Uziel, I do not want another Ruby Ridge or Waco on our hands. Now that's pretty clear, isn't it? You get my point, don't you?"

"Yes, sir. We were aware of the risks—"

"And yet you went anyway."

Uzi sighed. "I'm sorry if we upset them, sir." Actually, he wasn't—but he sensed a bit of contrition was called for.

"Did you find anything?"

"No."

Coulter tossed his pen onto the desk. "Agent, Mr. Ripclaw did us all a favor by calling my office instead of filing harassment charges and sending a copy of his complaint to the *Post*. The Bureau's had enough black eyes the past several years. We don't need any more. What you do reflects on me, and I don't want to have to answer for it, do you understand?"

Uzi looked away. "Very clearly, sir."

"Good. Now—" The buzz of Coulter's phone gave Uzi a second to think. Coulter lifted it, listened for a moment, then said, "Send them in."

Marshall Shepard and Douglas Knox walked through the door. Uzi felt the heat rising beneath his collar, and he immediately wished he'd removed his leather overcoat before entering Coulter's office.

Coulter exchanged a glance with Knox and Shepard. "Agent Uziel and I have been having a little chat. Weren't we, Agent?" Coulter paused, looked hard at Uzi.

"Yes sir, a little chat."

"I got a call from Hayes Patino Sinclair Ripclaw," Coulter continued. "Seems Agent Uziel and his partner have been harassing Nelson Flint and his colleagues. Went to Mr. Flint's place with their firearms drawn."

Shepard and Knox simultaneously looked at Uzi. They were not wearing their happy faces.

"The managing partner gave us a heads-up before filing charges."

"Uzi," Shepard said, "you've got some explaining to do."

When one of the most influential attorneys in the country lit a fuse, the resulting fallout often consumed those in close proximity. Like a neutron bomb, it left the office standing but destroyed the people inside it. Uzi hoped Shepard could escape the damage. Still, he should've seen it coming: taking the heat for the actions of people under your command came with the territory. Shepard was guilty by rank and proximity.

Coulter held up a hand to silence Uzi. "Save it. I don't want to hear it."

"I don't mean to be disrespectful," Uzi said, "but how about our side of the story? Since when does the FBI kowtow to an attorney whose client slithers into his office crying harassment?"

Coulter stood from his seat. "Since I became attorney general. And since I decided to clean up our image. And since it's *my* decision to make."

"Sir, the second time we were there, we never stepped foot on their land. We stayed outside the fence and—"

"And nothing," Coulter said. "Victor Ripclaw isn't a hack. He's a powerful and influential lawyer, and I don't want him on my back. We've got enough important work to do in this office without fending off lawsuits from attorneys who know how to bury my people in paperwork. But most of all, Agent Uziel, he gives scum like Nelson Flint credibility. If he's Flint's mouthpiece, we've got problems. He knows how to play the strings of public opinion. And I don't want to see anything in the papers about trampling citizens' constitutional rights." He turned to Shepard. "Did you know anything about this?"

Shepard's gaze was still locked on Uzi. "No, sir."

"Why the hell not?"

Uzi turned away. He could feel the perspiration beading down from his sideburns.

Shepard took the smart way out, treating Coulter's question as if it were rhetorical. Like a suspect in handcuffs, he remained silent to prevent further damage.

After an uncomfortable moment of silence, Coulter continued: "Do us all a big favor, Douglas. Rein in your people. Make sure they stay away from Nelson Flint unless I authorize it."

Uzi knew this was an extraordinary measure; the attorney general did not usually micromanage FBI affairs. In fact, any directive from Coulter would normally flow directly to Knox, who would then deal with Shepard and/or Uzi.

"Agent Uziel, we're through here."

So much for getting an opportunity to ask the attorney general about overriding Knox's blocking of the NICS database. Any inquiry regarding Knox's political interference in the investigation would have to come from someone else.

As Uzi turned to leave, he caught the frowns of Shepard and Knox.

He felt he should apologize, but what could he say—especially in front of Coulter? Instead, he put his head down and moved between the two men, parting the sea of anger and walking clear out of the room without looking back.

6:07 PM
115 hours 53 minutes remaining

"I heard all about your meeting," DeSantos said as he and Uzi strolled along Pennsylvania Avenue.

Ninety minutes after leaving the Department of Justice, Uzi received a call from DeSantos telling him they needed to meet. Now, walking along the district's main drag, the air was crisp and their breath sent vapor trails snaking behind them.

"Sorry you had to face it alone."

Uzi waved a hand. "It's over. I'll get past it. Hopefully my boss will."

"I wish it were that easy."

A taxi roared by them, the wind ruffling the bottom of Uzi's overcoat. He looked at DeSantos, his partner's last comment taking a moment to register. "What do you mean?"

"Some shit going on behind the scenes. This is DC, boychick. You know how it goes. What you see ain't what you get."

The meat of rush hour had passed, the mass of people pouring out of government buildings slowing to a trickle. Uzi dodged a couple of women in business suits scurrying to hail a cab. "So what's the rest of the iceberg look like?"

"Knox wants you to keep investigating ARM."

Uzi stopped and watched as DeSantos took another few steps before realizing his partner was not keeping up with him.

He came back to Uzi and shrugged. "C'mon," DeSantos said. "We need to keep moving." He glanced around, then nudged Uzi with a shoulder. They turned and began walking.

Uzi waited a moment for DeSantos to elaborate. He knew Knox was the preeminent power broker, operating behind closed doors in ways no one else would dare dream, but he never expected to be part of his inner circle. Nor did he want to be. He needed rules and structure.

"Knox asked me to deliver a message," DeSantos finally said. "But he needs to know you're on board."

"On board with what?"

"He wants you to continue looking into ARM, but Coulter and Shepard can't know."

Uzi knew what this meant: he was, indeed, being invited in. Perhaps not to the inner circle, but he was being asked to dip his feet in the water. Get them wet, feel the temperature. Then make a decision as to whether to go in all the way. Or not. "Santa, the attorney general is the FBI's 'boss.' I may not like the guy, but he specifically told me to back off Flint. If I keep poking around . . ."

"Knox will insulate you."

"Knox answers to Coulter. How's he going to insulate me?"

"Technically, he answers to Coulter, but he's . . . Don't worry about it."

Uzi looked up at the sky, as if it held answers. "I don't get it. First your buddy Knox plays political games by blocking us from getting into the NICS database—something that could help our investigation. Now he wants us to ignore the AG's direct order and go after ARM."

"Don't try to make sense of Douglas Knox's actions. I can tell you that if he's blocking you from something, there's gotta be a reason. Other than politics, would be my guess."

"Why not use OPSIG?"

"Knox has his reasons."

"That's not much of an answer."

DeSantos sighed. "Just tell me what you need."

Uzi shook his head. "We need access to the NICS. I was hoping to convince Coulter to override Knox's order, but I never got the chance."

"What do you need gun records for?"

Uzi explained the link between Wheeler and Ellison. "And Vasquez probably knew about it, but kept his mouth shut. Any idea why? Does Knox have some secret relationship with Vasquez or someone else in the Marines? Maybe one Marine killing another would be bad PR, so this way, he prevents us from getting at the truth."

DeSantos slowly perused the surrounding street, chewing on what Uzi had just told him.

"This guy could be a key to our case, Santa, but without gun records we don't have shit. We need them to get a warrant. I wanna put this guy in the box and sweat him out."

"He's a Marine. Be a waste of time. But I'll talk with Vasquez and see what he knows." DeSantos was silent as they crossed 6th Street NW. Finally, he said, "Doesn't matter what's going on behind the scenes. Knox still wants us looking into ARM. Just you and me. We'll keep Shepard out of the loop."

Uzi hesitated, then shook his head. "Shepard's my friend. I don't like keeping stuff from him. He's stuck his neck out for me a lot of times, especially when I needed a job—"

"Exactly. You're helping him here, not hurting him. Deniability. The less he knows, the better. He can't get into any serious shit if he doesn't know about it."

Uzi wanted to say that if this insulated Shepard from "serious shit," it implied that Uzi would be stepping *into* the smelly stuff himself. Ultimately, Knox would make a choice: him or Shepard. And the lower ranks always took the heat first. But he chose a different tack. "That's not what happened today. Coulter made a point of implying that even if Shepard hadn't known what we were doing with ARM, he should have."

DeSantos waved a hand. "Just a show of power. Nothing will come of it. Trust me."

"Santa, I've got enough to handle running this investigation without pushing the envelope any more than I already have. It's not like Shepard asking me not to do something. He'd get pissed, let off some steam, and everything would be okay. But Coulter is the boss of all the bosses. Despite what you think, if Coulter wants my ass, there's nothing Douglas Knox is going to be able to do to save it."

DeSantos's pace had quickened. "You can make a lot of mistakes in life, Uzi. But the biggest one any of us can make is underestimating Douglas Knox."

Uzi felt DeSantos's gaze bearing down on him. He didn't want Shepard hurt again, and if this went sour in any way, the fall guys would be himself and Shepard, he was sure of it. Still, if the FBI director wanted this done and ordered him into secrecy, who was he to object—or disobey?

"There's something else you should think about. This order Knox imposed, preventing you from accessing the NICS. I think you're poking around the wrong neighborhood."

"Don't try to defend Knox."

"Hear me out," DeSantos said, holding up a hand. "A good chunk of the guns bought by militia members come from gun shows. You know why?" DeSantos didn't wait for Uzi's response. "Because there's a loophole in the Brady Law. The law says you can't sell a gun to someone without a background check, without paperwork being filled out. But see, the interesting thing is that the law doesn't apply to hobbyists." Uzi started to say something, but DeSantos continued. "And you know who sells guns at gun shows?"

"Hobbyists," Uzi said.

"No, professional gun dealers. They only say they're hobbyists so they can avoid the law."

"Okay, so the law sucks—"

"You know who created that loophole? A simple clause quietly added to the bill at the eleventh hour." DeSantos smiled. "Winston Coulter. Senator Winston Coulter."

Uzi sucked on his bottom lip. "That's interesting."

"Thought you'd think so."

They stopped walking at the intersection of Pennsylvania and 10th Street.

"So Knox isn't the bad guy. He always has reasons for what he does. You hear what I'm saying? Do what he says. There's a bigger picture here, I'm sure of it. You need to trust him."

Uzi sighed. He looked out at the red taillights of the cars in front of him. "It just doesn't feel right. And I don't want to be responsible for ending a friend's career."

The light changed and the pedestrians started to cross the street. DeSantos leaned close to Uzi and said, "Knox knows about your time with the Mossad."

Uzi's brow crumpled. He stopped in the middle of the street. "You told him?"

DeSantos held up his hands. "I didn't tell him anything. He told me."

"But how—"

"The real question is, 'How'd you get into the Bureau in the first place?'"

Uzi turned and they continued walking across the street. He understood DeSantos's point: the FBI would not have approved Uzi's application if they knew he had worked for a foreign intelligence service. Avoiding DeSantos's gaze, he said, "Don't ask, don't tell."

DeSantos stopped walking and grabbed Uzi's arm. "Bullshit. They do ask."

Uzi shrugged off his hand. "Okay, they asked. I didn't tell. I needed the job. Right or wrong, I didn't disclose it, and no foreign intelligence service discloses the identities of its operatives." Uzi looked away. He felt awful about having deceived the Bureau—and even worse about having to admit it now to his friend.

"Knox knew you lied on your app. He said I should tell you it's a federal offense. He also wanted you to know your secret is safe with him. But he wants you to do this in return."

Uzi looked out at the oncoming headlights and thought he knew how a deer felt. "What choice do I have?"

DeSantos took him by the crook of his elbow and led him toward the sidewalk. "I guess if you wanted to throw away your career and do prison time, you could say no."

Uzi nodded. He figured as much. Before he could launch into a complaint about being blackmailed, his cell phone rang. He glanced at the screen and saw that the call was from a blocked number. "Uzi."

There was a second of silence before the caller spoke. "This is the person who met with you last night. Your colleague's friend."

Uzi recognized the voice as Tad Bishop's. "What can I do for you?"

DeSantos moved closer, clearly tuned into the fact that the call was related to their case. He leaned close to Uzi, who tilted the Nokia so both could hear.

"I need to meet with you. Now. Wolf Trap Park, do you know where it is?"

"It'll take me a bit to get there."

DeSantos motioned with an index finger to indicate that he was going to come along.

"There'll be two of us coming."

"Agent Koh?"

"No, but it's someone you can trust." Uzi knew this was not going to be an easy sell, but he had to give it his best shot. Perhaps meeting Bishop would help convince DeSantos there was merit to his claims about Knox.

"I'm not comfortable with that," Bishop said.

"I understand. But he can help us. He's my partner, and I trust him."

Bishop was silent for a moment, then said, "Fine. Thirty minutes?"

"Maybe forty. We'll do our best." Bishop gave Uzi the exact location of where they were to meet. Uzi ended the call and turned back in the direction from where they came. "Looks like I'm gonna be late to my dinner with Leila." He pulled out his phone to text her about the delay.

"This that Bishop guy? The paranoid schizophrenic?"

Uzi frowned at DeSantos. "Let's go see what the problem is. He seemed uptight."

"He's paranoid. Being uptight goes with the territory."

The drive to Fairfax, Virginia, took them longer than Uzi thought it would. But they drove around, surveilling the area like all Special Operational Forces did. Looking for routes to E & E—evade and escape—should it be necessary. Assessing risk, evaluating the terrain.

Satisfied as to the meeting place, they parked and waited. A car pulled up behind them, half a block away. Its headlights flashed twice; Uzi looked at DeSantos, who was stifling a laugh.

"Go on, flash your brake lights," DeSantos said.

"What's so funny?"

"This guy thinks he's one of us."

Uzi popped open the door and got out, then headed into the park with DeSantos a few paces behind him. Bishop waited while the two of them walked down the path, then stopped and faced one another as if engaged in conversation.

"Now what?" DeSantos asked.

"He likes to make sure the area's secure before he'll come over here."

"You're shitting me."

"I shit you not."

DeSantos turned and looked at Bishop's car.

"Don't stare," Uzi said. "It'll just make him nervous."

"And you said this guy wasn't paranoid?"

"I'm saying I understand his situation. He digs into volatile issues. There's a lot of money at stake, a lot of power. He pisses off a lot of people in Washington."

DeSantos shrugged. "So do I."

Bishop's car door opened and he emerged from the darkness wearing a wool hat with ear muffs pulled down over his head and a black trench coat with a turned-up collar.

As he crunched a path across the grass toward Uzi and DeSantos, DeSantos turned away. "Oh, man. This guy's a piece of work."

"Keep an open mind, will you? Just listen to what he has to say."

"Fine. But only if I can keep myself from laughing—"

"Gentlemen," Bishop said.

Uzi gestured at his partner. "This is Hector DeSantos, Department of Defense."

"Department of—"

"Relax, Mr. Bishop. He's on my task force. And I've known him a long time. What's on your mind?"

Bishop glanced around and spoke to the air around him. "I'm being followed, I think my phone's being tapped, and I've had a number of hang-ups today."

"How do you know you're being followed?" DeSantos asked.

"Mr. DeSantos, would you know if you're being followed?"

"I've had extensive training—"

"I used to be a private investigator," Bishop said. "I know what I know, sir. And I'm being followed."

"Right now?"

"I know how to deal with it. I'm clean at the moment, but I don't know how long it'll last. They may have some sort of tracking device on my car somewhere."

DeSantos threw Uzi a sideways glance. Uzi knew DeSantos was stifling a laugh.

"And the phone tap?" Uzi asked.

"I took apart the handset, but didn't find anything. They must be tapping in at the switch box. There's clicking on the line, and it . . . it just sounds different, is all. I can tell."

DeSantos nodded slowly, his gaze taking in Bishop from head to toe. Sizing him up.

"Mr. Bishop," Uzi said, "I can arrange for someone to look into it. Hoshi can do it. Do you want me to call her?"

Bishop nodded.

As Uzi pulled out his phone, Bishop turned his head to check over his shoulder. He swayed a bit, but DeSantos reached out to steady him.

"I'm okay," Bishop said. He pulled his arm from DeSantos's grip. "I haven't been able to sleep. I'm a little light-headed is all."

Uzi eyed Bishop with concern, then dialed Hoshi. "Is that all you had to tell me?" he asked as he pressed Send.

"No." Bishop's eyes danced around the park. "It's about our AG."

His smartphone beeped in rapid succession. Uzi ended the call, looked at the flashing red light, then brought an index finger up to his mouth. He pressed a button to silence the beeping, then held the device near Bishop's body. "Number's busy. I think we should do this tomorrow, anyway. Schedule a time when we can meet with Hoshi in person." The flashing light became steady. Uzi nodded, then slipped the device into his pocket. "That okay with you, Mr. Bishop?" Uzi nodded animatedly, then again pressed an index finger to his lips.

Bishop's eyes were wide. He clearly understood what was going on. "Yeah, yeah, that's fine. Hopefully I can get some sleep tonight, then my head will be a little clearer."

"Tomorrow night," Uzi said as he helped remove Bishop's jacket, "Nine o'clock. Same place. I'll bring Hoshi with me." He held the jacket by the collar and said, "Take care." He carefully set the jacket on the ground and motioned for Bishop to follow him down the path.

When the three of them had walked thirty feet, Uzi removed his phone again and ran it over Bishop's body. The red lights remained off.

Bishop whispered, "Listening devices?"

"Probably sewn into your jacket," Uzi said.

"We don't know that," DeSantos said. He turned to Bishop. "Do you have any electronic devices in your pocket? An iPod, smartphone, GPS—"

"Santa, I'm sure. I programmed this myself. The only thing that would make it react like that is a device that puts out a very specific low-voltage wireless signature."

DeSantos sighed deeply. "I still don't buy it. There could be other explanations. But we'll take the jacket with us, Mr. Bishop, have the lab analyze it, okay?"

"Yeah, yeah, sure. I appreciate it."

"I bet," DeSantos muttered.

Uzi gestured at Bishop with his chin. "You were saying. Winston Coulter."

"Shh," Bishop spat. "No names.

DeSantos elbowed Uzi. "What's the matter with you? Directional microphones." He faced Bishop. "Right?"

Bishop nodded. "Can't be too careful with these people."

DeSantos shook his head. "Okay, enough. I've had just about all the bullshit I can han—"

Uzi grabbed DeSantos's right forearm. "Santa. Take it easy." His voice was calm, but firm. "Chill out, let's hear what he has to say. I think he's on the level, and I think his . . . paranoia is legit. Go with me on this."

DeSantos rolled his eyes, then shoved his hands deep into the pockets of his overcoat. "Go ahead. I'm listening. The AG. . . ."

Bishop twisted his body and glanced back toward his car. "He's in this thing as deep as the . . . the man we talked about last night."

"The Director," DeSantos said.

Bishop glared at him.

DeSantos shrugged both shoulders, keeping his hands buried in his pockets. "What. No names."

Bishop pulled his eyes from DeSantos and settled again on Uzi. "The man's also a member of the organization."

"The organization."

"Yeah," DeSantos said. "The organization of paranoid sociopaths." He grunted. "I tried, Uzi, but I can't listen to any more of this." He turned to walk away.

Uzi reached for his shoulder, but the subsonic whiz piercing the air stopped them both as they instinctively whirled to locate the direction of the signature noise.

Before Uzi found the source of the sound, Tad Bishop crumpled forward into his arms—a large bloody hole where his left eyeball used to be.

6:57 PM
115 hours 3 minutes remaining

"Jesus!"

Like a defensive lineman, DeSantos wrapped his arms around Uzi's waist and toppled the big man, who was supporting the weight of Tad Bishop's dead hulk.

After hitting the ground, Uzi and DeSantos crawled along the cold, dirt-littered asphalt path, attempting to make themselves more difficult targets.

"There!" Uzi said, indicating a large pine directly ahead of them. They pulled themselves up slightly against the wide tree's trunk. Both of them had their weapons in hand.

"What the fuck is going on?" DeSantos asked.

"Other than the fact that a sniper took a shot at us? That our CI is lying there dead with a freaking bullet in his brain?"

"Yeah, other than all that shit."

"Despite what you think about the guy, he obviously had good reason to be paranoid."

"Fine. Want me to apologize to him?"

Uzi looked at Bishop's prone body, a shimmer of moonlight reflecting off the man's puddled blood. "Just a guess. I don't think he's in a position to accept it."

"Where do you think the shooter is?"

Uzi did not dare peer around the tree. He closed his eyes, trying to picture the landscape behind him. "Up on the ridge maybe. Hard to say. He could be five hundred yards away."

"Or more if he's properly equipped."

Uzi replayed the subsonic whiz in his mind. It seemed to be multi-directional, which only meant one thing. "Based on the sound, I'd say it's safe to make that assumption. Fitted with a suppressor, is my guess, to disperse the sound."

"So we can't key in on his location and return fire."

"We're dealing with a pro here."

DeSantos's eyes roamed the immediate vicinity. "Think he's gone?"

"Only if he was after Bishop. If he was after you or me, we'd better get the hell out of here. These toys against his cannon aren't much of a match."

DeSantos suggested they split up and run jagged routes back to the Tahoe. Uzi agreed.

They dropped to a knee, nodded at each other, and took off. Sprinting in opposite directions, they circled around toward Uzi's car. As soon as they got in, Uzi started the engine and peeled away from the curb.

He shoved the Nokia against his ear, said, "Call Shep," then waited as the device initiated his voice command.

Two rings later, Shepard answered. "Uzi—"

"Yeah, it's me. Listen, we've got a problem." Uzi turned the corner, doubling back to where he estimated the sniper had been located.

"Another one?"

"I'm serious, Shep. DeSantos and I were just shot at. Sniper fire. Whoever it is, he's a pro."

"What?"

"He took out our CI. We had to leave the body, but we're staying close by."

"Where the hell are you?"

Uzi gave him their location.

"There," DeSantos said, pointing. "Park us over there, behind that building."

"We need a team out here," Uzi said, "see if we can find the shooter's roost."

"I'll alert HRT and get forensics on it. Meantime, you guys stay safe."

Uzi ended the call and pulled behind a building that gave them some cover, maneuvering the SUV in a way to afford them a view of the park. "He's sending Hostage Rescue and an Evidence Response Team."

"Fucker'll be long gone by the time they get here," DeSantos said. "We've gotta go after him now." He peered out into the darkness. "Where do you think his nest is?"

Uzi reached beneath his seat and pulled out a small black case. He opened it and removed a monocular night vision lens.

"You keep that in your car?"

"Like my American Express card. I don't leave home without it." He brought the device up to his face, then scanned the park, his eyes first finding Bishop's car as a reference. He then shifted his gaze fifty yards into the park and located the man's body. He dropped the lens from his eye and played back the seconds before the shot. He looked to the right, then back to the path where they had been walking. The only direction the shot could have come from was across the park, over a small ridge where a couple of houses were located. "There." He pointed, but DeSantos had already keyed in on the same place.

DeSantos reached up, disabled the dome light, then popped open his door. "Let's go."

7:07 PM
114 hours 53 minutes remaining

They scampered in the moonlit darkness, keeping beside the tall brush that shouldered the road. They turned a corner and came up on the other side of the houses.

Uzi took a moment to assess the angle of the shot that killed Bishop, then narrowed the possibilities to one of the homes. "Second story gives him a damn good view of the area where we were standing. Or the roof. But he's a pro, not like he's gonna be sticking around waiting for us to break down the door and haul his ass away."

"Unless we're the target, in which case he *is* waiting for us to come through the front door."

"Good point," Uzi said. "May as well wait for HRT."

"Fuck it. He just tried to kill us. I'm goddamn pissed. Let's go in. If he is still there—"

"Hang on a sec." Uzi brought the night vision lens back to his face. They were now about thirty yards from the two-story gray Victorian. "It's a business, not a residence. Providian Arts Council." He shoved the monocle in his pocket. "I'll go first, take a position along the right side."

DeSantos agreed, and Uzi took off, running a zigzag pattern across the lawn of the nearest house until he could take cover behind a brick column that contained a built-in mailbox. He signaled DeSantos, who followed the same path.

"You want the back door?" DeSantos asked.

"Shit yeah." Uzi strapped the night vision device to his right eye and rolled left, his Glock leading the way.

He arrived at the back door and tried the knob. Locked. He pulled a small pad from his pocket and peeled away three pieces of self-adhering film from its wax backing, then placed them beside one another on the door's window. He then took the butt of his handgun and slammed it against the glass. It cracked with a crunch, rather than an ear-shattering smash. He carefully peeled away the tape containing the broken window fragments, then inserted his right hand and felt for the deadbolt. With a quick turn, he had the door open.

Inside the house, moving slowly. Darkness. The grainy viewfinder of the night vision eyepiece illuminated the kitchen's interior in monochrome hues of green. Uzi stepped lightly, hoping a creaky floorboard would not give him away. He assumed DeSantos was likewise making his way toward the stairs. They would meet there, then proceed up.

He caught sight of his partner slinking through the living room and gave him a hand signal. Uzi ascended the staircase, DeSantos followed, and they fanned out, Uzi going left and clearing the rooms toward the front of the building. DeSantos went right.

A few moments later, Uzi came upon the room that provided the view of the park the shooter would have needed. He waited in the hall until DeSantos appeared, then flashed him a thumbs up sign. Uzi knelt low, turned the knob. With DeSantos at his side, he flung open the door.

Quiet. No movement, save for a ripple of air blowing through an open window. Uzi scanned the interior with his night vision eyepiece, then proceeded in.

Newspapers and magazines, a standard oak office desk, and metal file cabinets cluttered the area. Uzi cleared the room, then turned his attention to a walnut hutch against the wall adjacent to the window. He opened the drawers and sifted through the contents. A mailing label on one of the magazines contained the name of the subscriber, as well as what appeared to be the building's address. The name meant nothing to him.

He looked back to DeSantos, who had taken a position where he could keep an eye on Uzi's progress while he covered the door.

He knelt down in front of the window and scanned the ground. Nothing. He lowered his hand and felt around, sliding it beneath the hutch and the desk he had searched. His hand hit something that rolled away. He lay down on his right side, pulled out his smartphone, and activated the flashlight app.

Against the wall lay the object he had been hoping to find. He removed a pen from his inside jacket pocket and snared the metal item. He got to his feet and held it up to show DeSantos.

His partner backed into the room, maintaining his view of the doorway, then glanced down at the brass casing perched atop Uzi's pen. "Smoking gun?" he whispered.

"More like the empty metal cartridge of the smoking bullet."

DeSantos nodded toward the window, where, in the distance, a large black truck was pulling to a stop behind Bishop's parked car. "Cavalry's arrived. Let's go fill them in."

7:14 PM
114 hours 46 minutes remaining

Law enforcement personnel swarmed the area. Outside the boundaries of the yellow police tape, news crews and reporters jockeyed for position as close to Tad Bishop's body as they could get. Keeping to accepted convention, the police established two distinct crime scenes: the first where Bishop was killed, and the second where the sniper was hunkered down. Either way, definitive answers were a long time coming.

A core contingent from Uzi's task force had been notified, and as they arrived he attempted to connect the dots for them—without leading them to Knox or Coulter. But with a couple dozen agents sniffing around, chances were decent they would eventually stumble onto the Knox connection, lessening the blow Shepard would endure when the dust settled.

But even if they didn't identify the connection, all was not lost. Knox had something on Uzi; it couldn't hurt for Uzi to have something on Knox as well. It might just keep everyone honest.

Hoshi arrived in the second wave of cars that descended on the scene. She approached the area cautiously. At first Uzi thought it was because she was using her analytic skills to appraise the logistics of what had gone down. But when she reached him, he realized her face was white and her eyes moist.

"Hoshi, I'm sorry."

"I don't know why I feel this way. It's not like I knew the guy well. He was a source, someone who fed me info. Half the time I just let him ramble on about how the NFA was controlling our government. After a while, I think I became numb to all of it. I stopped listening." She looked out over the body bag the coroner was zipping twenty feet away. "And now this."

"Hold it," Uzi said. "You did the right thing putting me in touch with him. Bishop was on to something, and whether or not he told us, he was already on their radar. Someone didn't want his nose where he was sticking it."

"Maybe I could've prevented it. Warned him somehow. Protected him."

Uzi took her by the shoulder and led her away from the body. "The guy used to be a PI. He knew there were dangers in what he was doing. He was naturally paranoid. He knew something was up but he felt he had to keep digging."

"Yeah, but—"

"Listen to me. He felt he had to do this. He didn't do it for Hoshi Koh. He did it for Tad Bishop. He had his reasons."

She bobbed her head. "I guess."

"'Guess' all you want. You know I'm right." He stopped walking, dropped his arm from her shoulder, and faced her. "It's tough to lose someone like this. I know, it's happened to me. But the kind of work we do . . . These are the risks we face."

Uzi caught sight of DeSantos talking to Douglas Knox, who had arrived at the scene. In the distance, it appeared as if his partner was filling in the director on what had gone down. Uzi excused himself and started toward them, but a hand hooked on his forearm and stopped him in midstride. It was Leila.

"Hey. What are you doing here?"

Her eyebrows rose. "Nice greeting. Did they teach you that at the Academy, or am I seeing one of your undesirable sides?"

"Abruptness? One of my undesirable sides. But you didn't answer my question."

"I'm on M2TF. Didn't Shepard tell you?"

Shepard's name sent a pang of guilt through him.

The moment was approaching when he'd have to lie to his friend about Knox's personal directive to continue the ARM investigation. Friendships didn't come easy to him, but when he did find one, he held onto it dearly. Until this blew over, at which point he'd level with Shepard, he would avoid him whenever possible.

"I haven't seen him much. I've been a little busy." Uzi shrugged. "Don't get me wrong. I'm glad to have you on board." *And I'll get to see more of you this way. How could I complain about that?* "You got my text, I take it."

"If I hadn't, I'd think you stood me up and I wouldn't be so civil."

"True." Uzi caught a glimpse of one of his agents approaching with a member of the forensic crew. "So welcome, officially, to the team. Do you know what your role is here?"

"ADIC Yates and ASAC Shepard assigned me to you, as the liaison between M2TF and JTTF." She raised her eyebrows seductively. "And I always know my role, Uzi." She turned and walked off, leaving him to gaze at her rear as she moved down the path.

"Uzi."

He turned to see one of his task force agents approaching with a forensic tech at her side. "Well, well, well. Tim I-never-met-a-steak-I-didn't-like Meadows," Uzi said, extending a hand and flashing a broad smile. "How you doing?"

"You two know each other?" the agent asked.

"Best high-tech guru we've got in CART," Uzi said. "'Course I know him." He turned to Meadows. "What are you doing out and about? I didn't think you ever left your lair."

"Very funny, Uzi. I see you haven't lost your sense of humor. Oh, wait a minute. You never had one. This must be something new you're trying out."

"I'll leave you two to talk shop," the agent said, then moved back toward the secondary crime scene.

"Seriously. This isn't somewhere I'd expect to find you."

"I got a call from Shepard," Meadows said. "He needed a favor."

"I don't see any motherboards or hard drives out here."

"You think that's all I can do?"

"I guess I know better than to assume that."

"I told Shepard it'd cost him a meal at Angelo & Maxie's. He said to talk to you about it."

"If your info's any good, you got a deal."

"If my info's any good?"

Uzi clapped him on the back. "Glad you're here. We need all the help we can get."

"I've already got some stuff. You want to hear it?"

Uzi crossed his arms over his chest. "No, Tim. Keep it to yourself."

"There's that biting humor again. I'm beginning to think it borders on sarcasm."

"No borders about it."

"Did someone say sarcasm?" The voice emanated from their left, in a patch of darkness. Stepping forward into a spot of light was Karen Vail.

"Well, there you go," Meadows said. "The very embodiment of sarcasm."

"Glad to see you here," Uzi said.

Vail shrugged. "You know how it is. No desire to have a life, always at the Bureau's service." She sang, 'You just call out my name and I'll be there, yes I will. . . .'"

"James Taylor," Meadows said.

Vail looked over her shoulder. "Where?"

Uzi rolled his eyes, then nodded at the plastic evidence bag hanging from Meadows's left hand. "What've you got?"

"Oh. This. Yeah, this is that empty brass casing you found . . . 7.62 round, I'd say. Exactly what type of round, I don't know yet. There are a lot of similar 7.62 cartridges. When I get back to the lab, I'll throw it under the microscope. I should be able to tell you which type of rifle was used."

"Our guess," Uzi said, "is that the guy used a suppressor. The sound was kind of dispersed—"

"Very good. Yes," Meadows said. "A suppressor will scatter the crack of the shot. The cartridge travels faster than sound and makes a fairly loud sonic boom. In a sniper situation, using a suppressor doesn't mask the sound, especially on a round as big as this one is. What it does do is change the sound signature enough that the target is unable to determine which direction the shot came from, so he can't return fire."

"We already knew that."

"I didn't know that," Vail said.

"You know serial killer shit," Meadows said. "None of us expect you to know about high-powered sniper rifles."

Vail tilted her head. "'Serial killer shit'? You think that's all I'm good for?"

"Tim." Uzi shook his head. "Tim, my man. You just stepped into some seriously rank horse poop."

Meadows looked from Vail to Uzi and back to Vail. "That is what I said, but it's not what I meant. I mean, we all have our specialties. And you're so good at what you do that I don't look at you as having such a broad knowledge base dealing with the kind of minutiae I wade through."

"I accept your lame apology," Vail said. "Mostly because you're a tough guy to stay angry with."

Meadows shifted his feet. "Do you? Know a lot about rifle calibers and the science of suppressor technology?"

"Hell no," Vail said. "I know serial killer shit. Other things, too. But not that kind of picayune stuff. Especially suppression technology."

"Suppressor," Meadows said with a frown.

"Speaking of suppressors," Uzi said. "Can a device like the one our shooter used affect the accuracy of a shot?"

"Unlike our Renaissance-ish FBI profiler," Meadows said, "you ask good questions. Have I ever told you that?"

"Couple a dozen times."

Meadows zipped the jacket up to his neck, then began walking. "That's debatable. My sense is that it depends a lot on the particular weapon matched with a specific suppressor. Good match, less chance it'll divert the shot. But it definitely shouldn't affect accuracy to the point where a trained sniper would miss completely."

Uzi's head snapped up. "How'd you know that's what I was asking?"

"'Cause I'm smart and I know how you guys think."

Uzi frowned. "Here's the deal. Three guys are standing around talking and one of them gets popped from three, four hundred yards away. So was the guy actually aiming for me or my partner and missed? At four hundred yards, an inch or two is only significant to the guy who gets nailed and the guy who lives to tell about it."

"As good as I am, as we all are—Karen excluded—I don't think I can answer that one. As much as I want to ease your mind."

Uzi stopped walking, and Meadows and Vail did likewise. "It's more than just easing my mind. It's a matter of pointing us in the right direction. This investigation takes on a different flavor if I'm the target—or my partner—instead of Tad Bishop."

"Understood," Meadows said. "I'll do my best to answer whatever questions you've got."

"I have an opinion on this," Vail said.

"You mean a guess?" Meadows quipped.

"Uh, no, Tim. An informed opinion. If this is the work of a pro—and that seems to be the case here—a pro would match his equipment well, wouldn't he? The best suppressor to the best rifle, just like he measures dew point, humidity, wind conditions, and so on to make sure that when he pulls the trigger, he stands a damn good chance of hitting his intended target. Not the guy standing next to him."

"Well, well," Meadows said. "The distinguished lady from the BAU does know a thing about snipers."

"Yeah," Vail said. "Or two."

Uzi pulled a toothpick from its plastic wrapper and stuck it in his mouth as he looked off, surveying his colleagues swarming the area. "Deductions are great. But I want as definitive an answer as possible."

Meadows pulled another evidence bag from his pocket. "I'll get right on it."

"Let me know as soon as you figure it out."

"I know, you need it yesterday."

Uzi held out a hand. "Hey, did I say that?"

"No, but I'm so used to hearing—"

"This one I need day *before* yesterday."

Meadows stared deadpan at Uzi. "It's almost nine o'clock. I was off three hours ago."

"And now you're back on."

"You suck, you know that?"

Uzi nodded. "That's what they tell me."

"McCormick and Schmick's. That's where I want to go."

Uzi winced. "That hurts, Tim."

"A little pain is healthy, didn't you tell me that once?"

Uzi jutted his chin back. "I never said that."

"Well, someone did."

"I did," Vail said. "When I kicked you in the balls for insulting my new haircut."

"You never kicked me," Meadows said.

"You're lucky. I really wanted to."

Uzi pointed at the Ziploc-enclosed brass casing. "I want the answer, Tim. Fast. Even if it means working through the night."

Meadows groaned.

"The way I see it," Vail said, "sometimes you just gotta bite the bullet."

Ninety minutes later, most of the task force members had secured what they needed and left. The forensic crew thinned as well, most of the evidence collection having been accomplished in the first hour at both crime scenes. They focused on the assassin's perch, hoping to find an errant identifying mark in or around the house. With a handful of technicians remaining to finish combing the grounds, Uzi found Leila hovering around Bishop's vehicle.

"Find anything?"

"Nothing useful. Just the usual stuff we all keep in our cars. No tracking devices. Most importantly, no smoking guns."

Uzi cringed. "That was bad."

Leila grinned. "I thought it was quite clever."

He grabbed a peek at his watch. "So much for dinner at Amir's. How about something that's still open?"

"According to Shepard, you're the boss. If you say it's time to quit, we quit."

"One thing you'll learn about me, Leila, is that I never quit. But all good intelligence officers know that when you're facing uncertain or unstable situations, and you get a chance to eat, you take it—because you never know when you'll get another."

"Very good. I didn't realize you were ever in intelligence."

"Actually," Uzi said with a chuckle, "intelligence is something I've never been accused of." He motioned toward the street, then led the way to his car.

Uzi helped Leila pull her chair up to the small, square table in the rear of Georgetown's Thunder Burger & Bar. Despite the hour, the place was abuzz with talk and laughter. Uzi sat down heavily, then leaned back as the waitress set two cocktail napkins on their table. Uzi picked up the menu—which was surprisingly diverse—and offered it to Leila. "Hungry?"

"Very. But it's late. I'll just have a Caesar salad."

A rush of grief washed over Uzi. Dena made the best Caesar dressing he had ever tasted: just the right amount of garlic and anchovies. It was so good he would lick out the Cuisinart bowl while they were cleaning up the kitchen. Dena could whip up something sumptuous from scratch, with whatever ingredients she had in the apartment.

Uzi couldn't cook a can of soup, let alone figure out what all the different mixing bowls and oven settings were for. His mother never taught him the ways of the kitchen, but to be fair, he'd had no desire to learn. He was too interested in playing football, a tag game known as Ringalevio, or riding his bicycle.

"You there?"

Uzi focused his gaze on Leila. "What?"

"You were spacing out on me."

"Sorry." He turned his attention to the menu. "I've never been able to eat Caesar salad in restaurants." He glanced up and noticed the confused look on Leila's face. "My wife made the best Caesar in the world. Ordering it in a restaurant would always be second rate. Or worse."

"You're married?" Her question carried the tone of an inquiry, not an accusation.

Uzi buried his face again in the menu. "Used to be."

"Oh." After a moment, she said, "Nasty divorce?"

His eyes shot up. "No, no. Nothing like that. She was . . . murdered."

Leila's face remained impassive. "Murdered."

"Murdered."

"How long ago?"

"Six years."

She seemed to examine his face a moment, then said, "It still carries a lot of pain for you."

Uzi didn't respond. *If only she knew.*

"That's a long time to suffer."

Uzi closed the menu. "It'll be with me the rest of my life. That kind of pain never heals."

The waitress turned from the adjacent table and asked if they were ready to order.

"Caesar salad for the attractive young woman, and the falafel sliders for me." He looked at Leila. "Bottle of—"

"How about a Pinot Noir?" she asked.

"We've got an '09 Acrobat from Willamette Valley," the waitress said. "Cherry and blackberry, firm tannins, with a silky mouthfeel. One of my favorites and reasonably priced."

"Sold," Uzi said.

The woman collected the menus and headed off.

Uzi dipped his chin. "Dena liked Pinot."

Leila smiled. "She had good taste."

"Yeah, she did." Uzi lowered his eyes. *All this talk about Dena—* After his session with Rudnick, the old can had been opened and he was now sloshing around amongst the worms. Too many emotions to deal with now. He had a job to do, and walking around with a heavy heart and drudging up old feelings of guilt were affecting his focus. Maybe he should talk to Shepard, ask for a temporary reprieve on his counseling sessions. If he could make the case that it was impacting his performance in running the task force, he might allow him to forego treatment for a while. Then again, could he face Shepard after conspiring with Knox?

"You're doing it again."

Uzi shook his head. *A beautiful woman is talking to me and I'm zoning out on her.* "Sorry. I've got a lot on my mind. This investigation, other things . . ."

"I lost a loved one, too," she said. "My only brother."

Uzi looked at her, and instantly saw the pain in her eyes. Why was she telling him this? To make him feel better—as if that would help his pain?

"Murdered, too."

Uzi tilted his head. "Really."

She nodded. "In Gaza."

The waitress appeared with the bottle of Pinot Noir and two glasses. She placed them on the table and seconds later had twisted the cork from the wine. She poured an inch and waited for Leila to taste it and nod her acceptance. Leila did and the two glasses were filled.

Uzi took a sip and let it float over his tongue. Memories of Dena again. Sitting in Venice on their fifth anniversary, sipping Chianti and watching the water taxis depart for Murano. They had taken one themselves, wandered the glass galleries and finally bought a bud vase that still sat on his dresser today, filled with a desiccated red rose. A constant reminder of their trip together. A constant reminder of her. *Dena got pregnant with Maya on that trip—*

He realized he had been staring at the table. "Spacing again, sorry."

Leila was refilling her glass with more wine. "I'm beginning to think I'm poor company."

Uzi forced a smile. "If anything, I'm the poor company here."

She set down the bottle and swirled her glass. "You've hardly touched your wine."

"Brings back memories." He lifted the glass to his lips and drank.

"You're thinking about your wife."

Uzi's eyes drifted down again. "And my daughter. She was killed too."

Leila leaned forward. "Same time?"

Uzi nodded.

Leila reached out and touched Uzi's right hand, which was resting on the table near his glass. The contact made him flinch.

"I understand the pain," she said.

Uzi gently pulled his hand away and lifted the glass for another sip. "Did your brother live in Gaza?"

"Live there?" Leila snickered. "He was part of an IDF patrol."

"How did you deal with his death? If you don't mind me asking.'

Leila sucked in some air and blew it out slowly. "Anger, anger, and more anger. Some grief thrown into the mix somewhere along the line. Guilt, then more anger. The usual, I guess."

"How'd it happen?"

"Remember back in 2001 when Hamas killed a bunch of IDF soldiers? He was one of them." She studied her wine. "Terrorist sons of bitches."

Uzi tightened his grip on the glass. "I wish they could feel the pain they cause. I wish on them what I've had to live with the past six years."

"They'll get theirs," Leila said. "Sooner or later." She nodded, apparently lost in thought herself. She took a long drink of Pinot.

"When did you leave Israel?"

"Shortly after. I needed a change of scenery."

I totally understand. "Is that when you went to Jordan?"

Leila's brow lifted. "How do you—"

"You CIA spooks aren't the only ones with good intel." He grinned.

"First I went through training at The Farm. Then, yeah, they placed me in Jordan."

The waitress approached the table and set down their two dishes.

"I think I need this," she said. "The wine, empty stomach . . ." She threw her hands out to her sides, swayed in her seat, forced a smile.

They finished their food, Uzi paid the tab over her objections, and they headed out to his Tahoe.

As he left the parking lot, he asked, "Back to the crime scene to pick up your car?"

"No, I got a ride there. Take me home."

They arrived at Leila's Hamilton House apartment building on New Hampshire Avenue NW a few minutes before midnight. A doorman stood just inside the lobby, unsure if he should approach the car. Leila waved and he nodded back, understanding that she did not need his assistance.

Uzi pushed the gear shift into park and crooked his neck to gaze up at the nine-story, block-long monstrosity that looked more like a hotel than an apartment building. "Nice place."

"I've lived in caves, tents, and the desert. Compared to that, this is the lap of luxury. But really, home is what you make it."

Uzi knew she was right. He looked at her large brown eyes and felt something in his chest. He struggled to define the sensation. Warmth? "Your eyes are so beautiful." He saw the pleased look on her face before he realized what he had said. "I'm sorry. I didn't mean to say that. I mean, I didn't mean to make you feel uncomfortable."

"Do I look like I feel uncomfortable?"

Uzi turned away. "No. I think it's me who's uncomfortable."

She pointed to the ignition. "Shut the engine."

He craned his neck to look out at the No Parking placards at the curb. "I can't park here."

Leila tilted her head. "Alec and Jiri are my buddies. They'd do anything for me. Don't worry about your car. Give Alec the keys. He'll move it if there's a problem."

Uzi looked from Leila to the windshield, but still had not turned off the engine.

"Go on. Shut it off and come up with me."

This was moving faster than he'd intended. Faster than he was prepared for. He had clearly indicated his attraction and the desire to get to know her better off the clock. She picked up on those signals—but now Uzi was unsure if this is what he really wanted. He was a healthy male and Leila was a beautiful woman; of course he wanted this. *But am I ready for it?*

"Problem?"

"I . . . I'm not sure I should come up."

"You don't like good company? Do you think I'm inviting you up for sex?"

"No, I— I don't know. No."

"No, you don't like good company?"

Uzi blew some air through his lips. He wasn't used to being so flustered around anyone—let alone an attractive woman. "It's not that."

"Then let's go." She reached over, turned the key and removed it. She clutched the fob in her hand and popped open her door. She swung her feet out and glanced back at him over her shoulder. "You coming?"

Leila's apartment was an orderly one bedroom, generously appointed with a large living room and an equally small kitchenette. The parquet wood floor was well maintained, with an earth-toned Indian area rug providing warmth and muted color. Two loveseats sat around a glass coffee table, where a hand-carved matchbox rested alongside a couple of porcelain candlestick holders.

Uzi picked one up and examined it. "I recognize the artist. From the Old City?" he asked, referring to that section of Jerusalem.

Leila smiled. "For Shabbat. Hard to break old habits."

"I lost interest after Dena's death. Lost my faith, I guess."

"You've always got to have faith, Uzi. No matter what happens, you need to believe in your cause. When things hit bottom, that's the time to turn inward and renew your faith, not lose it."

Uzi took a few steps into the hallway. A few carefully placed framed photos hung on the far wall, sporting images of people he didn't know—but places with which he was intimately familiar: a younger Leila hiking in the Golan Heights, a few street shots from the artist colony, Tzvat, and Leila in a bikini on the beach in Tel Aviv.

"You still wear your star." Leila motioned to the Star of David necklace peeking through his shirt collar. It was an unusual piece consisting of two separate gold triangles, one pointing up and one pointing down that, when they overlaid each other, formed a six-pointed star.

He touched the necklace. Most of the time he forgot he still wore it. Nevertheless, it had special meaning to him. "My wife gave it to me."

"It's very cool, very modern. I've never seen anything like it."

"Do you know where the star comes from?"

Leila pursed her lips. "Never gave it much thought."

"The triangles represent the Greek letter 'D,' or delta, for David. Archeologists say the layout of the two Ds was meant more as a design than a star or religious symbol. It was King David's logo, which he wore on his shield whenever he went into battle."

She seemed to study his face a moment, then took his hand. "Come," she said, pulling him back across the room to the coffee table. She picked up the small carved wood box and removed a match. "It's way after sundown, but it's still Saturday." She glanced at the wall clock, which had ticked past midnight. "Well, sort of. Let's light the Havdalah candle, anyway," she said, referring to the ceremonial prayer that signified the end of the Sabbath. She made her way to an armoire tucked into the corner of the room.

Uzi bit his lip. He felt terribly uncomfortable but found himself moving the few steps toward her.

Leila reached into the walnut cabinet and removed a silver tray that held a long, tri-braided candle and a brass spice box. With the match, she set the wick alight and began chanting the blessing.

She nudged Uzi with an elbow and he joined in. The melody, the pungent scent of fresh sulfur, and the flaring candle warmth on his face transported him back to the rare Friday and Saturday nights when he was home to share the beginning and ending of the Sabbath with Dena—and then, after she was born, with Maya, holding the little girl in his arms, teaching her how to recite the prayers.

The memories pained him like a hot poker in the pit of his stomach.

Leila lifted the candle and placed it upside down into the silver cup, extinguishing it.

"How long have you lived here?" he asked, hoping to avoid more probing questions.

"About six months." She walked into the kitchen and pulled a bottle of Prager Tawny port from the cupboard. "I used to live in Georgetown, but I wanted to get into the city. Into the heart of things." She pulled the cork and poured a couple of glasses.

Uzi took one and sipped it. "Mmm. This is very good."

Leila took her glass over to the loveseat and settled gently into the cushion. "When did you move to the states?"

"A couple of months after." That's how he thought of his life: before death and after death. Two different lives—one enriched, the other hollow.

"What did you do in Israel?"

Uzi sat down beside her and set his glass on the coffee table. He was inclined to tell her the truth—but couldn't bring himself to fight through the oath he had taken with Mossad so many years ago. He had caused Rudnick some pain for access to such info. For now, he took the safe road. "I was a design engineer for Intel. I spent a few months at the development center in Haifa, then moved to their fab in Kiryat Gat." Technically, it was the truth—which was fine by him, because he didn't want to base a relationship on a lie. Then again, he wondered how much she could find out by digging through the CIA database.

"Fab?"

"Manufacturing plant. I led the team that turned out the Pentium 4 chips."

"That sounds very . . . serious. Long hours. No time for fun."

Uzi shrugged. "It was intense, yeah. But we found time to mountain bike in the hills outside Tiberias. It's beautiful there." His thoughts drifted to Dena.

"I used to go rock climbing with my brother. In the ruins by the cliffs of Arbel."

"I went climbing there, too. We used to bring a lunch, hike around a while, do some climbing, then hike back." He laughed. "We had some great times." His smile faded.

Both of them remained quiet. She placed a hand on his arm. "You've got a right to be happy, Uzi. It's not like you have to be miserable for the rest of your life."

"I know. I know you're right. But it's not that easy."

"You just have to decide that life goes on and know that you've suffered enough."

"Now you sound like my shrink."

She raised an eyebrow. "You don't strike me as the type to go for counseling."

"Shepard's idea. More like an order."

Leila leaned forward to place her drink on the table, then slumped back on the couch. Her shoulder rested inches from his. "I talk a good game, I know. But I don't always put my own advice to work. When my brother died, it took a while for it to sink in. I was numb for so long. Numb to the pain . . . but not the anger. All I wanted to do was get even. I still do."

Uzi wanted to tell her he felt the same way, but was afraid he would break down. It was too difficult to discuss what he'd gone through in the days after the murders. He realized she had gone quiet. He craned his neck a bit to see her face and saw a shiny streak coursing down her cheek. "You okay?"

"Tell me about this shrink you're seeing."

"I really like the old guy. I've only had a few sessions with him, but I feel very close to him. He's a good man. And maybe a little too good at what he does."

She sniffled. "Is he helping?"

"He's dredging up all sorts of things. I'm telling him stuff I never thought I'd tell anyone." He looked off at the wall of photos. "Is that good? I'm not sure."

She brought her knees up onto the couch and reclined onto Uzi's thigh. His hand instinctively rolled off the back of the couch and came to rest on her left shoulder. "Sometimes I wake up crying. In the middle of the night."

"Me too."

He began stroking her hair, thinking of the times when Dena would lay across his lap and he would gently run his fingers across her scalp, around her ears. She would fall asleep and he would follow. They would remain like that until he would awaken hours later, the two of them sprawled out on the couch in each other's arms.

He closed his eyes and was instantly back in Haifa, the warm wind rippling his T-shirt, enjoying his time off between missions. Remembering the last time they'd gone there, only days before Dena and Maya were killed. They had picked flowers and he'd snapped some photos of Maya, photos he never looked at. Photos that were still on the SD card in his camera. Memories too painful to remember.

He shut his eyes and, moments later, fell asleep.

DAY FIVE

1:15 AM
108 hours 45 minutes remaining

Soft lips against his, hands pulling at his belt buckle. He kissed back, hearing himself moan. *Feels good.* She was touching him, her body against his, her warm tongue on his neck, her hair falling into his face.

He awoke from his dream, a dream where he had been lying in the tall grass with Dena. He opened his eyes and saw Leila, her head back as she moved slowly, rhythmically, as if seduced by a love potion. Her breath deep and regular, her hands unzipping his pants as her tongue trailed across his cheek and penetrated his mouth.

Uzi wanted to resist, but couldn't. He wasn't sure if he wanted her to stop. The guilt was strong—the sense that this wasn't right tangling with feral desire. The warmth, the intimacy, the comfort of being close to someone, of being touched and caressed. Her lips wandered down his chest, slowly making their way toward his waist.

He shut his eyes and cleared his mind. It felt too good to resist. He deserved this, he kept telling himself. Enough grief, enough anger, enough feeling sorry for himself. He relaxed and let his head fall back, lost in the moment.

The morning came upon him suddenly. Uzi awoke with a start, disoriented to time and place. He glanced around the room, saw the two glasses and the empty bottle of Port, Leila asleep in his lap. He wiped his face with a hand, then blinked several times to clear his vision. Leila stirred, then moved to her left and curled up with a crushed velvet pillow that lay beside her on the couch.

Her clothes were askew, a knit afghan draped across her dark skin.

Uzi rose, stiffness in his back causing him to straighten slowly. What time was it? He twisted his watch so he could read the face, and yawned. Five-sixteen. He gathered his shirt and jacket, fastened his pants, then walked lightly to the door and left the apartment.

Downstairs, he found his car where he'd left it, no ticket attached to the windshield. A different doorman was on duty, but apparently Alec or Jiri had left instructions to look after Uzi's vehicle. When Uzi asked for his keys, the man knew exactly where they were.

As he drove home, his mind started to clear. He replayed the evening's events—starting from when they were sitting in the car—and suddenly flashed on Leila awakening him at some point during the night, her lips trailing across his lips, his face, his stomach. He missed his street and cursed under his breath.

"We had sex," he said into the still air. "Or did I just dream it?"

As he turned down his street, he slipped into cop mode and thought of how he had found himself when he had awakened: his pants undone, his shirt lying on the floor. If it were a crime scene, the clues would be too few to be of value.

He pulled into a spot near his townhouse, the possibility that he had made love to Leila weighing on his thoughts. What did it mean? How could he deal with it if it were true?

Of course it was true. He remembered it: she had awoken him from a deep sleep. He was dreaming of Dena at the time— How riddled with guilt could he possibly be?

He made himself a cup of coffee, threw a couple of ice cubes in it, then downed it quickly. He still felt sluggish, and he needed his mind sharp, so he could think, try to figure out what he was feeling, what it all meant.

Having finished his drink and reached no resolution to any of his dilemmas, he pulled out his phone and found Dr. Rudnick's home number. He did not like using it, but he figured the doctor had given it to him for just such a reason. The phone rang twice before Rudnick picked up. Uzi explained the situation and asked if he could meet him in forty-five minutes, knowing that the answer would be yes, regardless of the doctor's schedule and despite the fact that it was Sunday.

He showered and dressed, then drove to Rudnick's office, unsure of what he was searching for. He felt like he needed to do something.

But what it was, he did not know.

7:03 AM
102 hours 57 minutes remaining

Uzi sat down heavily and stared ahead at the desk, or the wall, or whatever happened to be in front of him. His mind was a flurry of confusion.

"Talk to me," Rudnick said. He took a seat directly in front of Uzi and rested his forearms on his knees.

Uzi rubbed his eyes with thumb and index finger. "My informant was taken out by a sniper. His bullet missed my head by a few inches."

Rudnick studied his patient's face. "How do you feel about that?"

Uzi merely shrugged his shoulders. "How should I feel about that?"

"We're not here for me to tell you how to feel." Rudnick shifted his legs. "Were you aware your informant's life was in danger?"

"He thought it was. That's one of the things we were discussing when he was killed."

"But you're not bothered by the fact that this man was killed. I'm not saying you weren't affected by his death, but you've been in the trenches, this type of thing has happened to you before. So tell me what's bothering you."

Uzi shrugged.

"Is it Dena? Are you upset about what we talked about during the last session?"

Uzi rose from the chair, ran his fingers through his freshly combed damp hair.

"Guess my hammer still has some good aim left in it."

Uzi turned to face the doctor. "What?"

"I hit the nail on the head. We'd touched on the source of your stress the past several years. Your feelings of guilt over the death of your wife and daughter."

Rudnick's words hurt. But he realized the man meant no harm; Uzi had asked his doctor to be direct and Rudnick was only doing as he had requested. "There's more to it than that." He hesitated, then decided to just say it. "I met someone. A woman."

"Ahh," Rudnick said with a knowing nod of his head. "And this bothers you."

Uzi thought for a moment. "I feel dirty."

"Unfaithful?"

He nodded. "Yeah, I guess."

"Uzi, my friend, these are normal feelings. It's nothing to be ashamed of or upset about."

"I think it's bothering me because I let it happen, or because it felt good even though I feel bad about it." He sighed and looked up at the ceiling. "Does that make any sense?"

Rudnick grinned. "You say you're not in touch with your emotions, but you really are. I think you're very astute."

"Then here's another astute observation: being told that my feelings are normal doesn't help."

"I can only offer you an outlet to talk about what you're feeling, help you understand why you're feeling it, and let you know it's okay. But I can't get rid of the pain."

Uzi sat down heavily in his chair. "You mean you're giving me permission to feel guilty?"

"I wouldn't exactly put it like that, but I guess the answer would be, yes." Rudnick tilted his head. "Tell me about her."

Uzi blew air through pursed lips. "Her brother was killed by Hamas in an ambush."

"So you two have an instant bond, common ground. You can feel what she feels. Such bonds can make for a solid foundation on which to base a relationship."

Uzi looked away.

"Tell me more about her."

"I'd rather not."

"Sounds to me like you aren't ready to admit you're attracted to another woman."

If only it were that simple. "It's more than that, doc. We . . . made love. Last night."

"I see."

"I mean, how can I tell the difference between love and just being hard up? You can talk about 'bonds' and 'solid foundations,' but maybe I'm just horny after not having been with a woman for six years. I mean, I let down my guard and I'm suddenly in bed with a woman."

"Letting down your guard is a good thing. Sooner or later, it had to happen. Don't you think?"

"I don't know. Who would've thought six years later the guilt would still be so fresh?"

"Some people go through their entire lives lugging around excess baggage, never learning how to let go. Never coming to terms with it. You're just now finding out how. You might want to feel proud of yourself rather than guilty." Rudnick put the palms of his hands together in front of his nose. "I make it a point not to tell my patients how to feel, but rather steer them, help them figure out how to feel on their own. So I apologize for steering you a little bit strongly there.

"But I want you to view your actions positively, not negatively. We only get one go-round in life, Uzi. You've seen how fleeting it can be. Here today, gone tomorrow. Don't let yesterday's pain become tomorrow's sorrow. It's healthy to move on. Not to learn how to forget, but to learn how to remember. Remember constructively, Uzi, not destructively." He stopped to appraise his patient. "But I think you've finally figured it out for yourself."

Uzi sat there, absorbing every word Rudnick was saying. *Learn how to remember. Maybe that's the key.* He sucked in his breath, rose from the chair and extended a hand to his doctor. Rudnick stood and shook it.

"Thanks," Uzi said.

"I'm just here to listen and give you some perspective. The rest you're doing on your own."

8:10 AM
101 hours 50 minutes remaining

Uzi arrived at the Hoover Building shortly after eight. Moments later he was exiting the elevator on the fourth floor, where the lab was located. He entered the sprawling facility and saw Tim Meadows sitting in front of a monitor, clicking through a pictorial catalog of rifles and rounds. An iPad sat propped up a smidgen to the right of his screen, a writing stylus lying beside it and electronic notes scrawled across the virtual yellow pad.

As Uzi neared, he noticed that Meadows was wearing a pair of small headphones with a molded band that conformed to the back of his head. Uzi pulled them off and slipped them over his own ears. "What is this?"

Meadows grabbed back his headphones. "You're shouting."

"You've got the volume cranked."

"You crank rock music," Meadows said. "This is New Age. By turning up the gain, the ethereal sense of being in the woods, or lounging by the ocean, is that much more sensual."

Uzi scrunched his brow, then indicated the screen. "Can we put the forest and ocean aside for a moment and talk about more gut-wrenching topics, like large-caliber rounds?"

Meadows frowned. "You've got a violent streak, you know that? A lot of bottled up hostility. Ever consider taking meditation classes?"

"I'll put it on my To Do list. *After* I break this case. But that's got no chance of happening if you don't start talking."

"You should cut a guy some slack. It's Sunday, okay?"

"Tim. The rounds."

"Okay, the rounds. Here's what I've got." He swiveled in his chair, facing Uzi head on. "Wait. If I give you this, and it's real helpful, you owe me dinner, remember?"

"For doing your job?"

"Doing my job means you get the report in a couple of weeks, not overnight."

Uzi grabbed a chair to his left and sat down. "Dinner, fine." *Didn't I already agree to that?*

"O-kayyy," Meadows said gleefully, spinning in his seat like a kid on a counter stool in an ice cream shop. He faced his monitor, then hit a few keys. A highly magnified image filled the screen. "This, my friend, is a bullet."

Uzi's gaze shifted from the high-resolution photo to Meadows. "No shit."

"Not just any bullet, Uzi. It's your bullet. It's what would be inside the brass casing you recovered at the scene last night."

"And what does it tell you?"

"Well it brought up some very interesting challenges. First of all, it's Russian."

"Russian. You sure?"

Meadows gave him a look. "Yes, I'm sure. Look at the shape of the cartridge. Right here," he said, pointing at the screen. "Russian cartridge has a rimmed case. American doesn't."

Uzi nodded. "Okay. So it's Russian. Type of weapon?"

"Traditional army-issue Russian sniper rifle is the Dragunov SVD. It's not considered to be the best choice because it's a semi-auto, and inherently less accurate than a bolt action. A new high-quality Russian bolt-action rifle was designed in 1998, the SV-98. Here's where it gets interesting. The SV-98 is chambered for either 7.62 x 54mmR or 7.62 x 51mm NATO rounds. The 54mmR round isn't used in many other rifles. The 51 NATO, however, is very common."

"And my casing fits . . . which?"

"The fifty-four."

"Less common. Good," Uzi said. "But how rare are we talking about?"

Meadows struck another key. A different photo appeared. "The fifty-four is common to only two rifles, the SV-98 and the obsolete Russian/Finnish Mosin-Nagant. The Mosin-Nagant was the Eastern Block sniper rifle in World War Two. Both rifles have four lands and grooves in the barrel, and the rifling in both rifles twists to the right. The difference between these two rifles is that the SV-98 has a barrel twist rate of one in twelve-point-six inches, and the Mosin-Nagant has a twist rate of one in nine-point-five inches."

Uzi looked at Meadows again. "How do you keep all this shit straight—I mean, how many hats do you wear?"

Meadows leaned close. “I gotta confess, Uzi. You know me, mister honesty. When it got down to the nitty-gritty I had to ask a buddy of mine next door. I got the Mosin-Nagant but I couldn’t accept it. It didn’t seem to fit. I was racking my brain till he told me about the SV-98.”

“So a Russian SV-98,” Uzi said, rubbing his chin with the back of his right hand.

“Probably. I did some checking with the ME, found out the round he recovered from your friend Bishop had a one-to-twelve-point-six twist ratio. That’s why I say ‘probably,’ because it’s possible to have a gunsmith change the chambering on a rifle to almost anything within reason. Just to throw us off.”

Uzi chewed on his lip. “What’s the most likely?”

“Depends on who you’re dealing with, but if you’re looking for ways to focus, I’d say you’d have to be dealing with someone who really knows his shit—and who doesn’t want to get caught.”

“None of ’em want to get caught, Tim. But maybe they’ve got significant exposure—in other words, they’re easily connected to the rifle. This is a way of disguising themselves.”

“Could also mean that by choosing a Russian SV-98, they’re trying to throw you off. They’re a tad bit rare in the US.”

Uzi chewed on that a second, then realized something. “Is the SV-98 a bolt-action rifle?”

“Yup. Why?”

“So the bolt has to be manually cycled after each shot to eject the spent case, and then manually moved forward to chamber the next round. Right?”

“Yeah.” Meadows tilted his head. “So what?”

“Just something that’s bugged me. We found a casing at the crime scene. Now I can accept that after the guy ejected the casing, it rolled away from him in the dark and he couldn’t find it and he had to get the hell out of there. But what’s bothered me is that he ejected it in the first place.”

“A pro would only need to take one shot and there’d be no need to chamber another round.”

“Exactly.” Uzi looked again at the on-screen image. “Law

enforcement and military snipers are generally taught to automatically chamber a round to be ready for any eventuality, even if they don't expect to have to shoot a second time. Target could sneeze just as you stroke the trigger and your bullet passes through thin air instead of the guy's eye socket." Uzi shrugged a shoulder. "Of course, that doesn't mean our assassin is an ex-cop or military-trained sniper, but it sure makes it interesting, doesn't it?"

"'Interesting' to me is a hard drive that contains encrypted data. That's the kind of stuff that gets me going. This investigative stuff is more your speed."

Uzi rose from his chair and gave Meadows a pat on the shoulder. "I'll be in touch. As soon as this case breaks, we'll do dinner, okay?"

"McCormick and Schmicks, that's where I want to go. The lobster's to die for."

Uzi snorted. "Again with the McCormick and Schmicks. GS-15's a solid salary, Tim, but isn't their lobster like forty bucks?"

"I think it's closer to sixty."

"Sixty." Uzi's hand covered his wallet. "You're killin' me, man."

"Oh—oh—wait a minute. I hear violins playing."

"Yeah," Uzi said with a grin. "It's that New Age shit you listen to."

Uzi left Meadows and took the elevator up to the sixth floor to meet with the Bureau's expert on militia groups, Pablo Garza. Hoshi had set up the meeting but hadn't had time to assemble a background sheet on the man. At a minimum, Uzi liked to know the agent's FBI pedigree—most importantly, was he known among his peers as someone whose information could be trusted? Was he a diligent investigator? Did he accept the information given to him as fact, or did he dig to verify?

He located Garza's office and rapped on the door with his knuckles. One thing was sure: Garza worked out of HQ, a floor below the director. Proximity to power meant you had some yourself.

After knocking, Uzi heard a noise to his right. Down the hall, staring at Uzi as if he were Osama bin Laden risen from the dead, stood Jake Osborn. Uzi turned back to the door, hoping to avoid a confrontation so close to the director. He wondered what Osborn was doing in the Hoover building. On a Sunday, no less.

As Uzi raised his fist to knock again, the thick wood door swung open. Uzi almost rapped Garza in the face.

"Agent Uziel," the agent said, "come on in."

"Call me Uzi," he said as he glanced over his right shoulder—and saw that Osborn had moved on. He shoved his hands into his dress pant pockets and stepped into Garza's office.

Papers were stacked haphazardly across the desk; magazines, folded back to specific articles, and a variety of textbooks sat beneath official reports and periodicals.

But Pablo Garza the man painted a different picture: with a starched white shirt and burgundy tie, charcoal suit and gold cufflinks, he looked like a show-quality FBI purebred. Crisp and professional. Self-important.

What grabbed Uzi's attention, however, were his dark, deep-set eyes.

"What can I do for you?" Garza asked, standing behind his desk.

Uzi was tempted to sit down, more by instinct than fatigue, but with Garza remaining on his feet, Uzi felt compelled to do the same. "I was told you're the man to see about militia groups."

"I'll accept that. What would you like to know?"

"I'm heading up the task force on the downing of Marine Two. We have reason to believe ARM might be involved."

"Wouldn't surprise me."

"Why's that?" Uzi asked.

Garza waved a hand dismissively. "Just a feeling. After a while dealing with these people, you get a feel for who might be capable or inclined to do what to whom."

"Just a feeling?"

"You want evidence? Can't help you. You'll have to do your job yourself."

Uzi felt his face flush. What was this guy's problem? He'd never asked anyone to do something for him he could do himself. "How about just telling me about ARM— Any unusual activity in recent months?"

Garza thought for a second, then shook his head. "Nope. Nothing comes to mind."

"So you feel ARM is capable of bringing down Marine Two."

"Like I said," Garza said with a shrug, "just a feeling."

Uzi twisted his lips in frustration. "What can you tell me about them?"

"Don't you have someone on JTTF that handles domestic militia groups? Osborn, right?"

Uzi forced a grin. "I'm interested in your perspective."

Garza hiked both shoulders, then launched into a monologue that lasted a solid two minutes, delineating the beginnings of ARM, including the rise to power of Jeremiah Flint, and how son Nelson succeeded him. It was all info Uzi already knew, most of which he'd gotten from DeSantos, the Internet, or Bureau database.

Uzi realized he was wasting his time. Either the Bureau was horrendously ill informed about ARM, or his colleague Garza was purposely withholding information. He was inclined to think it was the latter, but his FBI loyalty forced him to conclude it had to be the former.

Uzi thanked Garza for his time. Don't ever come knocking on my door, pal, he felt like saying. But he kept his mouth shut.

He was in the elevator, heading back to his car, when a thought occurred to him. There was another source of information on extremist groups, one whose sole purpose was keeping tabs on organizations like ARM. He just about ran the rest of the way to his car, buoyed by the possibility that he might actually gain some insight that would help push his case to the next level.

9:42 AM
100 hours 18 minutes remaining

The Washington offices of the Anti-Defamation League, or ADL, were located in a nondescript highrise in the heart of downtown. The building's only distinguishing characteristic was the modern entrance that conspicuously jutted out onto the sidewalk.

Uzi flashed his credentials at the lobby guard, then took the elevator up. He slid his badge and ID through the bulletproof glass pass-through, along with his business card. The receptionist examined them, then picked up a telephone to make a call.

There was no shortage of surveillance cameras—those he could see, as well as those he couldn't, even though he knew they were there.

He figured the woman was calling the number on the card, verifying his identity. At least, that's what he would be doing if he were them. And because of who they were—the target of just about every racist, hate-mongering group in the world—they had to exercise extreme caution. Some considered their safeguards paranoiac, but Uzi knew better. He sat down and absently thumbed through a magazine while his mind ticked through the various facts he had thus far amassed.

Ten minutes later, the receptionist ushered him down a hallway, past several dark and vacant offices, to a modest-sized room. The door was slightly ajar, as if the room's occupant was expecting him. The woman pushed it open, stepped back, and cleared the way for Uzi to enter. "Would you like something to drink? Coffee, juice, water . . . ?"

"Coffee would be great. Black, two sugars, if you don't mind."

The woman nodded and moved off.

"Agent Uziel." The voice came from the man behind the desk.

Uzi stepped in and extended a hand. "Call me Uzi. Sorry to drop in on you like this."

"Uzi," repeated the man. "I'm Karl Ruckhauser. Karl, if you don't mind. And it's not a problem. It gives me a break from the daily grind."

"Even on a Sunday?"

"'Hate' doesn't take weekends off."

"No, it doesn't." Uzi took the seat to his right and gave the office a quick once-over. Like Garza's office, there was a storm of paperwork, journals and books—but Ruckhauser's desk was organized as if it sat in a model home of a new tract of houses. Uzi wondered if the comparison between the two men's offices bore any significance to the extent of their knowledge base.

"What can I do for you?"

"I'm here about American Revolution Militia. I'm in the middle of a sensitive investigation, so I can't go into details. But I have reason to believe they may be . . . involved."

"Involved in what?"

Uzi squirmed a bit in his chair. "I can't say."

Ruckhauser nodded. "But it doesn't take a genius to put the recent assassination attempt together with your question about a large, well-armed domestic militia, now, does it?"

"Guess not."

Ruckhauser took a seat behind his desk. "So you want some background information. Who they are, who's in charge, who they're in bed with, what they're capable of, what they've been up to lately. Right?"

A small smile tickled the corners of Uzi's lips. "Exactly."

"Kind of like a newspaper article: who, what, when, where, how, and so on." Ruckhauser waved a hand in the air. "I was a journalism major. They stamp it in your brain."

"Got tired of writing stories?"

"I saw the demise of the newspaper business a mile away. Decided to jump ship before others got the same idea. But what I do here is pretty much the same thing when you get down to it. I dig for information, do my investigative stuff, and use it to help people like you keep tabs on people like ARM."

The door opened and the receptionist entered with two steaming, jacketed paper cups. She set one down on the desk beside Ruckhauser, the other in front of Uzi; they thanked her and she left.

"Why don't we start with some basic background on domestic extremism? That'll help you put it all into perspective." Uzi nodded for him to continue. "How much do you know about it?"

"With all that's gone down the past several years, foreign threats have taken all my time. But after Fort Hood, we've scrambled to beef up a separate group within my task force dedicated to homebred terrorists. But their focus has been on Americans who've got ties to Pakistan, Yemen, Somalia . . . wherever training camps spring up. My own knowledge base is limited to what we get in our threat assessments.

"But all of us have studied Oklahoma City. And obviously I've been fully briefed on the more recent stuff, like Nidal Hasan at Hood, the Hutaree in Michigan, Faisal Shahzad in Times Square, the Northwest Airlines underwear bomber, and a bunch of other attempts we cut off at the balls and were able to keep out of the media. That good enough?"

"Not really," Ruckhauser said, "but let's start with Oklahoma, because it opened our eyes to well-armed, obsessively antigovernment fanatics and neo-Nazis. Basically, we're looking at disaffected loners who frequent the gun-show circuit and camouflaged paramilitary 'officers' who dress in fatigues and go out into the backwoods of the South and Midwest. They used to get together to play soldier, but now they go on extended maneuvers and train hard for combat like a serious militia, with high-tech gear and high-powered weapons. And they're angrier and more volatile than they used to be. They see themselves as revolutionaries, plotting to attack America in order to save it—no matter how many innocent people they take with them."

Ruckhauser sipped his coffee before continuing. "But let's back up a bit, because there's a deeper history here. People know Oklahoma City because of the sheer magnitude of the carnage. But if you're asking if a militia is capable of doing what you're asking, my answer is definitely."

"Let's hear the deeper history."

"History can be boring, so I'll hit the high points. You'll catch the pattern. Blue Ridge Hunt Club, which was really a militia, recruited a gun dealer into its ranks so they could get their hands on all sorts of untraceable firearms. The dealer, a sympathizer, would merely 'lose' the paperwork. When ATF raided their compound, they found illegal machine guns, suppressors, grenades, and explosives. Not to mention elaborate plans on a computer for raiding a National Guard Armory, blowing up bridges, airports, and a radio station."

Ruckhauser swirled his coffee cup and leaned back in his chair. "Then there was the Tri-State Militia in South Dakota. It was going to bomb several buildings that belonged to civil rights groups, including an ADL office in Houston, abortion clinics, and welfare offices. Luckily, the Bureau got a tip from an informant. Sure enough, when arrests were made, the plans—and explosives—were found. The White Patriot Party. Ever hear of them?"

"Can't say I've had the pleasure."

"You're not the only one. They were led by an ex-Green Beret. They stockpiled thousands of dollars of stolen military hardware and got active-duty military personnel to train its members to use antitank weapons, explosives, and land mines. The leaders were arrested and got short prison terms. But that only pissed them off. When they got out, they planned to rob a restaurant to fund the purchase of stolen military rockets so they could blow up the office and kill the attorney who prosecuted them. When that plan fell apart, they tried to blow up a hydroelectric power dam. Dumb luck led police to a dozen of their explosives stockpiles." Ruckhauser sipped his coffee.

"Another group," Ruckhauser continued, "had plans—and explosives—to detonate bombs at the Olympics. During the raid, your colleagues also found a hit list containing the names of a dozen prominent citizens they had a beef against. You get the point?"

"Loud and clear."

"None of that is common knowledge. It gets a small blurb in the morning paper, but because no one was killed, because there were no gruesome images on TV playing over and over for weeks at a time, everyone forgets about it. But when McVeigh hit . . ."

"It caught everyone's attention."

"Even the FBI seemed to have a short memory. It treated McVeigh like an anomaly, as if the threat of homegrown radicals who would act on their fantasies to take down government institutions was either never going to happen again, or a distant reality."

Uzi was under no illusions that the Bureau was perfect. Mistakes were inevitable. The key was doing your best to prevent them, and learning from those you did make so they weren't repeated many years later when institutional memory faded. "There must've been a reason why we thought that."

"After 9/11, Islamic radicals and the war on terror became the big deal—along with Iraq, Afghanistan, Iran's nuclear program, the hunt for bin Laden, unmanned drones, and so on. But there were factors that seemed to support the FBI's theory about domestic groups posing a lesser threat. The economy was going strong, people were prospering, the militias were suffering from infighting, and there wasn't much of an increase in their influence after Oklahoma City. Certainly nothing like what happened after Ruby Ridge. If McVeigh meant it as a call to arms, it fell on deaf ears. For the most part."

"But you gave me the impression Oklahoma City was significant."

"Personally," Ruckhauser said, shifting uneasily in his chair,

"Timothy McVeigh scared the crap out of me. Not because of what he was, but because of who he was."

"I don't follow."

"He didn't exactly fit your typical far-right race-hating workingman. He came from a middle-class upbringing; he was articulate and polite. This guy was different from, say, Nelson Flint. That's what made him so scary. He didn't fit the profile of the people we watch—not unless you dug deep and looked at him after the fact. He slipped under our radar. He had loose affiliations with a few militia groups, but did most of his work alone—a brilliant strategy, actually. Small, independent cells are harder to track."

"Sounds like a tactic out of the Middle East book of terrorism."

Ruckhauser's eyebrows rose. "Interesting observation. On September tenth, 2001, your typical militia considered all people of color—Arabs included—to be the devil. Suddenly, on September twelfth, the average Neo-Nazi and militia member thought of the al Qaida terrorists as heroes. Anyone willing to fly a plane into a building to kill Jews had to be admired.

"Since then, I think we've seen a convergence between the radical right and some elements of the radical left—conspiratorial anti-globalists and hard-core anarchists in particular; and, most recently, support for foreign anti-American terrorists. It's a disturbing trend. Even mainstream, nonviolent movements— At the fringes of the Occupy Wall Street movement, people were spouting stereotypical rhetoric about the Jews being the bankers who took their homes away."

Uzi took the wood stirrer and sloshed his coffee. Steam rose like a ferocious snake suddenly awakened from its sleep. "Anti-Semitism's been around for centuries. It's not going away anytime soon."

"Do you know the basics of ARM's history?" Uzi nodded. "Okay then. Stop me if I start wasting your time. ARM had been stuck in a financial rut. They'd made a lot of their money by robbing banks— Took in a little over three million until four of them were caught and thrown in jail."

"Around '99 or 2000, right?"

Ruckhauser nodded. "The money was seized, and the heat was

on, but their comrades refused to roll on them. So they were cash-strapped until about six years ago when they merged with SRM, Southern Ranks Militia. SRM's leader, 'General' Lewiston Grant, was a progressive thinker who realized they needed to expand their reach.

"After the merger, they had big membership numbers, but money was still an issue because their plans grew more grandiose. But Grant wanted to raise the funds legally, if possible, because it wouldn't do the group much good if any of them got thrown in jail. He saw an opportunity and took them into business. Instead of selling copies of their racist manifesto, they bought low-end servers and embraced the Internet. They started an entity called Southern Ranks Internet, doing business as SRI—"

"The web-hosting service?"

"That's the one."

"Holy shit," Uzi said. "I had no idea who was behind that."

Ruckhauser's lips spread into a sardonic smile. "That's why they call it SRI. You won't find Southern Ranks Internet spelled out anywhere. We only knew because we were plugged into what they were doing. Their outlay was minimal but the payoff was great. Grant was a self-taught computer whiz, and he set it all up on his own. Within months, they had a steady inflow of money from their members and other white power/neo-Nazi/militia groups. They got everyone to be their marketing force, talking up SRI as a low-cost web-hosting service. Their members who were businessmen switched their websites over to SRI and they had a steady stream of cash coming in every month to cover their maintenance and startup expenses."

"That can be a cash cow business."

"Exactly— Especially when they started getting businesses from beyond their own circle. They started buying cheap server space in India and reselling it. Pure profit. That's when the money really started to flow. That's also around the time when we got some intel that they were purchasing less traceable foreign weapons."

Uzi had taken a drink of coffee, but suddenly pulled the cup from his lips. "Foreign weapons? From where?"

"I don't know."

Uzi nodded slowly, realizing he might have finally found the connection he needed to start building a case against ARM. "If you had to make an educated guess?"

"The field is relatively narrow. Russia, China, and North Korea top the list."

"How much money are we talking about?"

"SRI's obviously privately held, so they don't have to file financials with the SEC. But my people feel it's enough to give them serious spending money—and with that, comes influence."

"Influence. With who?"

Ruckhauser smiled. "You like mystery novels, Uzi?"

"Thrillers mostly. My life can get a little boring at times. Fiction adds some spice." Uzi hesitated, realizing the depth of the truth behind that statement.

"Then here's something that'll raise your eyebrows." Ruckhauser leaned forward in his chair and the spring squeaked. "How about ARM and the NFA in bed together?"

Uzi leaned forward as well, resting his forearms on the desk. "Really."

"I don't know if you heard about it, but there was a guy killed yesterday who was looking into it. You should check it out. Name was Tad Bishop."

"You knew Bishop?"

"Judging by your reaction, I take it you did, too."

"Not well. Met him a couple of times. Was the guy legit?"

"Oh, he lived in his own world. Used to be a private investigator. He left because he couldn't pay his bills, but I think deep down he loved the hunt."

"Credibility-wise—"

"A bit quirky, but he was a straight-shooter. From what I could tell, he was well grounded."

Uzi nodded. "So he was looking into the ARM-NFA connection?"

"Suspected connection," Ruckhauser said. "We had lunch a few weeks ago. He mentioned the players he was looking into. I put two and two together. He wasn't a good friend or anything, just someone I could get together with and shoot the breeze about common stuff."

"Did you know what Bishop was working on—what he'd found out?"

"No." Ruckhauser hesitated. "But based on what he was telling me, I started poking around myself."

"And?"

"And I think there's probably some money laundering going on, a way of passing the cash from the NFA to ARM. I'd guess they're doing it through one of their companies or subsidiaries. Or a well-to-do member who owns a lucrative business."

"Any proof? I can't do anything with theories."

"I gave everything I had to one of your guys at the Bureau. I talk to him a few times a week. Everything I know, everything I've got, he gets. Name's Pablo Garza. Good man."

Uzi thought of his encounter with Garza an hour ago. "Good man" were not the words Uzi would use to describe him. "When did you give him this info?"

"Couple of days ago. Delivered it myself."

Uzi sat there, getting as hot under the collar as his coffee. He rose from his chair. "Then I guess I should go talk with Agent Garza."

"You need anything, give me a holler. Or stop by. When I'm not out sleuthing, I'm right here."

"Yeah, well, be careful. The people who took out Tad Bishop don't want anyone sniffing around their business. You gave us the ball, let us run with it now."

"That's not the way a former journalist thinks."

"Tell that to Daniel Pearl." The *Wall Street Journal* reporter had been kidnapped and murdered by al-Qaeda terrorists—a videotaped beheading shown on the Internet.

"I knew Danny," Ruckhauser said. "The *Journal* lost more than a reporter that day. It lost a brilliant mind and a gentle soul." He looked down at his desk. "Point taken. I'll be careful."

Uzi thanked him, then headed out. He suddenly had an unscheduled appointment, and he had a feeling it was not going to be pleasant.

12:12 PM
97 hours 48 minutes remaining

Uzi did not even acknowledge the sixth-floor receptionist as he breezed past her desk.

She rose from her chair. "Hey, you can't—"

"Watch me," Uzi said under his breath as he rounded the corner. He grabbed the knob of Garza's office and flung open the door.

The room was empty. "Shit," Uzi said. He set his hands on his waist and stared at the empty chair twenty feet in front of him.

"Back so soon?"

The voice came from behind him. He spun, his right hand instinctively reaching for the handle of his Glock, as he'd done so many times before when his brain screamed "imminent danger." But he stopped himself before he'd drawn the weapon, the adrenaline subsiding a bit when he saw Garza standing behind him.

Uzi clenched his jaw. "You're an asshole, Garza."

The agent slid past Uzi into the office, making his way toward his chair. "No, I'm really not. I'm actually well liked by my staff and colleagues. Unlike yourself." He stopped, looked at Uzi, and grinned.

"What's your problem? What did I ever do to you?"

"Why are you here?"

"You didn't answer my question."

Garza took a seat behind his desk and lifted the phone. Uzi flashed across the room like a bobcat, his hand slamming the handset back onto the receiver.

"You seem a bit pissed."

Uzi kept his hand firmly atop Garza's. "You think?"

"Guess I'd better be careful. I don't want to get a visit by OPR," he said, referring to the Bureau's internal affairs police.

Uzi stood up, releasing his grip on Garza's hand. "What?"

"Jake Osborn isn't just my friend, he's a top-notch agent."

Osborn. That's what this is about. I should've seen it coming.

"Jake's paid his dues to get where he is, and then some punk foreigner comes along—"

"Stop right there, asshole. I'm a US citizen. I was born here. Even if I wasn't, so what? Osborn fucked up. He was unsafe. People could've gotten killed. He didn't follow established protocol, which means that if I look the other way, I'm as guilty as he is. It's bad for me, bad for the Bureau. It isn't what we get paid to do."

"We get paid to make the country a safer place. That's what Jake was doing."

"I could've referred him for an OPR, made things a lot worse for him. But I didn't."

"He engaged the suspect against orders because he felt the asshole was dangerous and could've killed others if he'd gotten away. Jake did what he thought was right."

"So did I." Uzi looked away. He had important matters to discuss with Garza, and this wasn't one of them. "I'm here to talk about ARM and the NFA."

Garza spun his chair to face the large picture window that looked out over downtown DC. "We already had that discussion."

"We're gonna have it again. Only this time you're not going to bullshit me. You're gonna tell me what you know."

"What makes you think I didn't already do that?"

"Obstruction of justice is an ugly thing to appear on your resume," Uzi said. He leaned both hands on Garza's desk, and waited.

"You're so good, I figured you'd find out whatever you needed on your own."

"I'm not kidding, Garza. You hindered an investigation, obstructed—"

"Give me a break. Where's the harm? A couple hours of your time? You're back here, asking questions. Maybe it proves you're a smart guy, a decent agent." He turned to Uzi and grinned a one-sided smile. "Then again, maybe it doesn't." He turned back to the window.

"Agent Garza, it's my responsibility to direct the investigation into the attempt on the president-elect's life. Do you understand the implications of all this? If you don't cooperate, the next time I give my report to the director—or the goddamn president—he's gonna know I've hit a roadblock. Call it ratting out, call it tattling, call it whatever the hell you want. I've got a thick hide, and I've heard it all. But I've gotta get to the truth, and no one, not some two-bit punk—and certainly not another agent—is gonna keep me from it. You understand what I'm saying?"

Garza seemed to be weighing the risks. His gaze still on downtown, he said, "I hear you."

"Good. Then tell me about the ARM-NFA connection."

"What do you want to know about it?"

"Karl Ruckhauser sends you all the info that ADL gets their hands on, their intelligence data. You've seen it all. There anything Karl doesn't know about?"

"There's no connection. I couldn't find anything."

"Ruckhauser seemed to think there might be. You sure about your conclusions?"

"All he had were theories. Theories are good for conspiracy theorists like your dead informant. But they don't do jack for us."

"How far did you look into it?"

Garza spun his chair and drew a bead on Uzi's face. "What the fuck does that mean?"

"It was a simple question."

"I did what I was required to do, what we all do to investigate an allegation. I went as far as I could. Without something substantial, there was nothing more to do, nowhere for me to go."

"What do you know about Lewiston Grant?"

"Guy's a dead end. He died in a fire in Utah."

"Find a body?"

"No. But with the level of destruction—"

"How hard did you look into his death?"

"Hard enough. Guy's credit card, bank accounts, apartment, everything went dormant after the bombing. No one's seen him. He's dead."

Uzi reserved judgment on that statement, but let it drop. "What's your gut say? On ARM."

Garza turned back to the window. He seemed to be giving the question some serious thought. Or maybe he was deciding whether or not he wanted to share his opinions with Uzi.

"I think they're involved. If there was a way to get at them, I'd be all over their case."

Uzi pushed off the desk. He had not gotten what he had come for;

however, though he still had no hard evidence against an ARM-NFA alliance, he at least had another supporting opinion from someone with knowledge and experience in dealing with these groups. And that was more than he'd had only a few hours ago.

1:19 PM
96 hours 41 minutes remaining

Uzi answered his cell phone as he entered the Hoover Building's elevator, headed toward the parking garage.

"I found something," Tim Meadows said.

"Cool. What do you got?" Uzi pressed the elevator button to stop the car at the next floor. If Meadows had something significant, he could be there in a couple of minutes.

"After you left, I ran those brass casings through the spectrometer. Turned up some really interesting readings. So I took it upon myself to do some more digging."

"That's what I like about you, Tim. Always going the extra mile."

"Yeah, that's what the section chief says. He loves my work ethic."

"Least you could do after twisting my arm over dinner."

"Well, I think by the time I'm done with this case, I'll have made it worth your while."

The elevator stopped at the next floor. "I'm listening."

"Come by. I'll show you."

Uzi pressed the floor button for the lab. "I'm headed up now. I'm in the building."

"That makes one of us. I'm supposed to be off today, remember? I went home. Come by my house."

"You're working at home? On your day off?"

"That's what the section chief loves about me. My work ethic."

"You said that already."

Meadows chuckled. "He really means it."

After jotting down the directions to Meadows's house in Arlington, Uzi called DeSantos and invited him along for the ride. They arrived at the small two-story colonial residence half an hour later. A tattered American flag hung on a brass flagpole cemented into the front corner of the brown lawn that was dotted with hearty green weeds. Uzi found the doorbell and rang it.

Meadows's voice came from nowhere. "Who is it?"

"Uzi. And my partner."

A buzzer sounded. "Come in and go directly down the stairs to your left."

"Nice setup," DeSantos said to Uzi.

"Thank you," Meadows responded through the hidden speaker.

As they descended the staircase, the scent of mildew poked at Uzi's nose. "Jeez, Tim, you should do a little disinfecting."

"You talking about bugs, or bugs?" Meadows asked from somewhere behind a line of free-standing, floor-to-ceiling metal shelves.

"The mildew kind."

The basement was unfinished. Curtained windows poked through the tops of the cement walls at ten-foot intervals. Spider cracks in the concrete extended in several directions, like tree roots branching out in search of water.

Their heels clicked against the brown tile flooring as they strolled down one of the rows, taking in dozens of half-finished projects that lay in various stages of completion.

"What is all this stuff?" DeSantos asked.

"I dabble in my free time," Meadows said. He squinted at DeSantos. "You are?"

"Sorry," Uzi said. "Hector DeSantos, DOD. He's on the Marine Two task force, coordinating with JTTF."

Meadows cocked his head, sizing up DeSantos. "DOD, huh?" He extended a hand, and DeSantos took it.

"Uzi said you found something."

"Yes, yes," Meadows said, then motioned them to follow him across the room.

As they passed a six-foot-tall black lacquer safe, Uzi said, "You in the banking business?"

"More like munitions," DeSantos said. "This is a gun safe. A big gun safe."

"I keep my projects in there. And my backup data. Media's kept in a smaller compartment, though. Had to build it myself. Tolerance to one hundred twenty-five degrees. Otherwise the SSD drives melt."

"SSD?" DeSantos asked.

Uzi said, "Solid State Disc drives. Flash memory. Safer and more stable than a regular hard drive, which is an electrical-mechanical device that's destined to fail."

DeSantos tilted his head back and looked at Uzi through the lower half of his glasses. "I knew that."

"Yeah," Uzi said. "Of course you did."

"And yes, before you ask, I've also got cloud backup." Meadows moved a few paces to his right, where an LCD monitor stood on a makeshift table that consisted of a plywood board resting on two beat-up sawhorses.

They followed Meadows and stopped behind him, then watched as he tapped at the keys. "After you left, I did some more digging on those large-caliber rounds."

Uzi turned to DeSantos and explained what they had learned about the Russian SV-98 sniper rifle and the spent brass casing they'd recovered from the scene.

"I found an unusual residue on the inside of the casing."

"How unusual?" Uzi asked.

"Unusual enough to be able to give you a specific location of manufacture. Like the former Eastern bloc. Czech Republic."

DeSantos nodded. "That goes with the weapon. And begs the question of who these people are, who they're affiliated with. This is all good stuff. We need to get this info over to the Agency, have them start working it up."

"I'll give it to Leila. She's now on the M2TF, liaison to JTTF."

DeSantos leaned back. "Is that right."

"Don't give me any shit. I had nothing to do with it. Shepard's idea."

"Uh huh."

A series of long, shrill beeps emanated from across the oblong room. Meadows's fingers played across the keyboard and a three-dimensional diagram filled the screen. He leaned closer to the monitor and studied it, as if trying to locate a small side street on a city map. He struck another key and the beeping stopped. "Sorry about that."

"What was that?" Uzi asked.

"'That' was *that*." He swiveled in his chair to indicate a ten-foot-long table on the other side of the room, barely visible behind one of the rows of shelving. "My crown jewel."

"Part of your dabbling?" Uzi asked.

"I've got twenty-three patents already."

DeSantos raised an eyebrow. "Any of them worth anything?"

"Not a dime. Yet. But I don't do it for money, Mr. DeSantos, I do it for the challenge."

"And what kind of a challenge is your crown jewel?" DeSantos asked.

"Come, I'll show you." He rose from his chair and led the way. He stopped in front of the long table. Old-fashioned vacuum tubes projected from wood and metal boards, which were crisscrossed several times with multicolored wires bundled at regular intervals with plastic lock-ties.

"What does it do?"

"It's a new kind of sensor that can detect all kinds of nasty stuff."

"'Nasty stuff'?"

"Bombs, guns, knives, trigger mechanisms, you name it. If it can be made into a weapon, this thing will find it."

"Even plastic resin or carbon fiber composites?" DeSantos asked.

"Yup."

"Don't we already have something like that?"

"Yes and no. We've got all kinds of fancy sensors, most of them developed after 9/11. But they can't do all the things this can do. Most check for metal or metal alloys. Some sniff for explosive materials. Some can detect certain kinds of resin composites. But this thing can find it all. Along with the software I'm writing for it. Best yet, it'll do it for a fraction of the price these companies are charging the government for their high-tech gizmos. With an off-the-shelf Intel chip, this thing'll only run a couple hundred bucks, assuming it's mass produced with economies of scale."

"Yeah, but does it really work?" Uzi asked.

"Seeing is believing. Here, I'll show you."

DeSantos checked his watch. "We really should get this info over to Leila—"

Meadows turned to a shelf behind him and dug into a shoebox full of parts. "It'll only take a couple of minutes. You gotta see this."

Before DeSantos could object, Meadows was handing Uzi a tiny square of light gray plastic. "Hide this somewhere."

Uzi did as instructed, dropping it into his left jacket pocket. Meadows lifted the screen of a nearby laptop and hit a button that woke it from sleep. He poked another key, then grabbed a thick, brushed stainless steel wand fitted with blue LEDs. "It's all wireless," he said proudly.

Meadows started at Uzi's head and brought the wand down slowly. The device was silent, until the same shrill beep they had heard moments ago blared from a console on the table.

"Hmm," Uzi said. "Impressive."

But Meadows's gaze was still directed at the wand. He continued to wave it over Uzi's coat, two LEDs flashing blue, then three, then four. And then the wand began vibrating.

"Take it off for a sec," Meadows said.

"This is all fun stuff, I'm sure," DeSantos said, "but we really should go."

But Meadows had already grabbed the collar of the coat and was peeling it off Uzi's body.

"What's the problem?" Uzi asked as he pulled his hand through the sleeve.

Meadows turned the jacket around and continued to wand the inside lining, watching the LED patterns change. "What have you got in here?"

"Just my phone."

"No, it's not your phone. See, this is your phone here." He wanded the right pocket and the pitch of the alarm changed. "And this is the resin block I gave you." Again, the sound changed. "Here," Meadows said as he glanced over his shoulder at the laptop, "is something else."

"Something else?"

Meadows pulled a Leatherman from his pocket and opened the knife.

"Whoa," Uzi said, "wait a minute. What are you doing?"

Meadows sliced through the lining of the jacket, along the lower seam.

"Jesus, Tim, that jacket cost me five hundred bucks—"

"Here, look." Meadows prodded and poked at the silk lining with his fingers and produced a plastic disc the size and thickness of a dime. He held it up between thumb and forefinger, then brought it close to the wand. The shrill beep sounded, the wand vibrated strongly, and the lights flickered and flashed as if it were a Geiger counter passing over uranium.

Uzi squinted at the small device. *What the hell is that?*

Meadows contorted his brow. "Jesus, Uzi, you didn't tell me you had a spare phone battery in your pocket." He put his index finger to his lips, then nodded across the room where his PC sat.

Clearly, Meadows felt the small device was a bug, and until he proved or disproved his theory, they had to operate as if it was. "My Nokia sometimes goes into roam and drains the battery in forty-five minutes," Uzi said, hoping to make the conversation seem realistic. "Hasn't happened in a while. Sorry. Forgot I had it in my pocket." *Why didn't my own sensor pick up the bug?*

Uzi and DeSantos watched as Meadows pulled a microscope from the shelf below the computer and plugged it into the PC's USB port.

"Not a problem," Meadows said. "But I told you this thing worked."

"When do you apply for a patent?"

"Already applied for." Meadows turned the knob on the microscope and an image appeared on the screen. "Takes a while to get a number. That's why you always see 'Patent Pending' on products. But I think it's too sensitive." Meadows found the area of the device he was looking for, then pointed at the monitor. "I need to make some refinements in the design. Mind if I take down a few notes? Only take me a minute."

"Go ahead," DeSantos said, squinting at the hyper-enlarged image.

Uzi pulled out his smartphone and pressed a couple of buttons, then moved it over the device Meadows was examining. Nothing.

Meadows double-clicked the Word icon on his desktop. He typed at the cursor:

> This is a very sophisticated listening device. It contains no magnetic parts. Its components appear to be resin and gold.

> Nothing that would be detected by conventional sensing equipment.

Yeah, no kidding. Uzi moved in front of the keyboard and typed:

> I'll bring it by the lab in the morning. We can't disable it or we'll tip them off. Can you examine it without destroying it?

Meadows:

> Yes.

Uzi leaned over the keyboard:

> There could be others. Does the Bureau have anything that can detect these things?

DeSantos nudged Uzi aside and typed:

> NSA's got a handheld unit, the NX-590. I can make a call, have one waiting for us by the time we get there.

DeSantos rooted out his BlackBerry and moved off to the far corner of the room.

Meadows said, "Almost done with these notes. Give me another minute," as he typed to Uzi:

> I know that unit. Not as good as mine, but it can pick up gold and other weak metallic conductors.

Uzi tapped out:

> We should let NSA take a crack at this thing, see what they can figure out.

He clapped Meadows on the back. "We've really gotta go, Tim.

Always a pleasure." Uzi winked. "If you find anything more on that ammo, let me know."

Meadows removed the listening device from the microscope and handed it to Uzi, who dropped it into his intact jacket pocket.

"Wish I could've done more."

"Hey," Uzi said, "you earned yourself an appetizer."

Meadows's face brightened considerably. "Oysters?"

Uzi threw a protective hand over his wallet. "You're killing me, Tim."

Meadows indicated Uzi's jacket pocket and said, "I think that may be someone else's job."

4:03 PM
93 hours 57 minutes remaining

The drive to Annapolis, Maryland, was strained. Uzi had removed his bugged coat and placed it in the rear compartment, then turned on the stereo and faded it to the back of the SUV as a cover.

"I've never been here," Uzi said. "Tell me about the NSA. Behind the scenes stuff." He turned onto the Baltimore-Washington Parkway and accelerated. Noting his partner's questioning eyes, Uzi explained: "We've got at least another half hour to kill."

"I signed a nondisclosure agreement."

"Give me the abridged version. Nothing classified. Just some highlights and background."

"Highlights and background." DeSantos pursed his lips. "Don't you know this stuff?"

"Probably some of it. But our agencies aren't exactly best pals. Assume I'm a blank slate."

"Okay. Let's start in 1919."

"We're talking serious background here."

"It was called The Cipher Bureau, or The Black Chamber, in those days. I think it was a one-room vault that held all the intelligence we had at the time, stuff we'd collected by cracking codes we intercepted from the Japanese and Russians. But the Chamber didn't exist, at least not as far as the government was concerned. Know why?"

"Uh, because it was a secret?"

DeSantos chuckled. "You're being a wiseass, boychick. But you're close. The Cipher Bureau operated out of New York and was a front business for The Black Chamber's real work, which was breaking codes. They were doing some great work until the secretary of state found out about it and shut it down because he didn't believe in reading others' letters and mail."

"You're joking."

"No joke. The Chamber closed up shop. The data they'd collected was thrown into a vault and remained on ice until 1930 when the Army realized it needed an advantage over unfriendly governments. They asked their chief cryptanalyst, a guy named William Friedman, to build the Signal Intelligence Service with the help of three of his math teacher buddies. He hid the SIS, its employees, and its budget from everyone. And we were back in the spy business."

DeSantos turned away. He seemed to be lost in thought, but then said, "Just like the Black Chamber was a closet, the NSA is literally the size of a city." He turned the stereo up a bit more and leaned closer to Uzi. "Crypto City's got 10 million square feet of offices, warehouses, factories, labs, schools, and apartments. Tens of thousands of people live and work there—and no one outside its walls knows what they do for a living or that the place even exists."

"Tens of thousands?" Uzi had known it was a lot, but that was a number far exceeding even his highest guestimates.

"Bigger than the CIA and FBI. Combined, by a long shot. And growing."

DeSantos continued his dissertation for another twenty minutes, until they arrived in Annapolis Junction. Uzi turned off the Baltimore-Washington Parkway onto a hidden exit ramp bounded by berms and dense foliage, then drove through the maze of barbed-wire fences, where yellow signs warned against taking photographs, making notes, or drawing sketches.

"Typical intelligence agency," Uzi said. "A bit paranoid."

"That's like saying the US Army has a few guns."

Uzi laughed. "Bet their surveillance cameras are better than ARM's."

"Trust me. You don't want to find out."

Uzi parked near Operations Building 1 and waited for DeSantos to complete his business. In the twenty minutes he sat there, three different guards approached, inspected his identification, then questioned his reason for being on-site.

When DeSantos mercifully returned, he said, "If they come up with anything, they'll let us know." DeSantos shut his door. "Actually, they'll let *me* know."

They left Crypto City and made their way to Uzi's office at WFO. After parking in the underground garage, they took the elevator up to the third floor. While DeSantos used the restroom down the hall, Uzi did a complete sweep of his work area. Satisfied it was clean, he set the scanning device on his desk and reached for a toothpick.

"Nice digs," DeSantos said, his neck craning around to take in all the wall hangings.

Uzi turned slowly, taking in the décor. "Guess it's a work in progress." Despite lithographs from noted American artists, there were only three personal items in the office: a framed photo of Dena, Maya, and himself standing among the ancient ruins of Beit She'an, south of the Sea of Galilee; a six-inch square Lucite block containing one of the first Pentium 4 chips to come off the Intel line bearing the inscription: "In recognition for a winning design, this is hereby presented to Lead Engineer Aaron Uziel, Intel Pentium 4 Willamette Development Team"; and a ratty, battle-worn canteen with a large bullet hole in the side, from Uzi's required duty tour with the Israel Defense Forces.

DeSantos lifted the canteen from the bookshelf. It clattered like a baby's rattle.

"Canteen from my Efod." Noticing DeSantos's confusion, Uzi said, "An Efod is an equipment vest."

DeSantos shook it a bit, then held it up and looked through the hole. "What's in it?"

"Syrian sniper's bullet. That hollow piece of tin saved my life."

DeSantos returned the canteen to the shelf. "I ever tell you you've got strange keepsakes?"

Uzi sunk down into his leather chair. "You've never been here?"

"Shit no," DeSantos said. "We always meet somewhere. You've never been to my office either. It's always a park or a restaurant or a car or something."

Uzi, sucking on the toothpick, spread his arms wide. "Welcome to my humble office."

"Humble?"

"For a peon task force head."

"Oh, yes. A peon." DeSantos said, using his fingers as quotation marks in the air. "Right. That's why you have an office instead of a cubicle."

"Well it ain't because everyone here likes me."

"I like you. Doesn't that count?"

"I think that may work against me."

DeSantos took a seat in front of Uzi's desk. "Go to hell."

Uzi pushed aside the stacked messages on his desk. "So . . . where are we?"

"Given what we found in your jacket," DeSantos said, "maybe now's the right time."

"Right time for what?"

"May I?" He indicated the laptop Hoshi had been using, then sat down and logged on to the Pentagon's Intelligence Support Agency database. He played the keys for a moment, then leaned back and turned the laptop so Uzi could see the screen.

"I had my buddy at NSA take some photos of the ARM compound."

"Sat photos?"

"With those KH-12s," DeSantos said, referring to the Strategic Response Reconnaissance Satellites. "The ones usually trained on Cuba. I had them rotate their axis a bit."

Uzi's brow rose. "No shit?"

"No shit. Had my guy do something like this a few months ago for Karen. Worked like a charm."

Spying on US citizens was not a good road to travel. But when terrorism was suspected and lives were at stake, well . . . Uzi had struggled with that issue on many occasions. But each time information led to the preemption of an attack, and he knew it was the right call. But it still bothered him. He glanced at DeSantos. "And?"

"There are three buildings that pique my interest." He struck a sequence of keys and a split screen of four images appeared. "Two sheds and a garage. With some unusual activity the night of the ninth. Trucks backing up to it making what I'd guess were deliveries."

"Deliveries? What kind of trucks?"

"Trucks. Plain cab-over cargo deals."

"So? Could've been delivering food. Or office supplies for the compound."

DeSantos peered over the tops of his glasses at Uzi. "Yeah, right."

"Wait a minute. The ninth. The hospital was bombed on the tenth."

DeSantos elevated his eyebrows and tilted his head.

"But what would they need trucks for?"

"Don't know. But we need to get onto the compound, take a look around those three buildings."

Uzi lifted the phone. "I'll get a warrant."

DeSantos reached across the desk and disconnected the call. "Put that thing down."

"Why?"

"No judge in his right mind would give us a warrant. For what? What's ARM done that we have proof of? Besides," DeSantos said, lowering his voice, "even if Knox said to continue investigating them, I'd rather not tip our hand yet that we're still on their case. Not till after we're in and out, and hopefully know more about what to look for."

Uzi's intestines twisted and turned. This was wrong—even if the director of the FBI gave the order, and even if President Whitehall had told him to do "whatever it takes to get the job done." He stared at the screen, attempting to rationalize his involvement. No matter how he turned it over, this was outside his comfort zone. "They've got security cameras all over that damn compound," he finally said.

"Not a problem." DeSantos returned to his seat and struck another series of keys. "We go at night, wear dark clothing and ski masks."

"Those cameras are infrared. They'll definitely pick us up."

DeSantos found what he was looking for and clicked on a file.

"Take a look." A grainy photo appeared on the left, a line diagram with callouts and descriptions to its right. "They look like Night Prowlers, manufactured by CCT. Computerized Camera Technologies. Standard motion sensor activation, sensor range up to fifteen feet at night. No night vision capabilities."

"Looks like them, but how can you be sure?"

"Because I'm sure."

Uzi studied the image on the display, then said, "They might have motion-activated spotlights. If that's the case, image clarity rises and the range of the cameras just about doubles. Sometimes that's better than night vision."

"Right on both accounts. But we'll be fine if we move carefully and wear the new light-absorbing clothing DARPA's been working on," DeSantos said. The Defense Advanced Research Projects Agency developed all sorts of new—and often futuristic—technology for the DOD. "B-one stealth technology." DeSantos clicked again, and another four photos appeared: uniformed soldiers acting like the military's equivalent of GQ, depicting the latest in warfare garb.

Uzi leaned close to the screen, examining the images with the care a jeweler uses to appraise a gem. He moved the toothpick to the other side of his mouth, then leaned back. "I still think it's too risky. Even with this special clothing, even if we're careful, we're letting it all hang out. No backup. Not to mention the law's working against us. We'd be totally on our own. Anything happens, no one will sanction what we've done. It'll be like we jumped in a tub of horseshit. No one will go near us."

"That's why we have to make it work," DeSantos said. "That's why we'll need a diversion."

Uzi leaned back in his chair.

"Are you hesitating because you don't think we can pull it off," DeSantos said, "or because it's a black op on US soil?"

Uzi smiled out of the corner of his mouth. "Does it really matter what I think?"

"It matters to me."

Uzi's tongue played with the toothpick. After a long moment, he sighed deeply. "What do you have in mind?"

"My buddies, at OPSIG."

"You said OPSIG was off limits."

"All I said was that Knox had reasons for not using OPSIG. And no, I don't know what those reasons are."

"So what's changed?"

"This is a more involved, sensitive operation. To work, we need help. Experienced help. The best of the best."

"What do you have in mind?"

"Still working it through. But whatever we do, they'll help execute it. They'll make it work."

"Aren't these the same guys you said would protect Knox to the end of time?"

"I didn't exactly say that—"

"But it's true."

DeSantos shrugged. "Yeah."

Uzi stood up and walked over to his office window. He didn't know who was in whose pocket: the NFA, Knox, apparently Coulter to some degree . . . OPSIG. DeSantos? "I'm not real comfortable with this."

"What happened to you, boychick? You used to be ready to go and do. If the plan made sense, you were on the next bus."

"Yeah, that was then. This is now."

DeSantos joined Uzi at the window. "That's a bullshit answer."

Uzi knew DeSantos was right. He sighed. "Remember at the crash site you asked me about Leila, and my wife? And I told you it wasn't something I wanted to get into?"

"It's important we don't have any secrets from each other. If there's something that'll affect the way you'd react—"

"It's not like that."

"Sure it is."

Uzi hesitated, then shoved his hands into his back pockets. "Yeah, I guess it is." He sighed, then decided to press on. After spilling his guts to Rudnick—and then Leila—it didn't feel like sacred ground anymore. "My wife and daughter were killed by terrorists six years ago. A Palestinian terror cell affiliated with al-Humat found out where I lived, and slaughtered them. Tortured them first, then slashed their throats, nearly down to the spine. Then they set off a small bomb to announce what they'd done."

Uzi stared out at the city below, seeing not Washington but his little villa in Israel, the police cars and emergency vehicles strewn at odd angles in the street out front. The cloths draped over his family's bodies, then the body bags as the Israeli medical examiners and rabbis, in well-practiced fashion, carted away the corpses.

"I hadn't followed orders. I broke with protocol. And because of that . . ." A tear coursed down his cheek. "Because of that I'm here. And my family isn't."

DeSantos swung his left arm around Uzi's shoulders and pulled him close. "I'm sorry, man. I didn't know."

Uzi was in another world, sorrow and longing numbing his body, the pain of nightmarish memories stinging his soul like a poisonous spider. Wishing he was alone, or with Rudnick.

"If you don't want to do this, I'll talk to Knox. Maybe he'll understand and let me pull someone from OPSIG to take the point with me."

Uzi pushed away, then wiped his sleeve across moist eyes. He was never one to shirk his responsibilities. And Knox wouldn't understand: he'd interpret it as a psychological inability to perform, impacting his position as head of the Joint Terrorism Task Force—perhaps even costing his job as a field agent. Right now, he had enough to lug around without adding the loss of a career to his burden. He sniffled, then squared his shoulders. "I'm in, Santa. My job is to defend the United States against terrorists, and no one's going to prevent me from doing that."

"Even if it means breaking protocol?"

Uzi looked away.

"Uzi, we all make mistakes in life. I made one that left my partner dead and his wife widowed. You met her. Trish, back at the house, with Presley. My goddaughter. I don't blame myself because I know Brian wouldn't blame me. We went on missions with the understanding that we'd always do our best no matter what. We'd watch each other's backs like brothers. But nobody's perfect. Missions get fucked for reasons beyond your control. Sometimes it's because of what you do. You make a split-second decision and react. Most of the time you're right. But that one time you're wrong . . ." He shook his head. "We knew all that. We'd even talked about it a few times. We told each other that if one of us made a mistake and only one of us walked away, those are the risks. We do a very dangerous job. Death comes with the territory."

Uzi appreciated DeSantos's words. But Dena and Maya were innocent victims. They didn't know what he did for a living and they had no such pact with him. In an insane world where going to a café could end with a suicide bomber blowing a dozen citizens to bits, terrorism was a fact of life. But leading the enemy to his family's doorstep was an error for which he could never be absolved.

He turned toward the window and looked out. The FBI director and the president of the United States were supposedly backing this mission. A big part of him wanted in, and if he continued to show conflict, DeSantos would go to Knox, and Uzi did not want that.

"Let's do it," he said.

"You sure?"

Uzi pulled out his chewed toothpick and tossed it in the garbage. "That diversion will make or break us."

The corners of DeSantos's lips lifted slightly. "I'll show you what I've got so far."

5:26 PM
92 hours 34 minutes remaining

Uzi sat through DeSantos's presentation, which was laid out point by point in hushed tones at his desk. DeSantos's OPSIG comrades were to fly a Black Hawk helicopter to the front gates of ARM's headquarters. They would take an erratic flight path and dump gray smoke out the rear, courtesy of the countermeasure ports designed to create a smokescreen for pursuing enemies.

But this would be a smoke screen of a different sort: simulated damage to the fuel tank that forced the helicopter to land. ARM's front gate sat in a small clearing considered too narrow to set down a Black Hawk. For OPSIG's crack pilots, however, it was another skill-sharpening exercise.

Uzi saw where the plan was going as DeSantos continued: once the chopper was over the compound spewing smoke, conveniently illuminated by the helicopter's aftermarket rear spotlights that were now being installed, Uzi and DeSantos would infiltrate the grounds half a mile away, on the far side by a stretch of double chain-link fencing topped with coiled barbed wire.

DeSantos tapped the screen, indicating the exact point of entry. "Piece of cake."

Uzi had to admit, the plan looked good. The diversion would be effective—and would no doubt cause all of ARM's parasoldiers to scurry to the main gate to defend their property. The sight of "black government helicopters" landing at their front door was tantamount to their worst paranoiac dreams coming true. By the time the ruckus quieted and the OPSIG troops explained they were having mechanical problems, Uzi and DeSantos would be inside the compound looking for proof of the group's involvement. At least, that was the plan.

After DeSantos left, Uzi played it through in his mind, employing a technique a senior Mossad agent had taught him many years ago: treat the planned action as a film, going through each step of the operation as if he were watching it on a screen, seeing every detail, considering all possible scenarios. That way, when a drama occurred, he wouldn't have to think; he'd simply react based on what he had visualized in his "film." In theory, this method of visualization worked. In practice, it helped the team leader prepare his team. But because there were myriad variables, each with its own inherent problems, there was no way anyone could predict with certainty what was going to happen.

Uzi would leave the planning of the Black Hawk portion of the operation to DeSantos; he would have to pour over the satellite images DeSantos had left on his PC and devise a plan of action from their own point of entry to the selection of targets, successful penetration, and extraction—all without leaving sign.

Now alone in his office, Uzi saw Hoshi appear in the doorway.

"Got a minute?"

"Before I forget," Uzi said, "I just emailed you a profile drawn up by Karen Vail at the BAU. Have someone cross reference all known offenders and see if it gives us anything worth following up. I meant to get it to you sooner, but I haven't been at my desk long enough to make sense of my dictated notes."

"Will do."

He struck a key to close the encrypted satellite photo he had been studying, then swung his feet off his desk and faced her. "Okay, now you."

She entered carrying a folder and grabbed a seat.

"I've done some more digging. And it definitely gets interesting." She flipped open the file to a well-organized stack of papers, then paged to a specific document. "President Whitehall was basically elected on the strength of the NFA. Not just money, like they contributed to Knox's senatorial war chest. They did that for Whitehall, too, for his first campaign—and in a very creative way. They set up a nonprofit, the American Liberties Consortium, which was allowed to raise unlimited funds—in Whitehall's case, the tally was twenty-seven million dollars. The ALC then contributed all twenty-seven mil to the Committee for Preservation of American Liberties, which can spend an unlimited amount on getting Whitehall elected."

"Why bother with the nonprofit shell?"

"It keeps their donor list private."

"Of course." Uzi frowned. "Sounds like legal money laundering."

"There's more. They also donated three-point-five million directly to the Republican National Committee, another fourteen million to support 'unaffiliated' groups, TV and radio ads, you know the drill."

Uzi reached into his drawer for another toothpick as he absorbed the numbers. "Go on. You said their 'contribution' wasn't just money."

"Right. While still governor of Texas, after Whitehall declared, he corralled some key NFA people. Haven't been able to confirm it yet, but I'd guess he called in some chips. NFA had their own agenda, too, so it might've just been a mutual feeding frenzy. They knew the threat to their values the Democrats would've forced down their throats, and they knew that Allen Moore, the Democratic challenger, was a major force. So they mobilized a grassroots get-out-the-vote campaign against Moore. They used the gun issue to win votes. It was a brilliant tactic, really. They went right to the heart of the Democrats' support—and monetary—network."

"Organized labor?"

"Yup. They polarized the union members by playing to their fears about losing their rights to own guns. First line of attack was the media: magazine articles drumming home the point that NFA was not antilabor, using smoke and mirrors to point out everything they did to protect jobs. Their reasoning was circular, but it didn't matter: they repeated the lie so many times it was eventually accepted as fact. Second line of attack was convincing the members that the only difference that mattered between the Republicans and Democrats was their position on gun policy. They developed a catchy phrase: Vote Whitehall. Keep your jobs. Keep your money. Keep your guns."

She flipped another few pages. "The strategy was extremely effective. According to a friend of mine who worked on Moore's campaign, the split of the union vote was like a dagger to the Democrats' heart. Basically, NFA was pivotal in defeating Moore in West Virginia, Tennessee, and Arkansas. If Moore had won even one of them, the White House would've been his. And the gun lobby would've taken a big one on the chin. They'd probably still be on their heels today, playing defense instead of offense."

Uzi leaned back in his chair, chewing on his toothpick. "So their strength comes from their alliance with Whitehall's administration?"

"That's only part of the story. They took their victory and power and parlayed it into more of both. They're well funded and very well organized. And they have millions of members committed to the same goal. They took in two-hundred-fifty-thousand new members in the last eighteen months alone. These are people who tend to feel threatened by the government—and they're willing to take action to secure their rights and maintain their power base."

"Sounds like a militia mentality."

"That's because they were in danger of becoming extinct, but were 'saved' by 9/11. Fear swept over the country. People from the fringes of society—the militias—found strength in numbers, so they took matters into their own hands. They joined in droves. They all shared a common mentality: they loved guns, cherished conspiracy theories, distrusted government, hated gun control, were politically active—and united against a common enemy."

Uzi shook his head. "Still, the mix doesn't seem like a formula for rising to power like they've done. Militias have been around for ages, but they've never advanced beyond a certain point. How did NFA go from militia ally to right-wing powerhouse?"

"There was another big shift," Hoshi said as she flipped back to the front page of the file. "Nine years ago. They merged with the American Gun Society. AGS was a small, growing organization that wasn't on our radar. The merger seemed insignificant at the time, and nobody paid attention to it. But it brought an influx of new leadership, which was important because they were battling a powerful adversary: the NRA. Both were going after the same base. But the merger with AGS gave the NFA critical mass. Within a year, after a nasty grab for the top spot, Skiles Rathbone rose out of the dust."

"This was around the same time Knox became director?"

Hoshi did not need to consult her notes. "Six months before."

"So Rathbone and Knox rose together. Coincidence?" It was a rhetorical question, Uzi thinking aloud, but Hoshi was sitting on his words.

"Possibly." She closed the folder. "NFA is now the leading lobbying organization in the country. It's got its own national newscast, over a million political organizers, an army of pollsters, and its own telemarketing company. It's a lobbying machine."

Lobbying. "Do me a favor, check on Russell Fargo's lobbying firm, see if there's a connection—any at all—to NFA."

Hoshi nodded, gathered up the folder, and rose. "Anything else?"

"Yeah, get with Pablo Garza at HQ on a guy named Lewiston Grant. Supposedly died in a fire in Utah, but I've got my doubts. Garza won't be much help, but he might tell you more than he'd tell me. Charm him."

Hoshi lifted her brow. "Okay."

"Anything comes up, let me know."

She turned and headed out, stopping only when Uzi called her name.

"Excellent work," he said.

She smiled, then shut the door behind her.

6:36 PM
91 hours 24 minutes remaining

Echo Charlie reclined in his car seat, the Sat phone pressed to his ear. In the failing daylight, he watched a man dressed in threadbare jeans and a ragged cloth jacket search trash cans in the park, extracting a few spent Coke bottles and shoving them into a ratty canvas bag in his shopping cart.

"He knows about our . . . instrument," Charlie said into the encrypted handset. "Our route of information is compromised."

After a moment of silence, Alpha Zulu asked, "Can you replace something like that?"

"My people have some ideas."

"*Ideas*? Things are in play. If you can't fix it—soon—we'll take care of it ourselves."

Even though it was chilly inside his car, beads of perspiration were forming across Charlie's brow. He flapped his overcoat to cool himself. "We've got it handled," he said, only half believing his own assurance. He hoped his voice was not betraying him.

"If you'd let us do it our way in the first place," Zulu said, "this wouldn't have happened."

Charlie blew some frustration through his lips. "Give us a day to get it fixed."

"A day is all you have. The time is—"

"I'm aware of the time, thank you very much."

The man with the shopping cart was headed in his direction, drawing Charlie's attention. Charlie tucked his chin and started to turn away—but something about the guy's face seemed wrong. It took a moment, but he finally realized what it was: the man was clean shaven.

"I've gotta go," Charlie said. "I'll contact you when I have something to report." He ended the call, then tapped his brakes three times, signaling his colleague dressed in a park police uniform thirty yards back. If this homeless person was, in fact, someone sent to spy on him, within five minutes he would be questioned and killed, his body expertly searched, ID confiscated, fingerprints and DNA samples taken.

And then the corpse would be disposed of with Jimmy Hoffa efficiency.

8:29 PM
89 hours 31 minutes remaining

Uzi remained at the office another two hours, stopping only to grab a snack to maintain functional blood-sugar levels. With less than twenty-four hours before they infiltrated the ARM compound, he logged off his PC and closed his mind to further intrusion. He was tired of thinking and needed to unwind.

He left the WFO parking lot, driving without thought to where he was going. Ten minutes later, he found himself stopped at a traffic light at 21st and N Streets, half a block from Leila's apartment building. He leaned forward, chin kissing the steering wheel, and trained his eyes on the eighth floor of her building, peering through the barren tree branches, wondering if she was home.

Remembering that her living room looked out over New Hampshire, he tried to estimate which balcony would be hers. One was lit, while several adjacent windows were dark.

He waited for the green light, then pulled in front of her building and saw the tall, wiry Alec in the lobby, jotting something into his journal on the stand by the door. Uzi parked his car in the passenger loading zone and tossed Alec the keys. Jiri, standing behind the reception desk, raised a bushy eyebrow in surprise, then told Uzi he would take care of his car for him.

Uzi proceeded up the elevator to Leila's floor, all the while wondering why he was there, and if Dena was looking down on him with disdain. As the doors slid apart, he stood there, lost in thought, until they started closing. He stuck out his hand and they snapped back. He walked out of the elevator and strode the twenty feet down the carpeted hall to Leila's apartment.

Uzi raised his hand to knock, but left it there, poised but inactive. Showing up unannounced, after only their first intimate date, was a bit strange, for sure. Would it show weakness, that he couldn't go a full day without seeing her? If so, was that bad—or was it good?

How could he be thinking of such things? How could he betray Dena like this? *She would want me to get on with my life; she'd want me to be happy. But I got her killed. I was responsible. How can I be with Leila? I don't deserve to be happy—*

Uzi turned and started down the hall, back toward the elevator. Five long strides and he had pressed the down button.

But before the car came, he heard a latch throw and the jiggle of a doorknob. Rather than turn around, he focused on the closed doors, willing the elevator to arrive.

"Uzi?"

He twisted his neck. Dressed in a suit and high heels, Leila had one foot inside the apartment and one in the hallway, a bulging Hefty bag in her hands and the door resting against her buttock. She put the garbage down in the middle of the threshold, then started toward him.

He turned his body fully toward her, regretting the question he knew would be on her lips.

"What are you doing here?"

And there it was. "I thought I'd stop by, surprise you," he said, taking the honest approach.

"I didn't hear the doorbell," she said, looking back at the door as if the glance would explain why it hadn't worked.

"Did you eat?" he asked.

"I just got home," she said. She took another few steps toward him, her long legs grabbing his eyes and refusing to let go. "I was going to cook up some eggplant parmigiana. Why don't you stay, have some with me?"

He stood there, his feet riveted to the ground as if stuck in cement. The arriving elevator dinged. He turned his head to look, but before he could make a move, he felt fingers hook his left elbow, gently urging him forward, toward her apartment.

Leila called to Uzi to turn on the oven while she changed out of her work clothes. He stood there staring at the digital readout, trying to make sense of the display. He was a whiz with a keyboard or circuit board, but in the kitchen, it was like the intelligence got sucked out of his brain cells. After several failed attempts, he pushed the right buttons and the oven began to heat.

Looking over the LED readout, satisfied he had initiated the preheat process and not a countdown toward a nuclear launch, he let a smile of accomplishment creep across his lips.

He found a bottle of Niebaum-Coppola Estate Merlot and poured two glasses, flashing on the first day when he had met Leila at the crash site. Aloof, unwilling to let him into her life—and now, a warm savior, taking him by the arm and pulling him to safety.

He lifted the wine glasses off the counter, then turned toward the living room. He nearly slammed into Leila, who was right behind him, standing there in a white lace negligee and spiked high heels. Her hair was tousled and she was wearing glitter lip gloss.

Uzi had to fight from losing his grip on the glasses. She leaned forward, between his occupied hands, and let her lips brush his. He could hardly breathe. His chest was tight, the heat from the oven suddenly unbearable.

She reached up to each of his hands, removed the glasses, and placed them on the counter. She then turned and walked out of the kitchen, her buttocks sliding beneath the short negligee, pulling him forward, inviting him to follow.

DAY SIX

6:00 AM
80 hours remaining

Uzi toweled off as he walked toward the living room, leaving Leila to finish showering. The sun was beginning to wake up along with the rest of the district. The evening was past him, the guilt simmering beneath the surface, new fodder for internal conflict. What had been a wonderful night with Leila had turned into "buyer's remorse" in the morning.

He lifted the phone and dialed Rudnick's home number. He kept his request short: he needed to talk. With the op scheduled for this evening, he needed to get this off his chest so he could be fully focused on the mission. In the past, he would've pushed it out of his mind and stuck it in his emotional closet, shoved back behind boxes and old memories. But if there was one thing his sessions with Rudnick had taught him, it was better to deal with such issues sooner, rather than later, before they morphed into painful, longlasting complications. He thought of the old computer monitors, and how images would get burned into the screen if left there indefinitely. He needed to avoid the burn-in factor.

As he hung up, he became aware of Leila standing behind him. She wrapped her arms around his waist, her hands reaching down through the towel that draped across his front.

"I've gotta go," he said. "An appointment."

She groaned disappointment, but withdrew her hands without protest.

He kissed her lightly on the lips, then moved into the bedroom to dress.

Uzi arrived at Rudnick's office, his thoughts in greater disarray than his rumpled clothes. He waited outside the doctor's main entrance, pacing back and forth, absently running both hands through his damp hair. Back doors, secret entrances were no longer a concern.

He was making his third pass when Rudnick exited the elevator, moving as fast as his short legs and arthritic knees would permit. Rudnick cancelled the alarm, then nudged his patient through the door. He flicked on the fluorescent lights and they hummed loudly, as if complaining because they had been called into work earlier than usual.

Rudnick disappeared into a narrow anteroom beside the reception area. "Coffee or tea?"

"Absolution. Got any of that in there?"

Rudnick poked his head out the door. "Got some in here," he said, an index finger pointing to his temple.

"I sure could use some," Uzi mumbled. He walked into Rudnick's treatment room, turned on the doctor's desk lamp, and studied the books on the shelf: *Caring for the Mind*; *Psychoneuroses*; *Handbook of Dissociative Disorders*; *Relationship Issues; The Psychology of Living*— Uzi stopped on the last one and was tempted to page through it when Rudnick walked in, a steaming coffee mug in hand.

"If this gets any earlier, I'm going to have to buy a futon to keep in my office."

"Sorry," Uzi said. "I've got a lot of stuff on my mind and I've felt things I haven't felt in years. Maybe never. I don't know what to make of it, how to handle it. And I've got this important . . . mission tonight, and I—"

"How about taking a seat. Relax."

"I can't, I don't feel like sitting. I need to . . . to move around."

"Okay," Rudnick said with a lilting voice. "Let's start with what's happened since our last visit."

"It's Leila. I know we talked about this, but I'm having problems getting past Dena. I keep coming back to her. I don't know what it is. I mean, there's guilt, I've got that one nailed. But there's something else. There's something about Leila. I'm drawn to her and I enjoy being with her, but every time I'm around her I get these visions of Dena."

"And you don't think it's guilt?"

"The guilt hits me at other times, like when I'm thinking about going to see her. But this is different. This happens when I'm with her."

"The mind is a very complex thing, Uzi. Sensory cues can set off visions, memories that transport us through time and space. Maybe there's something about her that reminds you of Dena. And those cues are stimulating these memories."

Uzi stopped pacing for a moment and was standing in front of a wall adorned with a framed lithograph of a late twenties Conde Nast cover. But he was not looking at the print. He was thinking about what Rudnick had said. "That can't be right, Doc, to be with a beautiful woman and be daydreaming about someone else. That's not normal."

"The way we process our senses is not completely understood, Uzi. But we know the brain forms associations with certain sensory memories and imprints them so that when we get a sensory impulse—a scent, a sound, a certain song—the brain references the memory we've associated with that sensation. Maybe by unlocking these emotions, you're discovering all sorts of imprinted sensations you weren't aware even existed."

Uzi listened intently to Rudnick's explanation, paced a bit more, and then stopped. "Maybe." He found the chair beside him and sat heavily, draping his long arms over the armrests.

"Perhaps we need to explore the concept of guilt more closely. It's a very powerful emotion. It can motivate or it can suffocate. It can remain beneath the surface, or come to the forefront with such a vengeance that it can affect our ability to socialize. It can permeate every facet of our life, including how we relate to coworkers, friends, significant others." He waved a hand. "But you didn't come here for a lecture. It's best if you do most of the talking."

Uzi sat there, lost in thought as the seconds passed.

Finally, Rudnick said, "How do you feel about this woman?"

"How do I feel about her?"

"First thing that comes to mind."

A grin broadened Uzi's face. "You don't want to know the first thing that comes to my mind."

Rudnick raised his eyebrows and nodded. "Okay. So there's a sexual component to your feelings. Completely understandable."

"I find myself thinking about her. I want to be with her. My heart aches when I want to be with her, and can't. Is that ridiculous or what? I mean, how can a heart ache? But it does . . ."

Rudnick leaned back in his chair. "Yes, Uzi, the heart can ache. With pleasure as well as with pain." He seemed to be waiting for Uzi to continue. "I think this all comes back to letting go of emotional ties to your past. Not the memories. The emotional baggage. Including the guilt."

Uzi pulled a wrapped toothpick from his pocket, fiddled with the plastic and finally poked the point through. He leaned forward, gathered himself, and rose from the chair. "Thanks, Doc. I've got a lot of shit to take care of and very little time. But I'll work on it."

"I'm serious."

Uzi stuck the toothpick in his mouth. "So am I."

10:33 AM
75 hours 27 minutes remaining

Uzi met with his task force group heads and exchanged information on what each was working on and where it was leading. He had other meetings and briefings scheduled for this afternoon, but while there were various theories and angles being pursued, there was little in the way of evidence or leads that could be considered "promising."

He explained to them their investigation was being closely watched by many heads of state, the president, their own director, the director of Central Intelligence, the attorney general, and the director of Homeland Security. Though he was stating the obvious, hearing the stress in his voice would hopefully make *them* feel the pressure *he* felt.

When he returned to his office, Madeline informed him that he had a call holding.

"Who?" he asked as he settled in behind his desk.

"Supervisory Special Agent Garza."

The mention of Garza's name caused a flurry of mixed emotions as Uzi reached for the phone. *Is the guy going to help me, or scold me again for ratting out his buddy?*

Uzi hit the line button and leaned back in his chair. "Uzi."

"We need to talk," Garza said. "Off-site. How about Union Station in twenty minutes?"

"What do you want to talk about?"

"Stuff. Stuff we discussed yesterday. I need to ask you some questions."

Uzi looked at his desk, littered by a stack of unreturned messages and a running list of emails. Still, Garza would not have called him if it wasn't important. He set a specific place to meet, grabbed his coat from the corner stand, and minutes later was leaving the parking garage.

Union Station was an intriguing architectural marvel: old-world charm melded with the sleek lines of high-tech design and function.

Uzi made his way up the ornate staircase to the second level, sauntered over to the Ann Ricard boutique, and pretended to browse the window. He figured a male wouldn't look out of place standing in front of a storefront casually perusing female lingerie, but when his eye caught the one in white lace, he flashed on Leila, and his emotions were off and running again.

He realized he was staring when he suddenly became aware of the warmth of someone's body standing beside him.

"A guy looks hard-up when he stands in front of a storefront staring at lady's lingerie."

Garza's voice was like an alarm clock blaring at five AM.

"I wasn't . . . I'm not—" Uzi turned and saw that Garza was sporting a large grin. Uzi relaxed and smiled as well. They turned away from the window and fell into step with the mass of travelers scurrying along the walkway.

"I've been thinking about Bishop," Garza said. His head bobbed from side to side as he shoved his hands into his suit pant pockets.

Uzi watched Garza go through his gyrations and figured he was performing casual surveillance of his surroundings, ensuring no one had followed either of them. His movements made Uzi suddenly paranoid.

"I was trying to make sense of his murder," Garza continued. "I mean, on the surface, it seems obvious someone affiliated with that organization he was tracking was responsible." His head rotated some more, glancing from left to right and then back behind them. "But things don't add up. I was wondering if you were involved somehow."

Uzi slowed his pace, causing Garza to take a few steps forward before matching Uzi's smaller strides. "You called me here to ask if I was involved in Bishop's murder?"

"No, no," Garza said, motioning with his hands for Uzi to keep it down. "I mean, did anyone else on your team know what Bishop was looking into?"

"Just Agent Koh, you spoke to her a few days ago—"

"Other than Agent Koh."

Uzi continued striding in silence. He couldn't think of anyone else he had told about Bishop. Had he mentioned Bishop to DeSantos before the night they went to meet him? He couldn't remember. "Why would you assume I'm the link? There could be a shitload of other people Bishop had told. Colleagues, employees—"

"He had no employees, and he was a paranoid shit who didn't trust his mother. If he talked to you about it, he must've felt he needed some help." Garza stopped in front of an ice cream stand and glanced into the display case. "Rum Raisin," he said to the vendor.

Uzi was thinking about what Garza had said when he noticed the man looking at him, waiting for his order. "Uh, mocha chip. Small."

While the man went to work digging his scoop into the tub of ice cream, Uzi turned his back to the glass counter and watched the commuters shuffle past. Across the way, a crowd of school kids was being corralled by their teacher, who was using her arms to herd them against the far wall. The girls cooperated, but a group of boys preferred to continue goofing off, grabbing each other's gloves and hoods. The teacher dropped her arms, tilted her head in anger, and moved into the epicenter of her frustration to separate the boys.

"My informant tells me he overheard something," Garza said. "I don't have any specifics, but I thought you should know your name came up."

"My name?"

"This person doesn't know you, probably doesn't even know you exist. Said he heard the name 'Uzi,' and I got to thinking, there aren't too many people with that name."

"In case you didn't realize it, there's a very popular submachine gun—"

"It was in the context of a person—an agent, not a weapon."

Uzi took the cones from the vendor and faced Garza. "Your contact?"

"Someone on the inside. That's all I can say."

Uzi licked away a dollop of mocha chip perched on the cone's edge. "On the inside? Inside of what? What the hell does that mean?"

Garza took a bite of his ice cream.

"You're supposed to lick it," Uzi said.

"I bite mine, you mind?" Garza took another mouthful as they moved off into the crowd again. The teacher had gotten her group sorted out and was moving them off in single file.

"Anyway," Garza said, "I just thought you should be aware of things, people around you. People close to you."

Is Garza trying to tell me something? People close to me. Shepard? With the weird things going on, with what DeSantos and Knox had asked of him, his relationship with Shepard felt strained. But his friend, mixed up in a plot to assassinate citizens? On the other hand, Knox and his cadre . . .

He became aware of Garza again doing his surveillance scans of the area as they neared a bookstore at the end of the station. Could DeSantos be involved in an assassination plot? He had participated in numerous black ops for just that purpose. But all were carefully orchestrated missions on foreign turf to take out rogue leaders, dictators, or terrorists—people who had designs on killing others, or whose purpose was to harm America, her citizens, or allies. Carrying out targeted hits on US soil was unheard of, even for his group of operatives.

That aside, why would DeSantos want Bishop dead? And how

did the NFA/Rathbone/Knox connection figure into this? How much could he tell Garza, and how far could he trust him?

"I need to know more about your contact," Uzi said.

"Can't. Not without jeopardizing his life and others around him."

Uzi's cone had begun to melt, so he lopped off a coagulating hunk with his teeth.

"I thought you're not supposed to bite ice cream."

"You're not giving me much to go on. How can I take this seriously when I don't know the source? You're passing on unconfirmed hearsay and expecting me to accept it as fact."

"Hearsay?" Garza said. He stopped walking. Uzi faced him. "This isn't a court of law, Uzi. We're talking a series of murders here, carried out by someone who could be entrenched in our own infrastructure." His eyes danced around the area. "You hear what I'm saying?"

"Yesterday you wanted to ram your fist down my throat for ratting out your buddy Osborn. Now you're passing me info you say you got from a confidential informant. Info you say will supposedly help me out. But things have to make sense to me, Garza. If they don't, I tend to go fucking crazy. It eats at me, so I get out my shovel and dig as deep as I have to dig to get at the truth. You hear what I'm saying?"

"I shouldn't have brought Jake into this. That was personal, and we've got a job to do. I'm sorry, it was unprofessional. I'm better than that."

Uzi looked him over, trying to assess Garza's intentions.

"I was wrong, Uzi, okay? You may still be a type-A, constipated, by-the-book bureaucrat with his finger up his ass, but I need to trust someone on this. And you're it."

Uzi looked away. "I'm not type-A."

Garza laughed. "That still doesn't excuse what you did to Jake, but you and I can deal with that when this case is over. Right now we've got some bad shit that needs our attention."

"But you still won't tell me who this insider is."

Garza tossed his nearly finished cone in the garbage pail to his left. "Keep me in the loop. I promise to do the same for you."

Yeah, in the loop. A loop with so many knots it was impossible to tell which strings tightened the noose and which ones loosened it. Uzi licked at his melting cone, watching with overt disinterest as Garza headed off into the crowd. But inside, his mind was churning.

4:41 PM
69 hours 19 minutes remaining

Following a briefing at Homeland Security, Uzi emerged from the parking garage as the longer shadows and yellow-tinted hue of afternoon daylight began the lazy transition to dusk. He needed to meet DeSantos in ninety minutes for pre-op planning.

As he drove toward the hangar at Quantico, where they would review and then commence their operation, he tried to sort out his thoughts on DeSantos. Before initiating a risk-filled mission, it was crucial to know the people you were going in with, the people to whom you were trusting your life and career. Until recently, Uzi had no doubts whatsoever. While his newfound unease was based on suspicions and spurious information, it still bothered him.

Adding to his uncertainty was the discovery of the surveillance chip in his coat. How had it gotten there? It appeared to be constructed of sophisticated materials to make it impervious to detection by most sensing devices, including the one with which Uzi had rigged his cell phone—the one DeSantos knew about, the one he'd seen in action. Coincidence?

DeSantos made no effort to disguise his disdain for Bishop; were those his true feelings, though, or was he attempting to discredit the informant in Uzi's eyes? From what he knew of DeSantos, he could make a case for both: the man clearly had seen things, had participated in missions, that would be fodder for fantastic action movies, things the average citizen would discount as being beyond belief. Little did they know that stranger things happened in real life, under the cloak of black ops.

Still, DeSantos was like Uzi in that things had to make sense to him. Unlike Uzi, however, if he sensed that theories and unrelated incidents were being fabricated and strung together into fanciful scenarios laced with conspiracy, he would point his efforts in the opposite direction, build a wall and be closed to anything that person had to say. Uzi himself had come dangerously close to alienating his partner in this manner, he now realized.

But if he was spying on Uzi, what would he hope to accomplish? Was it to keep Knox informed of his progress on the case—or was Knox running a parallel investigation, using leads and information Uzi was gathering to accomplish some other result? But what would that result be? Help Rathbone, and therefore ARM, escape scrutiny? Or something worse: was Knox involved with Rathbone and Flint in a plot to kill Rusch to help further NFA's agenda? Or did it have something to do with Whitehall's covert peace talks?

Uzi shook his head. He was falling into the conspiracy theory trap. He had spent his life analyzing intelligence, sorting out who the enemy was, then working on ways to neutralize them. In his latter days with Mossad, he was often given his assignment, provided background information, and pointed in the right direction. For the rest of the op, he was on his own. Clarity of thought, the ability to peel away layers to get at the truth, lay at the core of his talents.

It was a skill he had largely abandoned—or lost—when Dena and Maya were murdered. He refused to accept that he no longer possessed the skill set, however. He wanted to believe that if the situation arose, he could slip back into that mode. But it was not as easy as flipping a switch. It was a mind-set, a way of operating, with which he had now been out of practice for several years. In many ways, though the FBI had saved his life, it had retarded his skills.

And now, as he approached the main gate to Quantico, he couldn't shake the nagging sense that he was missing something.

Uzi drove into the hanger, killed his headlights, and shut the engine. DeSantos was already dressed in his mission attire, a black divers' skin sheath that conformed to the curves of his toned body. He was talking with another man in a weathered brown-leather bomber jacket and jeans, who stood a few inches taller than DeSantos.

As Uzi moved toward his partner, he wiped all doubt about him from his mind. Not only would DeSantos read it on his face, he didn't want it influencing his actions on the mission. He felt reasonably certain DeSantos wanted this op to succeed—given the invested resources and effort, DeSantos could've devised a simpler ruse to throw Uzi off the trail. He would keep his eyes open—but his mind had to be totally committed to mission success. He'd reassess and sort things out after the op was in the books.

DeSantos turned as Uzi approached. He elbowed the man standing beside him, then indicated Uzi with a tip of his head. "Aaron Uzi, this is—"

"Troy Rodman." DeSantos's colleague's voice was deep as James Earl Jones's, though not as rich and resonant.

Rodman's dark eyes were devoid of emotion. "You're a tough dude, I hear."

"That'll be on my headstone some day: Uzi. Tough dude, didn't know when to quit."

Rodman didn't react. Uzi, usually a quick judge of character, didn't get much from this man. Either Rodman wasn't sure what to make of Uzi, or the big guy didn't warm up to people easily.

DeSantos indicated Rodman with a tilt of his head. "Hot Rod's going to be flying the bird."

Uzi pulled his eyes off Rodman and turned to DeSantos. "How are we doing?"

"Team's assembled and ready for the briefing."

"Black Hawk?"

"Fueled, prepped, ready to go." DeSantos reached into the back of an adjacent pickup and pulled out a medium-sized gym bag, then shoved it into Uzi's chest. "Go change."

Five minutes later, Uzi emerged from the head, clad in the same skin-tight insulated material DeSantos was wearing. He was glad he kept in shape, as this outfit hid nothing. He tossed the sack, now filled with his clothing, in the back of the truck and joined the rest of the team in the corner of the hangar.

There were six other men gathered around DeSantos, each of them wearing military gear. He didn't know if they were authentic or not, and didn't care: in all the confusion they would generate, all they needed to do was look and act the part while Flint's team tried to figure out what was going on and what to do about it.

As Uzi approached, the jovial jousting came to an abrupt halt. Uzi thought of the old saying, "Don't stop laughing on account of me . . . unless you're laughing on account of me." He figured with his investigation of Knox, their fearsome leader and the object of their diehard loyalty, Uzi was not their favorite mate just now.

"Listen up," DeSantos said. "Final mission briefing."

Uzi would not be formally introduced to the other six members of the team. He needed to know Rodman's name because he would be running the show from the chopper. Other than that, these men's identities were classified, on a need-to-know basis. For now, Uzi did not need to know.

DeSantos, his right foot on the lower rung of a metal chair, motioned for Uzi to join him by his side. "My partner and I will enter the South fence, make our way toward the two storage sheds marked A and B on the Sat photos we reviewed. You guys will do your thing at the front gate."

DeSantos spent the next couple of hours reviewing the full complement of aerial images and briefing the team on mission details, escape routes, local law enforcement response times, commo procedures, and perhaps the most important element of a covert operation: the FUBAR scenario—Fucked Up Beyond All Recognition. If the situation suddenly degenerated, the team needed a predetermined set of guidelines to minimize collateral damage and exposure of the group's assets, affiliations, and identities.

DeSantos rose from the ladder and stretched. "You each know your roles. Bottom line: make it convincing. Be confrontational because they're paranoid shits and that's what they'd expect. But we don't want to provoke a gunfight. Remember, some of these militia guys are ex-Army Special Forces, so they know what they're doing and they probably trained their comrades. We're landing just outside their front porch with a huge fucking machine. It'll intimidate without us lifting a hand. So keep your guns stowed. And remember: do not dismount under any circumstances." DeSantos turned to Uzi. "You got anything to add?"

"I'm good. Let's do it."

DeSantos hit a large green button on the wall and the hangar doors rolled open. Beyond them was the Black Hawk, its still rotors drooped in repose. The group high-fived each other, then moved off. One of the larger men stared Uzi down as he brushed past him on the way out.

"Just a crazy question," Uzi asked, appraising the helicopter from a distance. "Our FUBAR scenario. Every part of that bird is traceable. Not to mention our team."

DeSantos shook his head. "We've got complete deniability. None of these guys will show up in a print or biometric database. All taken care of by a techie holed away in the bowels of the Pentagon. As for the bird, it was decommissioned five years ago. The guts have been totally stripped, completely changed out with untraceable parts. Not a fingerprint to be found anywhere. Officially, no one owns this thing."

"I've seen some of those aftermarket parts," Uzi said, his voice staying level despite the whine of the helicopter's engines starting up. "Not very airworthy."

"It'll fly. For a mission like this one, we should be fine."

Uzi's head whipped over to DeSantos. "Should be?"

"A lot's gone into making it a deniable craft. OPSIG wouldn't be too happy if they lost it."

"They're landing outside their property line, right? You're sure Hot Rod won't *hot dog* it."

"Man, you worry too much. Yes, outside the property. Despite what I said to the team, Hot Rod'll make it as nonthreatening as he can. He'll be walking a fine line, but I've put my life in his hands lots of times. He knows what he's doing."

DeSantos received a thumbs up from Rodman, who was now settled into the pilot's seat. DeSantos acknowledged the sign, then slapped Uzi in the chest with an open hand. "You ready?"

Uzi looked his partner in the eyes, trying to read them while disguising his own. He wasn't picking anything up other than a squint of deep focus. He pushed his residual doubts about DeSantos from his mind and nodded. "Ready."

The chopper was over its position twenty minutes later. Uzi and DeSantos rappelled into forested land a mile outside the compound. They would hike their way to the perimeter while Rodman moved off, returning when DeSantos signaled that he and Uzi were nearing their target.

Aside from his stint in the Israel Defense Forces, Uzi had never been on a mission in which he had to dress in military garb. He had always operated in the backstreets, alleys, and shantytowns of the Middle East and Europe, wearing whatever the natives wore, his first objective being to blend in with the locals, to be invisible. Here, his goals were the same, with an important distinction: he needed to be not only figuratively invisible, but literally as well. He and DeSantos couldn't be seen by anyone. Hence the need for stealthy infrared- and light-absorbing clothing.

They carried nothing that could identify them in any way. Of course, if they ran into Nelson Flint or his lieutenant, Rodney McCourt, identity would be the least of their problems. Uzi and DeSantos were banking on their assumption that the men in charge would be busy at the main gate with Rodman and his group.

Their equipment was sparse as well; they were unarmed except for a multi-purpose Navy Mk III Combat Knife. Capable of surgical incisions and slicing through bone as well as cutting through brush, the blade featured a stainless, black-coated finish that was both durable and anti-reflective. The knives were concealed by a slim resin sheath that strapped to the outside of their left thighs. While Uzi usually carried a Puma tactical knife, as well as a Tanto around his neck and a smaller boot knife—habits from his days with the Mossad—this mission demanded a single versatile weapon that could be explained away.

From this point forward, they would employ only commercially available two-way radios, using their squelch bursts as a crude form of code. It was far from ideal, and from Uzi's high-tech perspective a throwback to the dark ages of the fifties or sixties, but it was a wise precaution. If they were captured by roving guards, any high-tech gadgets would put them in Flint's crosshairs regardless of what Rodman was doing—and perhaps because of it. Should their movements be detected, they felt confident they could split up and each successfully make their way to a predetermined location two miles from the perimeter of the ARM compound where, earlier in the day, DeSantos had left an unmarked car.

Aside from their low-tech squelch code, the mission demanded silence going forward, so all close-contact communication would consist of hand and arm signals. While they had been able to evaluate ARM's video surveillance capabilities from the heavens, they did not know what other security measures the compound sported. This was the part that bothered Uzi most. They were taking calculated risks and making educated guesses, but they were risks nonetheless.

Twenty-five minutes later, they approached the South fence, along the back end of the property. They pulled black ski masks over their heads and settled nonreflective infrared sunglasses over their eyes. The glasses would not only block shine and sparkle, but the lens coating focused all available light to brighten the visual field. While they were not nearly as effective as NVGs—night vision goggles—to the untrained eye, they were indistinguishable from regular sunglasses, preserving their low-tech look. Of course, wearing sunglasses and neoprene tights at night might raise some suspicion, but anyone detaining them would be more concerned about their presence and assessing their potential threat than their odd clothing or eyewear.

DeSantos signaled Rodman with three short commo bursts followed by a long one. To anyone listening in, it would merely sound like background static. Ten seconds later, Rodman responded with two short bursts.

Per their plan, Uzi checked the fence for anticlimb sensors like the ones he had seen at the front gate. Because of the expense of deploying such technology over miles of land, he did not expect to find them—and as suspected, they were absent. He signaled that they were free to proceed, and then reached into the rucksack DeSantos was wearing and pulled out a coarse, densely woven fiber roll they would use to traverse the barb-tipped fence.

Inside Uzi's pack was another low-tech solution to the ten-foot chain-link wall: a homemade device consisting of a wood dowel with protruding nails. The nails served as hooks, providing Uzi and DeSantos purchase while they positioned the fiber roll over the barbed wire.

Three minutes later, they were grasping their makeshift claw hooks with one hand while holding the fiber roll with the other. DeSantos used a bungee cord and holes in the fiber to secure it in place, then nudged his partner. Uzi would go first. He shifted his weight carefully, trying not to cause too much shake and rattle in the chain link. Noise of any sort was their enemy.

While Plan B would have involved using a bolt cutter to peel away a section of the fence, their goal was to leave the grounds without any physical evidence of having been there.

Uzi hooked his homemade claw around the chain links, and boosted his right leg up and onto the fiber sheath covering the barbed wire. He maneuvered his left leg over the fence, then steadied himself while DeSantos repeated the movements Uzi had just completed.

They had done this once before over a decade ago in Estonia, when Uzi was with Mossad. The stakes were far greater then, as they were attempting to snatch-and-grab a Russian scientist who was threatening to provide the Iranians with blueprints and enough enriched uranium to construct their own nuclear reactor. Although Uzi and DeSantos were successful, Iran eventually obtained their information and materials through other means.

This particular mission also carried far-reaching implications: if ARM was involved in the attempted assassination of the vice president, they had vaulted onto another plane of domestic threat—with no limit to what they would try next.

They unhooked the bungees, then lowered themselves to the ground and tightly re-rolled the fiber before covering it with pine needles and branches. If things went sour and they had to get out fast, they would use a set of mini-bolt cutters they were now burying by the fence line. At that point, leaving any physical sign would be moot, and their priorities would shift: escaping without discovery of their identity would become paramount.

Packed up and ready to part, they gave each other a gloved thumbs-up, then set off in opposite directions: DeSantos headed for Target A, Uzi for Target B.

Uzi's deliberate movements made him feel as if he were watching a baseball game in slow motion. But that's what this op demanded. They had to keep from triggering the motion sensors. While light-absorbing clothing was an advantage, defeating motion detection was an inexact science; a passing animal, or merely brushing against a branch, could set it off.

So Uzi moved with caution, staying in the path of tree trunks—natural obstructions to the sensors. He slowed his movement in those areas where surveillance measures and other sensing devices were most likely to be placed. Ten minutes later, he came upon a clearing that contained a structure a bit larger than a modular trailer. His projected method of entry had also been determined by aerial surveillance. Though the doors were padlocked, they contained external hinges. Uzi circled to the back of the structure, shrugged off his rucksack, and removed a screwdriver. Using the back end of his knife, and limiting his movements, he used short, firm strikes that he shielded with his body. The screwdriver handle was coated in rubber, absorbing much of the noise.

After half a dozen blows, Uzi had the oxidized brass hinge pins in his pocket. He entered the building, flipped on his quarter-size red-beamed LED flashlight, and began taking inventory.

Across the compound, DeSantos was approaching his target, a twenty-foot-tall, flat-roofed structure that appeared to be a modestly sized storage facility of about a thousand square feet. DeSantos opened his backpack and removed a coiled length of thick rope, fitted with a grappling hook at one end. With a looping, underhanded toss, he sent it to the top of the building.

As feared—and expected—the quick movement of his arm was more than enough to stimulate the motion sensor. A tree-mounted spotlight snapped on.

Uzi divided the building's interior into grids and methodically carried out his search. Thus far, he had found a cache of weapons with filed-off serial numbers, ammunition, and boxes of spare computer parts. He wished he could take photos—or better yet—that he could make arrests based on what he found. But he was there illegally, trespassing at best and breaking and entering at worst.

After finishing his survey, he returned to Grid 3 and stuck the flashlight in his mouth. He was looking for ammunition with Russian markings—a potential link to Bishop's murder.

Uzi finished rummaging through the cartons, taking care to replace everything the way he'd found it. If he had the time, he would've used his phone to take photos of the interior after breaching the shack. That way, he could replace everything the way it had been with reasonable precision, then reformat the memory card to delete the pictures. But he had to be quick and be gone. No time to be perfect—and he could not afford to make any blatant errors, either. He had to hope that no one would notice a book or box slightly ajar.

Frustrated at not finding what he came for, he turned to make one last sweep of the area. As he pivoted, he noticed a removable floor panel that shifted under his weight. He knelt down and studied the seams of the metal plate, then removed the knife from his thigh holster. Using the sharp tip, he pried up the edge enough to get his fingers underneath.

When he lifted the panel, he saw four steel steps leading down to . . . What? A basement? A crawl space? After descending the stairs and lowering the hinged plate back into place, he took his flashlight and shone it around his immediate vicinity. Not a basement. Not a crawl space.

"Holy shit." Before he could take another step to explore, the storage building began rattling, followed by a rumbling deep in his gut.

DeSantos stood with his face and body pressed up against the side of the building, the dark stealth clothing protecting him from detection. If a guard was watching his security monitor, he'd see the light snap on—but, theoretically, would not see a black-clad male figure trespassing on their property. DeSantos had been told that in such a situation, if he remained absolutely still, he would probably appear to blend into his surroundings. He had told his DARPA buddy that he didn't like the "probably" part of his comment, but knew that with so many variables and limited field testing of the new technology, he would have to hope for the best.

As he waited for the lights to turn off, he realized he was wasting valuable minutes. One thing they couldn't determine from satellite reconnaissance was the length of time the motion sensors were set to burn. And with each second he remained pinned to the side of this building, the less time he would have to look around inside it. If he could just move his left hand a few feet, he'd be able to click his squelch key and signal Rodman to make his approach.

As he debated what to do, he felt the thumping of the rotors followed by the roar and whir of the Black Hawk's engines. The chopper blades' pounding of the air was intense, vibrating deep in his throat and hammering away at the inside of his chest like a heart stimulated by a massive adrenaline infusion—which wasn't far from the truth.

As if his airborne team had read his mind, Rodman was beginning a zigzag descent over the compound, stirring up all sorts of shit in wind buckets and dramatically lighting up the night sky with black and gray smoke spewing from the chopper's tail. DeSantos had hoped to be inside the structure by this point, as the strong wind generated by the Black Hawk would set off the motion sensors all over the compound. Instead, he counted to five, allowing all the members of ARM's security detail to get a good long glimpse at the noisy chopper putting on its show over their land. Then he grabbed the rope, and with catlike quickness, pulled himself up.

Rodman wiggled the control stick, giving the appearance of substantial instability in the chopper's flight path, then lowered the bird with lurching movements toward the ground. The performance was spectacularly frightening, particularly if you were a group of paranoid militia members who spent every waking moment obsessing about this very event. In some ways, it was a dream come true for them—a chance to grab their high-tech rifles and semiautomatic submachine guns to defend their property from an onslaught of invading black-helicopter Feds.

In another sense, it was their ultimate nightmare—for the very same reasons. They had powerful weapons and a common conspiracy-laden mind-set that kept them banded together, aligned against an overwhelmingly virulent enemy—ingredients for a potentially explosive environment. Rodman knew this. Trained or not, it was the inability of these men to properly analyze a situation under duress that made this situation so volatile.

Yet the same factors that infused this mission with risk were precisely the things that each of the OPSIG operatives craved. Whether on foreign or domestic soil, adrenaline was a drug for them.

As the chopper neared the ground, Rodman positioned the cockpit as close as he dared to the main gate without risking danger to his craft from the surrounding trees. He landed parallel to the fence line, clearly outside their property, taking care not to antagonize more than necessary. He sat there calmly in his seat, throwing switches that needed to be thrown, and some that didn't. Drawing out the moment and soaking up as much time as he could until he received the squelched signals from his land-based team indicating they had achieved mission success.

Like famished ants finding food, guards poured out of the nearby structures, Kalashnikov assault rifles slung over their shoulders. They hit the ground in choreographed fashion, dropping to one knee and pointing their weapons with practiced precision. Perhaps DeSantos had misinterpreted their level of expertise. Rodman's heart beat furiously as his outward calm belied his sudden sense of anxiety. He tried to ignore the troop maneuvers taking place in front of him as he spoke into his encrypted headset. "Uh, boys, we've made contact. They're well armed and seem to be itching for us to make a hostile move. Stand by."

Rodman engaged the external speakers. Phase two of their charade was about to begin—a bit earlier than planned.

Uzi had felt the chopper approaching before he heard it; the vibrating rumble in his gut told him he needed to get moving. But he couldn't, not yet—not after finding this hidden chamber. He walked down a long, narrow tunnel that led to another set of steps—and what appeared to be a larger, deeper room. After assuring himself that no one was there, he stepped down into the darkness.

Beyond a fire door lay an area that stood in stark contrast to the environs of the building he had just left. Rows of polished stainless steel racks held computer modules stacked neatly one above the other, color-coded cables feeding each of the units. Uzi knew exactly what he was looking at, having played a role in developing the earlier generation microchips running these very servers.

The chill of air conditioning and metal honeycomb flooring told him that whoever designed this facility for ARM clearly knew what he was doing. According to Ruckhauser, Lewiston Grant was a self-made computer expert. Looking at this subterranean setup and its advanced technology, Uzi had to agree. Unless they hired a contractor who could be trusted with their secret—or unless ARM had another networking guru in their ranks—Grant was alive and well, and keeping his knowledge base sharp.

Uzi did a quick walk-around, his knife clenched in his right hand, ready to be thrown or thrust should someone challenge him. He made his way to the end of the room, looking for the administrator's desk. It could be anywhere, really, but Uzi had a feeling they would have someone down here overseeing the equipment. He turned down a corridor created by the rows of shelving, and saw a free-standing PC resting on a desk against the bunker's cement wall.

He didn't have much time. But the thought of poking around and hacking the server was so tempting he would almost be willing to risk getting caught to see what he could find.

On the desk was a half-empty Styrofoam cup of coffee. He removed his glove and stuck his index finger into the drink. It was relatively hot. Whoever had left it had done so to respond to the chopper out front. They could return at any moment.

He rummaged through the desk drawers and found standard office supplies and various computer peripherals: a mouse, networking cables, a discarded hard drive. He reasoned that ARM used a RAID setup, which stored data redundantly, spread out over multiple disks. If one failed, a replacement could be slipped in and the system would automatically recover, without any data loss. While the drive in his hand had likely been trashed, he was certain CART could retrieve its information. But if he got caught, his cover would immediately be blown. There could be no excuse for having it in his possession.

He gave one last look around the desk and was about to close the drawer when he saw a small yellow notepad tucked beneath a book. He scanned the pages, which contained scribbled notations at varying angles. Whoever took these notes had no use for ruled lines. As Uzi read the various entries, he realized it was a scratch pad, kept by a phone, where reminders, names, and events could be scribbled, transferred later to their respective repository: a calendar, a contact list, a database program.

While it would not be something someone would miss, he played it safe nonetheless. He removed the second and fourth pages, figuring Tim Meadows could use alternative light sources and other forensic techniques to raise the imprinted notes taken on the pages directly above them.

Uzi grabbed a pen from the drawer, unscrewed the two halves, and removed the refill. He deftly rolled the two sheets of paper into a tight tube, then slid it into the hollow case. He slipped the pen into his backpack, then checked to see how much time had elapsed. He was three minutes behind schedule. *Patience. The easiest way to find trouble is by cutting corners.*

He positioned the chair the way it had been before he sat, then retraced his steps toward the tunnel, moving swiftly. Rodman and crew were now doing their thing. He needed to do his.

The militia members began pouring out of a pedestrian gate several feet to the left of the guard house. The men fell into position encircling the grounded chopper, with several peering into the cabin glass. But the windows were deeply tinted, and with the near total darkness inside and the security spotlights brightening the front of ARM's compound, they would be staring into mirrors.

Rodman waited, drawing it out, not making a move until forced to do so. Finally, one of the men walked up to the cockpit and rapped on the front side window with the muzzle of his assault rifle.

Rodman keyed the mike. "Back the fuck away!" He needed to establish authority without delay. Although he was accustomed to relying on his size, in this case broadcasting his deep baritone voice over the external speakers served as his sole means of intimidation, leaving him less confident of success—particularly considering the neutralizing roar of the copter's turbines and rotors. But the sooner they realized they didn't have a pushover in the command chair, the less likely they would be to aggress. Yet he had to be careful not to incite them. It was a fine line.

The man behind the submachine gun quickly dumped his own

testosterone into the mix by bringing his Kalashnikov up to his cheek and taking aim through the side window, in the general location of Rodman's head.

Rodman knew his chopper was made to fly soldiers into combat. It had a built-in tolerance to small-arms fire and most medium-caliber high-explosive projectiles. His team could withstand an assault, but he doubted the cockpit glass was impervious to a high-powered round fired at such close range.

He flipped the commo to the internal channel and informed his crew of the situation and ordered them to stand ready for countermeasures: the release of more smoke from the specially-installed exhaust pipes near the tail. The parasoldiers would likely back off for fear of explosion or asphyxiation.

Rodman switched back to the external speakers. "We've got problems with our bird. Didn't mean to land in your front yard, but we didn't have much choice. We're making repairs, but there's still danger of explosion. Stay back."

He kept his explanation and warnings incomplete and cryptic, to make them think—and waste time while they debated what to do. But at some point his friends would become frustrated with one-sided communication. How long did he have?

He got his answer faster than he had hoped: ten more armed men moved into position and brought their weapons to eye level. Beads of perspiration oozed from Rodman's forehead. Their sudden and unexpected reaction made him feel weak—an emotion he did not often experience. Whoever was calling the shots for this group was either a battle-tested military commander, or a decisive and impulsive individual. Either scenario was not good.

Rodman's eyes stung from dripping sweat. He scraped a shirt sleeve across his face and tried to remain clear-headed. He told himself it wasn't fear so much as nerves—the lack of control over an unstable situation with an unknown, and unpredictable or underestimated, adversary. If he was only free to deal with these yahoos the way he'd been trained to do, he'd feel much better.

But for now, he had to stare the enemy in the eye and refuse to blink. Action was his strength, not diplomacy. He silently urged

DeSantos and Uzi to hurry—then dabbed at the pimples of sweat, and waited.

DeSantos lowered himself into the small building through the roof vent. He landed on the floor with both feet, leaving his rope dangling in midair as he started his search. He was aware of the time limitation but pushed it out of his mind, focusing on his mission objectives: searching the interior's contents as quickly as possible, without leaving trace evidence behind.

He turned on his mini flashlight and moved through the storage building, which he estimated at twenty by fifty feet. Large, freestanding rusted shelves were arranged end to end and back to back, dividing the space into aisles. He took mental inventory of the shelves' contents—primarily sequentially numbered boxes stacked atop one another—then pulled down one of two unmarked cartons. After slicing through the tape with his knife, he lifted the flaps—and froze.

Having made his way back through the tunnel, Uzi closed the floor panel and gave one final pass around the interior. After he shut off his flashlight, two long squelches blurted from the radio: he was out of time. He fumbled with the brass pins to get the door lined up and restored to its original state, then took off in a sprint, less concerned now with the motion sensors. He figured—hoped—that at this point everyone on the compound would be dealing with the Black Hawk.

But he was wrong.

Twenty or thirty smaller boxes emblazoned with Cyrillic letters stared back at DeSantos. He pulled one out, stuck his thumb under the edge of the flap, and pried it open.

Egg crate packaging separated and protected the three-inch Russian rounds. Match-grade ammo—the kind used by snipers for accuracy. He removed one, bagged it, and shoved it into an inside pocket of his underwear. Positioned properly, despite his skintight outfit, it might pass as a part of his anatomy. He hoped it wouldn't come to that.

He rummaged through his backpack for the roll of packaging tape.

He resealed the box, restoring it to the condition in which he'd found it, and rotated it to the bottom of the stack.

As he packed himself up to leave, two squelches puffed over his radio transceiver. Time to go. He grabbed hold of the dangling rope and pulled himself up toward the roof.

Uzi was nearing the rendezvous point when he stepped in a camouflaged hole and went down hard, smashing his head and right shoulder into a sawed-off tree trunk. Sharp pain shot through his face and neck. He tried to pull himself to his knees but lacked traction on the wet leaves and slippery pine needles.

A flashlight beam hit him in the face.

"Who the fuck are you?" the voice behind the light said.

Uzi raised his left hand as a shield—his right was pinned behind him, preventing him from reaching his knife—and tried to make out the silhouetted figure against the glare. *Is he armed?*

"I said, 'Who the fuck are you?'"

"I was out hiking and got lost. You know how I can get out of here?" Uzi knew it was a bullshit excuse, but he figured it would buy him some time while he sorted out his jumbled thoughts and tried to reason a way out of the jam. Keep the captor talking and you had a chance. If he made you lay down and tied you up, the guy was a pro and you were in deep shit.

The man lowered his flashlight a bit, but still kept it pointed at Uzi's face. Dimly lit by the penumbra of the beam's errant light, his face sported sharp features and thin lips. Combined with military-short hair, dark stubble, and pseudomilitary accouterments, he fit Uzi's image of GI Joe.

"Take off your glasses and mask," Joe said. He waved his light as if underscoring his words.

It was an expected request. See your adversary, watch the language of his face. People inadvertently give away a lot about themselves and their motives by the simple involuntary ticks, creases, squints, and frowns woven into subtle facial expressions. Uzi was going to try to do the same with Joe.

"Now! Take 'em off!"

Uzi reached up with his left hand and complied. Joe took a step forward, his head creeping forward and tilting slightly, studying Uzi's face as if he recognized him from somewhere. If Joe was one of the ARM members who'd seen him on one of his prior visits, Uzi was in for a rough time. Uzi again thought of the knife and began moving slowly in an effort to free his right arm.

"Do you know how I can get out of here?" Uzi asked again.

Joe tilted his head left, then, with his eyes locked on Uzi's, lifted his chin toward Uzi's right.

Was he showing him the way out? Letting him go? Or was he toying with him, planning to shoot him in the back when he turned to leave?

But before Uzi could test the veracity of his new friend's offer, DeSantos appeared at Joe's side, his knife drawn, the rough tooth-edged blade jammed up against the man's neck.

"Down!" DeSantos said into his ear.

Joe complied, the sharp edge being most persuasive. He lay prone on the ground, remaining completely still while Uzi did a quick search of his body and removed his weapons and radio. Joe obviously knew the drill. He had figured out that they had control of the situation, and the best thing he could do now was to comply and wait for an opportunity to bolt. DeSantos was making every effort to ensure that never happened.

Uzi emptied the ammo and then dumped the rounds into the camouflaged hole while DeSantos, with his left knee squarely in Joe's back, loosely fastened flexcuffs to their captive's ankles and wrists.

That done, he motioned to Uzi to follow him toward the fence. Joe's bindings weren't permanent, but would last long enough for them to make their escape. The man would then be able to free himself before anyone got to him. Partly out of embarrassment and partly out of a desire not to admit he had failed at his job, Joe would never speak of his adventure—unless it had been caught on video. Uzi hoped that was not the case.

As they stood in front of the fence, they pulled their homemade clawhooks from their backpacks, uncovered the fiber mat, and went to work.

Rodman's parasoldier adversaries were getting restless. He knew the feeling. He wished he would get some indication from either DeSantos or Uzi that they were free of the compound so he could lift off.

But his radio remained quiet.

Rodman tapped his foot, perspiration continuing to pour from his face. But his hands tightened on the controls when he saw the ARM team leader tug at his shoulder mike. Something was happening. Rodman watched with rapt attention as the men simultaneously touched their earpieces as if straining to hear their orders.

A few moved first, then the others got the idea and followed suit. They charged the chopper en masse and slammed the butts of their weapons against the doors and windows.

"Goddamnit!" The chopper rocked violently from the angry mob's fury. "Do not engage," Rodman said. "Bravo, give me more fog!"

Thick black smoke again poured from the chopper's rear jets. Rodman couldn't see their response, but he knew the men had to be choking pretty well about now. The banging slowed, then stopped.

Rodman accelerated the rotors, as he would normally do in preparation for liftoff. The mob instinctively recoiled, some abandoning their weapons as they ducked and ran a haphazard retreat.

They had waited as long as feasible. Rodman needed to get airborne. He switched the frequency on his radio, then squeezed off two long squelches. They blew some last coughs of smoke out the tail, then the chopper lifted off, banking sharply and paralleling the periphery of ARM's boundaries.

10:50 PM
63 hours 10 minutes remaining

While in the car on the way to Tim Meadows's home in Alexandria, Uzi and DeSantos inventoried their ill-gotten goods. This "evidence" could not find its way onto FBI grounds, or it could mean the end of their careers with a fanfare from which the Bureau itself might never recover.

"I like the pen idea," DeSantos said.

"Works well unless the person who interrogates you tries writing with it." After a moment's reflection on what had happened with the militia guard, Uzi asked, "Why do you think that guy was gonna let me go?"

"It was all in your head. You thought he nodded at the fence. But it was dark, man. Maybe he heard me coming and tilted his head, but couldn't place the noise."

"Doesn't matter. Lucky for me, you saved my ass."

They turned on King and Uzi quickly located Meadows's street.

As DeSantos pulled against the curb, he said, "Basement light's on."

Meadows, a night owl by nature, took the materials without asking where they had come from, but Uzi told him they were never to be brought onto Federal property, nor would he acknowledge ever having given them to him.

"You're putting me in a tough spot," Meadows said. They were standing on his porch, the tech dressed in a pair of threadbare jeans and an FBI sweatshirt with a pair of Wal-Mart reading glasses hanging from his neck on a gray pull-chain necklace. "What's the deal with this stuff?"

"You don't want to ask that question," Uzi said. He gestured at the light in the basement window. "How's your project going?"

Meadows folded his arms across his chest. "Don't change the subject on me, Uzi."

"You can have the oysters, okay? Two orders."

Meadows arched backward. "Two appetizers?"

"Maybe that way you won't order an entrée."

Meadows took the package. "Don't count on it." He nodded at Uzi's car, where DeSantos was seated, leaning back against the headrest, staring at them with glazed, disinterested eyes.

"What's wrong with your partner?"

"Tough night," Uzi said. In truth, DeSantos had told Uzi his presence might give Meadows pause before agreeing to take part in a federal offense. Uzi felt a pang of guilt over asking his friend to jeopardize his career, but if it all came apart and Knox did his thing to shield him and DeSantos, he'd make sure Meadows somehow got the same immunity.

Meadows eyed Uzi cautiously, then looked at the thick envelope before moving to open it.

Uzi held out a hand. "Not here."

Meadows frowned. "What do you want me to do?"

"One item is self-explanatory. I need it matched to the evidence you examined from the Bishop murder."

Meadows nodded knowingly. "Okay."

"The other thing is less clear cut. Give me the works—prints, DNA, cryptanalysis, alternative light source, spectrometer, and anything else you can think of."

"Looking for . . . ?"

"I don't know. Something."

"That's damn helpful, Uzi."

Uzi shrugged. "What can I say?"

"How about, 'I know this is an impossible job that'll dominate your evenings for the next week, but I really appreciate it.'"

"Here's the thing. You don't have a week. You've got two days."

"Two days? Two days, Uzi?"

Uzi held up his hands in mock surrender. "How about this: Thanks, man, I owe you."

Meadows grunted. "If I had a ten spot for every time I've heard that . . ."

DAY SEVEN

8:09 AM
53 hours 51 minutes remaining

With less than five hours' sleep under his belt, Uzi reported to the task force's new base of operations: the suite used by the standing Counterterrorism Task Force, a once-woefully small group of experts that, after 9/11, expanded faster than a filling helium balloon. Caught off-guard, the FBI revamped their thinking on terrorist groups. They reorganized with serious manpower and—something that had been lacking—budgetary support.

Uzi was there to receive status reports. At this point, he could not rally the troops behind an investigative assault on ARM; he would have to tread lightly in view of Coulter's orders to back off—despite Knox's covert orders to the contrary. Of more concern was that if Meadows found something suspicious in the materials he was examining, Uzi and DeSantos would have to find a legal reason for returning to the compound with a properly executed search warrant. And with the attorney general in the way, with no way of disclosing what they'd found, that would be difficult, if not impossible.

And knocking around his thoughts was that there were only two days remaining before he had to finger a suspect and report to the president. He felt something stir deep down in his stomach. He used to thrive on pressure-packed missions like these. The ARM incursion definitely rekindled a spark inside him, the pinch of spice that had gone missing in his stir fry of a life.

As Uzi left the task force meeting, he was handed a message that Marshall Shepard wanted to see him. He winced; he had known there would come a time when he'd be forced to face his boss. He'd just hoped it would be later rather than sooner.

He made eye contact with Shepard's secretary and got the nod to continue into the ASAC's suite. When he entered, Shepard was standing at the large window behind his desk, his back to Uzi.

Uzi took a seat, and for the first time he could remember, was nervous about seeing his friend. He unwrapped a toothpick and stuck it in his mouth as he waited for Shepard to acknowledge his presence. In the meantime, he would play it as cool as he could, hoping Shepard's reason for wanting to see him had nothing to do with his circumventing Coulter's direct orders.

"You were told to stay away from ARM," Shepard finally said. Still facing the bright window, his large form was silhouetted against the glare of a gray Washington December morning. "You were told to stay away not just by me, Uzi, but by the fucking attorney general."

"Shep, what gives? What are you talking about?"

"I have reason to believe you didn't drop it like the AG told you to do. You didn't drop it."

"Look, we're conducting an investigation. You know how that goes. It's hard doing stuff from a distance. But if that's what we have to do, that's what we have to do. You hear what I'm saying?" Uzi wasn't sure *he* understood what he was saying. Shepard must have been confused as well, because he turned around. But the window glare prevented Uzi from seeing his boss's face.

"Uzi, you're talking in circles and when you talk in circles it's because there's something going on. Tell me there's nothing going on, because I sure as hell don't want to find out about it from the director or AG. I fucked up once. My ass is on the line. And I like it here. I like my job. Now you wouldn't be doing anything to put me in a bad way, would you?"

Uzi swallowed hard, but tried to disguise it by shifting the toothpick around in his mouth. "Shep, your friendship means everything to me. I want you here for as long as I'm here." Given the covert raid of ARM's compound, he wondered how long that would be.

"Better fucking be telling the truth, 'cause I heard things. I heard that something went down at ARM last night, and that you were involved. I just wanna know that it's all bullshit. That you're clean. Are you? Clean?"

Uzi couldn't stand it anymore. He hated lying; it was something he hadn't had to do since his black ops days with Mossad. Worst of all, he had to lie to his close friend. And he had to do it by placing his complete faith in Douglas Knox, a man he did not trust.

But he also knew that telling the truth would have dire consequences. Uzi looked his boss in the eyes, squared his shoulders, and said, "Clean, Shep." He wondered if he had been successful at maintaining a poker face.

Shepard turned back toward the window. "I sure hope so, Uzi. Sure hope so." A few seconds passed in silence. Finally, Shepard said, "We're done here."

Uzi chomped hard on the toothpick, then pushed himself from the chair and turned to leave. He stopped in the doorway, wondering if he should tell Shepard what had happened last night. Could he be trusted? Would he keep a lid on it? Would Knox really stand by him, defend him, shield him from Coulter's inquiry? Was Knox as powerful as DeSantos seemed to think—enough to deflect Coulter? If not, Uzi's career was over—including those who had participated knowingly—and unknowingly. But Knox had not given him a choice. For the time being, it was best to keep it to himself. Even if it meant lying to his friend.

Uzi bit the toothpick in half, then walked out, leaving Shepard staring out the window.

12:22 PM
49 hours 38 minutes remaining

"Tango is on the move again."

Echo Charlie was standing in front of a street vendor's cart, ordering up a hot dog and Coke, the Sat phone pressed against his ear, his bodyguards scanning the area with trained eyes.

Charlie held up a hand. "No mustard."

"What?" Alpha Zulu asked.

"Nothing." Charlie switched ears as he handed the man a five dollar bill. "How are you able to still keep tabs on our man without the . . . device?"

"We're doing it. That's all you need to know."

"Then why are we talking?"

"I need some help understanding where he's been. I need the big picture."

Charlie tucked the handset between his shoulder and ear, then took his food from the vendor. It was a brisk day, and steam from the juicy, sauerkraut-smothered frank was fluttering away on the breeze. He wished his comrade would make it quick—before his hot dog was no longer true to its name. "What places?"

"Private house off King Street, Alexandria. Five-twelve Jasper. But the one that had us most concerned was a location just outside Vienna."

That caught Zulu's attention. "Vienna?"

"Yes, but our residents there don't know anything about it."

"I don't like that." Charlie started toward his bodyguards. "I'll check on both."

"He could be getting too close. You know what's at stake."

Charlie motioned one of his men to take the Coke from him. He shifted the phone back to his hand and turned away. "Then we need to throw him off. But be smart about it. If Tango . . . disappears now, it'll bring problems that we don't need. Even though he's only a thorn, if we cut it off, suddenly the whole bush will be in our face."

"Not if we do it right."

Charlie ground his teeth. "Let me dig around. Need be, we'll erase the trail. That works, our problem may be solved. If not, we can take it a step further. I'll be in touch."

Before Zulu could object, Charlie ended the call. He took a large bite of his hot dog, and then dumped the rest in the garbage. "Gentlemen," he said as he chewed, "let's get moving."

1:01 PM
48 hours 59 minutes remaining

Uzi headed down to his car. He needed to see DeSantos, find out how Shepard knew about their visit to ARM. Was Knox playing both sides of the fence? He wouldn't put it past him.

Would DeSantos tell him the truth even if he knew it? What if DeSantos was the leak? Uzi dismissed the thought, feeling that DeSantos wouldn't place his team in jeopardy. But the bond between Knox and OPSIG was inseparable, and even if Knox wouldn't keep his promise to defend Uzi, he would go to war to protect DeSantos and his men.

As Uzi turned onto M Street, his secretary called. He was to report immediately to headquarters to meet with Pablo Garza. His chat with DeSantos would have to wait.

When Uzi arrived at the Hoover Building, he was cleared by the FBI Police and drove over the retractable metal barrier, down the ramp, and into the underground garage. His mind was adrift with thoughts, trying to make sense of the facts they had amassed, when he entered the lobby.

But his eyes locked on a man standing in an elevator fifty feet away as the doors slid closed. *That face— I've seen it somewhere.*

There was something wrong with this man being here, like he was out of place, in the wrong context, or the wrong time. But Uzi couldn't fight through the mental cobwebs to figure out why.

He took the stairs up to the fourth floor, allowing his mind to sort through facial images stored in his memory—like a massive binder of mug shots of people he had met during his law-enforcement careers. Someone from his past? Or more recently, from his FBI tenure?

Uzi walked into Garza's office; the agent flipped a file folder closed and asked Uzi to shut the door. He took a seat and waited for Garza to speak.

"So you're a risk taker," Garza said. He opened another file and appeared to be perusing its contents. But Uzi could tell the man's heart was not in it.

"Is that a question or a statement?" Uzi asked. He kept working through the virtual photos in his mind.

"You're also very, very stupid. You can't skulk around behind the scenes. There are rules. You know that. We've discussed that as it related to Osborn—"

"Yes, Garza. I know that. Your point?"

"My point?"

The office door opened and in walked the man from the elevator. Bringing up the rear was Jake Osborn. Uzi's intestines immediately knotted.

And that's when it hit him, as hard and fast as a rubber bullet to the thigh. The mysterious elevator man Uzi had seen was almost certainly "GI Joe" from the ARM compound—the one who had stopped him before he reached the fence, the one DeSantos had handcuffed.

At first pass through his logic, that didn't make any sense. It was nearly impossible for an ARM member to be a Federal agent. How could anyone have access to both FBI Headquarters and one of the most notorious militia compounds in the US? Unless— *Holy shit . . . They've got an undercover operative at ARM.*

And he saw us there.

Nausea swept over Uzi as his mind raced through permutations on how to handle this. He needed to know what Garza knew, and what he was going do about it.

One thing was clear: he'd be getting answers soon enough.

Uzi tried to keep his facial expression impassive. "Yes, Garza. What's your point?"

"Let me lay it out for you. This is Special Agent Adams. Recognize him?"

Uzi looked at the man, then turned back to Garza. "Should I?"

Garza slammed the file closed. "Let's cut through the bullshit, Uzi. I know you were on that ARM compound last night. Adams was there. He works for us, he's an infiltrator. We placed him with ARM after they merged with Southern Ranks. He's been there two years, feeding Flint stuff here and there to keep his position with ARM intact."

"Some key insight offered at just the right moment keeps me in

Flint's good graces," Adams said. "He thinks I'm a freakin' genius, a brilliant strategic planner."

"We've given him some useless stuff along the way, then backed it up with some action to give it legitimacy. Flint thinks he's gotten away with something. And he thinks Adams is someone he needs to keep close."

"The militias started to get wise to us," Adams said. "They were on the lookout for infiltrators and informants. Some in the movement advocated splitting into small cells to make the groups harder to crack. If you've got five members in your closed militia cell, and they're all family or longtime friends, there's no chance any of them's a government plant."

Cell-based structure . . . Exactly what a lot of Islamic terrorist groups use. "Obviously," Uzi said, "ARM doesn't like that model."

"Most of them don't," Garza said. "With small cells you can't have leaders. Some call it leaderless resistance. But militia leaders are like preachers. Take away their followers, you take away their pulpit. No audience, no needy masses to look to them for guidance. No stage to preach from. Fortunately for us, the typical militia leader's ego is his own undoing."

"They don't suspect anything?"

Garza shook his head. "There are three things the militias are trained to look for in spotting infiltrators. Most obvious is the guy who tries to push the group into illegal activity. Infiltrators tend to volunteer for things like selling or purchasing illegal weapons, drugs, bombs, shit like that."

"I do the opposite," Adams said. "I try to point out the danger in getting too aggressive. That way, when I do suggest they go on the offensive, it's got credibility. Because there may be five other times I've steered them away from doing something risky."

"You've been there two years. Don't you have enough on them?"

"Flint may seem like an idiot, but he's got decent instincts. He's very careful to insulate himself. He never directly gives the orders to do something. The weekly radio address, streamed over their website, comes from someone called "The General." I don't know who he is, and no one's talking, if they even know. He's the guy we want."

Uzi shook his head. "If we'd moved on them sooner, the attempt on the veep never would've happened—"

"There are other reasons for taking it slowly," Garza said. "If we moved against ARM based on what Adams gave us, and the prosecution failed—"

"How could it fail?"

"A sharp defense attorney convinces one juror Adams was trying to entrap them. It's happened, more times than I wanna admit. We couldn't take the chance." Garza leaned back, satisfied he'd quieted Uzi. "If they got off, our internal source is gone. We'd never get another mole in. But if we move on them based on other evidence, stuff that can't be traced back to Adams, our ears stay in their organization until we've got enough to take another shot at them."

"So far it's worked real well," Adams said.

Uzi grunted. "Yeah, it's worked so well that our veep and more than a dozen other people were blown out of the sky. Did you know about those plans—before it went down?"

"I don't like what you're implying," Adams said.

"I'm not implying anything. I asked if you knew they were planning to assassinate the vice president."

Garza held up a hand. "Let's not lose our focus, gentlemen."

Actually, losing focus would be a good thing for me at the moment. "How do you feel about gun control, Adams? Better yet, are you a member of NFA?"

"Right now," Garza said, his eyes locked on Uzi, "we're discussing what you were doing on that compound last night. Adams's political views aren't the issue here."

"If he knew about the plot and withheld the information—"

"The question on the table right now is why you were on the compound."

Uzi turned away, his eyes finding the carpet.

"This is the fucking FBI, Uzi. You can't land a goddamn Black Hawk in someone's living room just because you feel like it—"

"You don't know what you're talking about."

"Enough of this," Adams said. "He was there last night with some other guy. I don't know who he was, but he definitely had Special Forces training."

Uzi stood up. "This is a waste of time."

"Is this the way you follow procedure?" The voice from behind him pierced the thick tension in the room. It was Osborn. He'd been so quiet Uzi forgot he was there. Uzi turned slowly, his hands curled into fists. "What was that?"

"He said, 'Is this the way you follow procedure?'" Adams, a few feet from Uzi, tilted his head, daring Uzi to make a move.

"Two sets of rules," Osborn said. "One set for you and one for everyone else. You're a fucking hypocrite."

Uzi charged forward, but Adams grabbed him around the torso. The two men struggled, but Garza was now out from behind his desk and in the mix. Uzi squirmed against their hold for another few seconds, then backed off.

"Doesn't matter what I think," Osborn said. "Our reports have been filed. Now you've gotta answer to the director. Or are you gonna try to punch his lights out, too?"

Uzi sorted himself out. He had to get Osborn and Adams out of his head. He needed to think of the here and now, of the implications of Osborn reporting his ARM visit to Knox. Would Knox then be obligated to inform Coulter, to protect his own ass? Where did that leave Uzi, Shepard, and Meadows?

"Wait a minute," Uzi said, swinging his gaze to Garza. "Knox knew about Adams?"

"Of course."

Uzi ran both hands through his hair. *If Knox had someone on the inside, at the very least, why didn't he tell me? Had he told DeSantos?*

"You placed a very sensitive Bureau op in danger, Uzi." Garza shrugged a shoulder. "I don't think they did anything wrong by filing reports with the director. Like it or not, they were just following procedure."

Uzi's insides tensed. "Were they? Or was there more at work here—like revenge?"

"Hey," Osborn said, "you made your own bed. Don't blame me for having to sleep in it."

Uzi steeled himself against the urge to pummel Osborn's self-righteous smirk into the plasterboard wall. The man knew nothing of the pressures he faced, the tug of war he had been living through. The pawn he had become. To Garza: "He was the source you told me about at Union Station. Why didn't you tell me you had a guy on the inside?"

"It was need-to-know. And I figured you might connect the dots anyway."

Uzi didn't reply. It explained why Garza didn't tell Uzi—but why hadn't Knox? It seemed like too important a detail to leave out. Then again, knowledge was power—and as Uzi was learning, Knox's clout was bolstered by the inside information he was able to amass.

He needed to get out of there, to get some answers. Was Knox setting him up? Uzi never heard Knox actually say he should continue pursuing ARM; it was a message delivered to him by DeSantos.

Uzi decided he couldn't make any admissions to Garza—certainly not in front of Adams or Osborn—until he knew more about who was involved and how it all fit together. For now, he would take his chances.

After giving Garza a parting glance, Uzi turned toward the door. He found himself nearly face-to-face with Osborn.

The two of them locked eyes for a moment. Then Uzi pushed past him and walked out.

5:26 PM
44 hours 34 minutes remaining

Uzi left a couple of messages for DeSantos. While the Osborn-Adams situation burned at the lining of his stomach like bad whiskey, he realized it was something out of his control. What was going to happen would happen, and he would have to deal with it. All Uzi could do now was focus on the million other balls he had suspended in the air.

His biggest concern was that he had more questions than hours left before he had to give the president an answer. He returned to WFO and immersed himself in work. But when his PC clock showed 7:00, the realization hit that he was getting nowhere. He stopped into the Command Post and poured through the thousands of tips the agents had taken, none of which were panning out.

As he stood in the elevator on the way back to his office, he rolled his neck around, the tension burning his muscles like a flame. He closed his eyes and, with the subtle movement of the elevator, felt like he could fall asleep if he were somewhere horizontal. But the tone of his phone stirred him. It was Leila, calling to tell him she had a surprise planned for the evening.

"I'll have to take a raincheck," he said as the doors parted. "Just too much damn work and too little time."

"You know what they say about Jack," she said. "Want me to think you're a dull boy?"

"Maybe Jack is running a major investigation. Cut him some slack." He walked into his office and sat down heavily in his chair. "Tell you what, though. In a few days I'll make sure you don't confuse me with boring old Jack. But for now, I just can't leave."

"You have to get some rest, give your mind a break. Have you even eaten dinner?"

Uzi glanced at the clock. It was almost eight. Where had the day gone? "No, mother, I haven't eaten."

"You have to eat sometime. Let's do it together. I won't keep you long."

His stomach rumbled on cue. He rested his head in his hand, stifled a yawn. He really did need to eat, if nothing else to keep him awake.

"Meet me at HeadsUp Brewery," she said. "A few doors down from Angelo & Maxie's. Ninth and F."

It was only a few blocks away. He could walk it, take in some cold night air. "I've got a couple things I have to wrap up. Meet you there in half an hour."

Uzi looked up from the menu. "I thought you said we'd grab dinner."

"First we do this. Then we eat." She must have read the disappointment on his face, because she placed a hand on his. "C'mon, you can spare an extra half hour."

Uzi sighed. She was right. He needed the time to clear his mind, return with a fresh perspective.

"Okay, I'm game. How does this thing work?"

Leila leaned over his shoulder, seductively touching his back with her breasts. "You brew your own beer. You choose what ingredients you want, mix it all together, bottle it, and label it. A couple of weeks later it's ready to drink." She pointed to a laminated placard that described the process. "Used to be a lot of these places, but the idea didn't catch. This may be the only one left."

Uzi glanced around at the mahogany paneling, the etched glass windows and brass fittings that lined the bar, tables, and light fixtures. "They're into this place for a bundle. You don't cover your monthly nut, you're done." He looked at Leila. "You sure this place will still be here in a couple of weeks when we come back for our beer?"

"Who knows if we'll be here in a couple of weeks."

Uzi raised his eyebrows. "That's a fatalist comment, don't you think? Or just pessimistic?"

Leila shrugged. "You never know, do you? No guarantees in life."

Uzi was looking at her but wasn't really seeing her. *No guarantees in life.* That's what the director general of the Mossad had said to him after Dena and Maya were murdered. Before the agency completed its analysis of what had gone wrong. Before Gideon Aksel removed him from the payroll and made him leave Israel in disgrace.

"No guarantees," Uzi repeated. He set the menu down and cleared away the gloomy memories. "I'm a dark beer guy. You?"

"I'm a dark beer guy, too." She smiled.

"Then let's get started."

They laughed their way through the process, realizing their beer may not taste any better than a can of Coors—but having a good time nonetheless. Uzi typed their assigned lot number into the computer and hit Enter. A wizard appeared, walking them through the process of creating a label.

They chose the design style they wanted—a delicate strand of grain draping across the top with a serifed Olde English font below it.

"What should we call it? Two lines, twenty characters."

Leila scrunched her lips. "Something fun." She grinned. "How about Spy Brew?"

Uzi looked over at her to see if she was joking. "How about something meaningful? To us. Like, Genesis . . . or New Beginnings."

"New Beginnings?"

"Because a relationship takes time to brew, just like beer." Uzi winked at her, then typed in the words. He clicked Finish and waited while the label was making its way to the color printer. He leaned back and interlocked his fingers behind his neck. "In two weeks we'll be enjoying this." He winked. "Assuming we're both still around."

Leila opened her mouth to respond but was interrupted by a chirp from Uzi's phone. As he reached into his pocket, Leila's cell began ringing. They both answered their calls, Leila turning away while she talked.

"It's Hoshi. I've got something you need to see."

"Okay, but I'm in the middle—"

"You'll want to see this now, Uzi."

He looked up at Leila, who was turning toward him. "Gotta go."

Leila held up her phone. "So do I."

Uzi sighed, then swiveled the handset back to his mouth. "On my way."

As Uzi made his way to Hoshi's fourth floor cubicle, his mind made the slow transition back to work mode. Doing the reverse used to be difficult—the Mossad required him to be "always on." Dena often complained that his inability to turn off the stresses of work and focus on her and Maya threatened their relationship. Although he knew she was right, he was never able to change the situation.

It eventually became a moot point.

He exited the elevator, swiped his ID card, then walked through the glass doors en route to Hoshi's cubicle. He found her there, squinting at her computer monitor.

"Hey," she said. "Pull up a chair. Got some things to show you."

Uzi moved in tight and looked at her screen. "Go."

She hesitated a second, then leaned back a bit and appraised him.

Sniffed, moved closer to his body and sniffed again. "Were you on a date?'

Uzi felt his face turn crimson. "What are you, a hound?"

"I don't think that particular perfume works with your body chemistry."

"You're jealous."

Hoshi turned to face her computer. "Maybe."

Uzi interposed his head between the screen and her face. "Really?"

She swiveled her chair toward a stack of files to her left. "I've been going through Tad Bishop's phone logs. His home and office lines were pretty sparse—but his cell's another story. I saw the call he made to you, a few he'd made to me. And then there were about two dozen over a two-week period to someone else."

"Two dozen? Short or long calls?"

"Most were a minute long."

"Leaving a voicemail?"

Hoshi shook her head. "Bishop didn't like to leave messages. For anyone."

"So if these calls weren't to leave messages, then what were they for? Setting up meetings?"

"That would be my guess."

"And who's the owner of this number?"

"Brady Haldemann. According to NCAVC," she said, referring to the National Center for the Analysis of Violent Crime, "he's got a sheet."

"This is a guy Bishop was meeting with regularly?"

"He didn't believe anything he couldn't independently verify. He was very careful."

"For now I'll accept that as fact. But despite what we may want to believe, he wasn't a cop and he doesn't know the standards we have to uphold." Uzi flashed on his ARM compound incursion and guilt stabbed at his gut. "What's on Haldemann's sheet?"

"Mostly petty stuff. Did ten months for assault, but that was twenty years ago. Pretty clean since. I did a search through Southern Poverty Law Center, and got hold of some articles Haldemann wrote for Southern Ranks Militia's monthly newsletter. He was pretty high up there, a Founding Tactical Commander or something like that."

"And the articles?"

"Typical stuff. The government's trampling our constitutional rights, the IRS is unfairly harassing hard-working Americans. Ruby Ridge—and lots of conspiracy garbage on 9/11."

Uzi lifted the phone receiver. "What's the number?"

She scrolled down her screen and read it off to him.

Uzi dialed and let it ring four times before a man answered.

"Brady?"

"Who wants to know?"

"A friend of ours suggested we meet before he . . . expired. I'd like to talk with you about the same things you discussed with him. I think you know who I'm talking about."

"You didn't answer my question. Who are you?"

"Let's just say I'm a friend. More than that I can't say over the phone. Let's meet. Judicial Square Metro station. By the big lion on the left as you face the sign. How about twenty minutes?"

"Come alone." The line went dead.

Uzi checked his watch. It was approaching 11 PM, thirty minutes since he had spoken with Brady Haldemann. But he figured the guy was at least as paranoid as Bishop was, and the best thing he could do was to stay put, look nonthreatening, and wait him out.

He leaned against the lion and glanced across the street at Hoshi, who was observing from a darkened ground-floor window inside the adjacent building fifty feet away.

Five minutes later, a bearded man approached wearing a baseball hat and canvas fishing jacket. Uzi waited till his contact was within ten feet, then slowly pushed himself off the statue. He didn't want to make any threatening moves.

Haldemann stopped a few steps away and thrust both hands into his deep coat pockets.

Normally, such a move would heighten Uzi's paranoia a notch: Did the man have a weapon secreted away? He fought to keep his thoughts in check and said, "I see you found the place okay."

"I'm here. Why, I'm not sure. But you've got five seconds to tell me who you are."

"Name's Uzi. I'm with the Bureau. Like I said, I was a friend of Bishop's."

"He never mentioned you."

"He never mentioned you, either."

"I thought you said—"

"He was working with me on some things that might involve your former group. Your name . . . came up." Telling Haldemann he was with Bishop at the moment he was killed wouldn't put the man's mind at ease. "I'd like to continue that relationship you had with him."

"I don't talk to Feds."

Uzi pulled a pack of Camels from his pocket. He didn't smoke anymore, but he wanted to look relaxed, as if he couldn't care if Haldemann cooperated or not. More importantly, he pegged Haldemann as a smoker, and sharing a hit of nicotine seemed a good way of finding common ground. He offered the man a cigarette, and he took it.

Seconds later, a smoke cloud hovered around them. "You're no longer with SRM," Uzi said.

"I didn't like the merger, didn't approve of what they were doing. But Lewis had his reasons."

"Lewis."

"Lewiston Grant. Guy's fucking brilliant. Born leader. Ex-Green Beret."

Grant . . . An ex-Green Beret. Interesting. If true, how come we didn't know that? "But you didn't see eye-to-eye with him."

Haldemann took a long drag. "He's also a snake. You know much about Southern Ranks and how it became ARM?"

Uzi shook his head. Even if he knew the whole story—which he didn't—an insider would provide a different take.

"Southern Ranks used to be about guys getting together because they didn't like the way the government was taking away our constitutional rights, telling us how to live. What chemicals we could use to fertilize our lawns, which guns we could or couldn't own. Didn't seem right to me how they could just take away our freedoms like that, how they could use affirmative action and NAFTA and shit like that to take away our jobs."

He dragged again on the Camel, left it dangling from his lips. "I saw a flyer on my windshield one day back in late ninety-two, just after Ruby Ridge. It said the same stuff about the government that I thought. So I called the number. It was Lewiston Grant, he was starting up a group to watch out for citizens' rights. I went to a meeting, and the guy really knew what he was talking about. Said he'd been to some big leadership gathering in Colorado, and it made him think long and hard about things. He wanted to start a group of his own. I mean, I sat there listening to Lewis, and I thought, Finally. Somebody who understands what I've been saying all these years."

Uzi leaned back against the lion and examined the cigarette. "So you two started Southern Ranks."

"It took off real fast. Lewis had all these great ideas. Pretty soon we had a couple hundred members and started having regular meetings. Lewis even wrote a book. *America's Second Revolution*. People started calling in from all over the country wanting to buy a copy. The guy worked at a cannery during the day, then soon as he got home he went to work on his computer. He was a freakin' machine. And a great speaker. You got goosebumps all over, he really got your blood going. Like a preacher. I mean it, he got you all revved up. Pretty soon, you're nodding your head, agreeing to do things you never thought you'd be doing."

"You're talking about him in the past. Is he dead?"

Haldemann chuckled. "You can't kill a guy like Lewiston Grant. I'm sure he's alive and kicking. He faked his death a few years ago, changed his identity, some shit like that. Nelson Flint's his lackey, a figurehead. People don't take Flint seriously, so they don't take ARM seriously. A blip on the radar, just the way Lewis wants it. Behind the scenes, Lewis is the brains."

This confirmed Uzi's suspicions and fit with the OPSIG intel DeSantos had assembled before their first visit to ARM. "You said you agreed to do things you never thought you'd do. What kind of things?"

"You think I'm stupid? I answer that, I'll find myself rotting away in some federal prison."

"We're off the record here. I'm investigating the assassination attempt on the VP. That's it."

"So you think I should trust you guys, just because you tell me to."

Uzi looked the man in the eyes, then took a drag. "Yeah. I got that." He stuck the Camel in his mouth, pulled open his jacket, and lifted up his pullover sweater. Haldemann looked down at his bare skin. "No wires," Uzi said. "No recordings. Just two guys talking about things."

Haldemann looked away, blew some smoke from his mouth. "Lewis said we had to find a way to pay for everything. He said until we had some money behind us, we couldn't get our message out to enough people. So SRM hit an armored car. That bankrolled our raid of a couple of weapons depots. Took in a ton of arms and explosives before two of our guys got killed."

"That was '97 or '98, right? Shootout near Fort Decatur. Three officers were taken hostage and killed, another infantryman was paralyzed."

Haldemann's eyes narrowed. "Yeah, '98. February sixteen. That was the last job we did. I'm sure the Feds figured it was SRM, but they didn't have anything tying it to us. I kept saying, too close a call, Lewis. Too close." He took a long drag. "Finally—reluctantly—Lewis agreed with me. Started looking at other ways of increasing membership. But the economy was good, and it's easier to get peoples' attention when they've lost their jobs and things are shitty."

"Like now."

"Like now." He took another drag, seemed lost in thought a moment. "Anyway, that's when Lewis started getting weird."

"How so?"

"He started talking more and more about a government conspiracy. See, most militias believe a secret group called the New World Order is gonna take over the world. They'll use the UN, which is run behind the scenes by a group of wealthy, powerful men. The UN's foreign troops will invade the US, enslave the American public, and install a global dictator."

"And just how are they going to get past the US military?"

"Oh, our government's in on it. According to Lewis, it's all being run by FEMA."

"The Federal Emergency Management Agency?" Uzi stifled a laugh. "They help people. After hurricanes and tornadoes and earthquakes. They get people back on their feet."

"Officially, yes. But their original purpose was an offshoot of the military, to help out after a nuclear war. Lewis says they're now a shadow government that's in bed with the UN. He said they've got executive orders in place that give FEMA control over our communication facilities, power and food supplies, transportation depots . . . and, they've got a hundred thousand Hong Kong police hidden in the salt mines in Utah, just waiting for the word to be given by the UN dictators." Haldemann took a puff. "Lewis used to mention the New World Order in his talks, how Yahweh commanded us to take up arms against it. But he never got so specific about it."

"Yahweh?"

"God. We— I mean, they—don't use the word God because it's 'dog' spelled backwards."

Uzi's eyes narrowed. "Go on."

"Lewis said he'd gotten hold of all kinds of 'proof' that the New World Order was real. He said it all started with Ruby Ridge and Waco, how they were dry runs for the Feds going door to door to arrest innocent people like us—good, hard-working Americans who fought to keep our constitutional rights. He said FEMA's got dozens of subterranean concentration camps set up all over the country, for people who challenge the government and fight the New World Order. They're gonna kill us all once the invading armies have control."

Uzi flicked away a train of ashes from his cigarette. "They really believe this crap?"

"Shit yeah. Hate to admit it, but I did, too. It's in the delivery. Like I said, Lewis is very good at what he does. He got all worked up, told everyone what was going on, and then showed them. Photos of the concentration camps. Hidden messages buried in laws Congress passed. Eyewitness accounts of black helicopters carrying UN troops into position, hovering over militia compounds, following members in their cars, and taking secret pictures of their homes. It was hard to disagree with what he was saying. It all seemed to fit. Everyone bought into it."

"Belief in a conspiracy keeps your membership active, interested in the cause," Uzi said. "It's no different with the Islamic terrorist groups. If there are powerful enemies plotting against you, your membership stays focused on stopping them. Gives them purpose, an us-against-them mentality." Uzi eyed Haldemann, gauging his reaction. If what he was saying made sense to the man, Haldemann was truly "over" the militia movement. Only a person outside the closed group could see the conspiracy for what it really was.

Haldemann dragged hard on his Camel but offered no response.

"So you were concerned about where Grant was leading the group," Uzi said.

"One day Lewis and I were out shooting in the woods and he said he wanted to bomb Camp Grayson, that National Guard base outside Bethesda. He had photos of railroad cars carrying Russian tanks into the base. He said it was the beginning of the foreign invasion, and that we had to stop it. He had this whole plan drawn up. Tell you the truth, it scared the shit out of me. I drove home that night and started thinking. SRM wasn't like it used to be. It changed. From trying to make people aware of government abuses to some big plot to take over the world.

"So I drove over to Camp Grayson and asked to talk with the person in charge. Some guy came out and I told him what the photos showed. He told me it was part of training exercises using Russian tanks we'd captured during Desert Storm, that if it was a conspiracy, they wouldn't have been transporting the tanks in open rail cars. I looked at him, and it hit me. Shit, this guy's right. I wondered if Lewis knew this and didn't care because he needed us to believe an invasion was in the works, or if he really thought they were coming for us. I went back and told Lewis what I'd done. He went ballistic, said I had no business going behind his back like that. I realized he didn't care about the truth, he needed 'the enemy' just so we'd all stay together, united against a common cause."

"Exactly," Uzi said, relieved that Haldemann was exhibiting signs of reason.

"He called off the raid. Next thing I knew, he was saying we needed bigger numbers so our voice would be heard. He changed his title to 'General'—he said Ulysses S. Grant was a Jew-hater, and he wanted to honor the man's legacy. So *General* Grant started talking to Nelson Flint about merging our group with his. Flint's group was the

American Revolution Klansmen back then. Their roots went back to Flint's father, a Klansman in West Virginia. Nelson took over after the old man pulled a gun on a state trooper.

"They expanded into government conspiracy, too, and that's where Flint and Lewis found out they had a lot in common. The two groups decided to focus on stopping the New World Order. Lewis sold Flint on the idea that together they were stronger. Really, Lewis just wanted numbers—the power he could get from having more men under his 'command.' By merging with ARK, he gained ten thousand members. Most of 'em were racist, white supremacist, card-carrying Klansmen, but to Lewis, that was a good thing. He said it made them more committed to the cause. So ARK and SRM became ARM. They drew up a charter, and first on the list was gun control."

"Gun control," Uzi said. He tossed his nearly untouched Camel to the ground. His senses were sharp, refreshed. He felt he'd stumbled onto something important.

"They figured the first thing the New World Order would need to do in order to keep control over the People was to take away our guns. The Brady Bill started it all, they said. Then came the attack on the Second Amendment. Lewis said that any gun law is unconstitutional. Main thing is, they're afraid that once the New World Order agents take away our guns, there'd be nothing we could do to stop the UN troops from moving in."

"How serious are they about all this?"

"Dead serious. The militias consider the Second Amendment to be holier than the Ten Commandments. Weapons are sacred to them. Every spare dollar is spent buying more guns and ammunition. Assault rifles, automatic machine guns, rounds and rounds of ammo. The way they see it, you can't have enough. To the militias, this is a holy war. Like them A-rab extremists."

"How far would they go to make sure their guns aren't taken away from them?"

Haldemann laughed. He took a pull on his cigarette, then exhaled and watched the smoke disappear into the night sky.

"Would they kill?" Uzi asked.

"'Would they kill?' You kidding? They'd find out whoever was responsible and blow the fucker clear to Kingdom Come."

Uzi thought of the C-4 on Glendon Rusch's helicopter. "Does Grant stream a radio show over the Internet to ARM members?"

Haldemann eyed him carefully. "How do you know about that?"

"Thanks for your time. I appreciate what you've told me." He offered Haldemann a card. "If you ever need anything."

Haldemann hesitated, then took it and walked off toward the Metro escalator. He glanced back at Uzi once, then stepped onto the stairpad.

As it began to descend, Uzi saw Haldemann toss the card to the ground.

DAY EIGHT

6:26 AM
31 hours 34 minutes remaining

Thoughts sped through Uzi's mind faster than he could process them. He'd slept fitfully, and finally decided to give up the charade and get out of bed. Now, sitting at the kitchen table, he drummed his fingers on the surface, trying to process what Haldemann had told him.

He glanced at the clock and realized he had to get in the shower or he'd be late for his session with Rudnick. *Fuck it. Can't deal with it now.* He pulled out his phone and texted Shepard.

skipping shrink appt. too much going on

He tossed his phone aside, opened his iPad, and began dictating notes when his Nokia vibrated. Return text from Shepard.

wisconsin resident agency is short an agent. pack ur bags.
naming osborn new head of jttf.

Uzi clenched his jaw. *Goddamn it, Shep. Cut me some slack.* He closed his eyes, took a breath, and replied:

dont like cheese. will make my appt.

He looked at his notes, realized he had lost his train of thought, and shut his iPad. Perhaps a cold shower would shake loose some useful ideas.

Uzi sat opposite Rudnick, his foot drumming a furious beat on the carpeted floor. Rudnick sipped his coffee and waited for Uzi to speak.

"Are you feeling okay this morning?" Rudnick finally asked.

"Me? Yeah, fine. Just a lot on my mind. Things are starting to come together, I think. You okay if we skip today's session? I've got a ton of things to follow up on and very little time left."

"When we last talked, you were having some issues with Leila. How's that coming along?"

Clearly, skipping the session's not an option. "So much has been going on with the investigation, we haven't had much time together."

"I see."

"I did run into Jake Osborn. That didn't go so well."

"The agent you wrote up, yes. So you were expecting a more favorable reaction?"

"No."

Rudnick took a long drink of coffee, then leaned back in his chair and seemed to appraise Uzi for a moment. "The FBI wasn't your first choice when you moved back to the US, was it?"

"You've been spending time in my personnel file."

"Just a bit. But there's really nothing in there. Just a note that you interviewed with the CIA."

"Their Special Activities Division," Uzi said. "Secret paramilitary operators that work undercover. They do everything the military does, and more—and with deniability. I was looking at hooking up with their Ground Branch."

"Sounds right up your alley."

"Because of, well, because of what had happened, I'd had my fill of covert missions. Enough following orders. I realized I couldn't handle it mentally anymore. I'd lost my edge, my mental toughness." Uzi forced a grin. "You realize what it took for me to admit that just now?"

Rudnick didn't smile. "You had 'enough of following orders,' yet you chose to work for the FBI, where protocols and procedures are vital to the performance of your job."

The grin evaporated from Uzi's face. "We're back to Osborn."

"We'll get to Osborn in a minute. First let's talk about 'what had happened,' as you put it."

"How about . . . let's not."

"I really think it'll help. Go back to your days with the Mossad. Was following orders something they stressed?"

Uzi's foot was tapping the floor furiously as he decided whether or not to answer Rudnick. Realizing the good doctor wouldn't allow him to sidestep the issue, he pressed on. "Mission success was the bottom line. They gave you the tools needed to get the job done and the rest was up to you. There were rules, yeah, but they were there to ensure survival. If you didn't follow those rules, you ended up getting caught and embarrassing Israel, or getting killed. Or both."

"What was your role?"

"I did what I did because it was necessary. But I'm not proud of it."

"It?"

Uzi looked away. He pulled a toothpick from his pocket. He could feel Rudnick's gaze on him as he fumbled with the plastic.

"Those toothpicks are like cigarettes for you, aren't they?"

"I used to smoke. These are a hell of a lot healthier."

"Are you embarrassed about what you did with Mossad?"

"Embarrassed? No. Not embarrassed. It was necessary. It was my job."

"Yes . . ." Rudnick said. "But there's something that still bothers you about it."

Uzi had to give the shrink credit. He was very intuitive. He read his patients as if their diagnoses were imprinted on their foreheads. "Killing someone would bother any law-abiding citizen, even if the people you killed were terrorists, horrible people who enjoyed killing others because they were different and had different beliefs.

"During wars, soldiers sit in tanks with a ton of steel between them and the enemy. Or they fly in jets a few thousand feet in the air dropping bombs on a faceless enemy . . . lie on a mountainside hundreds of yards away and pull a trigger . . . launch a missile from a drone. Or fire a machine gun across a ravine. But what I did was up close and personal."

A moment later, Rudnick caught on. "A kidon. A government-sponsored assassin."

"If our operatives found out about a terrorist plot and infiltrated the cell, they would call us in. It was our job to . . . neutralize that cell before they could do any damage."

"You killed them before they could kill innocent people."

"Only if they'd killed before and posed a known risk to the general population." Uzi chuckled. "Sounds so simple, doesn't it? It's not. You try to go about your business because you know what you're doing is right. But you still wake up in cold sweats reliving the mission."

Rudnick nodded slowly, then took a sip from his coffee, as if he were measuring his response. Finally, he said, "I would imagine it's a very difficult thing for anyone to live with, regardless of who your . . . targets are."

"Over the years I worked with other counterterrorism agents—Special Operational Forces, GSG-9s, MI5s, MI6s. We all felt the same way. Yeah, there were some who got off on it, the killing, but most did what we did for our country." He shrugged a shoulder. "'Course, knowing that didn't really make it any easier to live with."

"Your last job was before Dena's . . . death?"

Uzi felt his eyes tearing and looked away. He managed a nod, but couldn't get his voice to work. He cleared his throat and, staring at the floor, said, "A terrorist cell that'd assassinated one of our interior ministers was also responsible for three other bombings. A café, a disco, and a school bus. Seventy-nine were killed. They were planning an attack on the Knesset, to take out a major portion of the Israeli government. It'd be like 9/11, if the plane that crashed in Pennsylvania had made it to the Capitol building."

"It would've been . . . very demoralizing."

"And it would've triggered a war with devastating consequences. So the agents kept a watch on the group's activities, checked and double-checked everything. We found out how they were going to do it. They'd be able to defeat the building's defenses and hit different parts of the structure simultaneously. But we didn't know when it was going down." Uzi relived the events in his head as if they'd happened a month ago. "There was one point each day when the six terrorists were in separate locations. We knew where and when, and I was given the assignment of eliminating one of them. Another five kidons were dispatched to take out the others."

"Sounds like a pretty important mission they entrusted to you."

"The kidon they'd originally assigned got injured. I was the backup. I'd trained alongside him, so I knew the op as well as he did. Funny thing is, if I hadn't gone, my family would still be alive today. Strange how things work out, isn't it, Doc?"

"Uzi, you can't—"

Uzi held up a hand. "There are some things you have control over, and some you don't. Nothing I could've done differently on that. Luck of the draw."

"So what went wrong?"

"They didn't tell me till the morning of the hit that I was going in. They did that sometimes so you didn't stress over it. You trained for days, sometimes weeks, and then one day they just said 'Get your gear, you're going in.' That's when they told me who my target was. I couldn't believe it. I knew the guy. Ahmed Ishaq, one of our best informants. I told the director general there was some mistake, that Ahmed would never do this. He told me to carry out my orders, that our intel was good. He asked me if I could handle this mission, and I told him of course.

"But in the back of my mind, I had doubts. I thought that if I could just talk to Ahmed, find out what was going on. . . ." Uzi shook his head. "I just couldn't believe Ahmed was a terrorist."

"So you went to meet him."

"I should've followed mission protocols," Uzi said, pounding the knife-edge of his right hand into the palm of his left. "Everything was mapped out. Mossad had reconfigured their training facility to match Ahmed's safe house, so I knew the layout before I went in. I'd practiced the maneuvers so many times I could've done it in the dark." Uzi chuckled sardonically. "My grandmother used to say, 'Man plans and God laughs.' Because when emotions enter the equation, everything goes to hell. The best kidons leave their emotions at the door. That's the way I'd handled all my missions. Except this one."

"I take it the Director General was right about Mr. Ishaq."

Uzi was staring at the floor. Finally, he spoke without raising his eyes. "I wanted to give him every opportunity to come clean. But he couldn't, because . . . yes, the director general was right. And it all blew up in my face. One of his buddies was in the back room. I didn't approach the mission like I was supposed to do. I should've scoped out the house, known everyone who was in there. Bottom line, Ahmed was guilty and trapped. They started shooting. I got caught in the cross fire, pinned down. I couldn't even get a shot off. But Ahmed got hit, probably by a ricochet from his partner's gun. The other guy took off."

"What about the other five terrorists?"

"Eliminated."

"Then I don't understand," Rudnick said. He took a sip of coffee. "May not have gone as planned, but it sounds like the mission objectives were met."

Uzi was still staring at nothing.

"Right?" Rudnick asked after a long silence.

"We stopped the terrorist attack. So, yeah. But the guy at Ahmed's place who got away. That's where the problems started. When Dena and Maya were killed . . ." Uzi stopped, his voice choking down. He looked up at the ceiling. His eyes were moist. "A note was left. It read, 'For Ahmed.'"

"But you didn't kill Ahmed," Rudnick said. "His colleague—"

"His buddy couldn't admit he'd shot one of his own. I'm sure he told the others in his cell that I'd killed him. That *is* what I was supposed to do. I'm sure it wasn't hard convincing them that I was the one who'd killed him. Why would they question it?"

Rudnick nodded. "I see. So one of the remaining members of this terrorist group tracked you down and . . . effected revenge. And you blame yourself."

Uzi said nothing.

"Well, my friend, this explains a lot, doesn't it?"

The toothpick bobbed up and down on Uzi's lips. He was trying his hardest to fight back the tears. But a knock at the door interrupted his thoughts.

Rudnick's brow crumpled. He rose from his chair and cracked the door open.

Just then, Uzi's phone rang. The caller ID told him it was Marshall Shepard's private cell phone. "Yeah."

"Uzi, listen carefully. Some bad stuff's going down. I don't know the whole story, but I'm working on it. It's gonna take some time. Just cooperate and don't make it any harder—"

Uzi turned in his seat and saw a gray-and-black uniformed law enforcement officer through the doorway. The man and Rudnick exchanged a brief, muffled conversation—during which Uzi heard his name.

This is about me. Shepard's phone call suddenly made sense.

"I'm a psychologist," Rudnick said, louder. "I'm not at liberty to disclose who's a patient—"

"It's okay, Doc," Uzi said. He was on his feet, moving toward the door. "I'm Aaron Uziel."

A suited man nudged the door open and pushed through. It wasn't until he had entered the treatment suite did Uzi see there were a handful of officers in the anteroom. And their guns were drawn.

Definitely not a positive sign.

"Aaron Uziel, Detective Jack Paulson, Fairfax County Sheriff's Department. I've got a warrant here for your arrest. Do you have any weapons on your person, sir?"

"What's going on?" Rudnick asked. "You can't just barge into a doctor's office and arrest his patient—"

"We can and that's exactly what we're doing," Paulson said matter-of-factly. "Now step back, sir, and don't interfere or we'll have to take you in, too."

Uzi slowly spread his arms like an eagle, his Nokia still in his right hand. An officer stepped forward and patted down Uzi's body, removing the Glock from its holster. Next he found the Puma tactical knife in Uzi's pocket and then the Tanto hanging around his neck.

"I've got a boot knife, too."

The officer handed it all to Paulson, who squinted as he eyed the weapons cache, no doubt wondering why an FBI agent was so heavily—and unconventionally—armed.

"I'll ask you not to make any sudden moves," Paulson said. "You know the drill." Paulson turned around. "Chuck."

A man in a brown windbreaker stepped through the crowd of officers. He opened a small toolkit on the carpet and peeled a couple of wide swatches of adhesive tape from a plastic wrapper. He applied the strips to Uzi's hands, then removed and carefully packaged them.

Uzi knew what they were doing, and he didn't like the implications. "What's the charge?"

The technician nodded at Paulson.

Paulson nudged Uzi around, then pulled his prisoner's arms down one at a time and affixed a set of handcuffs.

"Aaron Uziel, you're under arrest for the murder—"

"Murder?" Uzi craned his neck to look at Paulson. "Of who?"

"John Quincy Adams."

"Is that a joke?"

"No, sir, no joke. And you have the right to remain silent."

"Spare me," Uzi said. But Paulson continued nonetheless. Uzi zoned out, searching his memory for the name John Quincy Adams—beyond the obvious American history reference.

Then it hit him.

8:25 AM
29 hours 35 minutes remaining

Uzi was driven by squad car to the Mason District station of the Fairfax County Police Department. A modern brick and stucco structure, it had the flavor of a small-town police station with all the technology and creature comforts of a metropolitan facility.

A single deputy manned the booking desk, where clipboards and files were stacked on end, with memos and rosters taped to walls. Everything Uzi expected to see that he had seen when he'd visited other police departments as a guest—phones ringing, keys clanging, printers spitting out documents—were absent.

He was led to a counter-mounted camera, positioned in front of a wall with measured hash marks, and given a metal identification sign to hold in front of his chest. The flash sparked and he was ushered over to a metal bench. Ahead stood several jail cells with thick, yellow bars.

"Wait here," Paulson instructed. He handed some paperwork to another deputy, who was operating the free-standing LiveScan electronic fingerprint unit. Uzi's ridges and whorls were recorded and stored digitally in an expansive electronic database. Uzi thought of the tour he'd taken of the Bureau's Criminal Justice Information Services Division, a state-of-the-art fingerprint facility in Clarksburg, West Virginia. The technology contained in the 100,000-square-foot computer center fascinated him. Uzi had wanted to spend more time learning about it, but never had made the trip. Now he was experiencing the front-line centerpiece of the system firsthand.

Paulson led Uzi across the hall to a small room where a rack of forms sat beside a Sony television. Mounted atop the TV was a PictureTel video conferencing unit linked with the magistrate on duty. The bespectacled judge was leaning back in her chair listening to Paulson outline the charges.

Uzi followed his better sense and kept his mouth shut. Mostly, he didn't know what to say other than to deny everything—something he was sure the cops and the magistrate heard often.

Paulson glanced down at his notepad. "Evidence includes a ballistics match to Mr. Uziel's Glock forty-caliber sidearm—"

"What?" Uzi looked at Paulson, his mouth agape.

"You'll get your chance in a moment," the magistrate said to Uzi. She gestured toward Paulson, and the detective continued.

"That should be enough for now, Your Honor."

"Indeed," the magistrate said. "Agent Uziel, now you may speak."

Uzi faced the monitor. He was a bit unnerved over pleading his case to a television screen, but pressed on without hesitation. "Your Honor, what time was Agent Adams murdered?"

The magistrate consulted her paperwork. "ME estimates five to seven hours ago."

Uzi knew the gunshot residue test the forensic technician had performed on him was only valid for up to six hours after firing a weapon—which meant he was right on the cusp of the timeline. Regardless, he was confident the GSR would come back negative since he hadn't fired his sidearm in nearly two weeks. But a negative finding might not do him any good because a good US Attorney would merely point out the test's limitations and the fact that several hours had elapsed since the murder.

Uzi looked directly into the camera. "Your Honor, I only met Agent Adams once—actually, twice," he said, realizing he had first seen the man on the ARM compound. "I had no animosity toward him. I've got no motive." He figured it would be best not to mention the argument in Garza's office, though he knew, of course, it would eventually surface.

"And how do you explain the ballistics match?"

Uzi absentmindedly shook his head. That was a good question. He couldn't. "I don't know, Your Honor."

"Well, for now we're just going to go with what we have. I'm sure you would want me to do the same thing if you were in Detective Paulson's shoes."

Uzi sucked the inside of his cheek. He wanted a toothpick desperately, but given the circumstances figured he would be better off asking for a phone call to an attorney.

"Okay then," the magistrate said. She looked down at the paperwork on her desk and scrawled her signature. "Officer Paulson, we're a go on this one."

Paulson nodded, then took Uzi by the elbow. "Thank you, ma'am."

"Your Honor, I'm running the investigation into the vice president's assassination attempt. I can't just—"

"Agent Uziel, as a rule of law, my hands are tied. They'll have to carry on without you. I hope, for your sake, you get this straightened out."

That makes two of us.

The detective led Uzi back across the hall to Room 162. He pulled open the door, and they walked into the quiet chamber that held six empty jail cells. Paulson grabbed the handle on unit number two and slid the gate aside. Uzi knew that was his cue to enter.

"I'll get you a phone in here as soon as I can. Meantime, make yourself comfortable."

Uzi sat down on the cot and watched Paulson close the door. His first thought was what this meant in terms of his task force and the investigation. He had barely a day left—not a good time to be locked up in a cage.

Then, as he stared at the cold iron bars, a weightier question gnawed at him: who had framed him— And how did they do it? But as the minutes ticked by, the reality of being imprisoned began to eat at him like necrotizing bacteria. The more he thought about it, the more he realized that whoever was behind the downing of the VP's chopper was probably responsible for putting him in this cell. And though the wheels of justice ground slowly, sometimes they got off-track, and bad people got away. Which meant, in his case, the good guy didn't.

He laid back on the cot and stared at the ceiling. Shepard said he was working on it. Uzi hoped to hell he was working fast.

9:04 AM
28 hours 56 minutes remaining

Alpha Zulu sat in a 2004 Dodge Stratus and watched Tim Meadows pull away from the curb in front of his Alexandria home. When Meadows's Ford disappeared down King Street and then turned, Zulu set his watch and waited. Because of the Fibber's expertise in detecting sensors and bugs, Zulu had to resort to low-tech human methods to track his target.

Sierra Bravo, in his equally nondescript and untraceable gray 2007 Mazda 6, was now following Meadows. If the Ford did an about-face and started heading home, a phone call to Zulu would alert him.

They used the same procedures to track Agent Uziel when they tailed his SUV around town. Zulu's people were skilled in city surveillance and kept reasonably close to their target. But determining what Uziel did once he arrived at his destination was more difficult.

But that was where strategically placed state-of-the-art equipment played a role: high-tech concepts with low-tech applications. Nevertheless, Zulu's extensive training taught him that relying less on devices and more on intuition, logic, and reasoning were more reliable methods of gathering accurate intelligence.

He pulled the baseball cap further down over his forehead, got out of his car, and quietly closed the door. He walked briskly across the street, keeping his eyes straight ahead, and went directly into the yard, where he had previously identified his method of entry: the basement window. Using a diamond-edge circle cutter and a suction cup, he scored an opening. After making additional slices, he removed enough glass for him to crawl through, bypassing the alarm.

The surveillance, the intelligence gathering, the mock maneuvers . . . they had their moments. But this was the part of his job he enjoyed the most; each situation was designed to confuse the authorities. Throwing a fastball when they were expecting a curve was pure art. No, it wasn't just art. Working covertly in a target's own home and manipulating law enforcement provided an indescribable sense of power.

But not the power politicians craved. It was more than that. It was the ultimate violation. And when executed to perfection, a rousing—no, explosive—culmination of a job well done.

10:53 AM
27 hours 7 minutes remaining

An hour and a half passed. Paulson had not brought the phone and Uzi hadn't heard anything from Shepard. He was fighting to contain his anger, but panic was worming its way into his thoughts. Scenarios were running through his mind, becoming more nightmarish as the moments passed.

order authorizing Fairfax PD to access the Academy's ballistic Why had they arrested him? Sure, he'd had an altercation with Adams, but so what? That's suspicion, not evidence. They were running a gunshot residue test on him—but that was being done to bolster the evidence they already had.

Uzi tried to compartmentalize his anger and fear to reason this through. If Adams was killed, it had to be someone from

ARM—someone who'd discovered Adams was a government agent. But Adams had been there two years. Who would suddenly betray him—and why now? Fallout from his and DeSantos's incursion on their compound?

Perhaps the incident had been captured on film and Adams was killed for incompetence—an example to the others of what would happen if they didn't do their jobs properly.

He stuck to known facts. They were running a GSR and had recovered a slug from Adams's body. It was from a .40 caliber Glock—the weapon Uzi, and just about all FBI agents, used. Combined with the altercation they'd had, someone must have convinced a judge to issue an arrest warrant. Yet no judge would authorize the arrest of a federal agent unless he had damn good proof. But the magistrate had said there was a ballistics match.

A ballistics match. How can that be?

He stood up and grabbed the bars, closed his eyes and leaned his head against the painted metal. This was not helping. He needed to know what the cops knew.

Suddenly the main door to the room cracked open. And Uzi's head snapped up. DeSantos pushed through.

"Boychick . . . I came as soon as I heard."

"What the hell is going on?"

DeSantos settled himself in front of the cell, placed his hands on the bars. "I wish I could tell you everything's under control, but things are all fucked up."

"What could possibly be fucked up? I didn't kill Adams. What could they have on me?"

"All I know is Coulter signed an profile database. They ran the slug they pulled from Adams. It's a match."

"For my gun."

DeSantos hiked his eyebrows. "Apparently."

"That's impossible, Santa. How could someone steal my gun, kill Adams, and then return it to me?"

"Unless the Glock you're carrying isn't really your Glock. If it was switched at some other time, say a few days ago, you wouldn't have known."

Uzi felt his heart skip a beat. He slumped down onto the cot. "Either way, I'm fucked."

"Not on my watch."

The two men turned to see Douglas Knox standing in the doorway to the cell block.

"Mr. Director," Uzi said, quickly rising to his feet. He glanced at his partner for an explanation, but DeSantos seemed just as surprised.

"Obviously, there's been a mistake," Knox said. "Detective?" He turned to the open doorway.

Paulson walked in, keys dangling at his side. He didn't look pleased. He unlocked Uzi's cell, then walked away without saying a word.

Knox shut the door to the room and stood toe to toe with Uzi. "GSR was negative."

Uzi knew that was a bullshit explanation—the GSR could've been negative even if he had killed Adams. And if that was the reason for his release, Knox would not have wasted his time showing up at the local police station.

"I'll leave you to get your belongings," Knox said. "Hector, with me."

DeSantos gave Uzi's shoulder a shove, then left with Knox.

As Tim Meadows made a U-turn, he took another glance at the sedan down the block from his house. It was one he hadn't seen before. Although some considered his self-preservation measures paranoiac, he had seen more of humanity's seedier slices than most individuals would experience in a lifetime.

And this car bothered him. Sure, its windows were tinted, but there was an intangible *something* about it that set off his internal alarm.

He checked his mirrors, then got out of his vehicle and hustled up the path to the front door. He disabled the house alarm and descended the basement steps to grab a pair of binoculars. He'd find a safe place where he had a clear view, get the license plate, and call it in.

As he lifted his Leupold Mark 4 tactical glasses from their case, he noticed something in the darkness. Rather, it was what he didn't see that caught his attention: the lack of green power LEDs that normally glowed from his PC across the room. He flipped on the lights. The computer—and a couple of projects on the workbench—were missing. And the door to his gun safe was ajar.

Meadows bit his lip. Someone had broken into his home and stolen his PC. Why? Was it related to the Russian 7.62 round Uzi had brought him? As he reached for his cell phone, his eye caught sight of a red light on the floor, attached to a device that wasn't supposed to be there: a detonation unit piggybacked by what looked like multiple blocks of C-4.

"Jesus Christ!"

Meadows darted forward, as fast as his thick legs would carry him, toward the basement's side wall. He grabbed the heavy gun safe door and pulled it open, then shoved his body inside, rotating his beer gut and squeezing himself against the velour interior.

He struggled to swing the door shut. But he couldn't lock it— This was a safe, with hardened steel lugs that latched into the frame. As long as he didn't secure the handle, he could get out. But if the mechanism engaged accidentally, or if debris piled in front of the door, he'd die from asphyxiation.

If the blast didn't kill him outright. He gambled the explosion would push the door tight enough for the duration of the pressure wave, then leave the path free of rubble for his exit. Gambling. With his life. Damn it . . .

Images flicked through his mind like an out-of-control movie projector. Calm yourself. Think!

He pictured the device, analyzing its setup. Reviewing his options. What options? Defeat it. Difficult, but not impossible. If he had time to study it. But if he guessed wrong, or if it was booby trapped, the fat lady would be singing so loud everyone in the neighborhood would hear her.

Then there was that car. If the bombers were sitting out there waiting for the right second to set off the device, they'd probably shoot him dead if he tried to leave the house.

No, there was no defeating it and no escaping. The only thing left to do was hope the safe would survive the explosion. It was fire resistant and blast proof. But even though the force would be directed upwards, he was so damn close to the bomb.

Just how blast proof was "blast proof"?

He was sure whoever planted it had to be associated with Uzi's case. Who else would want him dead? He was a likeable guy. No enemies, aside from that sixth grade bully he popped in the eye—

So freakin' hot in here. He struggled to breathe, wishing he'd stuck to the diet and exercise plan he'd started two years ago. Would've been a lifesaver in more ways than one.

Nothing to do but wait. His skin was clammy and fear-slick. Mere seconds had passed, but it felt like hours.

His arms ached from pulling on the door to keep it closed—but not locked—not locked!

Cell phone— Would it work in here? Call EOD. Yes! Before the damn thing goes off. But in the next second, that thought vanished.

The blast was deafening.

Uzi retrieved his belongings—sans his Glock—and met DeSantos in the parking lot. His partner started talking before Uzi reached him. "Knox said your palm had trace barium and antimony."

"From handling my weapon, putting it in my holster."

DeSantos nodded. "That was all they found. Otherwise, GSR was negative."

They got into DeSantos's vintage Corvette and swung the doors shut. "Santa, you and I both know they're not throwing out a murder charge based on a negative GSR. What gives?"

DeSantos turned the key and the massive engine roared to life. "Knox took care of it."

"Knox made a murder charge go away?" He snapped his fingers. "Just like that?"

"Don't worry about it, boychick. Just forget it. Let Knox do his thing, okay?"

"His thing?"

"You know his affiliation with OPSIG. His work with black ops. He has ways of dealing with shit like this."

"But—"

"He takes care of his people. I told you that. That's how he builds loyalty."

Uzi considered this as DeSantos headed out of the lot. Was this Knox's way of getting Uzi to back off his investigation of the director's NFA links? I take care of you, you take care of me?

"From what I know of Knox," Uzi said, "if he does something like this, it's gotta serve his interests. So I guess the question is, What are his interests?"

"Despite what you might believe, he only tells me what he thinks I need to know. And why he did what he just did is not something he thinks I need to know."

Uzi looked hard at DeSantos, trying to determine if his partner was being straight with him. "I'm not comfortable with this. Another thing for him to hold over my head."

"Were you more comfortable in that prison cell with a lethal injection in your future?"

"No."

"Then don't look a gift horse in the mouth."

"No shit. In this case I might find rotten teeth."

DeSantos frowned. "You're a hard man to please, you know that?"

As they approached the exit, a black Lincoln Continental pulled in front of the Corvette, blocking their path.

"What the hell is this?" Uzi asked, his right hand moving toward his empty holster.

DeSantos touched his partner's arm with calm assurance.

The Lincoln's blacked-out rear window rolled down, revealing the silver-haired Douglas Knox. DeSantos threw the gear shift into Park and got out of the car, Uzi close behind.

Knox, tracking Uzi's movements, said, "Agent Uziel, do you know who Danny Carlson is?"

Indeed he did. Danny Carlson was Nuri Peled's cover name. Was this a test? Or a trap of some sort? Unsure as to why Knox would bring up Peled's name, Uzi simply said, "Yes."

When Knox's expression did not change, Uzi concluded the man already knew the answer to his own question.

"Mr. Carlson was found dead an hour ago. In his garage, apparent suicide. He was a former colleague of yours, I believe, so I thought you might want to know." Knox waited a beat, then said, "JTTF should confirm cause of death. See to it." When Uzi did not respond, the window rolled up. A second later, the car drove off.

The air in front of Uzi turned Everest-thin, a dizzying array of colored pinpricks dancing around him, sparkling, swirling, shifting. In the next instant Uzi was sitting on the asphalt, DeSantos kneeling in front of him.

"You okay? Uzi. Look at me, man, look at me." He gently slapped Uzi's cheeks and, over the next few seconds, Uzi focused on his friend's face.

"I just saw him, Santa. Just spoke to him."

"Nuri was a good man. A good operative."

Uzi licked his lips. "You knew him?"

"You weren't the only guy in Mossad I worked with."

"After the chopper went down, I reached out," Uzi said, his voice coarse with pain. "To see if he knew anything about a Mideast connection. Nuri said there was nothing as far as he knew. But he'd heard a whisper that a new group had a sleeper operating in the States. He was checking it out for his employer. Not Mossad . . . He called it a 'friendly ally.' He shifted things into high gear because of the chopper crash."

Uzi lifted himself off the ground and straightened his jacket with a wiggle of his shoulders. "I spoke to him again the night I dropped by your place. He hadn't found anything but was working it. Obviously, the rumor was true and the group he was tracking is here. They must've found out he was on their tail." He looked up at his partner, his face lacking color. "Santa, did I get him killed?"

DeSantos held up a hand. "Before you slop another helping of guilt onto your plate, let's add this up. Knox said it looked like suicide. Gassed himself in his garage. Not exactly your typical hit."

"I know Nuri. He wouldn't do that. And he gave no indication of being in distress. It's bullshit."

"I agree. Then if it was a hit, they wanted to keep it low key, to minimize suspicion. So they staged it. But that's not a terrorist's typical MO, either." He regarded Uzi, then asked, "Your reaction to the news tells me Nuri was more than just one of your sources."

Uzi nodded, then looked skyward as if God could provide an answer. "He was my mentor when I joined up. Taught me a lot about staying alive. But I hadn't talked to him since I left Mossad. It was good seeing him. I didn't realize how much I missed talking with him."

"I'm sorry, man."

"I have to call Knox, tell him what Nuri was working on. If it wasn't suicide, and if a sleeper was involved, Homeland Security needs to know. And I need to get some people assigned to it. You call Knox, I'll call Shepard."

DeSantos nodded and rooted out his BlackBerry as Uzi dialed. But before Uzi could hit Send, the phone rang. It was Shepard. He started to brief his boss on Peled, but Shepard interrupted him. Uzi listened for a moment, then turned to DeSantos, who was ending his call. "How fast can this thing go?"

"My 'vette?" DeSantos chuckled devilishly. "How fast do you want it to go?"

Uzi started toward the car. "Fast."

Uzi and DeSantos ran into the Virginia Presbyterian emergency room, where Uzi flashed his credentials and asked where Tim Meadows was being treated. The nurse gave them resistance, but Uzi was in no mood for delays, and he made sure she understood his urgency. A moment later, they were striding down the hall looking for treatment suite four.

Gauze bandages covered Tim Meadows's head and hands. A moment passed before Meadows opened his eyes.

"My old pal," Meadows said, "the man with the cool name. Uzi. Aaron Uzi." He licked his dry lips. "It's got that license-to-kill feel."

"Tim, I really—"

"Feel guilty? Don't. I'd hate for you to feel responsible for nearly getting me killed."

"Tim . . . I really am sorry." He looked at the monitors attached to Meadows's body. "Are you okay?"

"What? You'll have to speak up because my hearing is, like, how shall I put this? Severely impaired. I was thinking of having a nametag made up to wear around the office: Speak up 'cause I'm freakin' deaf. What do you think?"

Uzi frowned. "What I said was—"

"I know what you said, I read your lips. So you want to know if I'm okay. Hmm. Let me think about it for a second. Several freaking blocks of C-4 exploded in my basement a few feet from where I was standing. I can still hear the explosion in my head. 'Course, I can't hear anything else."

"I'd say you escaped relatively unscathed."

"Yeah? Easy for you to say. Would you like a concussion and two broken hands?"

"Care to tell us what happened?"

"A bomb exploded. Specific enough?" He must have noted Uzi's pained expression, because he continued: "I saw this car on my street. Didn't look right to me. I went into my house to get my binoculars so I could grab the plate, have it run.

"I realized someone had stolen my PC and broken into my safe. That's when I saw it. Blocks of C-4 connected to a detonation device. I hid in the safe. But it took out a good chunk of my house. My goddamn house, Uzi."

"If you were in the safe, how'd you get so banged up?"

"I stayed put to make sure they weren't waiting around to finish off the job. There was so much garbage all around me I had a hard time pushing open the door. I finally got it open and climbed out, but twisted my ankle and went down hard, broke my fall with my hands—then all sorts of crap hit me in the head. I blacked out. Metro PD pulled me out of the rubble."

"Do you know who did this?" DeSantos asked.

Meadows's eyes moved over to DeSantos when he saw Uzi look at his partner. DeSantos repeated his question.

Meadows tilted his head. "Shouldn't I be asking you that? I assume the same person who wanted my PC and backup files. And, if I might guess, the same person who wanted that Russian round you gave me to analyze."

Uzi glanced at DeSantos, then looked at Meadows. "Your PC is missing?"

"I'm the one who's near deaf, Uzi. Do you really need me to repeat myself?"

Uzi rolled his eyes. "Are you sure they got the bullet?"

"Your concern for my health is flattering." He turned to DeSantos. "I thought he'd ask if I'll regain my hearing, and how long I'll be laid up here. Instead he asks about his bullet."

Uzi leaned on the hospital bed, getting closer to Meadows. "Tim, I can't tell you how sorry I am. I didn't mean for you to get dragged into this. And I sure as hell didn't want you to get hurt. You know that."

Meadows looked away. "Yeah, I know it."

Uzi ducked down, got in front of his friend's face. "You need somewhere to crash, I've got room at my place."

"I may take you up on the offer. But first things first." Meadows kicked back the thin blanket and swung his legs over the side of the cot.

"Where are you going?"

"Going? Nowhere without a freaking wheelchair." He pointed. "There's one over there in the corner."

As DeSantos turned to retrieve it, Uzi grabbed Meadows's arm.

"You sure it's a good idea for you to get out of bed?"

"First of all, I hate hospitals. Second, if you give me a hand, I might be able to access the data that was on my PC—including the ballistics results I took from that round."

Meadows looked at DeSantos. "You're all business, Mr. DeSantos. I can tell. Tell your buddy to get me over to a computer that's hooked up to the Internet, and not to waste any time because whoever stole my PC knows what he's doing. He'll be going through the hard drive. And that's when he'll find my trail."

"Your trail?" DeSantos asked.

"His online backup account," Uzi said.

"If it's still there. Our bomber may try to delete it. We should hurry."

"Where do we find a computer?" Uzi asked.

Meadows shrugged. "Doctor's lounge?"

Uzi helped him off the bed and into the wheelchair while DeSantos sorted out the wires and tubes so he could unhook Meadows from the monitors and take the IV stand with them.

"I tried to get the nurse to get me to a computer, but she clearly didn't understand what was at stake." He grabbed the armrests of the chair. "Whoa."

"You okay?"

"Just dizzy. They've got me a little doped up."

"If you weren't in such a bad way, I'd say that you're always a little dopey."

"I'm glad you restrained yourself. Your lack of humor might depress me even more." He closed his eyes for a second. "Head's killing me."

"Let's get going so we can get you back to bed as soon as possible." DeSantos gave the chair a push toward the doorway.

"So, since it damn near cost me my life, I'm a tad bit curious. Just what is at stake here?"

Uzi shared half smiles with DeSantos, and then leaned in front of Meadows so his friend could read his lips. "Believe me, Tim, you really don't want to know."

"You said the same thing to me when you gave me that Russian round to analyze. Still sticking with that line, huh?"

"It still applies."

The third floor doctor's lounge featured four computers sitting on a long work shelf against the far wall. Uzi pushed Meadows in front of one of the keyboards, and Meadows lifted his splinted hands. "Oh, Christ. This isn't gonna work."

Uzi pulled over an adjacent chair and followed Meadows's instructions to log into his SafeStor online data storage account. As Uzi scrolled down the list of hyperlinks, Meadows scanned the items, mentally ticking off each one.

"Well?" Uzi finally asked.

"There," Meadows said, pointing at the screen with a bandaged paw.

Uzi looked at Meadows's hand and then at the screen. "Can you be a little more specific?"

Meadows scowled. "Click that box where it says, 'Select all,' and then that green button that says 'Download.'"

Uzi did as instructed.

"Where are you going to put all of it?" DeSantos asked. "It says there's nineteen gigabytes of data. I may not know much about computers, but my former partner did, and I do know that when you're talking gigabytes, it's an awful lot of shit."

Meadows bobbed his head. "Yes and no. It's all relative." He pointed.

"We're going to borrow some room on the hospital's server. I'm sure they won't mind."

"Anything sensitive in here?" Uzi asked. "We really shouldn't—"

"Would you rather lose it? Because unless we move fast, in the time it takes for me to argue with you, all our data could vanish."

"Do it," DeSantos said. "Now."

Meadows directed Uzi to download all the data to a special folder they created on the hospital server. The green status bar began moving from left to right at a rapid pace.

"Looks like they're on a DS3 connection," Meadows said, "so this should go quickly."

Uzi swiveled his chair toward Meadows. "Give me the lowdown on that Russian round. Did it match the one pulled from Bishop?"

"It sure did. One hundred percent."

Uzi shared a look with DeSantos. Regardless of what his partner thought of Bishop's paranoia, the informant's fears were clearly justified. "Only one thing bothers me."

Meadows's brow hardened. "Only one thing?"

"How did they find him?" Uzi asked DeSantos.

DeSantos shrugged. "Good question. I'm sure he didn't broadcast the fact that he had the stuff we gave him."

Meadows's gaze shot back and forth between the two men as if he were watching a tennis match. "Will you two stop talking about me like I'm not here? And talk louder!"

"If we were tailed . . ."

Uzi nodded. "I'll check the car when we get out of here."

As the last bytes of data were being transferred to the Virginia Presbyterian server, a red dialogue box popped up. "Connection to SafeStor server lost. Authentication cannot be verified. Attempt to log in again or contact administrator for assistance."

DeSantos stepped closer to the screen. "What the hell does that mean?"

"It means we've either got a security issue on the hospital's end, or . . . we were a tad bit late getting this done."

"How much did we get?" DeSantos asked.

Uzi leaned back in his seat. "Ninety three percent."

"Try logging off and signing in again," Meadows said.

Uzi did so—but upon returning to the SafeStor account, the files were gone.

"Looks like our friends didn't want us getting at your data."

Meadows sighed. "If they were a few minutes faster we wouldn't have gotten anything." He nodded at the screen. "Click on our folder, let's see what we got."

A moment later, after scrolling through the file names, Meadows concluded they had retrieved everything that was important—both to him and to Uzi.

Uzi blew a mouthful of air through pursed lips. "So who would've gone to all this trouble?"

"That, boychick, is the million dollar question."

"We need a cover story," DeSantos said. "For him." He nodded at Meadows.

Meadows threw up his bandaged hands. "Again with the third person."

"You mean leak something to the press that Tim was killed in the blast. Or critically wounded and died here after surgery. We'll need to dummy up the records. What about the staff?"

DeSantos nodded. "Would've been easier at the military hospital. I'll have to see if OPSIG has anyone here on the payroll."

Uzi logged off the hospital's network. "You take care of that. I'll get a guy over here from CART to retrieve and wipe the data. Meantime, Tim, let's get you back to bed."

DeSantos pulled out his cell phone. "And a few agents to sit watch outside his door until he dies his unfortunate death in the OR."

Meadows's gaze bounced from Uzi to DeSantos, his mouth agape with horror. "Remind me never to get on your bad side. You guys are very dangerous, do you know that?"

3:39 PM
22 hours 21 minutes remaining

The Metro doors slid apart and Uzi walked out. He headed up

the long escalator and emerged a block away from WFO. DeSantos, meanwhile, stayed at the hospital to supervise Tim Meadows's untimely death and the secure transfer of his data from Virginia Presbyterian's server.

Uzi knew he should check in with Shepard but didn't feel like dealing with the questions he would ask. Instead, he went straight to his office to collect his messages—and his thoughts.

He draped his jacket around the back of his chair and rolled up his sleeves, ready to dig in. He wasn't at his desk three minutes before Hoshi appeared in the doorway, notebook in hand.

"You get my text about Tim Meadows?"

"Just got back from the hospital. Been a bit preoccupied. Sorry."

"How's he doing?"

Uzi glanced at his clock. "Officially, he's dying in the OR right about now, complications from the explosion. Unofficially, he'll fair a bit better. Probably be off work awhile." *And he may need a hearing aid.*

She took a seat in front of his desk. "I'd been trying to reach you for about three hours. Where were you all day?"

"What are you, Agent Koh or Mother Koh?"

Hoshi frowned. "Fine, be that way."

Uzi looked down at his desk and shuffled some papers. "I had . . . a problem that needed to be dealt with." He trusted Hoshi, but an innocent mention of his arrest could cause a tidal wave of rumor to sweep through the building—and the Osborn fallout had already caused enough damage. "I need two agents assigned to the death of someone named Danny Carlson. Shepard's got the details. Metro PD probably caught it, but we need to take it over ASAP. Do it gently— I don't want any hard feelings with MPD, okay?"

"Related to our investigation?"

"Hard to say. Could be a hit by a sleeper cell of Islamic terrorists, staged to look like suicide." His eyes found hers. "Get me two of the best agents we can spare, Hoshi. This guy was a friend of mine, I owe it to him to do a thorough job." Uzi grabbed for a toothpick, shoved it in his mouth. That was all he cared to say on the matter, and he hoped she would sense that. "How are we doing on Wheeler?"

"Nothing. I hate to say it, but unless we get access to the NICS, we're in a holding pattern. Surveillance hasn't given us anything. We're at a dead-end."

"Speaking of dead ends, anything on Lewiston Grant? He might be ex-Green Beret."

"Nothing more than Garza had. He basically disappeared. I put Cindy Caruthers on it."

"She's sharp. Good call." He sighed, dipped his chin and began massaging his temples. "What about Vail's profile?"

"Cindy's in charge of that, too. So far, nothing on that front, either." She hesitated. "I've got another problem for you. Or is this a bad time?"

Uzi's low-level headache was graduating and rapidly making a bid for migraine status. "It's a bad time. But there's never a good time for a problem." He leaned back in his chair and closed his eyes. "Hit me with it."

"I put together a background on Congressman Harmon, then did a cross match with all the other vics, and basically came up empty. On the surface, at least, there's no connection. Your software program didn't find anything, either."

"Dig deeper."

"Felder and Brown are on it, but they're getting some resistance. I hope to have something on your desk in a couple of days."

Uzi groaned. "We don't have a couple of days, Hoshi. Tell them to get me an answer by tomorrow morning." He pushed harder on his temples, but it only increased his headache. "That's not the problem, I take it."

"No, the problem is that the congressman seems to be one huge contradiction. I mean, at first look, he appears to be a left-leaning moderate, I guess. His policy speeches support a woman's right to choose, he's soft on the death penalty, and prefers fiscal responsibility over cutting taxes across the board for votes."

"Okay," he said, still massaging his head, searching for some magical headache release button.

"But when I examined his voting record, the legislation he either authored or voted for tells a different story." She paused, but Uzi's eyes remained closed as he poked and prodded. "Strictly far right," she said. "In fact, he wrote an article for *The Southern Sentinel* on gun control. *The Southern Sentinel* is a newsletter that used to be published by Southern Ranks Militia."

Uzi's eyes snapped open. "What?" He leaned forward, the arms of his chair slamming into his desk. "Do we have this article?"

She opened her notebook, pulled out a printed document, and handed it to him.

He set it down on his desk. "Give me the executive summary."

"The article probably went over most of his readers' heads. It's written like a law review article, with references and footnotes. But the gist of it attempts to use the Constitution to justify the right to bear arms and stand up against our government should it begin to repress the people."

Hoshi thumbed to a page of her notebook. "And he was quoted a number of other times. Get this: two years ago, he said, 'We can only have a true democracy when the Federal government is afraid of its citizens.' Or this one, after Oklahoma City: 'Sometimes a government pushes people too hard, makes it too tough for the average hard-working American to earn a decent wage. I think we have to stop squeezing the average Joe, and stop it now, because we're going to have a thousand Timothy McVeighs trying to stop us if we don't do it first.'"

"We can't condemn the guy for his opinion," Uzi said. "Still . . . this is a connection. Did you give all this to Felder and Brown?"

Hoshi gave him a look.

"Okay, of course you did." He rooted out a bottle of Excedrin from his drawer. He pulled out his toothpick, threw two tablets into his mouth, and began chewing.

Hoshi cringed. "Don't you need water?"

Uzi was staring ahead at his desk, his teeth crunching the pills and mind crunching the information she had just given him. "So what does this mean? Was Harmon an ARM collaborator? Just a sympathizer? Was he killed because he knew something?"

"Whoa. I don't think I've seen horses leap as high as you just did. Don't you think you're getting a little ahead of yourself?"

Uzi settled his forearms on the desk. "Am I getting desperate? Maybe a little. But look at the facts: at the very minimum, Harmon was a sympathizer with the militia cause, and ARM, a major player in the militia movement, is suspected of trying to take out the veep. But the plan goes south, and suddenly Ellison, Fargo, and Harmon are killed. And Bishop. And Adams, who'd infiltrated ARM." What he almost told her is that ARM was definitely responsible for Bishop's murder—but he caught himself in time.

"Adams?"

"John Quincy Adams. No, I'm not joking—Special Agent Adams. He was working out of HQ. You'll be briefed on it tomorrow morning." Uzi moved the toothpick around his mouth with this tongue. "They're getting rid of people who knew something, Hoshi, I'm sure of it. We just have to find out what they knew. What's ARM afraid of? Some other part of their plan they're about to implement?"

"Who's handling the Adams investigation?"

"Fairfax PD. And possibly someone out of HQ. But we need someone from the task force looking things over. Do me a favor, call Jake Osborn, ask him if he wants it."

Hoshi's eyebrows rose. "Jake Osborn?"

"Yes. Osborn. I think he'd appreciate it. Adams was a friend of his."

"Are you feeling okay?"

Uzi looked at her. "No, actually, I'm not. Please, just give it to Osborn."

4:01 PM
21 hours 59 minutes remaining

After Hoshi left his office, Uzi leaned back in his chair and closed his eyes, hoping the Excedrin would win the battle with the headache mallets pounding away inside his head. Fifteen minutes later, his cell phone jolted him awake. He rooted it out of his jacket pocket. It was Leila.

"How about dinner at my place? Chinese takeout. Soft music, a bottle of Rombauer Zin. Full bodied, fruity, with hints of sensuous raspberries. Irresistible, actually."

Uzi pulled his feet off his desk and sat up. "Are you describing the wine—or yourself?"

"I think you should take a tasting and decide for yourself."

"I'm there. Around seven?"

"Make it six. Then we'll have time for a bath, too."

He dropped the phone back into his pocket, then realized that the Excedrin had reduced his headache to a dull jab. He could live with that—and after the day he'd had, he could use a romantic evening to take his mind off Nuri Peled, the death and destruction of the past eight days, and the pressure that came with having few answers and many questions on the eve of an important deadline. Re-energized, he lifted his phone and began to dial.

The next ninety minutes seemed to crawl. He approved Hoshi's choice of agents for the Peled investigation—Danielle Phish and Bob Mason—then met with various task force members, cleaned up several dangling issues that needed to be addressed, and got status reports from a number of agents, including Felder and Brown, who were less than pleased with their newly imposed deadline. Heat at the top always trickled down to those below, Uzi told them.

Hoshi assured him they would find another way of getting the NICS database info, but Uzi wasn't so sure. He hated being handcuffed—literally and figuratively. As soon as the meeting broke, he went back to his desk and breezed through his emails, leaving him fifteen minutes to get to Leila's.

He paused at Madeline's desk long enough to say good-bye, but not long enough to get sidetracked. He wanted to get to the elevator, then his car, then the front door of Leila's apartment.

He pulled up in front of the Hamilton House at six, took his familiar spot in the passenger loading zone by the front curb, and dropped his keys with Alec.

"Miss Harel told me to expect you, Mr. Uzi."

"Thanks, Alec. I appreciate your help." Uzi hurried toward the bank of elevators, making a mental note to pick up a gift at the FBI Academy's PX shop—an FBI or DEA baseball cap or gym bag would no doubt make Alec and Jiri big shots with their friends.

He was at Leila's apartment moments later, his knuckles rapping on her door. He heard high heels clacking against the tile entryway, followed by the metallic slip of a lock sliding open.

She greeted him in a red negligee. Uzi stood in the open doorway, his mouth salivating like a wild cougar licking its chops as it looked down on a young doe. Leila reached out and took his hand, then pulled him inside.

They lay in the hot water, candles flickering around them, their glasses of Zinfandel—and the empty bottle—sitting precariously on the tub edge. Leila spread oil across his shoulders and rubbed, working out the knots with her strong thumbs.

"You're a mess," she said. "Even after the wine . . ."

"I didn't take this job because it was dull and boring. Stress comes with the territory. I'm sure it's the same with you." He thought of telling her about Nuri Peled's death, but as quickly as it leapt into his consciousness, he shoved it aside. He didn't want anything spoiling the moment.

"I know how to ease the tension. It usually works really well. Want to know my secret?"

Eyes closed, he absorbed the kneading relief of her hands. "You're killing me with the suspense."

"Yoga. Yoga is the key."

"Yoga."

"And meditation."

Uzi reached over and lifted the wine glass to his lips. "Yoga and meditation. Good to know."

"I'm serious. Have you ever tried them? I can teach you some moves."

"I can think of some other moves I'd like you to teach me."

She leaned forward, her chest resting against his back, as she drew her arms around to his front. "Are you ready? Here's the first one."

Uzi awoke at 11:20 and reached for his phone to make sure he hadn't missed any important texts or emails. It wasn't in his pocket or coat—but he had to pee badly, so he ran into the adjacent bathroom. On returning, he checked his jacket again—and noticed Leila stirring. He gave her a peck on the lips and she looked up at him, then smiled.

He knelt beside her, took her warm hand, and smiled back. "I didn't think I'd find happiness again," he said. "I figured I'd be alone the rest of my life."

"The pain must be unbearable, constantly thinking about your wife and daughter."

Uzi nearly jerked backwards. "Yes." How could such a heavenly moment come crashing down to reality so fast? "Unbearable." He could feel tears welling up in his eyes. *Shit. Why'd she have to bring that up?*

"You okay? Did I upset you?"

"No," he said. He remembered his phone, and needing a diversion before he started bawling, said, "Can't find my phone. Must've left it in the car. If anyone's trying to reach me . . ." He leaned on the bed and pushed himself off the floor.

"You're coming back?"

"Of course," Uzi said as he pulled on his pants. He slipped on his V-neck sweater, then grabbed his jacket and headed out.

His ride down to the first floor seemed to take longer than usual: alone with his thoughts, the guilt burrowed into his gut. Making such a precipitate emotional descent left him feeling like he was skydiving without a parachute.

He wiped the tears from his eyes as he stepped out of the elevator, then walked to the concierge's desk, where Jiri was reading a magazine.

"Mr. Uzi, is everything good?"

"Everything's fine. I think I left my phone in the car."

"Alec went to move it. Limo coming with the Chilean ambassador. We need the front curb open." Jiri craned his head to peer out the large windows that fronted the street. "You might catch him soon. He just leave."

Uzi turned toward the ornate lobby and took off toward the front doors, sidestepping the overstuffed chairs and sofa. "Thanks," he yelled over his shoulder.

If Alec drove off before Uzi could reach the car, he'd have to wait till the doorman parked the car and made his way back to the lobby through the parking structure on the other side of the enormous building. Then Uzi would have to get his keys, find his Tahoe, and retrieve the phone. This late at night, in his current frame of mind, he was not in the mood to go searching through a parking garage. He cursed himself for leaving it in the car. He shouldn't be out of touch.

As Uzi ascended the three steps to the canopied street-level entryway, he saw Alec in the Tahoe's driver's seat as the door closed and the glow of the dome light went out.

But before Uzi could take another step, a searing fireball exploded upward and outward. Heat slammed against his face, the blowback throwing him to the pavement like a rag doll. Metal and rubber flew past him. He curled into a fetal position and buried his head, trying to make sense of what had just happened. His brain was sluggish, his hearing muffled by the blast.

He felt someone grabbing his arms, dragging him along the rough brick, the heels of his boots scraping and kicking up with the jagged surface, bouncing down the three steps, and across a threshold.

The helping hands then dropped his arms. Cool air breezed across his face. Uzi looked up and saw the high, taupe ceiling of the lobby. His senses started to come back to him. He fought dizziness and rose to his knees, using the large, adjacent flower pot for leverage and support.

He touched his face, felt something thick and slippery, and immediately identified it as blood when he saw his smeared hand. The elevator doors opened and Leila came running out. She looked to her right, out the large windows, and saw the still-burning Tahoe. Uzi's vision was slightly blurred, and he wasn't ready to venture the few steps toward her, but at the moment all he wanted to do was run to her arms. He needed something—support? Confirmation that he was still alive? He wasn't sure what it was, but he reached out to her with his left hand while leaning his full weight on the flower pot.

She was still staring out the window, watching the car burn. Why wasn't she coming?

"Leila," he managed. "Leila—"

She turned and saw him, confusion crumpling her face. "Uzi! Oh, my God!" She ran toward him, grabbed his body and hugged him tight. "What happened— Are you all right?"

"Car bomb," he said. "I'm . . . okay. I'm alive." He looked at her eyes. "I am alive . . . aren't I?"

"I'm calling an ambulance. Come, sit down on the couch."

She disappeared behind Jiri's concierge desk. Uzi heard her talking, reporting the incident. A moment later, she was back at his side. When she sat down, her weight tilted the couch cushion toward her body. He started to fall into her, then stuck out his hand to steady himself. "Just a little off balance."

"Ambulance is on the way. I paged Shepard, too. We'll get you taken care of, don't worry."

"You're going to be fine," the paramedic said. "You've got a minor concussion, but you'll recover fully. Meantime, you might have some headaches and dizziness. If there's someone who can wake you every couple of hours, check your pupils, just to make sure—"

"I've got it covered." The voice came from behind him. Uzi turned and saw his partner standing there.

"Santa, glad you could make it."

"C'mon, let's get you out of here."

Uzi was feeling better—not as weak, his mind clearer, his hearing more distinct. "Where's Leila?"

"Outside, briefing Shepard."

"I should say good-bye—"

"I already took care of it."

"You? No, let me—"

"Don't worry about it."

"But what about Shepard? I should check in—"

"No." DeSantos's grip on Uzi's arm was suddenly firm. "Come on."

Uzi followed DeSantos into the garage, where a large black limousine was parked.

"Where's your 'vette?"

"You're lucid now, that's a good sign." DeSantos nodded at the limo. "This is our ride."

Uzi glanced at his partner seeking an explanation.

"Get in. There's someone inside who wants to talk with you."

Uzi tilted his head. DeSantos opened the door and nodded at the backseat. DeSantos followed Uzi inside, then shut the door. The driver accelerated, headed for the exit.

Uzi could make out a large figure sitting several feet in front of him, and another, broad-shouldered figure to the man's right. With the tinted windows and darkness of the garage, he couldn't see anything else.

The electronic door locks clicked. "Am I supposed to guess who's in the car with us?"

"You should tell him, Mr. DeSantos. He's not smart enough to figure it out."

Had he not just been blown ten feet by a car bomb, he would've exploded across the car's interior and pounced on the man.

Uzi knew the voice. Though he wished otherwise, it was one he would never forget.

DAY NINE

12:04 AM
13 hours 56 minutes remaining

Uzi turned to DeSantos, anger battling the fog clouding his thoughts. "Is this some kind of joke?"

"He's come to help."

"Bullshit. That man doesn't help me, Santa."

DeSantos pressed a button on the panel to his left and three interior lights came on. One, a ceiling-mounted halogen above the visitor's head, threw harsh shadows across the face of Mossad Director General Gideon Aksel. With coarse skin and stubby but strong arms and legs, Aksel was built more like a truck than a human, the years of battle-hardened maneuvers from numerous war fronts wearing on him like the bleaching effects of the sun on an abandoned car's hood.

"You were my best kidon, Uzi, and you threw everything away. First your family, then your career, then your life."

Uzi started to charge forward, but DeSantos grabbed him and threw him back into the seat. Aksel remained still, his face impassive.

Uzi struggled a moment, then relented. "Fuck you, Gideon!"

Aksel folded his thick hands across his lap. "Go ahead, let it out, if it'll make you feel better. Who knows, maybe you've done good things for the FBI. Then again, maybe not."

"Enough," DeSantos said. "Uzi's one of the Bureau's top agents, Director General."

Aksel turned away, waving at the air with a dismissive hand.

Surrounded by Iran, Libya, and Syria—with Hezbollah and Hamas a constant threat and Egypt's government under pressure—Israel's survival was dependent on an effective Mossad. And Gideon Aksel had adeptly restored the agency's tarnished reputation; no one was more aware of this than Uzi.

Still, after Uzi's personal tragedy, Aksel moved swiftly to dismiss him, to disgrace him publicly for causing the debacle that left his family dead. Right or wrong, Uzi felt it shouldn't have been made public—and it certainly was not something Uzi needed when he himself had been so close to the edge.

"This man has no business being trusted with things of importance to national security," Aksel said.

"I don't have to take this, Santa." Uzi looked toward the front of the limo. "Let me off," he shouted in the direction of the driver.

"Yes," Aksel said, "run away again—"

"I didn't run away, Gideon. I made a mistake. I blew it. I just thought we should've given Ahmed a chance to explain. I was wrong."

Aksel's brow hardened. "It's taken you six years to admit it."

Uzi looked away. "All that killing. On both sides. Maybe we should've given the Palestinians what they wanted."

"You have a short memory," Aksel said. He leaned forward in his seat. "We offered them almost everything. Everything. Arafat said no. Because he wasn't interested in the West Bank and Gaza. He wanted the entire state of Israel, and that was never going to happen."

"Maybe if we'd given them something, as a show of good faith—"

"Good faith?" Aksel pulled out his smartphone and began stabbing at it with a thick index finger. "We gave them a police force and armed them. They used the weapons against us. We gave them infrastructure, and they used it to build bombs to attack our people. We pulled out of Gaza and turned over the entire territory. We said, 'Here, it's yours.' What have they done? They've fired six thousand rockets and four thousand mortars at our homes and schools."

He turned his phone toward Uzi. "Look at the photo, Uzi. A kindergarten classroom destroyed by a Grad rocket." He swiped his finger and another image appeared. "A school bus, struck by a missile. They target our children and families." Aksel's face was blood red, engorged veins pushing from his temples. "Look at it. Don't turn away!"

Uzi, gazing at his feet, said, "The problem is with the terrorists, Gideon, not the Palestinian people."

"Of course. But Hamas was an *elected* government, by the people." Aksel sat back. "Even if you're right, do you honestly think giving them land and calling them a country will make the terrorists go away? It won't, for one simple reason: they refuse to recognize Israel's right to exist. They refuse to recognize it as the Jewish state. Their goal isn't just to have their own country. It's to have *all* of Israel for themselves."

Uzi looked out the black window, at his own reflection.

"With all due respect," DeSantos said, "that's not their official position."

"Of course not," Aksel said. "Their PR people and negotiators say one thing to the world, but their leaders tell a different story to their people. Uzi, you've seen the secretly recorded videos in Arabic. You know this is true."

Yes, I've seen them. But . . . Uzi turned back to Aksel. "Something should've been done. I don't know what. But something. All these years . . . all the killings . . . all the terrorist attacks. If I had to pick up flesh and body parts off the street one more time—"

"Israel has made concessions all her life to get peace," Aksel said. "We gave away the Sinai to Egypt. I was part of that negotiation team. And it was the right thing to do because Sadat was an honest broker. We had lasting peace for forty years. It takes a viable partner to make peace. Real peace. We didn't have that in Arafat. And we certainly don't have that in Hamas." He faced DeSantos. "Do you know the Golda Meier quote, Mr. DeSantos?"

DeSantos shifted uncomfortably. "Which one are you referring to?"

"She said, 'We will have peace with the Arabs when they love their children more than they hate us.' They strapped bombs to their children and called them martyrs." He swung his gaze back to Uzi. "They blew up their children, Uzi. Where do you think that leaves *us*?"

Uzi closed his eyes. *I can't deal with this now.*

"Living in America has made you soft," Aksel said. "Poisoned your thinking."

"It's given me distance. Sometimes we get caught in a never-ending cycle and we can't break it."

"Have you forgotten what the terrorists did to your family?"

Uzi ground his molars. "I'll never forget. It's with me every waking moment. I can't go anywhere without seeing my daughter's face, smelling my wife's perfume. You think the terror ended that day six years ago? That was just the beginning, Gideon. The pain is forever. My life's been a torture all its own. So don't you dare lecture me on getting soft."

"Then I've got some more pain for you," Aksel said, his eyes dark and penetrating. "You've put your government at risk. Again."

"Director General," DeSantos said, holding up a hand. "Please. Let me." DeSantos received a stiff upper lip and a slight dip of the chin in response.

DeSantos turned to Uzi, his eyes searching his partner's face. "I've got some bad news, and I really wish I didn't have to be the one to tell you. But I'd rather it be me than him." DeSantos nodded in Aksel's direction.

"Tell me what?"

"Man . . ." He looked to his right, out the limo's window. "It's about Leila."

"C'mon, Santa. Just tell me. What about her?"

"Part of it is my fault. I didn't do my job, I just saw what I saw and accepted it. And for that, I'm really sorry."

"Oh, for God's sake, Mr. DeSantos." Aksel leaned forward. "Your girlfriend is a terrorist with al-Humat. She's Palestinian."

12:24 AM
13 hours 36 minutes remaining

Uzi's mouth was agape as he looked from Aksel to DeSantos. Then he began to laugh. "Who put you up to this, Santa? Did he convince you this would be funny? We'll it's not, man, it's not. I finally find some happiness. . . . It's goddamn disgusting is what it is. I almost get fucking blown up tonight, and you lay this shit on me? Fucking joke, that's all it is."

Uzi grabbed his temples with both hands. His greatest fears seemed to be materializing right before him. *Was DeSantos working against me all this time?* "This is retaliation for going after Knox, isn't it?" He began to rock back and forth on the leather car seat. "Some kind of payback, that's what it is. Are you playing me? Who are you working for?"

"Uzi, I know it's a lot to absorb, and I really am sorry. If I'd done my homework on Leila that first day, I might've realized something wasn't right. But I just didn't see it. My buddy told me she's with the Agency. And he was right. She *is* with the CIA."

"It's all a lie," Uzi said, his face still down, his head clamped between his hands. "She's Jewish, her brother was in the IDF, he was killed by Hamas." *And she's got Havdalah candles in her apartment . . .* "Gideon, why are you doing this to me? Haven't I suffered enough?"

"She runs a sleeper cell for al-Humat," DeSantos said softly.

Uzi cringed. Al-Humat. The irony was not lost on him. The group whose name means "The Protectors" murdered his wife and daughter, the people *he* failed to protect.

"They get funding through a complex series of innocuous trusts," Aksel said, "that much we know. We've been watching al-Humat for a decade, and we know they're affiliated with al-Qaeda. But it wasn't until a few days ago that we discovered they had active cells in the US."

"Nuri was tracking them, too," Uzi said, his voice weak.

"Nuri?" Aksel looked from Uzi to DeSantos and back. "Nuri Peled?"

Uzi set both elbows on his knees and bent over, palms massaging his forehead. "He was found dead, a little over twelve hours ago. Staged to look like suicide. He was looking into a rumor that a new sleeper had set down roots here. It got him killed."

Aksel sat back, affected by this news, but absorbing it. "He wasn't working for us."

"I know."

There was a moment of silence before Aksel continued. "Your girlfriend might have been the one who killed him."

"No," Uzi said, his head still down, like a child who doesn't want to hear what his parent is telling him. Cover your eyes and ears and it won't be so. "She's a CIA counterterrorism expert. She's on my task force. Shepard assigned her, she's on my task force," he said, as if stubborn insistence made it true. "She works for the CIA, Gideon. They would've vetted her. They couldn't have missed that, not something like that, not after 9/11." He lifted his head. His face was hot and his eyes felt swollen with tears.

"There's a lot we still don't know," DeSantos said. "But we're telling you the truth, Uzi. I can't speak for the director general, but I've got no agenda. I'm not trying to hurt you. But your feelings aren't what's at issue here. It's Leila—"

"Batula Hakim," Aksel said. "Her name is Batula Hakim."

Uzi's head snapped to Aksel. "What? I know what Batula Hakim looks like, Gideon. I memorized every angle of her evil face. Leila Harel is not Batula Hakim." He turned to DeSantos. "Have you confirmed any of this with the Agency? I mean, how sure are you of this?"

"We have to be very careful. I've spoken with Director Tasset, no one else. If she is a mole, we don't know who else has slipped under our radar. These people are very good."

"My God, Santa . . . Do you realize what this means?"

"Yeah. And I'm really sorry."

"I don't think you understand." Uzi looked at Aksel. "You didn't tell him, Gideon?"

Aksel looked away.

Uzi ran his fingers through his hair, then let his head fall back against the seat. "This can't be. It's gotta be a mistake."

DeSantos's gaze ping-ponged between Aksel and Uzi. "What is it? What's the problem?"

Uzi closed his eyes and sighed deeply. "Batula Hakim is the terrorist bastard that murdered my wife and daughter."

12:30 AM
13 hours 30 minutes remaining

The wide eyes, the parted lips told Uzi that DeSantos's shock was genuine. His partner didn't know—if it was true—that Leila was the woman who'd murdered Dena and Maya.

That this could be the case was too horrific for Uzi to bear. Not now, not tonight. Not with all that had happened. He didn't know when he would be able to deal with such a thing. At the moment, he had to focus, remove all emotion from the equation—something he didn't do six years ago. The event that had set all this in motion.

He had to clear his head. He had to think.

He asked the first question that came to mind. "Why has she suddenly surfaced?"

"That is the question, isn't it?" Aksel said. "Why now, why here?"

Uzi and DeSantos shared a look. "She's involved with Rusch's chopper," DeSantos said. "Has to be. Her cell takes it down, then she inserts herself into the investigation. That way she can keep an eye on what's going on, know what we know."

"It's your job to turn the tables on her," Aksel said. "You must find out what she knows. She's a terrorist. To know what she's after, you have to think like she does."

"We have to figure out what her interests are," DeSantos said.

Uzi reached into his jacket for a toothpick, then struggled to rip it from its plastic. After sticking it in his mouth, he said, "Assuming she is who you think she is, we know the groups she's affiliated with. Their views are the same as most Islamic terrorist groups—" He stopped himself, the sudden realization like a knife wound to the lung: *The peace talks, the covert meeting tomorrow—no, today. Shit, it's today.*

"You need someone else on the case," Aksel said to DeSantos.

Uzi's face tingled as if he'd just been slapped. "I'm on the case, Gideon. In fact, I'm the one in charge."

"And you're the one who failed. Hakim was operating a cell right under your nose, and you didn't pick it up. Ultimate responsibility falls on your shoulders, Uzi."

DeSantos's face tightened. "With all due respect, that's ridiculous,

Director General. There's over a hundred joint terrorism task forces across the country—tens of thousands of intelligence agents in the US alone. None of them picked it up. It isn't one person's failure any more than 9/11 was."

Despite DeSantos's attempt to defend him, Uzi realized that Aksel was right. There are 104 JTTFs, but only one in Washington—clearly a center of activity for al-Humat, possibly even their US base. In his own backyard, and he failed to see it.

"He's right," Uzi said. He looked out the window. The limo was stopped at a light on 23rd, approaching L Street. Uzi knew exactly where he was. He popped open the door and got out.

"Uzi, wait—" DeSantos followed him out of the limo. "C'mon, man, he's just playing head games with you. You can't bear the weight of all this on your shoulders."

Uzi stopped but did not turn around. He felt like he was in another session with Rudnick—which, he was beginning to think, would not be a bad place to be right now.

"Boychick, listen to me." He gently pulled on Uzi's shoulder, then stepped in front of him. "Leila had the ultimate cover story. Working for the fucking CIA, for Christ's sake. No one would've thought to look there."

"But fourteen people died because of my failure to see it. Another mother and daughter are dead because of me—"

DeSantos grabbed Uzi's shoulders and looked into his eyes. "Uzi, listen to me. None of this is your fault. If anything, Tasset has to take responsibility. His agency is the one that hired her. They should've vetted her better."

Uzi chuckled. "Yeah, we both know that's foolproof. Look at me."

"Except that in your case, Knox knew who you were."

"If he knew from the beginning, why didn't Shepard?"

DeSantos let go of Uzi's shoulders and looked off at the building behind them. "I don't know. Knox has a reason. He's always got a reason."

"Maybe he figured I'd bring info with me that'd help in flushing out these groups. If that's what he was thinking, if that's what he was after, then I obviously let him down."

"Uzi. . . ." DeSantos looked at the ground, then rubbed at his forehead. "Batula Hakim is here, right? She murdered your wife and daughter, right?"

Uzi looked away, then nodded.

"You have an opportunity here to even the score. You hear what I'm saying?"

"I'm not a kidon anymore. I'm not part of Mossad. I'm not on a mission to eliminate a terrorist who's planning a massive strike on civilians." He thrust his hands into his jacket pocket. "When I went on a mission, it was never personal. I had no stake in the outcome other than to do my job. I work for the US government now. I'm a federal agent." He stepped closer and lowered his voice. "I can't just go out and . . . eliminate her."

"Yeah, but I can." DeSantos's voice matched Uzi's timbre. "I can arrange for her to go away." His eyes patrolled the dark recesses of the narrow commercial street.

Uzi did not hesitate. "No. We do it the right way. Gather evidence, make an arrest."

"You sure?"

Uzi nodded. "I'm not a killer, Santa. With the Mossad, I was a soldier in a war, with a mission to save lives. I'm on the other side of the world now. Different job, different life."

"But my job lets me settle the score for you."

Uzi shook his head. "We arrest her."

DeSantos shrugged. "Okay. Your call." He indicated the idling limo. "Let's get back."

As they turned toward the vehicle, which had pulled over to a curbside loading zone, they saw Aksel standing beside the open rear door, his head rotating slowly in all directions.

"We stopped without warning," DeSantos said to Aksel. "No one could know we're here."

Aksel turned to Uzi. "Did you get your issues settled? Do you feel better now?"

"Don't start with me, Gideon."

"We'll be doing this by the book," DeSantos said.

Uzi stepped closer to Aksel. "Just how sure are you that Leila Harel is Batula Hakim? Her physical appearance—"

"Is somewhat different." Aksel smiled. "Yes, it is, isn't it? When you saw a surveillance photo of her eight or nine years ago, she was a nineteen-year-old living in the backrooms of a terrorist lair. Tents, sleeping bags. But her body's matured. She lost weight, works out, wears makeup and tight dresses with high heels. She's had plastic surgery and uses her tradecraft well. She may be a terrorist, but she's a professional."

"A wolf in sheep's clothing," DeSantos said. "We know the type." He looked at Uzi and received an acknowledging glance.

"You didn't answer my question, Gideon. Just how positive is your ID? Confirmed by fingerprints, facial recognition, functional gait—"

"Intel," Gideon said.

Uzi tilted his head. "Intel? A CI?"

"Reliable intel," Aksel said firmly.

DeSantos brought a hand up to his eyes.

Uzi bit down on his toothpick and snapped it in half. He spit the fragments out and said, "So you're not even sure it's her. Who's doing sloppy intelligence now?" He turned around and began to pace. "How dare you come here and tell me this story—turn my life upside down again—without absolute proof? What if we move against her and you're wrong?"

DeSantos let his hand fall to his side. "You told me you were sure, Director General."

Aksel's jaw muscles clenched. "Leila Harel is Batula Hakim." His eyes were hard and cold. "You do what you want with this information. If you don't believe it, do your own analysis. Just make it fast."

Uzi noted the hard stare shared by both men, and then it clicked. "You wanted Hector to take her out. Because kidons don't operate on US soil." Uzi turned to his partner. "And you were going to do his bidding. No matter what I wanted—"

"No, Uzi. I mean, yes. At first. Knox said—"

"Knox?"

DeSantos held up a hand. "It's not what you think." He took Uzi's left arm and ushered him away. He looked over his shoulder and said, "Director General, the longer we're out here in the open, the more vulnerable we are. Please, get in the car. We'll join you in a moment."

DeSantos led Uzi toward a landscaped planter in front of Ris, an upscale restaurant at the corner of 23rd and L. They stopped by a line of covered patio tables, dark with inactivity.

"You asked me to help you arrest her, and that's what I'm going to do."

"But if Knox—"

"I'll deal with Knox."

"If we're going to arrest her," Uzi said, "we'll need evidence . . . at least a positive ID."

"Good news is there's a simple solution to this problem," DeSantos said with a shrug. "We get a positive ID."

Uzi extended his fist, and DeSantos touched it with his own.

1:56 AM
12 hours 4 minutes remaining

After the limo departed, Uzi sat on the curb, mentally spent. Angry, confused, frustrated—but despite his efforts to shove his emotions aside, they kept forcing their way to the forefront of his thoughts.

Finally, at nearly two in the morning, he began making his way from 23rd and L toward the Hamilton House. The brisk air gave him a chance to clear his mind and regain some lucidity. As he headed down New Hampshire Avenue, the apartment building rose from the asphalt like a block-long monolith, partially obscured by a dozen trees. A series of Metro Police barricades and warning lights were arrayed across both lanes, blocking the street. The crime-scene techs had finished their analysis of the blast site and the crowd had dispersed.

He felt naked without his tricked-out smartphone. But it was now history, so much cinder and ashes. He found one of the few remaining pay phones a couple of blocks away and accessed his voicemail. He paged through the thirteen messages, hoping to get an eleventh-hour handle on his investigation. There was one from Hoshi, left only ninety minutes ago. She was heading home, hoping to grab a few hours' rest. Because of the approaching deadline—since it was now past midnight, "D-day" was technically today—she urged him to call her as soon as he retrieved the message.

He dug more quarters from his pocket and dialed the number. Hoshi was in a dreamy half-sleep, but had enough wits to be oriented as to time and place. "I take it this line isn't secure."

Uzi nearly laughed. "Not even close."

"Okay." She grunted as if pushing herself into a seated position. "Phish and Mason said Danny Carlson called you twice, once on the tenth, lasting two minutes—remember, they round up—"

"Just one, Hoshi, he only called me once. The tenth sounds about right."

"There's also an outgoing call on the fifteenth, lasting only a minute."

"When yesterday? I never spoke to him."

"Best they could tell, he called you shortly before he was killed."

Uzi did the math. *Son of a bitch. He called while I was in jail.* "He might've left a voicemail." Uzi knew that cell service was notoriously unreliable, and sometimes the message notification didn't buzz back to his phone for days. "Have Phish and Mason look into it. Give them my password and find out if he left a message, and if he did, what it was. Tell them to coordinate with DeSantos. I'm a bit occupied at the moment."

"Occupied?"

"Occupied. We've only got about twelve hours, Hoshi. Go back to the office. I'll check in with you later."

He hung up and headed back to Hamilton House. Across the street were large brick-and-stone Victorian-style homes, where he would set up camp. As he passed in front of the apartment building, his eyes scanned the crime-scene-taped area.

Remaining across the street from Hamilton House, Uzi sat on the concrete steps beside a brick column. He wrapped his scarred leather jacket around his body and leaned his elbows on his knees. Through the barren trees—the ones that survived the fiery blast—he could see the dark window of Leila's apartment. On the walk over, he'd decided to continue thinking of Batula Hakim as Leila Harel—at least for now—because if he encountered her, he didn't want it slipping that he knew her real name.

If Gideon Aksel was correct.

The thing that gnawed at Uzi was that he had never known Aksel to be wrong. That's why he had been so successful as director general. He weighed facts and made informed judgments. But he always seemed to have such damn good facts. And if Gideon was right about Leila being Hakim, he was wasting his time with this exercise. Still, aside from law enforcement protocols, for his own peace of mind, he needed to know—quickly—if she was Hakim. He could then move forward . . . with the investigation, and with his life.

While he wanted to believe that meeting her was pure chance, at a crash site on a random event, he now knew that if she was Hakim, everything had happened by design. She played him like a skilled flautist coaxing music from a rusty flute. He bowed his head out of disgust. Gideon was right. Shame on him that he could be suckered so easily. That he'd let his guard down. That he hadn't done his job properly six years ago.

The time passed slowly. He almost dozed twice—and was tempted to grab a little shuteye because it was three o'clock in the morning and a prime rule of covert ops was that you took short naps at odd moments, whenever it was safe. He doubted he was in danger sitting where he was. Even before Dena's death, he was a light sleeper. He'd learned the skill when in training for Mossad. Under normal circumstances, if anyone came within twenty feet of him, it would awaken him.

But with a concussion and the recent physical and emotional stress, he couldn't risk falling into a deep sleep, putting himself in danger and missing his window of opportunity.

Across the street, as he watched the lighted traffic cones flash rhythmically on and off, his eyes settled on the area where the shattered Tahoe sat only hours ago. In many ways, his damaged psyche was not much different from the SUV: shattered from within, nothing more than a burned-out hulk.

Hoping that Leila was either asleep or not returning tonight, he entered through the parking garage, staying clear of the building's front entrance in case someone had been watching. He took the elevator to the lobby and saw Jiri sitting behind his large marble desk, shoulders slumped and head drooped forward. Uzi thought he was asleep, but as he approached, Jiri looked up. His face brightened a bit but it was clear the man was in a funk.

"I'm sorry about Alec," Uzi said.

"He was only twenty-six," Jiri said, his Czech accent thicker than Uzi had noticed in the past. "Always on time, always did good job." He closed his eyes. "These terrorists are, what do you say, pigs?"

Uzi had other words for them. He placed a reassuring hand on Jiri's shoulder. "I'll make you a promise, okay? We'll catch the person who killed Alec. You have my word."

Jiri tilted his head in confusion. "You'll catch . . . ?"

"I'm with the FBI."

Jiri nodded. "Miss Harel, she took hard drive for the camera. She said they may show person who planted bomb." He shook his head. "I know her a year and didn't know she was part of FBI."

Uzi didn't bother correcting the concierge. He looked above Jiri's head at the two black-and-white monitors, one of which was trained on the curbside of the Hamilton House's entrance. If Leila took the digital recording, she was probably going to erase it using Department of Defense secure deletion algorithms. It was taking a big risk, though, because the responding Metro cops—or someone else from the Bureau—should have inquired about the recording, too. "Anyone else ask you about the surveillance—about the cameras?"

Jiri nodded. "I told them I already give them to Miss Harel. That's okay, what I said?"

Uzi forced a smile. "Yeah, that was good." He glanced back at the security monitors.

"Are you okay?" Jiri asked. "I got you away from the fire best I could. Tried to find Alec, but—"

"That was you who pulled me away from the car?" Uzi noted a muted nod from the Czech. "I owe you, man. You ever need help with anything, let me know." He faked a wide yawn. "Meantime, I'm gonna head upstairs and get some sleep. Can I get the key?"

Jiri lifted his thick body from the stool and reached beneath the desk. He pulled Leila's apartment key from a drawer and handed it to Uzi.

"Thanks, man. Take some time off. Go for a drive. Clear your head."

Jiri checked his watch. "Someone supposed to come soon. I go home."

He gave Jiri's shoulder a gentle pat, and then headed for the elevator.

The doors parted on the eighth floor. Uzi stepped onto the thick carpet and strode slowly toward Leila's apartment. At three-thirty in the morning, nearly everyone on the floor was asleep. He put his ear to her door and listened. Quiet.

He inserted the key, gave it a slow turn, and then stepped inside. His main objective was to secure a number of items that would contain Leila's fingerprints—and preferably some DNA—without her becoming suspicious. One of the wine glasses they'd used should contain at least an index or thumb print and saliva. But reaching the kitchen meant crossing in front of the bedroom.

He slowed his breathing and waited until his eyesight had accommodated to the darkness. A moment later, he began inching along the wall, focusing his hearing, keying in on movement.

The bedroom door was open. He stood beside it, listening, trying to see as much of the interior without revealing himself—in case she was lying awake in bed. If she startled, he would merely explain that DeSantos had insisted he be examined by the Bureau emergency room doc, and that he was returning to get some sleep. He didn't want to go back to his place because if he was the target of the car bomb, it was no longer safe. And he didn't want to be alone. Coming back to be with her after a life-threatening event would be consistent with his recent behavior.

As he stood outside her door, he realized he had left his Puma and Tanto knives somewhere in the apartment. He remembered taking them off—but when? Probably when they started undressing one another. Where? *In the bedroom. No—the bathroom.*

He still had his boot knife, but a weapon in hand would blow his cover story.

Uzi waited by the door but heard nothing. He knelt down and

peered around the jamb at the bed. The side where he had been sleeping looked unchanged: the comforter was drawn to the side just as he had left it. His eyes trailed over to Leila's side, and the covers there, too, appeared to be folded back. He could not see her body. He decided to walk in, as if returning to her after meeting with DeSantos. It would make his job more difficult but not impossible: he would have to resort to his backup plan—use the bathroom and quietly search her medicine cabinet and drawers for items that might contain her prints. He rose from his crouch and walked into the bedroom.

It was empty. Uzi stood there, considering his options. Best to know if she was in the apartment before he started snooping around.

"Leila?" he called into the darkness. He walked into the kitchen, then moved into the living room. "Leila?"

He returned to the bedroom to find his knives—but they were not there. He searched his mind, replaying the evening. He remembered getting up around 11:30 and realizing he'd left the phone in his car. *Did I take the knives with me? No, I was just going out to the car to get my phone.*

He unsuccessfully searched the room again. Uzi bit his bottom lip, craving a toothpick like a smoker craves a cigarette. *Did Leila take my knives? Did she know I wasn't coming back because her group planted the bomb?*

There were no answers, not yet.

He stepped into the bathroom, his eyes scanning the surfaces, the floor—and then he remembered. The countertop, under the gold towels they had thrown on the vanity after getting out of the bath. He grabbed a handful of fine Egyptian terrycloth and tossed it aside—exposing his knives, right where he'd left them. *Cool.*

He slipped the Tanto around his neck and clipped the Puma to the inside of his pocket, and then moved back to the kitchen, resuming his primary task. But the dinner glasses they'd used were no longer in the sink. And the dishwasher was empty.

Beside the stove was a ceramic container filled with multicolored toothpicks. He grabbed one and stuck it in his mouth. He still needed to find something with a liftable set of fingerprints. Back in the living room, he noticed two DVDs on the end table beside a small briefcase.

He rummaged through the soft-sided leather attaché, but other than various books on counterterrorism and a blank notepad, he found nothing of value. But the DVDs . . .

He handled them by their edges and flipped them over. They had the purplish hue of "burned," or homemade, discs—as well as smudges, which looked like two partial prints. Without proper lighting and equipment, it was hard to tell with certainty. But even if there weren't any usable latents, the discs might contain incriminating data.

He walked back into the bathroom and slid open the drawers. He pulled several strands of hair from her brush, a few of which contained follicles—and DNA. As he turned to leave, a small makeup mirror caught his eye. He huffed on the surface, and a number of fingerprints appeared. *Gotcha.* He took it back into the kitchen, grabbed a couple of Ziplocs, and placed the mirror, hair strands, and DVDs in their own bags.

Now he had to get them to the lab.

4:30 AM
9 hours 30 minutes remaining

Uzi caught a cab and arrived at the Hoover Building at 4:30 in the morning, time melting away like an ice cube on a Phoenix street in August. He was greeted by the stout FBI policeman who had owned the lobby's graveyard shift the past two decades.

"Anyone in the lab?" Uzi asked.

The man snorted. "Hang out for a few hours and you'll have your pick of whoever you want."

"I don't have a few hours." Uzi went behind the security desk and lifted the receiver. He dialed the extension and waited. As he was about to hang up, the line was answered. The voice was groggy and raspy.

"Yeah. Lab."

"This is Special Agent Aaron Uzi—"

"Can you speak up a little?"

"I've got some latents," Uzi shouted. His voice echoed in the empty glass-enclosed booth. "I need them run through the system. Yesterday."

There was a loud groan on the other end of the phone. "Uzi, you're not really doing this to me, are you? Please tell me this is a dream."

"Tim? What the hell are you doing here?"

"They got me out of that god-awful hospital and wanted to transfer me to another god-awful hospital. Hate those places. Then they said something about a safehouse but I didn't want any part of that. So I had them bring me here. There's a cot in the back room. If I'm not safe here—"

"Jesus, Tim. Okay, listen. I'm serious about these latents. It's super important."

"You know what, Uzi? I've never said no to you before, but there's a first time for everything, right?"

"Tim—"

"No, I'm putting my foot down here. I just got my freakin' butt blown off. Have some compassion."

"These prints could be from the person who planted the bomb in your house."

There was a pause, then Meadows said, "Bring 'em right up. Let's get this bastard."

Uzi stepped into the break room and found Meadows reclining on the cot, eyes closed and his right shoulder scrunched against the wall.

Uzi nudged him in the side. "Sleeping on the job, eh?"

Meadows opened a lazy eye and groaned. "This is a nightmare, right?"

"We just talked on the phone, you told me to come up." The dazed look on the tech's face told Uzi to continue doling out clues. "The latents, the bomber . . ."

Meadows groaned again, then licked his lips. "Damn medication. Puts me out. Yeah, okay, fine, the bomber. I remember." He tried to push himself off the soft cot, but couldn't get much purchase. "Well, you gonna watch me struggle or you gonna help me up?"

Uzi grabbed Meadows's left arm and pulled him off the cot. "You should be in a hospital."

Meadows steadied himself against the wall with his right hand. "And when did you get your medical degree? Or are your FBI creds just a cover?"

Uzi pulled the Ziplocs from his pocket. "I don't think 'Doctor Uzi' would work. Might scare away the patients. Although I once saw a dentist named Payne." Before Meadows could comment, Uzi held up the bags. "I couldn't dust them, but I huffed on the mirror and saw a print."

Meadows slowly made his way into the adjacent lab. "You did what?"

"Huffed. You know, blew on it with— Just dust the damn sample."

Meadows sat down heavily on a stool and pulled a small kit from a drawer. His movements were clumsy because of the injury to his hands, but Uzi noted the doctor had removed the bandage wraps. Only casts remained, affording him some dexterity with his fingertips. Meadows dipped a wide brush into black powder, then tried to twirl it over the mirror. "Oops."

"Oops?"

He blew away some of the powder. "You try doing precise work with these things on your hands." He tilted his head to assess his work. "Don't worry, if there's something here, I'll find it."

Uzi yawned hard, then shook his head. "Sure hope so." He took the DVDs and, handling them carefully, slipped them into the drive of a nearby PC. He opened Windows Explorer and browsed them. There were two encrypted files from six months ago.

"When you're done with the latents, you've got a couple of files to crack."

"Oh, goody. You really don't want me sleeping tonight, do you?"

Uzi dragged the files onto the PC's hard drive, then brought the discs back to Meadows and grabbed a stool of his own. The tech looked at Uzi and seemed to appraise him for the first time.

"You look about as good as I did after the blast."

Uzi looked at his reflection in the glass cabinet above the slate work surface. Numerous abrasions covered his face and neck, and a dollop of dried blood was plastered just above his left eye. "Let's put it this way: you weren't their only target."

Meadows glanced sidewards at Uzi. "No shit?"

Uzi nodded at Leila's mirror. "Anything?"

"Looks like one on the front and another on the back."

"Okay. Run them through the system, dust the discs, and see what they show. I've also got some DNA. And no, I really don't want you sleeping tonight." He rose from the stool. "I'm gonna use the bathroom, clean up and try to make myself look a little less scary."

When Uzi returned to the lab, Meadows was asleep in a chair beside a computer monitor where digitized fingerprint images rolled by at astounding speed. Uzi walked down the hall to a vending machine and bought a Coke and a granola bar, both of which he downed in record time.

He joined Meadows, set another bar in front of the computer, then gently woke the technician. "Tim, time to eat. We've got green eggs and ham. Tim . . ."

Meadows opened his eyes to half mast, groaned, and then sat up. "I dreamt I was eating breakfast. Eggs and—"

"No dream." Uzi nodded at the granola bar. "At least your hearing's coming back."

"What?"

"Anything on the latents?"

Meadows looked at the screen, rubbed his eyes with a shirt sleeve, and struck a few keys. "This ain't easy with freakin' casts on." Finally, he leaned back. "Nope. No hits."

Uzi stood and leaned over the desk to look at the monitor. "How can that be?"

"Guess this person wasn't in the database."

"She's gotta be. Where'd you run it?"

"Everywhere. Even Interpol."

"Call up Batula Hakim."

"Hakim, that name rings a bell," Meadows said as he pecked awkwardly at the keyboard. He hit Enter and seconds later, the fingerprint for Batula Hakim appeared on-screen.

"Compare it to the ones you just lifted."

Meadows created a split screen, and the two prints popped up beside one another.

"Any matching points at all?"

Meadows studied the screen, then shook his head. "Not even close. See these whorls here? They're— Well, look for yourself. It doesn't take a computer to call this a nonmatch."

Uzi fell back onto his stool. Aksel was wrong. *He put me through all this for nothing.*

"Sorry. You thought we had something, didn't you?"

Uzi rose, nodded absentmindedly, and then turned away.

A beep sounded, and Meadows rotated his body to check the monitor. "But we do have a match on one of the latents from the DVDs."

"Yeah?" Uzi asked impassively. "Whose?"

"None other than our own Marshall Shepard."

"Shep?" Uzi spun around and looked at the screen. "What would his prints be doing on those discs?" Uzi began pacing. On the fifth pass, he mumbled, "I just don't get it."

Uzi looked over and noticed Meadows sleeping again, his head nestled in the fold of his elbow. Uzi guided his friend back to the cot and gently set him down. He then grabbed a backpack and made his way through the many rooms of the lab, helping himself to various supplies and equipment.

He had the sense that his answers did not reside in a database. For the next few hours, he'd have to figure this out on his own.

6:01 AM
7 hours 59 minutes remaining

Uzi signed out an unmarked Crown Victoria BuCar—Bureau Car—from the FBI motor pool and grabbed a cell phone from the communications center. If he had wanted to replace his Glock, he would have had to do so at the Academy's armory—and complete paperwork about his prior handgun, which was now evidence in Adams's murder. But he hadn't taken the time—and there certainly was no chance to do that now.

As Uzi headed for Marshall Shepard's home—where he hoped to obtain answers to at least a few of his questions—he decided he had to make one major assumption: that the DVDs containing the encrypted files were passed from Shepard to Leila. That conclusion seemed logical.

When Uzi left the Hoover Building, his intention was to confront his boss, ask direct questions, and gauge the honesty of his answers. But as he turned onto his ASAC's street, he realized that until he knew what was in the encrypted files, he didn't want to create hard feelings with the man who had done so much for him over the years, someone he considered a close friend. *If I'm wrong about all this, I don't want to throw all that away.*

Uzi parked a block from Shepard's townhouse in Foggy Bottom and slumped down in his seat. He wished he had his night vision monocle—let alone his Glock—but he had gotten by with far less on missions in the heart of Damascus and Tehran.

Fifteen minutes passed without activity. He wasn't even sure his surveillance was going to bear fruit, but the alternative—getting some much-needed sleep—was no longer an option.

Despite all that he and DeSantos had amassed, it seemed like a nest of disjointed information, fragmented pixels lacking the cohesion that could bring the picture into focus. Another week and he might have most of the answers. He needed at least another week.

I've got less than eight hours.

As the dashboard clock changed to 6:21, activity stirred near Shepard's townhouse. The porch light snapped on, and in the dim throws of the bulb's glow, Uzi recognized his boss's lumbering gait. Shepard descended the five brick steps that led from his front door to the cement path that ended at the sidewalk. Shepard got into his car and hung a U-turn.

Uzi followed with his headlights off, keeping at least a block away. He hated being in a BuCar, as the standard issue Crown Victoria was like driving in a red tomato. It stood out to those in the know, particularly criminals—and federal agents.

But if Shepard had any inkling he was being followed, he never let on. He took a direct route, with minimal turns. Uzi calmed his thoughts, reined in his paranoia.

His sense of tranquility lasted barely a minute, however, as Shepard headed up 23rd Street and parked near Dupont Circle. Uzi parked, too, taking note that he was less than ten blocks from Leila's apartment. He watched as his boss walked toward the large central fountain and took a seat on what probably qualified as the world's longest park bench.

Shepard sat alone for ten minutes before being joined by a dark figure Uzi would recognize anywhere as Leila Harel. He knew that body. Perhaps too well.

He watched as Shepard handed her a thick manila envelope; following a moment of dialogue, Leila disappeared into the darkness, dissolving into the surroundings like a practiced spook. Shepard, deskbound and long removed from field work, lumbered back to his car.

His ASAC drove to Millie's Coffee Shop, a greasy spoon in Georgetown that apparently catered to college students who needed an early place to get their off-campus caffeine fix before classes started. It was dark inside, with single-bulb original art deco lights hanging over each booth. The wood floors were varnished, but well worn in traffic areas to the point where a groove had been ground into the main aisle, with branching furrows leading to each table.

Shepard was nestled in a corner booth on the left side of the restaurant, the *Post* spread across the metal-rimmed Formica table with a plate of scrambled eggs and sausage by his right elbow. Uzi slid onto the seat beside him and peered over the top of the newspaper.

"Uzi. What—"

"What am I doing here? Well, let's see. It's been a hell of a night, highlighted by nearly getting blown into the heavens."

Shepard eyed his friend silently before speaking. "Uzi, have you spoken with your shrink? I mean, this is a really traumatic thing to go through."

"You know what, Shep? Nearly getting blasted to oblivion doesn't really bother me. Someday it'll hit me. It always does. But right now I'm pretty focused."

"I know this case bothers you," Shepard said. "Knox isn't just breathing down your neck, he's on my case, too. Today's the big day, and we've still got shit—"

Uzi slammed his hand down on the table. The silverware jumped. All heads in the small restaurant turned. "Damnit, Shep, don't fucking play games with me. I'm not in the mood."

Shepard raised his fork and pointed it at Uzi. "Calm the hell down. And watch your mouth." He glanced around the café. "What's gotten into you?"

"Where were you fifteen minutes ago?"

Shepard looked away. "What the hell business is that of yours?"

"Wrong answer, Shep." Uzi stared coldly at his friend.

"Anita," Shepard called across the counter, where a large African-American woman with hair netting was bent over the cooktop. "I've gotta take a walk. Will you keep this warm for me?"

"Sure thing, shugah," she sang. She slapped the edge of her metal spatula against the stove a couple of times, ridding it of a few stray pieces of cooked egg, then threw an evil eye at Uzi.

Shepard and Uzi got up from the booth and walked outside. The sky was a bit brighter in the east, but sunrise was still a way off. Vapor rose from their mouths in the morning chill.

Shepard walked a dozen feet, turned right down an alley, and put his big hands on his hips. "Okay. What the hell's going on?"

"That's what I want to know." He stared at Shepard but his boss was not volunteering any information. "Why did you just meet with Leila Harel?"

"Were you tailing me?"

"I'm asking the questions here, Shep."

"Fuck you, my friend. Who the fuck do you think you are? I'm still your superior, and friendship aside, you have no right to talk to me that way."

Uzi held up a hand. He was pushing Shepard in the opposite direction. He closed his eyes and tried to think of what to say, where to begin. "You passed her an envelope. What was in it?"

Shepard looked away.

"Your fingerprints were on encrypted DVDs recovered from her apartment. Explain that."

"Intelligence," Shepard said quickly. "It's a need-to-know basis—"

"I need to fucking know, Shep. I'm running a major investigation. If I ask you a question that might be related to that investigation, you have to answer it."

"Is it related?"

The two of them locked stares.

Finally, Shepard blinked. "Okay, you want to know what's going on? I'll tell you. But this goes beyond any level of trust we've ever shared. This is beyond top secret, beyond top secret, you hear what I'm saying?" His voice was low, barely above a whisper.

"Yeah. You know you can trust me."

Shepard put a hand behind his neck and squeezed. "Man, oh man. I knew this was a bad idea. I knew it." He walked a few feet away, through a few puddles and past a pile of litter, then returned to Uzi. "What do you know about Leila?"

"I'm not sure. Yesterday I would've had a different answer. Today, I just don't know."

"And yesterday's answer?"

"CIA. Counterintelligence. A member of M2TF."

"And today?"

Uzi closed his eyes. He couldn't bring himself to say it.

"A terrorist with al-Humat," Shepard said. "Is that what you're thinking?"

Uzi's eyes snapped open. "You knew?"

Shepard turned and started to walk down the alley. Uzi followed. "I've known for a while."

"How could you not tell me? I mean, don't you think that would be an important detail for me to have—not just as head of JTTF, but for the investigation?"

"I wasn't being difficult before, Uzi. It really is need-to-know. The order came from Knox. And from what little I know, I agree with his decision."

Knox. Why am I not surprised that all winding roads lead back to that man? "Do we have definite proof she's with al-Humat?"

Shepard chuckled. "You bet, Uzi. You bet. Hard evidence."

"I just ran her prints, they came up a big zero. We even pulled Batula Hakim's prints and compared them visually."

"Batula Hakim? That's the woman who—"

"Yes."

Shepard was silent a moment. "Leila's real name is Leila al-Far, and her prints aren't in the system because the CIA doesn't post their counterintelligence agents' identities anywhere. For obvious reasons, you know that." They walked another few feet before Shepard said, "What made you think al-Far was Batula Hakim?"

Now it was Uzi's turn to demonstrate some trust. "I met with Gideon Aksel last night."

"The Mossad Director General?" Shepard appeared to chew on that one a bit. "He's here for the terrorism conference. That explains part of it. But why would he seek you out?"

The conference. Only five hours left and I still don't have answers for the president. He felt a surge of urgency in his chest.

"I don't know," Uzi said. "Maybe Knox had something to do with it. But it seems Aksel's main purpose was to tell me that Leila was Hakim." Cold wind ripped through his jacket. He shoved his hands deep into his pockets and brought them together, pulling his coat closed. "Aksel has his agendas, just like Knox. But the man's a legend. He's not often wrong." It hurt Uzi to utter those words, but it was the truth.

Shepard turned to his friend and twisted his mouth. "As for having an agenda in telling you Leila is Batula Hakim . . . yeah, that's probably a good assumption."

"I told him I needed positive ID, and that I was gonna get it."

"Then he knows that sooner or later you're going to find out the truth."

They both stood silent for a moment, each seeming to process the puzzle in their own way. Finally, Uzi said, "What intelligence were you passing to Leila?"

"She was assigned to be the counterintelligence liaison between the Bureau and the Agency. Shit hit the fan when some of the info she was entrusted with ended up in the al-Qaeda manuals we found when we took out bin Laden. Only a few people had access to that info, only a select few. But she didn't know that. It took a long time to parse all the data and unwind the convoluted network of subterfuge, but Knox and Tasset narrowed it down to Leila. So Knox had us set up a flow of disinformation. When NSA intercepted some of that bogus intelligence being passed to al-Humat and al-Qaeda, we knew we had our mole."

"Why didn't you move on her?"

"Knox and his NSA cronies felt she was more valuable if we used her, controlled what information she passed on. Some of the security plans she's got for the conference are bogus. An added precaution just in case they were planning something. But NSA said it's been quiet. Which means our intel's limited, so we're blind. The conference is an obvious target, but it might be too obvious. Know what I mean?"

As Uzi's shoes crunched against the pavement, he thought of the president's clandestine peace talks. Shep didn't bring it up, so maybe it was something the ASAC did not "need to know." He shook his head. "Playing with fire, Shep. If this is true, Leila's dangerous. Leaving her in place at the Agency, giving her access—"

"Tasset had all access codes changed as part of a system upgrade. She was pigeon-holed, locked out of essential systems. It's all been taken care of."

Uzi couldn't help wondering if DeSantos, joined at the hip with Knox in so many ways and over so many secrets, knew about the covert op against Leila. And if he did know, why didn't he tell Uzi about it? Was he under a similar gag order from Knox? For now, Shepard's answer was the only available explanation as to why the information had been kept from him. And what did any of them know of Nuri Peled's "suicide"?

"Would've been nice to tell me of all this."

"Knox felt it would jeopardize the operation."

Uzi bit his lip. Did Knox not trust him with the information because of his Mossad past? If so, why would he let him head Washington's JTTF? *Because* of his Mossad past? "You should've told me all this, Shep. You should've trusted me with the info."

"I couldn't."

"C'mon, man, I thought you were my friend. You either trust me or you don't."

Shepard grabbed Uzi's arm to stop him. Though Uzi was sizable himself, Shepard's heft dwarfed even him, and his grip on Uzi was like an offensive lineman grabbing a quarterback from behind. "'You either trust me or you don't'? What a freaking hypocrite. Don't act so high and mighty. And don't ever question my friendship, don't ever do that."

They locked eyes. Shepard's were red with rage.

"ARM. Knox's order."

"Yes," Shepard said, nodding his head animatedly. "Knox's order. I know he told you to go after ARM. You may think I'm rusty around the edges, been behind a desk too long, but I've still got my instincts and my inside sources, Uzi, I've still got 'em."

"Look, Shep . . . Coulter specifically said to leave them alone. You were there, you heard what he said. I didn't want you taking any more heat for me. After I left, DeSantos told me Knox wanted me to keep on them. I couldn't tell you, not without dragging you into it."

"I asked you point blank about being on that compound, Uzi, and you flat out lied to me."

"To protect you."

"Bullshit. My ass is in the fire even if I claim I didn't know." Shepard rubbed his eyes with meaty fingers. "And why in hell would you defy the AG anyway? Knox tells you to break the law, so you just go and do it? You should've come to me, leveled with me, and let me handle it."

Uzi turned away. He closed his eyes tight and hoped he could vanish into the vapor pouring from his mouth. "I couldn't do that, Shep."

"Trust, remember? You trust me, I trust you. It's gotta work both ways."

"Knox has something on me."

Shepard tilted his head back and looked down on Uzi. "Is this another thing you should've told me about?"

"Shep, please don't make me—"

"Damnit, Uzi, what other freaking surprises do you have for me?"

"Just this one."

Shepard began pacing. "If this job doesn't give me a coronary, I swear, you're going to. Another seven years and I've got my pension. Another seven years. I'd hoped to go out an SAC, but with you under me, I'll either stroke out before then or get canned." He stopped in his tracks and turned to face Uzi. He folded his arms across his chest. "Well?"

Uzi stepped closer, then nodded in the direction of the street. They started walking. They'd gone a dozen feet before Uzi spoke. "I used to be with the Mossad." Uzi felt Shepard's angry stare on his back like the red laser beam of a sniper's scope.

"You didn't disclose that on your app." Uzi didn't reply. "Head of the Washington Bureau's JTTF, and you were once— Jesus Christ, Uzi.

I knew about Shin Bet, that was cool. But Mossad? Not cool, not cool at all. Jesus Christ."

"I'm sorry, Shep. I really am sorry. I needed to—to make a new life. Escape my past."

"I was there, remember?" Shepard kept his gaze forward. "But 'sorry' doesn't cut it. This is bad, very bad." He shoved his hands into the pockets of his overcoat. "Ohhh, man. If the press gets wind of this, we're fucked. Congressional inquiry. Front page of the *Post*. Bloggers. Twitter. *Politico*. You think the director will take any of the heat? No way, it'll be our asses."

"Knox has known for a long time, Shep. So he'd be in the shit, too. But he and DeSantos—and now you—are the only ones who know. It can stay that way." Uzi ventured a glance at his boss.

Shepard's face was hard, his brow thick, his gaze focused on the sidewalk ahead. He abruptly turned left at the corner. Uzi stopped. "Where are you going?"

"To finish my breakfast," Shepard yelled over his shoulder. "At least with that, I know what I'm getting. Eggs are eggs. No surprises."

Uzi stood there, watching the big guy trudge down the street, feeling the same sense of loneliness he'd felt six years ago. Despite all the intervening time and his attempts to repair his life and fill the void, the only friendships he'd managed to harvest were now rooted in uncertainty.

7:29 AM
6 hours 31 minutes remaining

As Uzi headed home, he realized the landscape of his case had changed substantially in the past twenty-four hours: he had been sure ARM was behind the helicopter bombing and subsequent murders; the brass casing recovered from Bishop's crime scene matched the Russian 7.62 round he and DeSantos had pilfered from their compound. That was a pretty damning connection. But if he took a hard, objective look at his "evidence," all it proved was that the person who assassinated Bishop had access to ARM's ammo—or their storage shed, or to the same ammo supplier. Or, he was a lone wolf affiliated with the group. After all this time and trouble, Uzi had hoped to have more substance behind his suspicions.

Yet the bombs that took out Fargo and Harmon, and the attempts on Rusch and himself—appeared to be connected. Even though the explosive devices and MO differed, Karen Vail said a bomb was a less traditional assassination tactic. In terms of most probable explanations, it was likely the bombings were all perpetrated by the same group. Who had the most to gain from taking out these people? Was it ARM, in coordination with NFA, the attorney general and . . . Douglas Knox? All to remove Rusch from power in an attempt to eliminate a staunch gun-control advocate?

Then there was Nuri Peled's death. Suicide? Not likely. Murder, then— But why, and by whom? The obvious answers could not be overlooked. Even if he'd been taken out by an al-Humat terror cell Peled had discovered, Uzi had no hard link, direct or indirect, to his case.

Perhaps his answers hinged on Leila. This was the question that gnawed deep inside him, the one that demanded resolution if he was to have any peace of mind going forward: Was Leila al-Far in fact Batula Hakim? It appeared not—the fingerprint discrepancy was absolute proof of that—but Aksel's intelligence was flawless. Unless he was purposely leading Uzi down the wrong path.

But if Leila was Batula Hakim, how would she and al-Humat fit into the equation? Or were they part of another equation—gearing up for an unrelated attack on US soil? The terrorism conference? Or the supposedly secret Israeli-Palestinian peace talks?

If she wasn't Hakim, the complexion of his case—of everything—would change. He thought back to when he'd first met her. Was it merely coincidence that he had gotten involved with her? After all, he had pursued *her*; she wanted no part of him. Or was that by design? Was she a honey trap to draw him in? A few hours ago, he'd been convinced it had been just that.

Yet again, all he had were mere suspicions, theories without substance. In many respects, a case without evidence.

His years as a Mossad operative came roaring back to him—the unease, the paranoia, the questioning of everyone and everything, of not knowing who you can trust. He was out of practice—if there was one thing Gideon Aksel had said that rang true, it was that living in America had softened him. Uzi did not want to admit it, but he also could not dispute it.

His survival skills had eroded substantially in six years. It was a natural effect of becoming an administrator and investigator rather than a covert assassin. Two different skill sets. Two different lives.

No matter. He needed to tap those rusty instincts and abilities. He needed to be on top of his game. Because the people he was facing were undoubtedly on top of theirs. Several corpses were proof enough.

After parking two blocks from his house, Uzi observed the immediate area, watching for and evaluating stray movement—especially people or cars out of place. Despite the paucity of time left, he reminded himself that patience was a strength. He moved stealthily, blending into his surroundings the way he'd been schooled so many years ago.

Rucksack on his back, he knelt behind a line of bushes and peered about. Convinced it was safe to approach his townhouse, he moved to a planter by the building's entrance. Well hidden by shrubs, he squatted and withdrew his boot knife. Sticking the tip into the moist soil, he dug around until he located a small plastic container that housed a tiny combination-locked metal case. He dialed in the numbers and pulled open the lid. Inside were three keys: one to his house, one to his Tahoe—which he wouldn't be needing anymore—and one to his Suzuki motorcycle.

Uzi quickly reburied the container and headed down the block to his bike. Reasoning it was more difficult to plant a bomb on a motorcycle than a car—almost everything was exposed—he moved swiftly, eyes keeping sentry over the street for unexpected movement.

As Uzi neared the corner, he snuck a peak at his watch: 8:10. He undid the rope tie holding the heavy vinyl-coated canvas cover and pulled it off the vehicle. He hadn't used the beast in two months, but figured it would start.

After a once-over to visually inspect for faux engine parts fashioned from C-4, he unlocked his black M-4 Bell helmet and removed the ski mask he stored beneath the seat. As he pulled both over his head, he thought of the day he'd bought the motorcycle—against the wishes of his parents. His mother eventually caved, saying he could only ride the thing if he wore the best helmet money could buy. He squirreled away cash for three weeks, then bought a top-of-the-line Bell, which he used until he mothballed the bike in his parent's garage. He gave the helmet to a neighbor's son who couldn't afford one—and it ended up saving the teen's life two weeks later when he collided with a truck.

Uzi unlocked the hardened steel cable, pushed the Suzuki off its stand and rolled it around the corner. He got it going at a decent rate down L Street, then hopped on and started it up. It idled rough, but when he accelerated hard, the engine responded as it had so many times in the past.

Helmet and leather overcoat disguising his identity, he sped away.

8:17 AM
5 hours 43 minutes remaining

Uzi parked his motorcycle a block from Leila's apartment and peered through a Hensoldt Wetzlar rifle scope—courtesy of the FBI lab—at his former girlfriend's window. Had she been back? Was she there now, getting ready to leave for work? He had no way of knowing.

As he eyed the garage entrance to his right and the building's charred and damaged entryway further down the street, he realized Tim Meadows had no way of getting in touch with him if he had awoken and continued analyzing the "evidence." He pulled the Bureau phone from his pocket: he had only two of five bars of battery life left. And no charger.

Nothing he could do about it. He dialed WFO and asked for Tim Meadows, concerned about having the conversation because he'd have to talk loud due to Meadows's hearing deficit.

"Nice of you to call," Meadows said. "I've got a good mind to tell you what you've put me through—"

"You probably don't remember because you were so doped up, but I already apologized about the . . . incident at your house."

"I'm not talking about that. And I remember everything. Or almost everything. Guess I wouldn't know if there was something I forgot, if I can't remember it."

"Tim—"

"Okay, here's something you'll be interested in. Those rolled up pages you gave me— Is this line secure?"

"No, and grab a look at your Caller ID so you've got my number. In case you need to reach me." *For as long as the battery lasts.*

"Here's what I've got," Meadows said. "Though I have to tell you there aren't many techs who could do an alternative light source on a tightly coiled piece of thin paper. ALS requires—"

"Tim? Here's the thing: I'm running out of time—and my battery's running out of juice. So get to the point."

"Fine. I lifted three phone numbers off the fourth page. I traced all but one. The first was to a computer parts supplier, the second to a White House extension, and the third—"

"White House? Which extension?"

"I don't know yet. I have to get clearance from the Secret Service for that. I put in a call to the detail's special agent in charge, but it may be a while before I hear back. It was the middle of the night and I don't think they considered it a matter of national security. Even though I told them it might be. But—you're gonna love this—that's not the best thing."

"Tim, the battery . . ."

"Okay, okay. The best thing is this third number. See, it's not listed anywhere. So I did some digging, and seems the number is for an encrypted mobile phone. Cutting-edge stuff. It's got some kind of information security software embedded into its commercial TETRA system—"

"More than I need to know. Bottom line: Who's using it?"

"I was in the middle of figuring that out when you called. Give me another few minutes."

"Call me back." Uzi hit End, then rested his right foot on the engine bar of the Suzuki. He sat there trying to figure out who would have access to such a device. Obviously, the military. But why would anyone in the military be associating with ARM? Then he remembered what

Ruckhauser had told him: that there were some active-duty members who were sympathetic to the militia cause. Some had pilfered equipment and supplies and passed them on to militias, while others joined the groups when they'd completed their tours.

Ten minutes later, as Uzi sat there tumbling it all through his mind, the phone rang.

"I've got a name," Meadows said. "How about Quentin Larchmont?"

"No way. You sure?"

"Absolutely. Don't ask me how I got it, because I kind of broke some rules—"

"Keep working on those pages. Get me the call history on that encrypted phone. And call me if you find anything else." He thought about turning off the handset to conserve battery life, but power cycling the phone used more juice than leaving it on standby.

Uzi shoved the device into his pocket, then twisted the key and revved the motorcycle.

8:49 AM
5 hours 11 minutes remaining

As the morning sky brightened with unexpected sunshine burning through a cloudy haze, Uzi approached the gothically gaudy Eisenhower Executive Office Building across the street from the White House. He parked his Suzuki, pulled off the helmet and ski mask, and fastened them to the bike. He looked in the side-view mirror and attempted to comb his short hair with his fingers. Realizing it wasn't going to do any good, he walked confidently up to the guard booth on West Executive Avenue. He pulled out his credentials and presented them to the officer. "I need to see the president. Tell him it's Agent Uzi."

The Secret Service Uniformed Division police officer raised an eyebrow at the name, wondering if it was a joke, but after inspecting the ID, he nodded, then lifted a phone from the counter. He spoke for a moment, then turned to Uzi, twisting the mouthpiece away from his lips.

"The president will be in the Oval in twenty minutes. Once he's there—"

"I need to see him now. Tell whoever you're talking with to tell the president it's a matter of national security. I'm working under his direct orders."

"Agent, I'm sorry, but—"

Uzi pointed to the phone. "Just tell him."

He saw the muscles of the officer's jaw tense as the man turned back to the phone.

Minutes passed. The officer finally hung up the phone and said, "Someone will be here in a moment to escort you." He handed Uzi a red clip-on visitor's pass, then turned away to make a note in his log.

Uzi shoved his hands into his jacket and began pacing. He hated wasting time. But two minutes later, another officer appeared and ushered Uzi to the West Wing. He was deposited in the Oval Office, a Secret Service agent hovering in the background near the door to babysit him.

Uzi gazed up at the dramatic concealed lighting that radiated from behind ornate crown molding, creating a halo effect around the presidential seal stamped in relief in the center of the ceiling. Ahead of him stood the stately and history-laden Resolute desk, only a handful of items resting on the glossy inlaid top. He walked to the middle of the room, where a steel blue and burnt sienna presidential seal was woven into the dense, oval-shaped area rug. Brown rays radiated from its center and tapered at its edges. Woven in an arch around the eagle logo's periphery were the words "Of the people, for the people."

Uzi took a seat on the sofa to his right, threw his left arm onto the back of the couch, and crossed his legs. From this seat he had a view out the three bay windows of the magnolias and Katherine crab apple trees beyond. Directly ahead and slightly to the right was the glass door that led to the covered walkway where President Jonathan Whitehall now stood, about to enter.

Whitehall stepped into the Oval, leaving his two Secret Service agents outside the door. Uzi quickly unfolded his body and stood. Whitehall was dressed in a navy suit, which, against his short salt-and-pepper hair, white shirt and red tie, gave him an air of clean, pressed confidence.

Uzi, not having showered or changed after being blown to the ground in a massive explosion just hours ago, felt somewhat underdressed for the meeting.

"Mr. President."

"Agent Uziel." Whitehall's eyes seemed to roam the length of Uzi's body, from his facial cuts and abrasions to the disheveled appearance of his clothing.

"I apologize for my appearance, sir. I narrowly escaped getting killed last night and haven't had time to shower and change clothes."

Whitehall motioned to the cream and taupe couch and took a seat himself on the matching sofa directly across from Uzi.

"Was this attempt on your life related to the assassination attempt on the vice president?"

"I believe so, sir."

Whitehall pursed his lips and nodded slowly. He then raised an eyebrow and said, "The message I received said you had something to discuss that was a matter of national security. I assume that means you have the answer I've been waiting for." He glanced at his Démos watch. "And with not much time to spare, I might add."

Uzi squirmed a bit on the couch. Comments Hoshi had made about NFA's massive contribution to Whitehall's campaign flittered through his thoughts. Yet, in spite of that, he trusted the man. And with time perilously short, he had little option; he had to press on. "You wanted me to get to the bottom of this mess, no matter the cost."

Whitehall dipped his chin slightly. "Go on."

"I've uncovered a lot of facts and information, some corroborated and some not, Mr. President. I'm not sure yet how it all fits together, but there are some things I am ready to report on because they require immediate action. I know we don't have a lot of time left." Uzi stopped, suddenly recalling that conversations in the Oval were recorded. "Can we take a walk, sir?"

"Not at the moment. Go on."

Trust notwithstanding, he felt uncomfortable discussing this if it could later be used against him. But with time short, he pressed on. "We obtained several pieces of paper from the Armed Resistance Militia compound the other day. They contained phone numbers, one of which was traced to an encrypted army mobile phone. That phone is being used by Quentin Larchmont." Uzi paused to let that fact sink in.

Whitehall's face suddenly bunched into a mask of wrinkles. "What in hell does that mean?"

"This information is only thirty minutes old, sir, so I can't answer that. But let's just say that there's no reason why anyone affiliated with ARM should have a coded mobile phone number for Quentin Larchmont. One might also ask what use Mr. Larchmont has for such a device."

Whitehall's eyes seemed to study Uzi's face as he digested this thought. The grandfather clock against the far wall over the president's right shoulder ticked softly in the background. Finally, Whitehall leaned back on the couch. "Frankly, son, you're going to have to give me more than—"

Uzi's phone began ringing. The president looked at Uzi's pocket with disdain.

"I'm sorry, sir. This is important." He pulled the cell and answered it.

"Hey, man," Tim Meadows said, excitement boosting his voice. "I got the logs for that certain group we've been tracking, the one that sounds like an appendage—"

"Got it, Tim. I'm meeting with the president right now, so if you could make this quick—"

"*The* president? Right, okay. The logs. Well, they've got a bunch of calls to the Executive Office Building. Daily, it looks like, going on for several weeks before they suddenly stop."

"Who were they calling?"

"I can't tell, at least not yet. But there's more. Some of the calls from that phone went to another encrypted mobile. And that one apparently belongs to someone named Lewiston Grant."

Oh, man. Uzi rubbed at his temple. "Are you sure?" His eyes flicked over to the president, who was listening intently to Uzi's end of the conversation. "It was listed under that name?"

"Gee whiz, Uzi, I didn't look it up in the phone book under 'Grant,' if that's what you mean. I had to dig. I traced a pretty convoluted strand that led me to this guy. I'm about as sure as I can be on short notice. It takes time to hack—I mean, to *obtain* this information."

"Great work. Really, really good. Call me when you've got more."

Uzi hung up and apologized to the president. "Again, sir, I don't know yet how this all fits together. But we've got encrypted phone calls from the militia to the Executive Office Building. And we've got a large caliber Russian round from their compound that matches one that killed one of our informants."

Whitehall straightened up. "Are these militia people in custody?"

"No, sir." Uzi looked down at the plush carpet. "Remember that discussion we had on the green when you were putting—"

"Let's take a walk, son." Whitehall rose from the couch and turned for the French door.

Uzi pushed off the sofa and followed.

"Benedict to Horsepower," the Secret Service agent said into his cuff mike as he pulled open the door. Horsepower referred to the presidential detail's command post beneath the Oval Office. The agent continued talking into his sleeve. "Authorized break on the Oval Colonnade door. Big Bear on the move."

Whitehall and Uzi stepped out onto the Colonnade's long, covered fieldstone walkway, stone columns to their immediate right and the Rose Garden beyond. When they'd cleared the range of the recording devices in the Oval, Whitehall nodded for Uzi to continue.

"On the lawn," Uzi said. "Remember sir, when you told me to 'just get the job done'?"

Whitehall kept his gaze on the ground as he walked. "Go on."

"The evidence gathered at the ARM compound was not obtained . . . legally. The attorney general ordered us to give the militia some breathing room, to back off our investigation of them. But Director Knox made it known in private that he wanted us to disregard that order."

Whitehall stopped walking and inserted his hands into his pockets. "So what you're saying is that none of this can be used against them."

"That's right, sir. But I believe Quentin Larchmont is involved with ARM and there could be a larger conspiracy involving other members of the incoming administration. And possibly yours." Uzi braced himself for the president's wrath. But none came.

"Has Assistant Director Yates been fully briefed on all this?"

"No, sir. I wasn't sure who could be trusted, so I've kept this info close to the vest."

"And the peace talks. What can you tell me relative to the Palestinians?"

I was hoping you wouldn't ask me that. "It's not looking good, sir. Al-Humat's mixed up in all this. Looks like they've had a sleeper cell operating here for years. But I'll need more time to get you a definitive answer." He hoped Whitehall would give him some room on this, that somehow the credibility he had just earned with his exposure of ARM vouched for the quality of his work and his ability to follow the president's orders.

The commander in chief was silent, his gaze off somewhere in the vicinity of the Rose Garden. Abruptly, he turned and headed back into the Oval Office. Uzi followed.

"Benedict to Horsepower," the Secret Service agent said into his sleeve. "Authorized break, Oval Colonnade door. Big Bear returning."

Whitehall walked to his desk and lifted the phone. He punched a number and said, "Get me Director Knox."

Uzi stepped forward. "Sir, with all due respect, I wouldn't recommend that. Director Knox might be part of—"

Whitehall cupped the phone. His entire body tensed. "What are you saying?"

"Until we're clear on the players, we should be careful about who we bring into this."

The president's eyes narrowed. "Do you have any reason to believe the director of the FBI is a co-conspirator?"

Careful, Uzi. "No evidence, sir, but I do have 'reason to believe' there might be a connection. Potentially even the attorney general." Uzi realized he was sticking out his neck extremely far, but given the gravity of the information he now possessed, and the time he had left, he felt he could remain silent no longer.

Whitehall shook his head but kept his hand firmly over the receiver. "I refuse to accept that. Either way, I have to bring in the FBI. It's not an option."

The two men locked stares, neither willing to give ground. "Yes," Whitehall said, quickly removing his hand from the mouthpiece.

"Douglas. Good to hear your voice. I've got something I need you to look into."

Uzi closed his eyes and bowed his head as the president laid out the information Uzi had provided. When he finished, the president listened for a moment, then said, "For now, Douglas, let's not discuss how I obtained that information. I would like you to move on it, however." Whitehall rocked slightly on his heels, his left hand tucked behind his back. He nodded a few times. "I understand that, Douglas. . . . Yes, I realize that. . . . That's for you to figure out. But please do let Director Zallwick and Secretary Braun know they might have an internal security problem. Keep me posted."

Whitehall hung up the phone. "Agent Uziel, I can tell you're not pleased with my decision. But I'm not some covert operative in the middle of Afghanistan. I have procedures to follow."

The comment was like a kick in the rear. Uzi cringed internally. He suddenly realized just how far he had strayed from "procedure." Whose orders was he now following—and were their motives genuine, or was he being used?

"Notifying the directors of the FBI, Secret Service, and Homeland Security we may have a serious breach of security is crucial to maintaining the safety of this country."

"Yes, sir."

The president turned right and headed for the door again. Uzi followed. Back out on the Colonnade, Whitehall started walking down the path, but this time did not stop. He gave Uzi a sidewards glance, then said, "Unofficially, I believe you've started something you would like to finish. Am I right, son?"

Uzi nodded, unsure of where the president was leading.

"I don't know if Director Knox is involved. I would find it hard to believe given his decades of distinguished service. But I've also been around the block a few times, and I know that men are sometimes driven by things people like me can't pretend to understand. For one, I could never do some of the things our covert operatives are paid to do. But they do them without hesitation. Whatever their internal motivation is, I don't know. Honor, duty, love for their country is what I'm told. But all I need to know is that when the call goes out they put their lives on the line and do what's necessary to get the job done." Whitehall turned to Uzi. "There's something about you, agent, that makes me think you understand such men and their motives. And that's why I'm asking you to continue doing what you need to do to get the job done."

Uzi's head snapped left. "But you just called the director—"

"Because until January twentieth I'm still president of the United States, and I have to follow procedure. But sometimes following procedure is ineffective. I think you've been around Washington long enough to understand what I'm saying."

Uzi nodded. But he wondered if Whitehall knew more than he was letting on. Was there more depth to his comment on following procedure or was Uzi to take it at face value? Had the president been briefed by Knox—or Shepard—about his clash with Osborn? He had no doubt that Whitehall had asked the Secret Service to prepare a full dossier on him after, or even before, their first meeting at the White House. But exactly how much Whitehall knew about his past was unclear.

"You're wasting time, son, and that's something we can ill afford. Now get going. And Godspeed."

Uzi pushed his thoughts aside, shook the president's hand, and was off.

9:29 AM
4 hours 31 minutes remaining

Alpha Zulu paced outside his car, rubbing at his forehead but keeping his Redskins ball cap pulled low over his brow. He was good at keeping cool under pressure; it was more a learned skill than an inherited personality trait. But with time growing short, he was in operations mode. Expectations rose along with tempers. This was not the time for things to go wrong.

At the moment, there were no serious indications the plan was in jeopardy. Like any successful business, safeguards were built in, redundancies and backups. The anticipated glitches caused by law enforcement's inevitable probing made the intricate strategizing vital, the challenge that much more alluring. It was a chess game on a grand scale, with pawns and queens, moves and countermoves.

Like a master, Zulu had drawn up a winning plan, yet continued studying his opponents—measuring their weaknesses, finding holes in their methods. Identifying ways to use their deficiencies against them to break down their defenses. In this deadly game, when all was said and done, preparation, patience, and experience were king. They planned to have the board cleared in a matter of hours. But if getting to checkmate took weeks, or days, or years, so be it.

He glanced at his scorpion-engraved pocket watch: it was time. He climbed into his car and slid behind the wheel. A moment later, a late-model sedan pulled up alongside his and stopped. Oscar Delta got out, adjusted his jacket, and then moved around to Zulu's back door. He got in and closed the door quietly.

Zulu cranked the engine and drove off. "Things are hot. There's a lot in play."

"We expected that."

Zulu's eyes roamed the street. "Yes." He glanced in the rear-view mirror at Delta, then continued. "Be ready in case we need to implement *Fallback*."

"You think it'll come to that?"

Zulu knew what this could mean to Delta, but he had never doubted the man's resolve. "Hard to say." Zulu made a U-turn and accelerated back toward the park.

"What does your intel indicate?"

"I'll evaluate and advise. For now, that's all you need to know." He saw Delta's mouth contort in rebuke. A moment later, Zulu stopped beside the sedan and looked off to his left. "Good luck."

Without a word, the rear door closed. The interior was quiet.

Another car door slammed, and the sedan drove off.

As Uzi walked along West Executive Avenue toward his motorcycle, he pulled out his phone and called Tim Meadows. After obtaining the number for Larchmont's encrypted cell, he got onto his Suzuki and peeled away, headed for the Rusch transition headquarters.

He did a couple of drive-bys, casing out the place and locating all the entrances and exits. It would've been a great deal easier to involve the Secret Service detail assigned to the vice president's staff, but Uzi's plan demanded he engage as few people as possible.

He called DeSantos, but it went to voicemail; his partner either did not recognize the phone number of Uzi's borrowed cell, or his phone was off. Regardless, Uzi hoped DeSantos checked his messages soon.

After making his third pass around the office building, he settled on his surveillance point. A reinforced black Suburban was parked at the front curb, twenty feet from one of the two exits. Uzi reasoned the Secret Service would choose the shortest unprotected path to the car, and this was, indeed, the door Larchmont had used when Uzi had visited him.

He parked his bike two blocks away and across the street. From this vantage point, the Hensoldt scope gave him a clear view of the building and the Secret Service's black Suburban.

He inserted a small Y-connector plug into the side jack of the cell phone, then pressed Record on a digital recorder in his pocket. He dialed the encrypted mobile, hoping Larchmont kept the phone on at all times. If not, this could take longer than he'd planned. And the longer it dragged out, the greater the likelihood Knox could take actions that would interfere with Uzi's plans. At this point, Uzi wasn't sure if that was good—or bad.

Ninety minutes later, after repeated attempts and Uzi's patience—and time—wearing thin, the call to Larchmont's encrypted mobile finally went through.

"Mr. Larchmont," Uzi began. "It's good to hear your voice again. I've been trying to reach you. Now don't hang up. I know, this comes as a bit of a shock—"

"Who is this?"

"Oh—sorry. Didn't mean to be rude. This is Special Agent Aaron Uziel. Remember me? We met—"

"What do you want?"

"Easy, Mr. Larchmont, easy. I've got a problem and you've got a problem. I figure maybe we can help each other out."

"And just what problem do I have, Agent Uziel?"

Uzi chuckled. "I know all about your work with ARM. Specifically, Lewiston Grant."

"You don't know anything because there's nothing to know."

"Really? See, I've got this phone number, now, don't I? And I know about your calls to the Executive Office Building. By the way, I should remind you that your phone may be encrypted, but mine isn't. Still want to discuss this so close to the government's probing ears?"

"You didn't mention what your problem was."

Uzi smiled. He had him. What had been a listing of suspicious phone calls and unusual circumstances was about to turn into hard evidence. Larchmont was sniffing the bait, weighing the risks, wondering if it was a trap. Whether or not Uzi could hook him and reel him in depended on his next comment.

"Let's just say that certain . . . undesirable details about my past have come to light that . . . threaten my career. And my pension. Before CNN gets hold of it and it all blows up in my face, I need you to make it all go away. In a few weeks, you'll be in a position to do that. You make that happen, and I'll conveniently forget about this phone number."

There were several seconds of silence.

"My next call," Uzi continued, "won't be to you, Mr. Larchmont. It'll be to the *Post*, where I have a really good relationship with one of the editors who'll pay me pretty well for the story. And then I'll write a book and hit the talk show circuit—and the loss of my pension won't matter."

"The warehouse near Union Station, Fourth and G. Meet me there in twenty minutes."

The line went dead. Uzi pulled on his ski mask, followed by the helmet, then brought the rifle scope up to his eyes and watched the entrance. Inside of two minutes, Quentin Larchmont appeared, followed by two dark-suited men—Secret Service agents. The chief of staff-to-be stopped outside the building's large glass doors and said something to them. One of them spread his arms wide and replied.

Larchmont motioned with his hand, and the agent on the left reached into his pocket and passed over a small object. Larchmont then turned away and climbed into the driver's seat of the SUV.

Uzi shoved the scope into his pocket and started the Suzuki. There was no turning back now.

11:53 AM
2 hours 7 minutes remaining

Echo Charlie squeezed the encrypted mobile so tightly his knuckles ached. He sat at his desk, wondering how the Fed had gotten this phone number. And how could he have known he was working with Lewiston Grant?

Charlie realized Uziel could've been bluffing—but still, he knew too much if he could place him in the same sentence with Grant. They were too close. No, *he* was too close. It sounded to Charlie as if the agent was working alone in hopes of pulling off a trade: silence for a favor. This was not unusual in the power-driven winds of Washington. But was it legit? He couldn't take the risk. This had to be taken care of—quickly.

Charlie consulted his silver pocket watch, then headed for the door. "I'll be back in an hour," he called to the secretary sitting at the front desk as he turned left down the hall.

"But sir, you have a meeting with Mr.—"

"I said I'll be back," he yelled, and kept on walking.

Two Secret Service agents fell in step behind him. With the assassination attempt an ugly blemish on their record, the Secret Service was taking no chances, and agents followed him everywhere he went offsite. Though it was annoying, Charlie reminded himself it was merely a constant reminder of the power he now wielded.

He called over his shoulder, "I'll be back shortly. I won't be needing you on this errand."

"Procedure, sir," the older one said. "We'll be accompanying you—"

Charlie pushed through the glass doors and stopped a dozen feet short of the curb. He turned to face the two men and said, "You guys are just doing your job, I understand that. But I'll only be an hour. I'd rather be alone for a little while. Surely you can appreciate that."

"Sir, we're not supposed to—"

"Actually, there is something you can do for me. Give me the keys to the Suburban." He extended a hand and wiggled the fingers. "Quickly, please."

The agents shared a look, then one dug into his pocket and handed over the keys.

Echo Charlie climbed into the armored-up vehicle, started the engine, and drove off.

12:02 PM
1 hour 58 minutes remaining

Uzi accelerated hard. He needed to arrive ahead of Larchmont—and whoever else the chief of staff was bringing with him.

He ran a couple of lights and took turns faster than he should have, but he wanted to give his plan every chance to succeed. He swerved down an alley and the warehouse swung into view.

He did not think the Suburban could have made it here before him, and in fact, his quick recon of the immediate vicinity indicated it had not. He made a tight circle with his bike in front of the dilapidated structure, located its only entrance, and went to work.

Despite stopping to pick up his four passengers, Echo Charlie was early—important because they wanted to do a reconnaissance drive-by to ensure they were not being set up. Once convinced the area was clear of law enforcement, they would take action. The operation required stealth: work swiftly, dispose of the body cleanly, then get rid of all evidence that they had been there.

Charlie turned the corner of the potholed, puddle-filled alley and slammed on his brakes. Spread across the pavement, blocking the narrow road to the warehouse twenty yards away, was an upended motorcycle. The driver, pinned beneath it and lying on his back, flailed his arms like a beached fish impotently flapping its fins.

Charlie rubbernecked left and right, hoping for a way around the biker. But the area was too narrow. He cursed under his breath as his eyes darted around the alley, which was bordered by two windowless brick buildings. It was unlikely anyone had seen or heard the spill the motorcyclist had taken.

"Go deal with that," Charlie said to the men behind him. "No matter what, keep him quiet. We don't want anyone calling an ambulance. Drag him into the warehouse, gag and blindfold him. I don't want him to be able to identify us—"

"I get rid of him," one of them said in clipped English. "He see our car, the license plate."

"Fine. Just be fast, quiet, and clean. And get the goddamn alley cleared. Go! Move!"

The three men left the Suburban, the fourth staying behind with his boss. Charlie gripped the steering wheel with white knuckles as his enforcers approached the motorcycle.

Uzi lay in wait. Seconds later, Larchmont's black SUV lumbered into the alley and ground to a stop. Uzi began flapping his arms, as if he were trapped beneath the motorcycle, which had tipped on its side, taking the driver down with it. At least that's what he wanted them to think.

Lying on his back wearing a bulbous helmet was not comfortable. But if he was right, he wouldn't be here very long. He activated his digital recorder as the two back doors opened and slammed shut. Three trim olive-skinned men dressed in dark suits hurried toward him. As the closer one approached, his jacket parted, revealing a large-caliber handgun.

"Help me," Uzi said, his muffled voice sounding even more desperate.

But these three did not appear to be American Red Cross types; they looked more like the Middle Eastern terrorists he had once been ordered to kill. As the larger man bent over him, Uzi whipped his Puma tactical knife from his pocket and sliced it through the henchman's neck with the swiftness of a magician. Arterial blood gushed from his carotid.

Uzi swung the blade back to his right, and with equal precision and speed, cut the second man's trachea. Both reeled back, unsteady hands clutching their fatal wounds.

The last man stepped back and drew his handgun. But Uzi was faster with his blade, and he flung it through the air, the sleek metal slicing the intervening dozen feet in a split second. It was over before the pistol could clear leather. Clumsily grabbing for the handle of the blade protruding from the left side of his chest, the assailant fell back toward the pavement.

Uzi leapt up, and in two long strides reached the man's shoulder rig. He drew the Smith & Wesson and fired twice at the SUV. The fourth henchman, who had just exited the Suburban's open front passenger door, got off an errant shot before Uzi planted a suppressed round in the man's forehead.

He brought the handgun down and put a bullet in the skull of the man still attempting to pull the Puma from his chest.

Quentin Larchmont, seated behind the steering wheel and watching with dropped jaw, grabbed for the gearshift. He threw the Suburban into reverse and started out of the alley, but a black Hummer pulled behind him, blocking the way.

Uzi reached down and yanked his knife from the dead man's chest as two men jumped from the Hummer and headed toward him.

These men also had olive complexions.

And they were also armed. With suppressed submachine guns.

12:13 PM
1 hour 47 minutes remaining

"Drop it!"

The order came from the stocky one, his weapon trained on Uzi's chest. And in a brief split second of irony, Uzi couldn't help but notice that their weapon of choice was the Israeli-made *Uzi* submachine gun. It appeared to be one of the newer, more compact Minis. Though smaller than its full-size cousin, the Minis killed just as efficiently.

In the *next* split second, Uzi realized he was in the shit. Two men, approaching from opposite directions, had him drawn down with superior firepower. And he was out in the open, with no way of getting to cover before they made his body resemble a block of Swiss cheese.

Santa, now would be a good time to show up.

"Drop it," the bearded one said. "Now."

Uzi flung the handgun back over his right shoulder. He had a fleeting thought of throwing the knife, figuring he might be able to take one of them out—but that would accomplish little. At this distance, with their automatic weapons already in hand and aimed at his chest, he'd be long dead before the knife struck its target.

He tossed the Puma to the same place he had thrown the gun.

Quentin Larchmont, sporting a black fedora pulled down over his head, got out of the Suburban, then slammed the door shut. "Get him inside."

The two men grabbed Uzi by the arms, spun him around, and shoved him toward the warehouse. One of them used a key to open the door while the other pushed him inside.

Buried beneath his shirt and around his neck, Uzi still had the Tanto—not to mention the boot knife. But getting to either was the problem. He was outnumbered—and his weapons, while nearby, might as well have been a mile away.

"Get his helmet off."

The stocky one yanked on the black Bell while the other stood guard. As he worked on the helmet, Uzi got a better look at the man's face, and realized his darker complexion was the result of hastily applied makeup: he was, in fact, the Secret Service agent Uzi had seen only hours ago in the Oval Office. *Benedict? Was that his name? Yes, Benedict. That could explain the calls to the Eisenhower Executive Office Building, the location of the Secret Service's command post. But what did this mean? Were other members of the Secret Service involved? What about Whitehall?*

"Secure him," Larchmont said.

The bearded man produced a set of handcuffs and handed them to Benedict, then fished keys out of Uzi's front pocket. He tossed them to Larchmont.

As Benedict ratcheted the restraints closed, Larchmont tilted his head, appraising his captive. Then his face hardened as he said, "Down on your knees."

But Uzi did not budge. Benedict, standing slightly behind Uzi and to his right, swung the butt end of his Mini into Uzi's ribs. Uzi crumpled to the ground.

After struggling to right himself, he knelt on his left knee. "I'm worth more to you alive," he said through a clenched jaw.

"I didn't think you'd say you're worth more dead." Larchmont removed his fedora and held it in both hands in front of his body. "We'll talk about your fate in a moment. First, you're going to do some talking. Based on what you say, we'll evaluate your future usefulness."

"I'm not in the mood to talk."

Larchmont looked at the bearded gunman and chinned a nod in Uzi's direction. The man shoved the point of his Mini into Uzi's temple. "Maybe this will help."

Uzi's heart rate jumped. He struggled to control it, knowing he needed to keep his wits, to remain composed and be ready to strike at a moment's notice, when an opportunity presented itself. Assuming one did.

But it was hard to slow your pulse and keep focused when a man was shoving the cold metal barrel of a submachine gun against your skull.

An image of his little girl floated through his mind. Maya. Tears instantly filled his eyes, but he quickly compartmentalized the thought. He couldn't crumble, not now. Maybe DeSantos would answer one of the voicemails he had left for him. The ring of the phone might distract them long enough for him to make a move. At this point, making an attempt was better than taking a bullet without putting up a fight.

"Does Lewiston Grant know your operation is in danger of collapsing?" Uzi asked, hoping to get something incriminating on tape; the recorder in his pocket was hopefully still running. "I think Lewis old boy would want you to hear me out and cut the deal I'm offering. Everyone wins."

But Larchmont wasn't taking the bait.

"Who else knows about my private cell phone?"

Uzi bit his lip. If he told Larchmont there were others who have this information, the next question would invariably be, "Who?" Those people would then be at risk—after they disposed of Uzi. If he told Larchmont no one else knew, he would be killed for sure.

He answered obliquely. "I've got a recording of our phone

conversation. If we can't reach an agreement, the whole world will know."

Larchmont took a step forward. "Where is it?"

Uzi sensed a window of opportunity opening. "It's on an SD card. If I give it to you, will you let me go?" An absurd question—but Larchmont didn't know Uzi well, and perhaps his pompous ego would allow him to think Uzi was just stupid enough to consider the notion that trading the recording for his life was a request worthy of consideration.

"It'd go a long way toward convincing me to make a deal," Larchmont said, apparently buying the stupid agent routine.

"It's hidden on my motorcycle."

Larchmont's lips got thin with the suggestion of a smile.

"But you won't find it. It's a micro-SD card, smaller than the nail on my pinky," Uzi said. "Uncuff me and I'll get it for you."

The politician's smirk blossomed into a grin. "I think we can manage." Larchmont motioned to Benedict, who slung the Mini over his shoulder and pushed through the doors.

His odds having suddenly improved, all Uzi had to do was find a way of disabling the man holding the Mini against his head. While still handcuffed.

"Can I have something to drink?" Uzi cleared his throat, dipped his chin, and coughed. "My mouth is dry as hell. Please . . ."

"Are there any other copies of the recording?" Larchmont asked.

Uzi coughed again. "I just recorded it." He coughed harder. "When could I have made a copy?" He bent his head down, and launched into a spasmodic coughing fit. Then he felt it. The machine gun barrel left his temple.

It was only a second, but it was long enough. In one swift movement, Uzi pushed up with his right leg while twisting his torso left. His head knocked the gun barrel aside at the same moment his right shoulder slammed into the man's stomach. The guard flew back, his weapon tilting away and unleashing an impotent volley of nine-millimeter rounds into the cement floor and wall.

The momentum carried Uzi into a shoulder roll. He slid his cuffed wrists beneath his buttocks and under his feet, bringing his hands to the front of his body. He lunged for the Mini and wrestled the tip into the dazed guard's chin, then squeezed the trigger. The man's beard blossomed with blood. Uzi yanked away the weapon and wildly sprayed the area with lead.

Larchmont was hugging the ground and had escaped the lethal volley. But Benedict, clearly having heard the suppressed rounds ricocheting off the floors and metal racks, ran back into the warehouse and caught a shower of bullets in the face.

Uzi's heart was pumping much too fast. Adrenaline had prepared him for war—but though the battle was over, he still felt crazed, out of control. He pointed the gun at Larchmont, who was on his stomach and clutching his head. Uzi walked over to him and with his knee in the small of the man's back, fumbled around the politician's jacket pocket for the handcuff key. He finally found it, and after struggling to insert it into the lock, removed his restraints.

Uzi took a few deep breaths to calm himself, then backed away. "Get up."

Larchmont slowly picked himself up off the concrete floor.

"Hands behind your back."

Uzi drove the Suburban and sedan inside and removed several fuses from both vehicles. He unlocked Larchmont, moved him to the SUV's driver's seat, and then recuffed his wrists to the steering wheel.

"Mind if I borrow this?" Uzi asked as he pulled Larchmont's suit handkerchief from the breast pocket. He stuffed it between Larchmont's lips, and fastened the politician's red paisley necktie around his mouth to hold the gag in place. An unusual use for such luxurious imported silk—and a damn fine embroidered design at that—but effective nonetheless.

Uzi stood outside the car for a moment and checked off his list. With the Suburban's fuses removed, Larchmont could lean on the horn all he wanted to. It would remain silent.

Almost done.

After dragging the three bloody bodies out of the alley, he went about gathering his things: ski mask and helmet, his knives, and the .40 caliber Smith & Wesson he had tossed aside earlier. He cranked the warehouse door shut, then got on his bike and fled the scene.

12:49 PM
1 hour 11 minutes remaining

Alpha Zulu knelt beside Leila al-Far. Zulu, dressed in repairman gray coveralls, dug through a metal toolbox, looking for a part to complete the electronic device he had been busy assembling.

Gripped in Leila's right hand was a Taser-type stun wand, and slung across her back was an AKS-74U shorty assault rifle, fitted with a PBS silent fire suppressor. "Well?" she asked Zulu.

"Another ten, then it'll be ready." He really would have liked to set the timer and leave, but his cohort had other plans. Though she insisted on taking this more obtuse route, he wasn't concerned about the overall success of their plan. They would do what they needed to do and get out. Whatever happened after that was merely above and beyond, as far as he was concerned.

After several minutes had ticked by, Zulu gave the nod and Leila approached their hostage, Leonard Rudnick, who was securely fastened to a wood chair. Squaring herself in front of the doctor, Leila cradled the stun wand in both hands, displaying it as if Rudnick were a jeweler preparing to appraise a ring. "This is one of my favorite tools, Doctor. It sends three hundred thousand volts through your body. Do you know how it works?"

The muscles of his jaw tightened but he gave no nod, made no attempt to speak.

"I'd think you'd be familiar with it because you've studied the mind, you know how the brain works. Its physiology. Right? This little device scrambles the nervous system, leaves you dazed and confused." She tilted her head, assessing whether she had his attention. "Oh—I almost forgot. The pain. It lights up your nerve endings like an arcade. Pain beyond your wildest fears." Failing to elicit a reaction, she held the wand in front of his face. "You've got one last chance to cooperate."

Rudnick closed his eyes and turned away. Had the doctor indicated a willingness to talk, Zulu would've removed the gag. But he couldn't risk the man screaming unless they were sure he was going to tell them what they wanted to know. A screwup now would be disastrous.

Leila shoved the tip of the stun wand into Rudnick's abdomen and gave him a short burst. He screamed a muffled cry and jerked forward, but the bindings kept him erect. A longer jolt would've altered their plan, as there wouldn't be enough time for him to regain his wits.

A tear escaped Rudnick's right eye and streamed down his face. Zulu looked on, knowing firsthand the intense pain induced by a stun gun shock to the stomach. This man was a tough bird, that much was evident. But as a health care practitioner, someone who had devoted his entire life to helping people with their own personal hells, the doctor would respond to the one last trick Zulu had in his playbook. In this case, he had no doubt whatsoever it would work.

"Enough," Zulu said. He stepped forward and brushed Leila back with his left forearm. He held out the compact black box he had been assembling. At present, its red LED screen displayed "00:00," but soon it would be programmed with numerals. And then the fun would begin.

Alpha Zulu grinned at Rudnick out of one side of his mouth. "This, Doctor, is a powerful explosive that'll destroy a good portion of this building. Now, your offices have been here for several years, and you know many of the hundreds of people who live and work here. I'm told there are about five hundred here right this very minute. What do you think?"

Rudnick's eyebrows pointed inward in defiance.

"Maybe you doubt our convictions." He held up the bomb and poked numbers into its keypad. "But that would be foolish." He tilted his head. "I know what kind of man you are. You'd rather die yourself than cause others harm. Very noble. But your life isn't what's at stake here, Doctor. You hold hundreds of other lives in your hands. Make the wrong decision and they all die. Innocent women. Young children. Their blood on your hands." Zulu paused.

"My sources tell me you have experience watching people die. Lots of people. Burned in ovens, gassed in chambers. Shot and dumped in pits. But—you've got a chance to prevent that type of mass murder from happening again." He allowed Rudnick to mull the magnitude of his decision. And the guilt.

"So this is what it comes down to," Zulu continued. "You're going to make a phone call. Do it well, everything will turn out okay. If you don't . . ." Zulu shrugged and bobbed his head. A malevolent smile pursed his lips. "Well, I'm afraid that's something you won't be able to live with."

Uzi dialed Shepard as he headed back to Leila's house. This time he wouldn't be skulking around in the dark. There was no time for that. He wasn't sure where to go, who to talk to, whose help to enlist. But he was certain of one thing: whatever was going down, it was going to happen in less than an hour. And he couldn't shake the sense that Leila sat at the heart of whatever was to come.

Uzi's call to Shepard was short and to the point: he needed his ASAC to coordinate with Knox and Yates, Homeland Security, his own JTTF, M2TF, and Director Tasset. It was hitting the fan, and until they could put it all together to figure out what it meant, they had to be ready for anything.

First priority was the International Conference on Global Terrorism, due to begin within the hour. A close second was the peace talks, but he left Whitehall to shore up those preparations. Whatever agencies the president wanted to enlist, and when, was not Uzi's call. Uzi's involvement in that particular state of affairs ended with his rendering a definitive answer as to whether or not a Palestinian group was involved in the VP's assassination attempt.

Shepard assured Uzi the conference was well covered and highly secure. But he would alert all the involved parties. Uzi gave Shepard's secretary his cell number, then hung a left onto New Hampshire Avenue. As he pulled up in front of Hamilton House, workers were using a bulldozer and dump truck to cart away the shattered chunks of pavement left behind by the explosion of Uzi's Tahoe.

As Uzi removed his helmet, his cell phone began ringing. It was DeSantos.

"Could've used your help," Uzi said. "Big shit's gone down."

"Sorry, boychick, I didn't know this was your number. I ignored the calls. I've been coordinating stuff with Knox. You put the scare into Whitehall—"

"Then he told you about Larchmont?"

"About your suspicions."

"Yeah, well, they're not suspicions anymore. He and his thugs just tried to kill me. We need to meet. Where are you?"

"Headed to the Hay-Adams. Me and my colleagues are there as support. Just in case."

Uzi knew that meant his OPSIG buddies. Made sense.

"Just so you know, Phish and Mason got something on Danny Carlson," DeSantos said. "A voicemail on your cell, left a little before he died. A warning about Leila and that you were in danger. He also said he's onto something big. He mentioned a DLB 'where the tracks meet.' I know the drop, I used it with him a couple of times. I sent Phish over to grab the package."

"Not looking much like a suicide now, is it?"

"If it ever did. I'll meet you at the hotel."

The moment Uzi hit End, the phone rang again.

"Agent Uziel, this is Dr. Rudnick."

"Doc? How'd you get this number?"

"You weren't answering your phone, so I called your office."

Uzi instantly realized he had missed his appointment. "Geez—I'm sorry, Doc, I totally spaced out my session. Things are coming to a head and I had to—"

"Uzi, listen to me. I need to see you, right away."

Rudnick's voice was unusually tense. Uzi got the sense the doctor was not simply admonishing him for missing his session. *Someone's there with him. Leila.*

"You sure it's gotta be *now*?"

There was a second's pause, then a muffled noise as if the handset was being covered.

"Yes. Come now. There's something I have to discuss with you, something we discussed during your last session. But we can't do it over the phone. How soon can you get here?"

"Fifteen minutes. On my way." He hung up the phone, shoved his helmet back on, started up the bike, and twisted the throttle.

In reality, Uzi was five minutes away—but in the likely event Leila or someone else was using Rudnick to lure him there, he didn't want them expecting him when he was scheduled to arrive. He hung a right on M Street and twisted the throttle, accelerating hard toward Rudnick's office.

Uzi arrived with the engine off, gliding to a stop on the slate tiles of the building's exterior entryway. He pushed through the cherrywood-framed glass doors and nearly slipped on the slick marble of the lobby. He decided to forego the elevator—the logical place for him to emerge on Rudnick's floor—in case his visitor was wise enough to know he had padded his ETA.

He took the steps two at a time. When he reached the fifth floor, he removed his helmet and set it down, withdrew the Puma with his left hand and the pilfered .40 caliber Smith & Wesson handgun with the right. He pushed up against the metal fire door and listened.

Nothing. Uzi opened it a crack and peered into the empty hallway. He moved out of the stairwell and stopped beside a fire alarm pull box. He threw his back against the wall and inched along the corridor, his eyes and ears tuned to any and all noises. He approached the taupe door—the "secret" confidential patient entrance—his best shot at a stealthy entry.

Slowly, he pulled it open. Again, all was quiet. He was now standing in the anteroom to Rudnick's office. He stopped and listened, heart pounding, mouth desert dry—and made his way across the floor to the opposite door. It was ajar. He crouched low and pushed it open with a foot.

In one motion, he stepped inside and swept the room from left to right with the Smith & Wesson. All clear. Except that sitting in the center of the office was the doctor, bound and gagged.

Uzi cleared the entire area, and, convinced there was no one else present, turned his attention to the bound psychologist.

"Doc, are you okay?" He slid his knife blade behind Rudnick's head and sliced away the bandana. "I'm so sorry. I didn't want to involve you."

Rudnick spat out the gag, and then looked up at his patient with sad eyes. "I should be the one apologizing. I didn't want to call you—"

"Who did this?"

"I believe it was Leila. And an associate." He swallowed hard. "They wanted information on you. About the investigation. They thought I knew something."

"What did you tell them?"

Rudnick lifted his head proudly. "Nothing."

That was when Uzi noticed it. A large black resin box behind Rudnick's chair that sprouted gray metal flex conduit which snaked to a flat device below the doctor's right shoe.

"Is that what I think it is?"

Rudnick bowed his head. "I'm afraid so."

Uzi grabbed the doctor's phone on the desk—but there was no dial tone. He dug out his cell and called his office. "Hoshi—it's me. Get EOD to 2311 M Street. Fast—we've got a hot one, and there isn't much time!"

"I'll try, but they're on special assignment because of the conference—"

"I don't care how you do it, just get them over here—now!"

He hung up, ran into the hallway, and pulled the fire alarm. At least there was a chance some of the building's occupants would get out in time. He ran back to Rudnick, got down on all fours, and began studying the devices.

There was a red LED display that read 5:58. The seconds were ticking down. *Shit!* He had six minutes to get him out of the building. But his foot was on what appeared to be a pressure sensitive device. Lift the shoe, the bomb detonates.

He dialed Tim Meadows. "Tim, it's Uzi."

"Good timing. I was about to call you. I found something—"

"You know something about bombs, right?"

"That's a bit of a sore subject, especially coming from you—"

"My friend's wired to one and I've got five minutes before it blows. There appears to be a spring-loaded pressure sensitive device under his foot. It's got a very small trigger, otherwise I'd try wedging something under his shoe—"

"Don't do that. Devices like that have redundancy mechanisms that'll make the whole thing blow if they're tampered with."

"There are no exposed wires— I'm guessing they're inside a length of electrical conduit that connects the two devices. Can I open the bomb's casing? Looks like a composite material, about two feet square—"

"These people know what they're doing when it comes to bombs, Uzi. I can tell you that from personal experience. It's booby trapped, I'm sure. If you touch it without knowing what you're doing, they'll be picking you up with a vacuum cleaner."

"Shit." He fisted a clump of hair and pulled. "Shit. So what do I do?"

"How about a fire extinguisher? Spraying it with CO2 might freeze the trigger mechanism long enough for you to take cover."

Uzi's knowledge of microcircuitry told him this wouldn't work. "The drop in temperature will contract the metal. It'll change the tolerance of the components. That alone may set it off."

"Jesus, Uzi, this is a tough one."

"Tim, I can't just . . . I can't just let him die."

"How about amputating his leg? You'd have to secure it to the chair with duct tape so it doesn't move—if that's even possible, which I don't think it is. You're talking about cutting through a big freakin' bone. Unless you cut through the knee joint. No," he said, discounting his own suggestion, "best thing to do is call EOD."

"This thing's history in a little over four minutes."

"Then I've got one last suggestion: get the hell out of there."

"That's it?"

"I'm sorry, man. If there was something you could do, I'd tell you—"

Uzi ended the call. He bit his lip and stared at the black and red screen as the numbers cascaded downward. Maybe this was just an elaborate joke to scare the hell out of him. Meant to send him a message. *Yeah, that's it. It's really not a bomb. It's fashioned to look like one, but it's really not. It's really not.*

Damn you, Leila. Damn you!

"Uzi," Rudnick said softly, "you must leave."

He got down on all fours and peered at the black resin housing. "Can't do that, Doc. But thanks for your concern."

"That wasn't a request, Uzi. It was an order. You need to follow your doctor's orders."

Uzi continued to study the device. "Always the joker. Have you always had such a keen sense of humor?"

"Uzi, look at me. Look at me," he said, schoolteacher stern. "At my eyes."

Uzi stopped what he was doing and looked up. "I've lived seven decades longer than God intended, my friend. I should've died as a scrawny kid in Buchenwald. Somehow, I survived and lived a whole lifetime. The time has come for me to join my parents and sisters."

"No, I can't just—"

"Yes, Uzi. You can. Promise me one thing—that you'll be the one to tell my son Wayne at the BSU. Tell him I love him, that you were with me and that I wasn't afraid."

"I will. I'll tell him." But Uzi was not ready to give up. He searched his brain, trying to think of a solution. He needed something—a stray thought from his training. Or—

"Doc, did they say anything about the bomb? When they were talking to each other. Anything at all."

"Just that it would take down a good part of the building. And that if I lifted my shoe even just a bit, I'd set it off." Rudnick hesitated before continuing. "The man was in a hurry, though. I think they were going to plant another bomb, a car bomb."

Uzi sat up straight. A car bomb? "Where? What makes you think it was a car bomb?"

Rudnick's gaze tilted toward the ceiling as he struggled to remember. "He said something about the axle, getting it on the axle by the brake. That it's set to go at two. Whoever gets in that car, Uzi, they're dead. You have to find out whose car, before more people die—"

Uzi closed his eyes. *First things first. Concentrate.* He looked at the display: three minutes left. The piercing fire alarm siren blared in the background. He sat there, frozen, watching the numbers tumble lower. *There's gotta be something I can do!*

"Uzi, it's time to go. You must live your life, just as I did. You still have many questions that need answers. But I'm going to leave you with one answer. I usually let my patients figure it out themselves—and I'm sure you would have—but time is a bit short." He forced a smile. "That question I kept asking you, about committing suicide. I'll tell you why you didn't do it. It's the same reason why I didn't do it after getting out of the death camp."

Uzi's eyes moved from the red numbers to Rudnick's face.

"I needed to preserve their memories, of my parents and sisters and my aunt and uncle. Because I was the only one left. Inside me, they lived on for another seven decades. I thought about them, told stories about them. Talked to them, if only in my mind." He fought back tears. "If I'd committed suicide, their essence would have died along with me. Now, Wayne will pass on those memories. Do you understand?"

"Dena and Maya."

"There isn't much time," Rudnick said calmly. "You must go."

Uzi looked down at the bomb. Ninety seconds left.

"Honor a dying man's request," Rudnick said. "Would you do that?"

Uzi could not bring himself to look at him.

"Find the people who did this, Uzi. Find them and make them pay."

With this uncharacteristic request from such a gentle person, anger welled up in Uzi's chest. He looked up and met Rudnick's gaze. He didn't know if this kind-hearted man actually meant for him to take vengeance, or if it was a clever psychological play to get Uzi to leave. Whichever it was, it worked.

Uzi stood up. His lips started to tremble. Tears sprouted spontaneously, and he cried. He wanted to hug the old man, to give him strength to face what was coming, and to thank him for all he had done for him. But Uzi knew that any movement could set the bomb off prematurely. Instead, he leaned over and kissed his forehead. "I'll keep your memory alive. I'll tell Wayne. And I'll find the people who did this to you."

Rudnick smiled, the kind of grin a proud father gives his son when he has accomplished something of great value.

And then Uzi tore himself away, and he backed out of the room, away from the man who, up until recently was unknown to him, someone he now felt he had known all his life. Someone he had come to respect as much as he had respected his own father.

He turned and ran into the hallway, where the piercing siren was incapacitatingly loud. He hit the fire door with his shoulder and entered the staircase, slipping twice as he turned landings.

Uzi wasn't sure how much time he had left, but his gut told him it was no more than mere seconds. He counted down from ten as he ran the steps, taking two or three at a time, using the handrail to propel himself forward.

He rounded the second floor when he hit five seconds and kept on going, then reached the lobby at the moment he figured the bomb would go off. A dense crowd packed the area, moving slowly, clearly unaware the building was about to come down.

"Get out," Uzi shouted, darting toward the glass doors. "Everyone out!"

He hit the sidewalk and ran into M Street just as the EOD van pulled up in front. Farther down the block, a fire engine was approaching, its siren wailing and lights flashing.

The fifth story windows blew out first, a massive explosion sending dust and glass and metal and cement cascading down toward the street below. People darted in all directions, car tires groaning to a stop as the debris rained onto the pavement.

Uzi joined the bomb squad technicians, who had taken cover beside and beneath their truck. Though he struggled to corral his thoughts, to push his sorrow aside, his oxygen-starved voice was nevertheless edged in pain. "I called it in. Device was on fifth floor. Might be another . . . a car bomb."

The commander, back pressed against the glossy black truck, asked, "Where?"

"No idea." Then it clicked. *Oh, shit.* He took off down the block, heading for the spot where he had left the BuCar.

"Wait!" the commander called after him.

As Uzi turned the corner, he was relieved to find the Crown Vic still there, a ticket flapping against its windshield. He fumbled for his key ring, got in the car, and drove off.

Though he tried to focus on where he was headed, his mind would not let go of Rudnick. The image of him bound to the chair, bravely facing death as Uzi backed out of the room, was too powerful to push aside. It would take time for him to absorb the impact of his loss. He would have an empty space in his life. Again. But now he knew how to get through these things.

Unfortunately for him, he had experience in such matters.

1:36 PM
24 minutes remaining

The Hay-Adams Hotel
800 16th Street NW

The Hay-Adams Hotel took its name from two of the district's most distinguished residents, Secretary of State John Hay and historian Henry Adams. In the late 1800s, the men purchased adjoining lots across from Lafayette Park and the White House. They erected majestic homes that became a social epicenter for Washington's elite, including Theodore Roosevelt, Mark Twain, and Henry James.

The Hay and Adams houses were razed in the 1920s in favor of a luxury hotel that, because of its grandeur, history, and location, became a preferred destination for heads of state and international business leaders. Short of being a guest of the president, it is the closest one can get to staying at the White House.

To retain a connection to its past, the wood paneling from the original Hay residence was used in the stately public meeting area, the John Hay Room—the grand social hall in which the International Conference on Global Terrorism was being held.

As Uzi approached Washington Circle, he pulled out his phone to call DeSantos. He now knew Leila and her companion—with help, no doubt, from her al-Humat cell—were in the Hay-Adams implementing the next phase of their plan. What Rudnick heard and mistook for a car bomb was not a vehicle's axle, but an assassination attempt on Gideon Aksel, the Mossad director general.

The explosive device at Rudnick's office was a diversion: resources would be mobilized to his building, and attention would be deflected away from the conference as the second bomb was about to explode—killing many of the world's prominent leaders, counterterrorism experts, and intelligence chiefs.

Uzi now knew something else, as well: the phone call Leila and her accomplice had forced Rudnick to make was designed to lure him there so he would either arrive just as the bomb was going off, or shortly thereafter, so he could view the aftermath. An added, personal bonus for Leila. And very efficient.

As he started dialing DeSantos, his phone began ringing. It was Meadows.

"Just heard. No fun being almost blown to bits, is it?"

"I'm in a hurry, Tim. What've you got?"

"You know me, I can't leave well enough alone, so I had a guy in my department do the fishing on the logs while I went back to those latents you gave me. I may've been a little drugged up, but I remember you had a hard time accepting that they weren't Batula Hakim's prints. And I really wanted to get those bastards who tried to kill me—"

"And what'd you find?" Uzi rounded the circle and came out of it on Pennsylvania Avenue. He glanced at the dashboard clock. One thirty-nine.

"An irregularity in the data storage file. The algorithm was altered—"

"Tim, I think we've got another bomb set to explode in twenty minutes—" Uzi swerved to avoid a bicyclist, then switched the phone to his left hand—"so get to the goddamn point!"

"Someone got into the digital file of Batula Hakim's fingerprints and changed the algorithm. I found the code they used and estimated what it would do to the print's pattern. After some reconstruction, I'd say it bears a much closer match to the ones we lifted off that mirror. Leila Harel appears to be Batula Hakim, just as you thought."

Uzi was silent as the news hit him right between the eyes.

"You hear me? Uzi?"

"Still here. Good work, Tim. No, awesome work. Now check everyone, check all the digital files of everyone in the administration. Secret Service, White House staff, FBI, CIA—"

"Whoa, you know how many people you're talking about?"

"Write a program to search for specific parameters."

"I guess I can put something together."

"Do it. Call me back if you find anything else."

Uzi ended the call and turned onto H Street while struggling to punch in DeSantos's phone number. As he pulled in front of a temporary barrier and security checkpoint blocking the street to through traffic, DeSantos answered.

"Santa—I'm two blocks away." He got out of the car, showed the FBI agents his credentials, and took off in a sprint. "Leila and one of her buddies just killed my shrink. Another goddamn bomb. But he overheard them saying something was gonna happen to Aksel at two o'clock. Get him out of there, Santa, get 'em all out. There's probably a bomb—"

"Whoa, hold on— Do we know for sure there's a bomb?"

"I don't have video of them planting the damn thing, if that's what you mean," Uzi said as he ran by three well-dressed businesspeople making their way toward the Hay-Adams.

"You wanna evac the hotel, cause a freakin' stampede—and panic world leaders, without confirmed intel? Other than an overheard comment, we've got zip. NSA, CIA, FBI all say we're clear. Maybe they're planning to take a shot at him when he leaves the building. I'll have SWAT sweep the rooftops again."

As Uzi neared the hotel, he wondered just how much he could rely on what Rudnick had told him. He'd heard Aksel's name, saw the device they were wiring to his foot, thought of the recent news reports, and made the assumption they were going to set off a car bomb.

Am I overreacting?

"Uzi, I'm asking you again. Are you absolutely sure there's a bomb?"

"No."

"Then get your ass over here and we'll figure it out. If you press the fucking panic button and you're wrong, Knox won't be happy. And Aksel will never let you live it down."

Uzi, bristling at DeSantos's last comment—but knowing he was right—rounded the corner. "I'm almost there. Meet me out front."

As he passed the free-standing brass Hay-Adams sign, he hit a human wall of dark-suited, ear-miked Secret Service agents. But there was no time to stop. He held up his credentials as he barreled past them, yelling, "FBI— Let me through!"

After hearing a shout of "Hey—" and expecting to be tackled

from behind, he saw DeSantos a dozen feet ahead, approaching on the run.

"It's okay, let him go, let him go!" DeSantos pulled Uzi inside. The lobby was crowded with overflow visitors attending the conference. "Let's talk. I just spoke to Knox."

1:43 PM
17 minutes remaining

Presidential Suite
Eighth floor
Hay-Adams Hotel

Leila Harel—aka Leila al-Far, aka Batula Hakim—peered out the eighth floor window while a black ski-masked Alpha Zulu finished affixing the flexcuffs to their hostage's wrists.

"Everything look okay?" he asked.

"All's good," Hakim said. A thin smile of smug satisfaction spread her lips. "Secret Service is clueless." And then she gasped.

"What?"

"Son of a bitch." Face flushed, she grabbed her assault rifle and started toward the door.

Zulu stood and caught her arm. "What do you think you're doing?"

"Uzi's downstairs."

"Impossible. Hassan said the bomb went off."

"I know what I just saw. He's in the hotel." She yanked her arm from his grasp.

"Let it go," Zulu said. "Let *him* go." He stole a look at his scorpion-themed watch. "They're all dead in fifteen minutes anyway." He drew his handgun and pointed it at their gagged hostage. "We need to set the timer and get out of here."

"No!" She pushed his arm down and brought the submachine gun up to Zulu's chest.

"What the fuck are you doing?"

"I want Uzi." She nodded at their prisoner. "And he's my ticket."

The room phone began ringing as Zulu looked down at the floor, where four bullet-riddled bodies of the foreign dignitary's security force lay on the carpet in their own pools of blood.

And beside them was the bound and gagged Gideon Aksel.

1:44 PM
16 minutes remaining

Lobby
Hay-Adams Hotel

Uzi stood with DeSantos at the concierge's desk, shaking his head. "I still think we need to get everyone out of here, regardless of what Knox says. If I'm wrong, it's on me. But if I'm right, and we don't do anything, a thousand people are gonna die."

"It's out of our hands, boychick. We don't get paid the big bucks to make the big decisions."

"Santa, think of the power sitting in that room fifty feet away. The heads of the US, British, and German counterterrorism agencies are in there—not to mention Aksel and fifteen other intelligence chiefs. If I was a terrorist choosing targets, I'd go for the most bang for the buck. Gideon and Earl Tasset. Whitehall would be symbolic, yeah. Morally degrading, embarrassing. But it's not critical because Rusch and Nunn take over in a matter of weeks."

"I hear what you're saying, but—"

"Think of the impact it'd have if they bring this building down with Tasset and Gideon inside. It's every terrorist group's wet dream. Their two worst enemies, gone. Regardless of my personal feelings about Gideon, he's a freakin' legend—and he's here," Uzi said, pointing at the ground.

"Knox says there's no way they got a bomb into this place. They've had scanners set up the past two weeks."

"This cell has been operating here for how long? Do we know? Sleeper groups have been here fifteen years. Leila's been here five. You don't think they could've brought the explosives in three weeks ago? A month? Why not six months ago, when the conference was first announced?"

DeSantos sighed, checked his watch, and then rubbed his chin. "So you think Aksel and Tasset are the targets."

"Knowing what I know now, yeah. One or both. That's my bet. Them and as many of those counterterrorism officials in there as they can take with them. Think like a terrorist— To blow up a counterterrorism conference, and to do it across the street from the goddamn White House—"

DeSantos brought his sleeve to his mouth and spoke into his mike. "This is Santa. Where are Director Tasset and Director General Aksel? Over."

DeSantos listened through his earpiece, then looked at Uzi with concern.

"Tasset's with his detail," DeSantos said. "But Aksel's late coming down and he's not answering his phone. Secret Service just went up to his suite to get him."

1:46 PM
14 minutes remaining

The Presidential Suite
Hay-Adams Hotel

Batula Hakim crossed the room and stood beside Gideon Aksel's prone body. "Get him up."

Alpha Zulu shifted his MP-5K compact submachine gun, then reached down and grabbed Aksel's arm. "Get up, old man."

Aksel, bound and gagged, could not respond other than providing resistance as Zulu struggled to pull the man to his knees, much like a tantruming toddler uses gravity in some super-secret high-tech manner to appear heavier than he is.

Frustrated, Zulu pointed the MP-5K at Aksel's head. "Get up, goddamnit, or I'll blow you away right now!"

Hakim threw out a protective hand. "No—"

"To hell with your personal vendetta," Zulu said. "We have a mission to carry out and we're running out of time."

Hakim set her jaw and looked hard at him. "We've got fourteen minutes. And I deserve every one of them."

Zulu stared back. But he knew that no amount of reasoning would change her mind. *Damn bitch. If we didn't need her and her group, we could've gotten rid of her a long time ago.* "Fine. But if things go to hell, we take Aksel and leave. Whether or not you get Uzi. Am I clear?" He got a slight nod in response. "But we're not going anywhere if we can't get him into the elevator."

Hakim stepped forward and viciously slammed the stock of her submachine gun into Aksel's temple. "Get the fuck up!"

Aksel's neck snapped to the side, and a trickle of blood appeared where the metal had ripped through the skin. He looked up at Hakim with bloodshot gray eyes that seemed to sizzle with anger. But the tough old bird shook off the pain and slowly got to his feet.

Zulu shoved him toward the door and was about to grab the knob when a series of firm knocks froze him in midstride. Zulu shoved the muzzle of his MP-5K into Aksel's ribs.

"Director General," called a voice behind the door. "Please open up. Agent Vickers, Secret Service."

Zulu motioned Batula Hakim to a hidden spot off to his left, then dragged Aksel backwards a few feet to the middle of the room near where his dead bodyguards lay.

Hakim removed a suppressed Walther from the holster on her belt and unlocked the deadbolt.

"It's open," Zulu yelled from across the room. "Come in."

The doorknob turned and two Secret Service agents walked in. In a fraction of a second, their gazes took in the scene—Aksel gagged and bleeding, his hands bound behind him—and four men lying on the floor in pools of blood. The agents reached for their weapons, but it was a fruitless maneuver.

Batula Hakim fired two headshots, and the men fell limp. She reached over, relocked the door, and walked across the room toward the phone.

1:48 PM
12 minutes remaining

Lobby
Hay-Adams Hotel

DeSantos was waiting for Director Knox to respond to his request for a modification of their operational plan when the telephone rang. The concierge looked up and cupped the handset. "Agent Uziel? Is there an Agent Uziel here?"

Uzi and DeSantos shared a perplexed look, then Uzi reached over and took the phone.

"This is Uzi."

"I take it you know who this is."

Leila. Batula Hakim. The woman who murdered my family. "Yeah, I know who it is." Uzi moved the phone so DeSantos could share the handset.

"I have something you want."

A few days ago, that statement would have brimmed with raw sexual tension. But now it carried visceral emotion filled with vengeance. "Where and when?"

"In the basement by the kitchen. Come alone or I'll kill another person you care about."

The line went dead. Uzi eyed the fire alarm panel across the room, to the left of the main entry doors. It had worked with Rudnick's building. It'd be a much more orderly way to evacuate the hotel than to announce there were terrorists about to detonate a bomb.

"Where did that call come from?" DeSantos asked.

The concierge looked at his panel. "Presidential Suite, eighth floor."

DeSantos's shoulders slumped. "Go to the basement. I'm going up to Aksel's room."

"What about OPSIG?"

"Too high profile. This is an HRT and SWAT operation. But I did bring along a little help." He brought his secure sleeve mike up to his lips and spoke into it: "Hot Rod, Santa. Come down from the roof, meet Uzi in the basement. Hakim may be en route. Armed and dangerous. Potential hostage situation. Hodges, meet me on floor eight, Presidential Suite. Same parameters. Rest of you, take support positions. Over."

"Tell Knox and get HRT and SWAT up to speed," Uzi said as he backed away. He ran to the fire alarm, and pulled the switch. A blaring siren started wailing.

A nearby bellman pointed at Uzi. "Hey! What're you doing?"

Uzi moved quickly toward him. "What's the fastest way to the basement?"

The young man with slicked back hair was frozen by Uzi's urgent tone. "The John Hay room," he shouted, squinting against the siren's blare. "Far left wall behind the divider." He gestured across the lobby.

"Get everyone out," Uzi said, backing away. "Emergency's real."

He ran past the bank of elevators, then turned right down the short wood-paneled corridor and pushed through the etched glass doors. The two hundred foreign dignitaries and press corps packed into the grand dining hall/conference room collided with one another as they rushed for the doors. Four Secret Service agents looked overwhelmed as they attempted to exact an orderly exit.

Uzi pulled the Smith & Wesson from his belt, but kept it beneath the flap of his jacket as he worked his way through the crowd of tables toward the far left wall. After slipping behind the tall folding room divider, he entered the stairwell that led to the basement. With his back to the wall and his weapon now out in front of him, he slowly descended the steps.

The long, white-tiled basement hallway fed into, and dead-ended at, the kitchen. A room service cart stood off to the right, opposite a black elevator door. Uzi craned his neck, trying to see around tall industrial plastic containers and boxes of Evian stacked six rows high.

Close quarters and impaired line of sight. Great.

About the only positive was that the fire alarm was not nearly as loud down here.

He turned right into the main area of the kitchen. Aside from adobe tile flooring, stainless steel dominated the room. Ovens, cook stoves, refrigerators, and deep sinks brimmed with the matte-finish metal. Sizzling steaks sat on the broiler to his left. With the fire alarm ringing, the cooks had shut off the burners and evacuated. Uzi pushed forward into the adjacent room, where a walk-in freezer swallowed the far wall. *Clear.*

He lowered his Smith & Wesson and took in the lay of the land: this portion of the basement consisted mostly of the kitchen—which itself was a dead end. Though there was only one way in or out, an elevator and two feeder staircases spilled into the corridor twenty yards away, near where he'd entered.

A rumble in that direction grabbed his attention. Stepping out of the elevator was a ski-masked man with a compact assault rifle, followed by a bloody, handcuffed Gideon Aksel.

And Batula Hakim.

Uzi swung his S&W toward Hakim's head. Their eyes met and he saw something in them he had never seen before. Deep-seated contempt. His probably said the same.

"Should I call you Leila Harel or Batula Hakim?"

"You're a fool, not to know the woman who killed your beloved wife and daughter." She spit the words, her tone full of disdain. "To make love to me, to dishonor your wife like that."

Uzi's glance fell to Aksel's eyes. They said nothing, if not agreement with Hakim's statement. Uzi did not bother defending himself, did not bother explaining that she looked vastly different from the grainy intelligence photo he had seen of her so many years ago. He stole a look at her masked conspirator—the man was letting the scene play out and presented no immediate threat. Uzi turned back to Hakim. "Your problem's with me. Let him go."

"You! The man who killed my brother—you think you can order me around?" She pressed her submachine gun against Aksel's temple. "Would it hurt you to see his brains blown out, Uzi? Would it?"

"I didn't kill your brother, Hakim. Your own man killed him. His bullet ricocheted. I was pinned down and couldn't get off a shot."

"Liar."

"Ask the Director General. He saw my report. If I'd killed Ahmed, there'd be no reason to say I didn't. I fucked up the op. If I'd said I killed Ahmed, I would've looked a whole lot better."

"He already told me what happened. Haven't you, Gideon?" She looked at Aksel and smiled out of the left side of her mouth, then turned back to Uzi. "Years ago he told me what happened."

Uzi's brow furrowed. *Why is she calling him by his first name? Why would he have told her anything?* "What are you talking about?" He looked to Gideon for confirmation. But the man averted his eyes.

With her free hand, Hakim yanked on the knot holding Aksel's gag in place, then tossed the rag to the ground. "Tell him, Gideon. Tell him who I worked for."

Aksel kept his eyes on the ground and said nothing.

"I worked for Mossad," Hakim said. "Just like you. Just like Ahmed. Yes, my brother was on Mossad's payroll the whole time he lived in Egypt. Both of us recruited by your friend here. A fact that remains hidden from everyone at Mossad even to this day. When you were sent to kill my brother, it was because Gideon discovered Ahmed was a double agent who'd given him bogus information. Ahmed was playing him. And it cost two agents their lives.

"Mossad was still in trouble after several high profile fuck-ups, and Gideon Aksel—brought in to 'save the day'—was going to take the heat if the new prime minister found out his grand master had been duped." Hakim looked at Aksel, drew back, and spit in his face. "My brother would never betray his allegiance to the Palestinian people."

The director general leaned away in disgust.

No. She's lying. "Gideon?"

Aksel still would not look at him.

Uzi faced Hakim. "You killed an innocent woman . . . a sweet little girl." He swallowed hard, fighting to keep his composure. "You're a woman, how could you have done that?"

"Their lives were unimportant. You killed my brother. It was my right to take revenge, to give you the same pain you gave me. Relentless emotional pain, tortured forever."

Uzi felt tears filling his eyes but fought back the emotion. "I told you, I didn't kill your brother!"

"Deny it all you want. But I saw the mission reports. Gideon showed me the classified file. He told me he was sorry for what had happened and wanted to set the record straight, that you were acting on your own."

Uzi looked at Gideon. "That's bullshit. Our mission was to take out Ahmed and his cell before they could bomb the Knesset. About the only thing I'm guilty of is not following orders. I couldn't believe Ahmed would do such a thing. I liked him, I wanted to give him a chance to explain." Uzi stopped himself, realizing that his assumption as to why Maya and Dena had been murdered was incorrect. *It wasn't the terrorist who escaped who lied about the ricochet killing Ahmed. It was Gideon. He told Hakim I shot her brother.*

"Why, Gideon? Do you realize what you did?"

Aksel looked up at Uzi with war-weary eyes. "It was a price that had to be paid, Uzi. It took me two years to clean up Mossad's reputation and restore its credibility; even countries we're supposedly at peace with give terrorists safe harbor, weapons, and money to attack us. You know that. An effective Mossad is essential to Israel's survival." He sighed, looked down, and then lifted his chin. "We made a mistake. I made a mistake. Recruiting Hakim and her brother . . . It was a fatal error. My fatal error. The only one I've ever made."

"You needed a scapegoat," Uzi said. "So you pinned it on me, falsified the mission reports."

"I never intended for her to kill your family, Uzi. I never meant for that to happen. For that, I *am* sorry. But what I did, I did for the survival of our country." He turned to face Hakim, the barrel of her gun jabbing him in the bloodied portion of his temple. "Uzi didn't kill your brother."

"He's a Jew," Hakim spat. "A Zionist. That makes him guilty. Whether he killed Ahmed or not, it doesn't matter. He deserves what I did to him. And you deserve what I'm going to do to you."

Uzi's arms were still extending the gun out in front of him. "You got your revenge, Hakim. But this is a different time, a different place. This is where it ends. Drop your weapon."

1:51 PM
9 minutes remaining

Basement stairwell
Hay-Adams Hotel

Troy Rodman leaned against the wall, his physique, black tunic, and assault gear leaving the ignorant bystander no doubt that he was some sort of Special Forces operative. Headset firmly atop his shaven scalp and the boom mike an inch from his lips, he stood outside the basement stairwell listening to the goings on thirty feet away and around the bend.

It had taken him longer than he would've liked to make it down from the roof after DeSantos's call, as he had to take one floor at a time, checking for gunmen or booby traps—making sure he got to the scene in one piece. It wouldn't do anyone any good if he arrived riddled with bullet holes and an extra pound of lead in his body.

He wished he had a fiber optic camera that snaked ninety degrees to his right so he could see the position of the hallway occupants. But he wasn't equipped for battle. He was on-site support, and his orders were to travel light—which meant stripped down gear. Enough for barebones recon and assisting SWAT, if necessary.

But SWAT, HRT, and Secret Service were occupied: they had less than ten minutes to find the explosives, evacuate the building, and look after the safety of the roomful of dignitaries. And that meant Rodman was on his own.

He fished through his pouch and pulled out a small dental mirror—the low-tech equivalent of a fiber optic camera—and knelt down low. He moved the device into position, taking care not to catch light and cause a flare—because that's when the shooting would start. And as much as he loved his MP-5 submachine gun, there were too many people around to start letting the lead fly.

But what he saw in the reflection was not good. The director general sandwiched between two well-armed mercenaries, with Uzi at one end of the corridor and himself at the other, in each other's line of fire.

Rodman withdrew the mirror and remained quiet, listening to the conversation, waiting for his window of opportunity to open. Because if all went south, it didn't really matter who was in the way, since rounds would be zipping about in all directions. The odds of anyone coming out alive were not high.

He checked his MP-5, brought it into position, and focused on what Uzi was saying: ". . . This is where it ends. Drop your weapon."

1:53 PM
7 minutes remaining

Basement corridor
Hay-Adams Hotel

"Drop my weapon?" Hakim asked. "You're out of your fucking mind, Uzi. I don't surrender. To anyone, let alone to you."

Alpha Zulu checked his pocket watch. "We're running out of time," he said firmly to Hakim. He glanced over his shoulder toward the stairwell that led to the hotel's side exit. "We've gotta go. Now." He grabbed Aksel's arm and pulled him backwards.

"Police! Don't move!"

In one motion, Zulu turned and opened fire in the direction of the voice. He hit the man, but he wasn't sure where, because the cop—or whatever he was—was firing too, and Zulu hit the ground hard, his Kevlar vest absorbing most of the rounds.

The corridor was an echoing mass of confusion, scattering bodies, and cacophonous submachine gun clatter. Zulu saw the gunman go down and slide back behind the corner—which was fortunate, because Zulu's magazine was empty. He tried reaching the spare in his pocket, but stinging pain in his left arm and leg prevented him from retrieving it.

He craned his neck, hoping to see Hakim—but heard the elevator doors closing, and he figured she had left him there to die. The firing had ceased, but he had to get out of there. More Feds would be arriving any second.

He rolled onto his injured side and began crawling along the tile floor, hoping to reach the exit, where he could make it to the street. After that, he wasn't sure where he would go. But he needed to go somewhere, because even if the cops didn't come running, remaining where he was meant instant death.

In less than five minutes.

Uzi saw Rodman's head a split second before his body appeared in the corridor, followed by the MP-5 muzzle and Rodman's resonant voice.

And then the ski-masked man's submachine gun fire muted everything around him.

Uzi's first instinct was to grab Aksel and get him to the ground. But an errant round had struck Aksel somewhere, and the hefty man dropped to the ground on his own. Uzi crawled forward and tried to shield the director general's body, but a row of rounds struck the tile directly in front of him and drove Uzi back. He fired at the moving target—the ski-masked terrorist—and scored several direct hits to the body.

But as Uzi swung his S&W toward Hakim, she ducked behind closing elevator doors. He got to his feet and saw her colleague crawling toward the stairwell. Uzi kicked away the assault rifle, sending it clattering across the slick floor. He shoved the barrel of his handgun against the back of the man's head. "Give me a reason to send you where you sent my friend."

Uzi made his point, because his prisoner did not even twitch a muscle. Uzi rooted out a self-locking flexcuff, then yanked his prisoner's hands behind his back. As he ratcheted the restraint down tight, the man jerked back in pain, and a silver pocket watch fell out of his pocket. Uzi shoved it back into the man's pants, and then moved past Aksel's prone body. The director general was still alive—Uzi felt it more than knew it—but he had to get to Hakim. He couldn't let her get away.

"Rodman," Uzi called out. "You okay?"

"Yeah, you?"

"Fine." Uzi glanced up at the elevator. The indicator light above the doors showed it heading toward the fourth floor. "Coming around. Hold your fire."

Uzi moved toward the staircase. Rodman was leaning against the wall, an MP-5 clasped in his left hand, tracking Uzi as he appeared around the bend. Uzi immediately noted a blood-soaked tourniquet twisted about the operative's thigh.

"Go get her," Rodman said.

"Get Aksel out of here, bomb's going off in—"

"Goddamn it, Uzi— Go get her!"

Uzi turned and sprinted up the stairs.

Uzi was making exceptional time, but tired as he hit the sixth-floor landing. He slipped on the slick gunmetal gray slate steps and thought about stopping and going back down and getting out of the building before it exploded. Hakim had nowhere to go but up—yet he had no way of knowing if she'd gotten out on one of the floors or if she'd taken the elevator to the roof.

Doubting he would be able to find her before the building came down, he questioned the wisdom of continuing. But his promise to Rudnick smacked him across the face. He had to go on.

His instincts told him Hakim would avoid the lobby because there would be armed agents there on the lookout for her. If she had gotten off at one of the floors, there was no way out of the hotel. But if she made it to the roof, she might be able to cross to the adjacent building.

Knowing Hakim, alternate escape routes would have been plotted out ahead of time.

Gotta be the roof.

Grabbing the black wrought iron staircase railing for leverage, he rounded the eighth floor landing and headed up toward the metal fire door.

Sweat blanketing his torso and face, his breathing labored, he burst forward onto the rooftop. The cold wind burned his dry throat.

Weapon out in front of him, he stepped onto the long, rectangular patio, which extended thirty feet ahead to his right and was bounded by the same iron railing that ran the length of the staircase.

Ahead of him: 16th Street, Lafayette Park, the White House. The Explosives Ordinance Disposal truck was no doubt parked below on 16th, alongside scores of Metro PD and Federal Protective Service cruisers.

She wouldn't be at this end of the building—no fire escapes or adjacent buildings.

Uzi jogged right, past a doorway that led to the elevator, then slowed and swept his weapon from side to side, expecting the building to start shaking and collapsing beneath his feet.

Movement— Off to his right. Hakim—by the edge, facing away from him, on a graveled area of the roof. He swiveled his S&W toward her—and realized he had no idea how many rounds he'd fired in the basement. Were there any left in the magazine? Was there even one left in the chamber? So much commotion, so many bullets flying, it was all a jumble. As he inched toward her, he had to accept that he had no way of knowing what he had left—without ejecting the clip, which he was not about to do.

Hakim must have heard the crunch of his heel against the hard surface, because she spun, settling the red laser targeting beam of her assault rifle dead square on Uzi's chest. Between them stood only a two-foot-high wrought-iron fence.

"So it's come down to this," she said with the confidence of someone who knew she was in complete control.

"You've killed three people that were very dear to me, Hakim. As well as countless others."

"Countless? I know exactly how many I've killed in my lifetime."

"That can't go unpunished."

"An eye for an eye, Uzi?"

He shook his head slowly. "You're going to stand trial for your crimes." He realized that with the laser burning a hole where his heart lay, and wearing no Kevlar vest, he was talking tough without the power to back it up. And with the building due to explode, she wouldn't waste any more time with him. She wasn't going to chance the possibility that he would—again—survive the blast.

Her right arm moved suddenly—and Uzi dove and rolled, and came up firing. But his round struck a vertical bar of the intervening fence.

Uzi squeezed the trigger again—and dry-fired an empty chamber.

Fuck.

He tossed the spent S&W aside.

Hakim squared her shoulders and smiled. She brought the rifle up to her face slowly, savoring the kill. The red beam once again settled on his chest.

Uzi turned and ran a zigzag route away from her while pulling his Tanto from its sheath. Like a driving rainstorm, bullets pricked the cement all around him. But in one motion, he spun and whipped the Tanto through the thick DC air.

It found its mark in her chest, slicing through breast and muscle below the fourth rib. Her body went rigid and she dropped the assault rifle. Her eyes bugged out. And the breath seeped from her lung.

Struggling for air, Hakim stumbled backwards, her hands feeling the front of her chest for the handle of the knife. Her left heel hit the low cement curb and she fell over the edge, disappearing from view.

Uzi sprinted for the adjacent rooftop. He hit full speed and leaped over the edge of the hotel, bicycling through the air across the twelve-foot gap before landing hard one story below, atop the United States Chamber of Commerce. Pain shot through his ankles and knees. He rolled and scrambled to his feet, then found the staircase that led to the street.

A moment later, Uzi headed up H Street, running toward the barrier where he had left his car. Behind him, the Hay-Adams was still standing, a glance at his watch telling him it was a few minutes past two. Either EOD had defused the bomb or his timing had been off. Or there hadn't been a bomb at all.

He pulled his cell and noticed that the battery had been jarred loose. He reseated it and powered up the phone. He tried reaching DeSantos—and got through.

"Hakim's history," Uzi said. "She went packing and had an awful trip."

"I noticed. She's sprawled out about ten feet away from me. You want your knife back?"

"Evidence now. Make sure it gets bagged and tagged."

"Hell with that. I think you deserve to keep it. Another tchotchke to put on your bookshelf, next to the canteen with the bullet hole."

Uzi didn't know how to respond to that. "How's Rodman?"

"Medic thinks he'll need surgery on his leg, but he's a tough fucker. Speaking of which, he got Aksel out. Old guy's pretty banged up. Nasty GSWs to the hip and arm, but he'll make it."

"What about the bomb?"

"There were two. The dogs sniffed 'em out. EOD defused them with six seconds to spare."

Uzi closed his eyes. *Six seconds.*

"Where are you? Knox is gonna want to debrief you."

"Headed back to my car. Debrief will have to wait. What about an ID on our masked avenger? Hakim's accomplice?"

"Guy's a freaking looney tune. Refuses to say anything, other than name, rank, and serial number. Says he's some kind of 'sovereign citizen,' exempt from federal and state laws."

"Classic militia claim."

"Get this," DeSantos said with a chuckle. "Guy claimed his name is *General Grant*."

Uzi stopped in midstride. "General Grant?"

"That mean something to you?"

"Maybe nothing," Uzi said as he approached his car. "Maybe everything."

2:08 PM

Before hanging up, Uzi told DeSantos to bring Knox to the warehouse where he had left Quentin Larchmont ninety minutes earlier. On the drive over, Uzi continued ruminating. He had secured vital pieces to the puzzle, but key parts were still missing.

Lewiston Grant in bed with Batula Hakim— How did that fit in with Quentin Larchmont and the NFA? With Knox? Was the Skiles Rathbone-Douglas Knox connection a dead end, or was it suddenly thrust to the forefront in view of the discovery of Larchmont's involvement? If someone that high in the administration could be a conspirator, why not the attorney general and FBI director? Then there was Secret Service Agent Benedict, one of Whitehall's security detail, a highly prestigious post—

Uzi forced himself to slow down; jumping to conclusions and accepting such a far-reaching conspiracy theory that involved the two highest law enforcement figures in the United States—and possibly even the president—might blind him to what was really going on. He needed to keep an open mind, to put things in play and see where they led.

And right now, with Knox and DeSantos on the way over to where Larchmont was being held, he would have two key figures in one place.

He called his office and asked Madeline to have Shepard meet them at the warehouse immediately. He still held out hope that, should Knox be wrapped up in this, Shepard would be the one to stand witness and support him in what needed to be done.

He hung up—and Tim Meadows immediately called through.

"Uzi, I heard about the hotel. This ain't your day, is it?"

"Hard to say, Tim. I'm still alive, I may be close to breaking this thing wide open—and I killed the terrorist who murdered my family."

"I don't want to be the bearer of bad news, but . . ."

"Bad news?"

"I found something else. I really think you should come by. We shouldn't talk about this over an unsecured line."

Never a fan of delayed gratification, Uzi said, "You got something important, now would be a really good time to tell me."

Meadows hesitated a moment, then continued: "I did that check you asked me to do, on the digital files of all the federal—"

"Still kinda short on time, Tim. Get to the point." Uzi pulled into the alley adjacent to the warehouse. The crimson blood spatter, though dry now, was still visible on the charcoal asphalt.

"My worm found some irregularities in another file," Meadows said. "And this is where it gets hairy—"

Uzi pulled to a stop and waited for Meadows to continue. When he didn't, Uzi asked, "Where what gets hairy? Tim?"

He checked the handset, then tossed it aside in disgust. The battery had finally died. He sat there for a second, wondering what digital file had been altered. Realizing that Knox and Shepard would be arriving soon, he got out of the car and headed into the warehouse.

He pulled out his Puma and moved carefully, as the building had not been secured while he was gone. After deciding it was safe, he searched the bodies of Larchmont's dead guards. He found another S&W, a spare magazine and . . . a cell phone.

As he neared the Suburban, he called Meadows. While it rang, Uzi looked in on Larchmont, whose eyes were wide with fear, no doubt wondering why Uzi had returned—holding a gun—and with no one else in sight.

Meadows answered. "Damn it, Uzi, I hit the climax of my amazing discovery, something that could get me the Presidential Medal of Freedom, and I find out I'm talking to a dead line."

"Battery went out on me. I told you, you talk too much."

"Okay, then I'll get to the point. Are you sitting?"

"Tim—"

"You're not going to believe this, but I've checked it five times. The altered digital file belongs to none other than Glendon Rusch."

2:23 PM

Uzi squinted in disbelief. "What?"

"Yessir, that's right. Our president-elect is not who he appears to be. Now you know why I wanted to tell you in person."

Uzi looked at Larchmont through the glass. He thanked Meadows and told him to keep at it in case there were other surprises. He then walked around to the passenger door and climbed inside. Larchmont turned his restrained body toward Uzi. His dark eyes were puffy, his face ashen.

Uzi held up the handgun. "I'm going to remove your gag and we're gonna have a chat. You cooperate and I'll let you go. It'll all be our little secret. You fuck with me, and I'll have to kill you. And I'm not shitting you, Mr. Larchmont. I used to kill people for a living."

Uzi detected a hint of fear glaze over the man's eyes, then removed the tie and pulled the sock out of the man's mouth. Larchmont smacked his lips repeatedly.

"Leaves it a bit dry, doesn't it?" Uzi grinned knowingly. "Okay now. Here's the deal. I tell you what I know, and then you tell me what you know. Honesty is the only correct answer. For each incorrect answer, I will put a bullet in your leg. Those are the rules. Pretty simple, really."

Uzi maintained eye contact, waited a beat for Larchmont to read the intensity in his face, and then continued. "The man lying in the hospital pretending to be Glendon Rusch is not Glendon Rusch. Who is he really?"

Larchmont looked away. "I— I don't know."

Uzi lowered the handgun and shot Larchmont in the right foot. The blast inside the closed SUV was deafening.

"Ahh! Oh my god, you fucking son of a bitch—"

Uzi grabbed Larchmont's hair with his left hand and yanked back. "I explained the rules to you," he said with restrained fury. "Don't lie to me again. Now, who's in Glendon Rusch's hospital bed?"

"Bryce Upshaw."

Uzi released his grip. "The ARM member who told the *Post* that Rusch would be sorry if he didn't change his position on gun control?"

Larchmont nodded. "He was picked from their membership. They went through over ten thousand applications. ARM started collecting vital stats on their members—height, weight, skin color, blood type. He had them email photos of their faces from all angles."

"Militia members are super paranoid. Why would they agree to that?"

"They were told it was for security, to prevent government informants from infiltrating their compound." He grimaced and looked down at his foot. "Didn't work, though, did it?"

Another piece to the puzzle. "They found out about Agent Adams."

"You were supposed to take the rap for his death. They changed the digitized ballistics profile on your gun, the one that's stored in the Academy's database."

"Who did? They'd have to be on the inside, have access to secure government servers."

"I don't know."

Uzi moved the gun toward Larchmont's right leg.

"I swear, I don't know their name!"

Larchmont maintained eye contact, leading Uzi to believe he was telling the truth. "What did Grant do with all this info he collected on the membership?"

"He ran the photos through a sophisticated 3D facial recognition program, then used medical prosthetic Computer-Aided Design software they adapted to evaluate facial configuration. They found someone with fairly close bone structure to Glendon Rusch. With some plastic surgery and a few months' work with a personal trainer to reshape his body and a half-inch heel lift, Bryce Upshaw was almost a dead ringer. Even his blood type matched."

That's why Upshaw disappeared six months ago, after making his statement to the Post.

"They started training him. He watched tapes of Rusch, practiced copying his mannerisms, intonations. I tutored him on his political career and family life. Everything. His upbringing, his closest friends, bitter enemies, gambling losses, women he dated before he got married. The one he had an affair with ten years ago."

"So Glendon Rusch died on that chopper."

"His body was switched immediately after impact. His real body—what was left of it—was cremated."

Uzi nodded slowly. It explained a lot. The extensive burns, for one. "Upshaw was willing to burn his face, hands, and throat, go through intense pain, multiple surgeries, live life disfigured—"

"All to be president of the United States. The most powerful man in the world. To further a cause he believed in with all his heart. Yes, he was."

"And Winston Coulter? Director Knox?"

"What about them?"

"What were their roles?"

Larchmont squinted but maintained eye contact. "They don't have anything to do with it."

This was important. Uzi had to know the truth. He shoved the gun against Larchmont's thigh. "I don't believe you."

"Don't shoot! I'm telling you the truth. I swear. They're not involved."

"And President Whitehall?"

"Not involved."

Uzi withdrew the gun. "And who made the changes in the IAFIS database?"

"All I know is we've got someone at CJIS in Clarksburg. I don't know who."

Uzi thought about this. It made sense that the fingerprint repository at the Criminal Justice Information Services Division was involved. "But why? Why go through all this trouble?"

Larchmont winced, looked again at his foot. "It's throbbing. I need to get to an emergency room, get some painkillers."

Uzi knew a gunshot wound to the foot was painful. But he had used this method of interrogation in the past, and in his experience, with all the adrenaline in Larchmont's system, it would be awhile before he'd feel the injury's full effects.

"We don't have a lot of time. Not if you want me to let you go before my buddies start arriving. And they won't be so anxious to cut you any deals. Now answer my question. Why go through all this trouble?"

Larchmont's face crunched into a pained expression. He looked into his lap. "Power and money. What else is there in Washington, Agent Uziel? It all comes down to power and money."

"Spare me the philosophical discussion."

"It's important, goddamn it!" Larchmont appeared to have been infused with energy, either from guilt over what he'd done or from frustration over the realization that his grand plan was now in shambles. "Without understanding why it was done . . ." He grunted. "Glen had this epiphany after his sister was killed. He thought he could solve all the country's problems by getting guns out of the population's hands. It's a stupid thought, let alone one that's totally wrong."

"I already figured this part out," Uzi said. "You and the NFA and ARM were stuck with Rusch and his newfound conscience. You wished he would just disappear. So you did the next best thing. You replaced him with someone you had total control over. Someone who would steer the policy of the federal government towards a loose interpretation of the Second Amendment, one that doesn't restrict an individual's right to own firearms."

Larchmont shifted his weight, then winced. "There's more to it than that."

"I'm sure there is. Groups like these usually can't work together. Egos, philosophical differences, get in the way."

Larchmont snorted. "Power and money, remember? So much to gain, too much to lose by bickering with each other. Especially with our other partner."

Uzi thought for a moment. *Who's that other partner? An influential intermediary? Or someone with leverage who could keep them together in spite of themselves— An outsider? Someone with leverage. An outsider.* "Al-Humat."

Larchmont nodded. "They funneled twenty-five million dollars to the NFA. And Russian and Chinese assault weapons, rocket-propelled grenade launchers, shoulder-launched surface-to-air missiles, and enough Semtex and C-4 to bring down two World Trade Centers." Perspiration had pimpled Larchmont's face, his complexion looking a bit pasty. "Please," he said. "My foot—"

"What's al-Humat's stake in all this?"

He blew some air through his lips. The pain was beginning to worsen. Uzi knew his time was growing short. He shoved his S&W into Larchmont's groin. "Quickly!"

"Power and money, goddamnit! Look at who their partner is, who's bankrolling them—al-Qaeda—and what their long-term strategy is. Control over our Mideast policy, for starters. They wanted us out of their affairs, our military bases off Arab soil—Turkey, Saudi Arabia, United Arab Emirates, Qatar, Bahrain, Kuwait— The Pentagon's one of the world's largest land owners. We've got over seven hundred bases in a hundred fifty-six countries." He wiped his moist cheek against his right shoulder. "They intend to close down as many of them as they can."

"To reduce our global influence. Shift the balance of power." Uzi tilted his head. "But even controlling the presidency, I can't see them running roughshod over the Pentagon and getting anything like that through Congress."

"I told them they had some unrealistic goals. But they didn't want to hear it and we needed them as partners. Still—it's not as far-fetched as you think. We'd save a trillion dollars over ten years by closing the bases and selling off the land. Our debt load's at unsustainable levels, and the people want more entitlement programs and fewer taxes. It doesn't add up. To the average American, this would be an easy, painless fix. But I certainly had no interest in letting them eviscerate us. I figured I'd do my best to make sure we got everything we needed, and they didn't get everything they needed."

"Remind me to pin a medal on your chest. And al-Humat's part?"

"What do you think? Internally, they want to wrest control from

Hamas. But in the US, their goals are to facilitate the destruction of Israel."

"And they really think they can turn the US against its only democratic ally in the Middle East?"

"Their plan's obtuse, insidious. They'd advocate for expanding the basic needs of their young country—the construction of an airport in Palestine. That would be followed by the demand for basic defensive military capability. I don't have to tell you that's a nonstarter for Israel."

And Uzi knew why. The country's geography made it virtually impossible for Israel to defend itself against a Palestinian air attack before massive casualties would be realized.

"The Palestinians would file an application before the UN Security Council," Larchmont continued. "And without the US to block it, they'd start a covert program to import offensive weapons through the Gaza-Egypt network of tunnels. It's not always easy to draw the line between offensive and defensive weapons. And with al-Qaeda their new partner in crime, the chances of pulling this off are pretty damn good."

Uzi's jaw muscles tightened—as did his grip on the S&W. "I get the power part. What about the money?"

Larchmont smirked, as if Uzi should know the answer. "Oil. Does that surprise you? Tie up our alternative fuels industry in red tape, slow it down, divert funding, hamstring it. Put moratoriums on domestic offshore oil drilling and shale gas fracking. Reverse the huge influx in Canadian and Mexican petroleum imports.

"Bottom line, they want America back on a steady diet of Persian Gulf oil. OPEC's bean counters hired some big-time consulting firm, commissioned a top secret report. America's shifting energy policy alone will cost them nine billion a year in lost oil revenue. Not even the explosive demand from China and India will make up that kind of money. If the US is able to move off oil, China will follow. It'd be the end of the only leverage the Arabs hold over the world. Their economies would collapse. They're a one-product region."

"But a president's hampered by the whims of Congress. These issues don't get decided by unilateral presidential decrees."

Larchmont stifled a sardonic laugh. "I've been in politics two decades, Agent Uziel. Never underestimate a popular president's persuasive powers—and the power of the presidency on foreign policy matters. At times he needs congressional approval, absolutely. But it always comes down to the commander in chief. There are lots of ways he can influence decisions, directly and indirectly. And with sympathies high for a man who survived a terrorist attack that killed his family, he'll start out with a tremendous bank account of compassion—and a very high approval rating. If Congress fights him too hard, they'll look like bullies."

Uzi couldn't dispute that.

"And they have plans to cultivate senators and congressmen who share their views. It won't be in your face like the Tea Party— It'll be done insidiously, bankrolling candidates who either buy into their scheme or who are downright co-conspirators. But," Larchmont said, "I think their biggest play is something they've kept to themselves. Provoke us into invading a Muslim country, make us look like the bad guys, the infidels forcing democracy down their throats, trying to destroy their religion—"

"And then, after multiple terror attacks against US assets, they draw us into wars all over the place, draining our money and manpower, bringing our economy to the brink of default by financing several wars on multiple fronts. I'm well aware of Saif al-Adel's treatise."

Larchmont winced and leaned forward to get a look at his foot. "It worked with the Soviet Union, and almost worked on us, with Iraq and Afghanistan. With their own commander in chief pulling the strings, reacting—or *overreacting*—to large-scale terror attacks here and abroad against our allies, their end game's to bring America to her knees once and for all. If you think a debt load of $15 trillion is bad, you haven't seen anything. And if China smells blood and calls their debt due, we'll be royally fucked."

Uzi squinted. "But China's interests are best served by America paying off its obligations and continuing to buy its products."

"China's a rising superpower. They know it's only a short time before they supplant the US. Their goal is to bring us down slowly—a soft landing, a slow decline. They're after our technology and resources, weapons expertise and military systems. That's why they've launched repeated cyberattacks on our government and corporations—"

"Best clandestine war ever."

"I believe their goal is to eventually 'own' the United States . . . force us into defaulting on our debt, leaving us vulnerable to just about everything." Larchmont leaned back and closed his eyes. "I was a partner in this, but that partnership only goes so far. I can be that inside source that keeps them in check." He turned to Uzi. "Make me a deal, send me back in there to give you a window into—"

"You've gotta be kidding. A bunch of your people are already dead or in custody—and you can add Bryce Upshaw to that list. There's nothing to send you back into."

Larchmont ground his molars. "I need a doctor. I've told you all I know—"

"What about the people who died—Fargo, Ellison, Harmon, Bishop—"

"Sleepers." Larchmont wiped at his perspiring cheek with a shoulder. "All except Bishop. Planted long ago. People whose personal beliefs led them to ARM or NFA. They were recruited and followed strict orders to keep their views quiet so they wouldn't compromise the plan. Ellison should've been the hardest one to get, but he actually came to us. This whole thing was on the table years ago in one form or another. Grant, it was all his idea."

"After he started Southern Ranks."

"Before that. But then about three years ago, al-Humat came into the picture. I don't know how, but whatever it was, Grant handled everything with them. They gave us the financial backing to make it happen and the plan was put in motion. Once Glen had his 'gun-control epiphany,' we realized we had to move. The parts were already in place."

"Why were the sleepers killed if they did what was asked of them?"

"They became liabilities, once-valuable assets who'd outlived their usefulness."

For the first time in their exchange, Uzi felt the cool malevolence emanating from the man.

Car doors slammed outside. Larchmont's head turned. He heard them too.

He looked back at Uzi, then lifted his bound hands. "Let me go. Quickly." His head whipped back toward the warehouse door, expecting it to burst open.

"Give me your hands." Uzi took the S&W and pressed it against Larchmont's palm and fingers.

"What are you doing?"

"You tried to grab the gun from me. It went off. Between that and what you told me, I think it's called shooting yourself in the foot."

Uzi popped open his door.

"No," Larchmont yelled. "You said you'd let me go, that was our deal!"

Uzi shook his head in disgust, then headed out of the warehouse.

A black Suburban was parked behind Uzi's BuCar. DeSantos and Douglas Knox were headed in Uzi's direction when a Crown Vic pulled up behind the government metal. Marshall Shepard unfolded his large frame, then joined the cadre of men in front of the warehouse's rollup door.

"Quentin Larchmont is in there," Uzi said, "and he's been very talkative."

"That right?" Knox asked. He eyed Uzi suspiciously. "What exactly did he have to say?"

Uzi summarized the facts of the wide-reaching plan ARM, NFA, and al-Humat had launched. The three men listened intently. When Uzi finished, they remained silent, each absorbing the ramifications and reviewing their options and obligations before making their thoughts known.

Shepard put a hand on his forehead and appeared to be rubbing away the wrinkles. "Holy Jesus. Rusch ain't Rusch. Man, oh man."

The FBI director, lost in his own thoughts, began pacing. He pulled out his cell and, once out of earshot, began talking. Shepard fished out his own phone and started punching numbers.

DeSantos stood there looking at Uzi but did not say anything.

"What?" Uzi asked.

"Nothing."

"That look wasn't 'nothing.' What are you thinking?"

"I'm proud of you, boychick. You did good. You did better than good. This was huge." He extended a fist. "You can work with me any day."

Uzi touched his partner's fist with his own. "You know, I had doubts about you. I wasn't sure whose side you were on. I wasn't sure whose side Knox or Coulter were on."

"And what did I tell you? That Knox was clean. Right?"

Uzi nodded. "I'm sorry I doubted you."

"Hey, you were doing your job. Shit got confusing. You did the best you could. It all worked out in the end."

Uzi thought of Leonard Rudnick, then shook his head. "Not everything. My doc. He and I got pretty close. He was in that building on M Street. I couldn't get him out in time. He deserved a lot better."

"I'm sorry, man. I didn't know." He regarded his partner's face, then asked, "You okay?"

"Numb. It'll hit me one day. Maybe tomorrow. Maybe next week." Uzi craned his neck skyward where gray nimbostratus clouds had descended over the district; the acrid air suggested an electrical storm was brewing. "What did Nuri leave in that DLB? Do we know yet?"

"A flash card with digital images. They're still analyzing it, but on my way over here I was told there were bank statements, wire transfers, and financial records from a Saudi businessman with ties to a Swiss financier who's in our database as a suspected AQ banker. Best guess is some of al-Humat's funds were supplied by the Saudi and an unknown donor. I'm betting Iran will turn up in the mix, too. The funds were sent through the Swiss banker to an intermediary—some trust on the Isle of Man—before being shipped out to a Virginian charity that's a front controlled by Lewiston Grant. Nuri did his usual thorough job."

A sardonic smirk twisted Uzi's lips. "They still think he committed suicide?"

DeSantos waved him off. "ME found subtle petechial hemorrhages, teeth impressions—"

"Suffocation." Uzi nodded slowly. "They'll also find a needle mark and trace pharmaceuticals in his tissues. You don't stuff a pillow in the face of a guy like that without some help."

"I'm sure they'll get to the bottom of it."

"And at the bottom they'll find Batula Hakim." He looked off at the nearby buildings. "Leila."

They stood in silence a moment before DeSantos slapped Uzi's shoulder with the back of a hand. "Hey, how about you stay with Maggie and me tonight."

"No funny stuff, right? Ménage à trois . . ."

"Man, what do you think we are, sex fiends?" He shook his head. "We'd never do that on the first night a guest stays over." He winked. "You can tell us about your doc, maybe that'll help."

"You know," Uzi said, gazing off in the distance, "when I lost my wife and daughter, I lost a part of me, too. I withdrew from life. I didn't go out, I lost touch with my friends. The doc gave me a lot to think about." His eyes found DeSantos's. "So did confronting Hakim."

"There's something you should know on that." DeSantos checked over his shoulder to see where Douglas Knox was standing. "Aksel told me what happened in the hallway, things that were said. There's stuff you don't know. I confirmed it with Knox on the way over. Because of my relationship with him, he leveled with me."

DeSantos looked at his feet, then met Uzi's eyes. "Knox was in on the operation that recruited Hakim and her brother into Mossad. The CIA office in Cairo was working with the LEGATT," he said, referring to the FBI's Legal Attaché. "Remember the bombing against the US Embassy in Argentina?"

"In 2002."

DeSantos nodded. "US intelligence got wind of intel that al-Humat was responsible, but they didn't have proof. So Knox and Tasset proposed a joint op with Mossad. Aksel was skeptical, but they sold him on it. He was new on the job, so maybe he wanted to start things off right with his US counterparts. The key was turning Hakim and Ahmed into double agents. But when Aksel got wind that Ahmed was two-timing Mossad and was planning a huge hit on the Knesset, he was furious and told Knox and Tasset he was pulling the plug on the embassy op, that his first obligation was to protect his country from a devastating attack.

"Problem was, Tasset refused to fold up the tent. He thought he could still make it work—until Muhammad bin Zayed escaped after his shot ricocheted and killed Ahmed. If it got out that Ahmed was on Mossad's payroll, the prime minister would've demanded full disclosure. It would've been a disaster for Mossad. But Tasset freaked because he was afraid Aksel would leak the US role to deflect attention off Mossad. Aksel said he was more worried about finding bin Zayed in case there was a backup plan for the attack on the Knesset.

"But Tasset didn't believe that an accidental ricochet killed Ahmed. He thought Zayed found out that Ahmed was working with Mossad, and he killed him for being a traitor."

"That's not what happened."

"But Tasset didn't know that. He freaked. He knew it could've meant the end of his power trip as director. So he pressured Aksel for deniability. He told him to create a lie to protect the CIA."

"And *I* was that lie. A scapegoat."

DeSantos nodded. "Aksel refused. But Tasset bluffed, told him that if Mossad wanted full CIA cooperation and intel going forward, he'd better play ball."

Uzi sighed deeply. "And because of that, my family was killed. I guess I owe Earl Tasset something. A punch in the face."

"Or something a little more permanent."

Uzi bit his lip. His eyes scanned the men standing out of earshot. "Someday. Right now, I just want to decompress. Reflect. Heal."

Shepard stuffed his phone in a pocket and rejoined Uzi and DeSantos. "Tasset's on his way. Not happy he wasn't invited to the party."

Uzi snorted. *Tough shit.*

Shepard squinted confusion, but said, "I've got agents on their way over to deal with Larchmont."

"Tell them he'll need a medic," Uzi said. "He accidentally shot himself in the foot."

Shepard looked at Uzi with a sideways glance. "Oh, yeah?"

"Bummer when that happens," DeSantos said.

Uzi shrugged. "Struggle for the gun."

"Right," Shepard said, appraising Uzi. "You and me, my friend. We've got some things to discuss. About following procedure. Following procedure is vital to a field agent's duties—"

"Shep? Shut up."

Shepard started to back away. “I’ll catch up with you at the office. And before you ask, answer’s ‘no.’ You don’t have the rest of the day off.”

Douglas Knox walked up to them, his BlackBerry extended toward Uzi. “The president would like a word with you.”

DeSantos raised his eyebrows. Uzi smiled, enjoying the moment of self-importance as he took the phone.

“Mr. President, this is Uzi.”

“Agent Uziel, my man of the hour. I want to congratulate you, son. I had faith in you that very first day we met. I appreciate what you’ve done for me. For your country.”

“Yes, sir.”

“You’ll be glad to know that at this very moment, two Secret Service agents are taking Bryce Upshaw into custody. And according to the insightful Constitution of this great country, the Twenty-fifth Amendment outlines an orderly succession to Vice President-elect Nunn. Thank goodness for amendments. I doubt the Founding Fathers could’ve envisioned such a scenario as we’re faced with today.”

“No, sir, I doubt they could have.”

“I’d like you to be my guest for lunch. Does tomorrow work for you?”

“My schedule’s suddenly clear, Mr. President. Thank you, sir.”

Uzi handed the phone back to the director.

Knox nodded at Uzi. It was a short, subdued dip of the chin, an expression Uzi took as a look of admiration. Though he felt he might be reading more into it than intended, he didn’t think so. He interpreted it as an acknowledgment of respect the director didn’t dole out very often.

But Knox’s next comment removed all doubt. “Welcome to OPSIG,” he said.

Uzi wasn’t sure whether he wanted to be one of Knox’s chosen few. Despite being clean in this instance, Uzi still wasn’t sure about the man. Nevertheless, he was flattered by the offer. “Thank you, sir.”

Knox gave DeSantos a “follow me” tilt of the head, then moved off toward his car.

Uzi shoved his hands into his back pockets. “I’ll meet you at your place in a couple of hours.”

As DeSantos walked off, Uzi felt something in his right rear pocket and pulled it out. It was the claim check for the beer he had brewed with Leila. *New Beginnings.* He crumpled the ticket into a tight ball. He was turning a new leaf—a new beginning, indeed—and the first thing he was going to do was bring that chapter of his life to a close.

With all that had happened today, he felt he was finally able to do that. He flashed on something Rudnick had told him: *Don't let yesterday's pain become tomorrow's sorrow. It's healthy to move on. Not to learn how to forget, but to learn how to remember.* Though it made sense at the time, Uzi didn't fully comprehend what the doctor was trying to tell him.

Now he understood.

January 20

The US Capitol
West Portico

The crisp winter wind wound through the barren trees along the periphery of the Capitol building. Heavy snow had fallen throughout the day yesterday, well into the late evening hours, snarling traffic and nearly shutting down the district. Inaugural event planners sat on their phones, ensuring vendors made their planned deliveries, while others worked their cells trying to arrange alternate routes of transportation for VIPs and invited guests.

The Secret Service poured over their blueprints and diagrams, grumbling about crowd control for two million people amid mounds of snow that had yet to be adequately cleared—wish-list cover for prospective gunmen.

Although thought was given to postponing the presidential Inauguration or changing its venue, it was an idea that garnered little support. If ever there was a time for America to show its resiliency and strength, it was now. Today. During the succession and transfer of power laid out by the Constitution. In accordance with our laws and customs. When and where it's supposed to happen. Pomp. Circumstance. Politics and power. All on display.

If God decided to blanket the land in white, so be it. Perhaps it was a purveyor of good things—of purity—to come.

And perhaps not.

Television cameras, their cables snaking along the winter-pale grass, rolled as black-robed, white-haired Chief Justice Wendell Harris faced President-elect Vance Nunn.

Uzi had an unbelievably close seat, slightly off to the side and just over Nunn's right shoulder, dressed in a pinstripe suit, beside Hector DeSantos, Douglas Knox, and outgoing president Jonathan Whitehall. Whitehall gently nudged Uzi's elbow and leaned in close. Uzi bowed his head.

"You should be quite proud right about now, Agent Uziel. Of anyone else standing here today, you are almost single-handedly responsible for this."

Uzi suppressed a smile, then turned to face the podium where President-elect Nunn and his wife, Doris, stood, their coats fluttering in the wind like the proud American flag atop the Capitol. Uzi did, in fact, feel good about the role he had played. But for the past few weeks, he couldn't help but feel that he'd missed something. An insidiously creeping feeling—a mosquito bite that wouldn't go away. Itching, scratching, red and swollen—always there, sometimes intolerable.

He'd been over things several times, and when he had continued to come up empty, finally confessed his unease to DeSantos. DeSantos chortled and punched him in the shoulder. Told him to relax, the job was done and everything ended happily ever after.

There were moments when Uzi was able to let it go, to revel in the knowledge he had done his job and done it well. Then there were the moments when it gnawed at him so much he had to go for a run. Or lift weights. Or shoot a few hundred rounds at the range.

He huddled with Tim Meadows and they dug some more, crawling through various hacked databases, an unofficial journey through official files, hoping to find other digital irregularities. Other than Rusch's altered electronic medical records file—doctored to contain data belonging to Bryce Upshaw—they found nothing. The identity of the CJIS technician, whose digital wizardry played a crucial role, remained a mystery.

Finally, having reached the conclusion he had done everything in his power, Uzi began to relax. He immersed himself in a new case with Hoshi, and that seemed to help.

But now, standing on the West Portico of the United States Capitol building, amidst the ceremony and splash of the official political event being watched the world over, that sense of disquiet crept back under his skin. The mosquito bite rose again.

"This is the part I lived for," Whitehall said by his ear. "Franklin Roosevelt was a fortunate man, yes sir. Term limits ought to be abolished, I've said it many times. I could've gone for a third term, you know. Seventy percent approval rating right up to the end."

Uzi forced a thin grin, his mind once again running through the details of the case. Searching for that one thing he might have missed.

As Uzi mused unproductively, Vance Nunn stood opposite the judge, his right hand held high and his left resting on the good book. "I do solemnly swear that I will faithfully execute the Office of President of the United States, and will, to the best of my ability, preserve, protect and defend the Constitution. . . ."

Having repeated the oath, Nunn firmly shook the hand of the Chief Justice, then turned to give Doris a kiss and hug.

Uzi sighed heavily and for some reason—perhaps it was Rudnick's comment about the need to "move on"—his apprehension caught the next gust and blew away, into the angry gray skies. It was over now, the final period at the end of a long chapter. It wasn't such a bad day after all, he realized. Democracy was being served—which was, of course, the purpose behind the oath he himself had taken: to uphold the laws of the greatest country on the face of the Earth.

A twenty-one-gun salute marked the change of command as the national anthem roared through the high-powered, stadium-style speakers. Vance Nunn appeared to fight back tears, then saluted the crowd. With Doris at his side, he turned regally to the large walnut podium to deliver his inaugural address. As the masses settled down and took their seats, the teleprompter operator queued up the speech. Nunn dug a hand into his overcoat, rooted out a palm-sized object, and glanced down at it. It was a pocket watch.

A sterling silver pocket watch with a gold-inlaid scorpion.

ACKNOWLEDGMENTS

Hard Target required input from professionals in a myriad of fields. Because my research spanned many years, some of their titles might presently be different from what I've noted below. I've made corrections where known, but otherwise left their positions as they were when I worked with them. Thanks to those individuals, named and unnamed, who gave me access to vital places and information:

Brian Mitchell, Master Sergeant, United States Marine Corps, at Quantico Marine Base's HMX-1. Brian patiently answered all of my questions and reviewed pertinent portions of the manuscript for accuracy relative to the operation and maintenance of the United States's executive detail's helicopter fleet ("HMX-1") and the vice president's transport, Marine Two. Brian has flown these birds, transporting presidents and vice presidents on missions around the world. He's walked the walk. I couldn't have written those chapters without his experience and assistance.

Lee Bassett, Master Sergeant, United States Marine Corps, for taking me on a tour of Quantico Marine base—particularly HMX-1. Given the stringent security requirements, this was no simple request.

Melissa Thomas, FBI Special Agent, and **John Adams**, Joint Terrorism Task Force Special Agent at the Bureau's Washington Field Office, for a behind-the-scenes tour of their facility, and for Agent Adams's detailed answers to my logistical and procedural questions.

Mark Safarik, FBI Supervisory Special Agent and Senior Profiler (ret.) at the Bureau's Behavioral Analysis Unit, for his behavioral analysis guidance and bomber profile information. In addition, his FBI and military contacts and thorough review of the manuscript for procedural accuracy proved invaluable.

Cole W. Cordray, Lieutenant, US Army Crisis Response Team (deceased), and **Brian Hains,** Special Reaction Team Officer, for sharing their expertise relative to knives, assault rifle weaponry, and their in-depth information on the Sikorsky VH-3 and SuperStallion helicopters.

Robert L. Snow, Captain of Detectives, Indianapolis Police Department homicide unit (and author of *The Militia Threat: Terrorists Among Us*), for his expertise and invaluable insight on militia psychology, structure, and organization.

Lee McDonald, United States Marine Corps veteran and ordnance expert, for his assistance, suggestions, and manuscript edits relative to explosives and bomb detonation scenarios. **Mike Fergus** at the FAA for his orientation and information on accident scene investigation. **Guyllermo Canedo**, Major, United States Marine Corps Headquarters Washington, for information regarding the USMC's procedures involving crash investigations.

Kai Barkhald, Chief Inspector, for his personal instruction on helicopters. Asking for information on how to blow up the vice president's helicopter met with . . . some raised eyebrows. Kai handled the questions with integrity and honesty. And without massive paranoia.

Steve Garrett, US Navy Hospital Corpsman Senior Chief (Diver/Free Fall Parachutist/Fleet Marine Force) (ret.), for his thorough review of the manuscript and for correcting my Special Operations Force terminology and procedures (as well as other military, medical, and governmental agency jargon). Details matter—and Steve's review made a huge difference in my "getting it right."

Bill Caldwell, armorer and police officer (ret.), for his knowledge and expertise on ballistics and weaponry, and for reviewing numerous excerpts for accuracy. **Gabriel Salgado**, former First Sergeant with the Israel Defense Forces (IDF), for background and information relative to his time with the IDF and the Shin Bet security service.

Marc Usatin, MD, for instructing me on the physiology and treatment of burn injuries. **Bill Kitzerow**, Lieutenant, Fairfax City Police

Department, for being my Virginia and Washington, DC, police presence and "eyes on the ground," and for helping me select an appropriate location for ARM's compound. **Michael Weinhaus**, ICE Special Agent and former Fairfax County Police Officer First Class, for a thorough tour of the Mason District Station.

Matt Nosanchuk, Senior Counselor to the Assistant US Attorney General, former Assistant US Attorney (Washington, DC), and former Litigation Director and Legislative Counsel for the Violence Policy Center in Washington, for helping me frame the issues relative to the fictional National Firearms Alliance.

Paul Ortega, Emerging Technology Executive at AT&T, and **Joy E. Lovell**, Client Solution Executive of the IBM eBusiness Hosting Services division, for their assistance with server backup technology.

Jack Nargil, head concierge, director Les Clefs D'or, the Hay-Adams Hotel, and **Andrew Crosby**, President of Crosby-Volmer Communications, for roof and facility access, information, floorplans, and historical background on the Hay-Adams.

Sue Stengel, Western States Counsel, Anti-Defamation League, for information on militia groups; and **David Friedman**, Director of the ADL office in Washington, DC, for his candidness and perspective. **Michael Brown**, Battalion Chief, San Ramon Valley Fire Protection District, for his detailed explanations of helicopter fire-fighting procedures.

George Q. Fong, ESPN Director of Security and FBI Supervisory Special Agent (ret.) for assistance with procedural issues pertaining to Jake Osborn's transgression. **Corey Jacobson**, Policy Analyst and Strategic Communications Associate with Purple Nation Solutions, for his information on campaign finance laws and electoral procedure. **Salem Wali-Ali**, linguist, for his assistance with Arabic translations.

RoseMarie Mirabella, Barns and Facilities Rental Director, and **Valerie Wheels**, Stage Manager of Wolf Trap Foundation for the Performing Arts, for providing access to their facility.

To those unnamed sources who provided information and background on the Mossad and the Department of Defense, thank you.

My agents, **Joel Gotler** and **Frank Curtis**, for their insight, decades of knowledge, and hard work on my behalf.

My editor, **Kevin Smith**, with whom I share a brain during the editorial phase. Sometimes we're so much in sync I think that if we were women, we'd be cycling together.

My publishers: On the "e" side, **Thomas Ellsworth, Daniel Tibbets, Hutch Morton**, and **Julie Morales** at Open Road Integrated Media. The gang at PDP are revolutionaries and outside-the-box thinkers in a constantly changing industry. It's refreshing to work with professionals who understand the landscape and who aren't afraid to adapt when they identify a trend. On the hardcover side, **Virginia Lenneville** and **John Hutchinson** at Norwood Press: their primary interest is to turn out a first-rate top-quality product. Their hardcovers look beautiful on the shelf and will last a lifetime, and I'm honored to be part of the Norwood stable of legendary authors.

My fans and readers, worldwide, and those who follow me on Facebook and Twitter: You're the best! A special shout-out to the active posters for participating in spirited discussions, and for spreading the word about "Alan Jacobson"; and a special thank you to the two administrators of my Facebook fan group, Terri Landreth and Sandra Soreano. There are three ways to stay socially networked with me: my official fan page, www.facebook.com/AlanJacobsonFans; my fan-run Facebook group, which you can find at www.FansOfAlanJacobson.com; and Twitter, @JacobsonAlan.

Ultimate thanks goes to Jill, my wife and life partner. It's not easy navigating the challenges an author faces dealing with an industry in perpetual flux, but having one's mate solidly behind him during that uncertain journey, which has now spanned eighteen years, makes it bearable (and possible).

Any deviations from fact that appear in the novel should not reflect on the above named professionals. On (very) rare occasions, certain facts were modified to protect national security interests.

ABOUT THE AUTHOR

Alan Jacobson is the national bestselling author of several critically acclaimed novels. In order to take readers behind the scenes to places they might never go, Jacobson has embedded himself in many federal agencies, including spending several years working with two senior profilers at the Federal Bureau of Investigation's vaunted Behavioral Analysis Unit in Quantico. During that time, Jacobson edited four published FBI research papers on serial offenders, attended numerous FBI training courses, worked with the head firearms instructor at the academy, and received ongoing personalized instruction on serial killers—which continues to this day. He has also worked with high-ranking members of the Drug Enforcement Administration, the US Marshals Service, the New York Police Department, SWAT teams, local bomb squads, branches of the US military, chief superintendents and detective sergeants at Scotland Yard, criminals, armorers, helicopter pilots, chief executive officers, historians, and Special Forces operators. These experiences have helped him to create gripping, realistic stories and characters. His series protagonist, FBI profiler Karen Vail, resonates with both female and male readers, and writers such as

Nelson DeMille, James Patterson, and Michael Connelly have called Vail one of the most compelling heroes in suspense fiction.

Jacobson's books have been published internationally, and several have been optioned for film and television. A number have been named to Best of the Year lists.

Jacobson has been interviewed extensively on television and radio, including on CNN, NPR, and multiple ABC, CBS, NBC, and Fox network affiliates.

Connect with the author through his website (www.AlanJacobson.com), on Facebook (www.Facebook.com/AlanJacobsonFans), Instagram (alan.jacobson), and Twitter (@JacobsonAlan).

THE WORKS OF ALAN JACOBSON

Alan Jacobson has established a reputation as one of the most insightful suspense and thriller writers of our time. His exhaustive research, coupled with years of unprecedented access to law enforcement agencies, including the FBI's Behavioral Analysis Unit, bring realism and unique characters to his pages. Following are his current, and forthcoming, releases.

STANDALONE NOVELS

False Accusations > Dr. Phillip Madison has everything: wealth, power, and an impeccable reputation. But in the pre-dawn hours of a quiet suburb, the revered orthopedic surgeon is charged with double homicide—a cold-blooded hit-and-run that leaves an innocent couple dead. Blood evidence has brought the police to his door. An eyewitness has placed him at the crime scene, and Madison has no alibi. With his family torn apart, his career forever damaged, no way to prove his innocence and facing life in prison, Madison must find the person who has engineered the case against him. Years after reading it, people still talk about the ending. *False Accusations* launched Alan's career and became a national bestseller, prompting CNN to call him, "One of the brightest stars in the publishing industry." Detective Ryan Chandler reprises his role in *Spectrum*.

FBI PROFILER KAREN VAIL SERIES

The 7th Victim (Karen Vail #1) > Literary giants Nelson DeMille and James Patterson describe Karen Vail, the first female FBI profiler, as "tough, smart, funny, very believable," and "compelling." In *The 7th Victim*, Vail—with a dry sense of humor and a closet full of skeletons—heads up a task force to find the Dead Eyes Killer, who is murdering young women in Virginia . . . the backyard of the famed FBI Behavioral Analysis Unit. The twists and turns that Karen Vail endures in this tense psychological suspense thriller build to a powerful ending no reader will see coming. Named one of the Top 5 Best Books of the Year (*Library Journal*).

Crush (Karen Vail #2) > FBI Profiler Karen Vail is in the Napa Valley for a vacation—but the Crush Killer has other plans. Vail partners with Inspector Roxxann Dixon to track down the architect of death who crushes his victims' windpipes and leaves their bodies in wine caves and vineyards. But the killer is unlike anything the profiling unit has ever encountered, and Vail's miscalculations have dire consequences for those she holds dear. *Publishers Weekly* describes *Crush* as "addicting" and *New York Times* bestselling author Steve Martini calls it a thriller that's "Crisply written and meticulously researched," and "rocks from the opening page to the jarring conclusion." (Note: the Crush storyline continues in *Velocity*.)

Velocity (Karen Vail #3) > A missing detective. A bold serial killer. And evidence that makes FBI Profiler Karen Vail question the loyalty of those she has entrusted her life to. Squaring off against foes more dangerous than any she has yet encountered, shocking personal and professional truths emerge—truths that may be more than Vail can handle. *Velocity* was named to *The Strand Magazine*'s Top 10 Best Books for 2010, *Suspense Magazine*'s Top 4 Best Thrillers of 2010, *Library Journal*'s Top 5 Best Books of the Year, and the *Los Angeles Times*' top picks of the year. Michael Connelly said *Velocity*is "As relentless as a bullet. Karen Vail is my kind of hero and Alan Jacobson is my kind of writer!"

Inmate 1577 (Karen Vail #4) > When an elderly woman is found raped and murdered, Karen Vail heads west to team up with Inspector Lance Burden and Detective Roxxann Dixon. As they follow the killer's trail in and around San Francisco, the offender leaves behind clues that ultimately lead them to the most unlikely of places, a mysterious island ripped from city lore whose long-buried, decades-old secrets hold the key to their case: Alcatraz. The Rock. It's a case that has more twists and turns than the famed Lombard Street. The legendary Clive Cussler calls *Inmate 1577* "a powerful thriller, brilliantly conceived and written." Named one of *The Strand Magazine*'s Top 10 Best Books of the Year.

No Way Out (Karen Vail #5) > Renowned FBI profiler Karen Vail returns in *No Way Out*, a high-stakes thriller set in London. When a high profile art gallery is bombed, Vail is dispatched to England to assist with Scotland Yard's investigation. But what she finds there—a plot to destroy a controversial, recently unearthed 440-year-old manuscript—turns into something much larger, and a whole lot more dangerous, for the UK, the US—and herself. With his trademark spirited dialogue, page-turning scenes, and well-drawn characters, National Bestselling author Alan Jacobson ("My kind of writer," per Michael Connelly) has crafted the thriller of the year. Named a top ten "Best thriller of 2013" by both *Suspense Magazine* and *The Strand Magazine*.

Spectrum (Karen Vail #6) > It's 1995 and the NYPD has just graduated a promising new patrol officer named Karen Vail. On the rookie's first day on the job, she finds herself at the crime scene of a woman murdered in an unusual manner. As the years pass and more victims are discovered, Vail's career takes unexpected twists and turns—as does the case that's come to be known as "Hades." Now a skilled FBI profiler, will Vail be in a better position to catch the offender? Or will Hades prove to be Karen Vail's hell on earth? # 1 *New York Times* bestseller Richard North Patterson called *Spectrum*, "Compelling and crisp . . . A pleasure to read."

OPSIG TEAM BLACK SERIES

The Hunted (OPSIG Team Black Novel #1) > How well do you know the one you love? How far would you go to find out? When Lauren Chambers's husband Michael disappears, her search reveals his hidden past involving the FBI, international assassins—and government secrets that some will go to great lengths to keep hidden. As *The Hunted* hurtles toward a conclusion mined with turn-on-a-dime twists, no one is who he appears to be and nothing is as it seems. *The Hunted* introduces the dynamic Department of Defense covert operative Hector DeSantos and FBI Director Douglas Knox, characters who return in *Velocity, Hard Target, No Way Out*, and *Spectrum*.

Hard Target (OPSIG Team Black Novel #2) > An explosion pulverizes the president-elect's helicopter on Election Night. The group behind the assassination attempt possesses far greater reach than anything the FBI has yet encountered—and a plot so deeply interwoven in the country's fabric that it threatens to upend America's political system. But as covert operative Hector DeSantos and FBI Agent Aaron "Uzi" Uziel sort out who is behind the bombings, Uzi's personal demons not only jeopardize the investigation but may sit at the heart of a tangle of lies that threaten to trigger an international terrorist attack. Lee Child called *Hard Target*, "Fast, hard, intelligent. A terrific thriller." Note: FBI Profiler Karen Vail plays a key role in the story.

The Lost Codex (OPSIG Team Black Novel #3) > *Two biblical documents. Ancient. Priceless. With revelations that could change the world as we know it.* In 930 AD, a revered group of scholars pen the first sanctioned Bible, planting the seed from which other major religions grow. But in 1953, half the manuscript goes missing while being transported from Syria. Around the same time, in the foothills of the Dead Sea, an ancient scroll is discovered—and promptly stolen. Six decades later both parchments stand at the heart of a geopolitical battle between foreign governments and radical extremists, threatening the lives of millions. With the American homeland under siege, the president turns to a team of uniquely trained covert operatives that includes FBI profiler Karen Vail, special forces veteran Hector DeSantos and FBI terrorism expert Aaron Uziel to not only find the stolen documents but capture—or kill—those responsible for unleashing a coordinated and unprecedented attack on US soil. Set in Washington, DC, New York, Paris, England, and Israel, *The Lost Codex* has been called "A masterwork of international suspense," "an outstanding novel," and "brilliant" by Douglas Preston and Jeffery Deaver.

SHORT STORIES

Fatal Twist > The Park Rapist has murdered his first victim—and FBI profiler Karen Vail is on the case. As Vail races through the streets of Washington, DC to chase down a promising lead that may help her catch the killer, a military-trained sniper takes aim at his target, a wealthy businessman's son. But what brings these two unrelated offenders together is something the nation's capital has never before experienced. *Fatal Twist* provides a taste of Karen Vail that will whet your appetite.

Double Take > NYPD Detective Ben Dyer awakens from cancer surgery to find his life turned upside down. His fiancée has disappeared and Dyer, determined to find her, embarks on a journey mined with potholes and startling revelations—revelations that have the potential to forever change his life. *Double Take* introduces NYPD Lieutenant Carmine Russo and Detective Ben Dyer, who return to play significant roles in *Spectrum* (Karen Vail #6).

More to come > For a peek at recently released Alan Jacobson novels, interviews, reading group guides, and more, visit www.AlanJacobson.com.

CPSIA information can be obtained
at www.ICGtesting.com
Printed in the USA
JSHW022205260122
22305JS00001B/28

9 781504 013383